The Passions of Roxanna

La Passione di Rossana

By

Gail Michael

The story of one woman's journey to find her passions

Eloquent Books
New York, New York

Eloquent Books
An imprint of AEG Publishing Group
845 Third Avenue, 6th Floor - 6016
New York, NY 10022
www.eloquentbooks.com

ISBN: 978-1-60693-113-4
SKU: 1-60693-113-X

This book is a work of fiction. Except as noted, names, characters,
places and incidents either are products of the author's
imagination or are used fictitiously. Any resemblance to actual
events, locales or persons, is entirely coincidental.

Printed in the United States of America

Book Design: Roger Hayes

PRAISES for The Passions of Roxanna

"If a person has never been to Italy this story and the beautiful pictures that Gail paints would leave a lasting imprint on your mind. Every adventure is woven with the landscape of this magical place. You almost taste the wine and the food that is much a part of story. All I can say is that Roxanna is one lucky girl. This is a great relaxing summer read."

Nancy Higgins

"It's a great read. I loved it! I didn't want it to end and wished I could look five years into the future to see where she would be then."

Ellie Niston

"…The imagery, the colors, the food, the wine…I could feel the breezes. It made me wish I was her."

Nora Sterns

"Years ago, I suffered heart ache that was pretty devastating. As I read the book, Roxanna's thought process was a lot of what I went through in my own head and finally, it made it all right for me. I felt like I was no longer crazy or suffering. She represented courage to me and gave me hope that I could find love again. She sort of gave me permission to go out and live life again. She moved forward where I hadn't been able to. Roxanna represents a lot of women and what they go through."

Karen Morris

"Heart-beating…provocative…delicious…adventurous…uplifting…compelling…courageous…"

Susan Chen

DEDICATION

I dedicate this book to my son, Troy, who loved me enough to allow me to follow my dreams to the other side of the world. Thank you for your unconditional love and support.

- M

I would also like to thank the sweet and loving people of AnaCapri who were gracious enough to take me into their hearts as one of their own.

And to my Beloved San Michele for guiding me on my journey.

ACKNOWLEDGMENTS

I am grateful to many people who supported me on my journey to write this book. Thank you, Troy my son for loving me through my insanities and my longing for this island in the middle of the Mediterranean. You were always the voice of reason and logic on the other end of the telephone line; and today, you inspire me for who you have become.

I thank all of my friends who didn't understand me as I wept for this great love that was an island; but loved me and supported me still. A thousand thanks to all of you who had the patience to read my long descriptive weekly emails as I slept with the demons inside my head who I needed to make peace with when I first arrived on the island.

Special thanks to Eloquent Books who had enough faith in my work to publish it. Thank you, Lynn, Liz, Vicki, Mark, Eleanor, Joanne and your team for you tireless efforts in assisting me through the process. Suzanne Hartzell, thank you for giving balance to my dreamy writing and for bringing my heartfelt words back to earth so that the rest of my readers could comprehend them and enjoy what I was trying to convey. Thank you, Gergana Injev, a true friend and brilliant artist for your breathtaking cover design.

I thank Santa Maria, San Francesco, and all who whispered to me and protected me throughout Italy and Greece.

Thank you Michael, for always being there for me. You were the force behind me who believed in me when I did not believe in myself. Each time I woke up in Capri with doubts, you sent me an angel with a message. Thank you for planting the seed and prodding me to go there; and for very carefully slicing my heart wide open like a ripened pomegranate, so careful with all the little seeds inside. You opened me up ever so gently, so that my love could spill out onto these pages.

For the people of Capri and those of you who I met along the way throughout Italy and Greece, I have used some of your names because they are so beautiful to me, and I have changed others so that your personal lives will remain just that. I have described some of you just as you look because I fell in love with your faces, your personalities and who you are. For others, I have changed you, or embellished your character with my imagination. All in all, it is a fabricated story that has come out of my mind and my heart.

Franco, I could not have done this if it was not for you. I thank you and your family for your undying love and support. I would also like to thank the Pannullo family who I love deeply, Federico, and all my other friends in AnaCapri. You all know who you are and what parts you played in my story. I thank you for showing me love and kindness and watching over me as I lived among you and wrote to my heart's content.

Thank you for sharing this great adventure with me. And for some of you (you know who you are), thank you for referring to me as *"Gay-**La** Me-**Kay**-la, the famous American writer"* as I walked the town. You gave me confidence to be what I have always dreamed to be.

With much love and gratitude, I remain Roxanna of Capri – Yours forever!

Gail Michael

Preface

The Birth of Roxanna -

While traveling in the south of Italy in 1875, a young Swedish doctor named Axel Munthe, sailed in a small boat from Sorrento to the island of Capri; and on a dare, climbed the 770 Phoenician Steps to the top of the island and the little village of AnaCapri. Once he arrived at the top, he came upon a peasant's house and the remains of a little chapel dedicated to the Archangel San Michele. He became intoxicated... enraptured with the village, its people, the vistas, and the chapel and knew he had to live there. He had found heaven on earth. He wrote:

"The soul needs more space than the body..."

So he built his home there.

I share a kindred spirit with Munthe because I too was intoxicated... mesmerized...breathless...when I first arrived in AnaCapri in 2004. I had heard of the island but knew nothing of it until my son and I were planning a tour through Europe – our first. One thing led to another and soon I was being nudged to go there. Little did I know that it would change my life forever. When I stepped onto the soil of Capri, I almost fell to my knees; for the power of the island was that strong for me.

Have you ever felt as if you don't belong anywhere and suddenly you come across a land that stops you in your tracks and takes your breath away? That is how Capri was for me...

...It feeds my soul and makes my heart sing...

When we returned to the States, Capri was in my every thought, my every breath, my every vision. It was a longing – a love affair I had to explore further. I hardly slept for weeks. I had to return...

After discussing my dreams with my son, he was supportive enough to let me go for awhile as long as I came back to him. So I went, not knowing where I would be staying or for how long. I only knew a gracious stranger from AnaCapri who promised he would find me a place once I arrived. So I trusted. I left the security of my job of 6 years, moved my son and me out of our home in Laguna Beach, and put my belongings in storage. He moved to his father's home to live fulltime for awhile. Did I feel guilt about any of this? Yes, every day that I thought about it.

But the pull from Capri was so intense that each night when I went to bed, I found myself back on the island. I'd awaken to a noise in my room, but as soon as I closed my eyes again, I was in AnaCapri, walking the cliffs looking out to sea.

As my life would have it, everything fell into place and nine months after my first trip with my son, I traveled back to the island that had stolen my heart. It was as if I was not in my right mind or dumbstruck; because for the first time in my life, I trusted that it was the right thing to do and that I would be taken care of every step of the way. I never worried about having a place to live. I never worried about my safety even though I was traveling alone in one of the most amorous and romantic places in the world; and I was told by many to beware of gypsies who lurked in crowds looking for tourists to prey upon. Everyone seemed to be looking out for me, both in this world and the next. I never had a negative thought, emotion, or experience the entire time I was in Italy and Greece.

I rested my ailing body, I healed, I dreamed, and I played. I was consciously awake every moment that I breathed. It was as if I had a sixth sense for what to do next. I spent the first six weeks at my little villa on this beautiful piece of land that overlooked the aqua Mediterranean, Mount Vesuvius, the Bay of Naples and the islands of Ischia and Procida. There were aromatic flowers everywhere that Capri is so well known for, gardens all around, grapevines, and *terrazzos* where I could sit, rest, or write. The highlight of each day was to watch the sun as it dripped diamonds onto the golden turquoise sea and then set into the water. I was in *paradiso*.

I was ecstatic as I sat and listened to the silence of the island. The only sounds I heard were those of the distant hydrofoils as they crossed the sea far below, the big June bugs that flew about, and the birds that chirped in the morning. Sometimes, I would hear a scooter in the distance or children's laughter, but mostly it was free from sound.

To the islanders, I must have seemed a strange American woman who kept to herself for the first six weeks, but then I eventually grasped the language and ventured out into the village more where I met the most wonderful people of AnaCapri.

Soon, I was speaking with them daily, greeting them as I walked by their shops as they worked so hard in the gloriously hot Mediterranean heat and humidity. Many of them looked out for me, telling me where to go, where to shop, where to eat. All became my friends, and the most pleasurable moments of my days were walking in to town for food and supplies, and stopping to say *ciao* and converse with each of them.

Once my body started to heal, I crossed the Bay and started to explore the mainland, and that is when Roxanna's (and my) adventures began. I took the train into Rome and then to Tuscany where I visited Pisa, Lucca, the Chianti countryside and Florence. On another trip, I look the train into Rome – always Rome that I loved so much, staying in the opera district – and then traveled to Assisi and on to Venice.

I traveled to Athens, Greece and then Mykonos, Delos and Santorini where I had the most extraordinary experiences. I was living an amazing life just waiting to be led to the next place! My playground was the Amalfi Coast where I roamed through Sorrento, Vietre sul Mare, Ravello, the town of Amalfi, Positano, and also Napoli. I visited the islands around Capri and also the lost city of Pompeii.

Two treasured friends from Capri took me to the *Compania* and *Basilicata* Regions and to Matera in search of my own Holy Grail to see every basilica, church and monastery dedicated to San Michele – the greatest gift I have ever received.

And even before I visited all of these incredible places, I knew I would be writing a book. But the character Roxanna did not fully form until I had healed (body, mind and spirit) and moved into a place of oneness with my own life, opening up to the passion and romance of it. Only then was I able to create a character such as this.

Roxanna starts out slowly as if she has been asleep for years…which she has…same as the author. But as the story unfolds, you feel her awakening with each new day and each new experience, following her heart as if she is blindfolded, free and without trepidation - the way we should all follow our own hearts and walk through our own lives. Only then is she able to have such magical and mystical experiences.

I have been asked, *"Did you really do all of these things? Which adventures are real? And did these things really happen with the people on Capri and in all your travels?"*

Good questions… I can tell you that I was on the 18th century schooner with three Greek men in the Cyclades, my modern day pirates. I was in the castle in the Chianti countryside, and I stood in front of "the David" in Florence when someone…never mind. I traveled to all of the locations and settings that Roxanna did...but I will not reveal any more secrets but instead leave all to your imagination.

Everything I have written about has happened somewhere inside my world – either inside my head or in my reality. Most of the events (Roxanna's adventures) that take place are "loosely" based on my own experiences. However, I am a writer with a wild imagination, an overstuffed heart, a connection to the other worlds, and I have also worn rose-colored glasses most of my life. I could not have written such a romantic tale in first person narrative if I was not all of these things. And as far as what is fact or fiction, does it really matter? The book is fiction.

This dream that I lived inside of for five months was the most wondrous and fulfilling adventure of my life that awakened me to my own passions and purpose. If you are a woman - or a man for that matter - in search of yourself that has seemed asleep for so long, I suggest you give yourself permission to follow your dreams and find your own Capri. Because once you find that place that feeds your soul, it will ignite that flame within you and bring you into alignment with your own passion and purpose.

Enjoy!

Gail Michael

Table of Travels

Chapter 1

L'ISOLA DI CAPRI

"Faster! Faster!" I feel the anxiety rise up inside me as the *Napolitano* taxi driver speeds through the streets from the train station to the port. The crowded city is sprawled out before me, a web of ancient buildings, honking taxi drivers, and people everywhere speaking in a foreign tongue.

"Please, faster! I can't miss the last boat!" I'm so sleepy – I feel as if I have been up for days, flying, with a five hour lay-over in Munich, then on to Rome, then the train to Napoli to get to the port for the last hydrofoil to the Isle of Capri. Why does it seem so hard to get there? Maybe because it's on the other side of the world in the middle of the sea…my brain is misfiring.

"Finally, I hope I'm not too late!" I speak my thoughts aloud to the taxi driver, unable to keep them inside my head.

"*Grazie, Signora.*" Throwing twenty-five euro through the window, I grab my backpack containing my laptop and my one small suitcase and run to the *biglietteria* to purchase a ticket.

"No, no. Gone. Last one. *Domani*! Tomorrow!" The seller says in his broken English as he prepares to close.

"You don't understand! I have to get there tonight!" I have to get there at all cost, although I know not why. He slams the window down all the while talking with his hands, as I stand there in shock. What now - how will I get there tonight? The fog inside my head…I feel drugged. Oh, I wish I could lay down here and sleep. No, I must get to the island. Exhaustion starts to take hold as I walk out to the water's edge and stand there not knowing what to do. I can feel it behind my eyelids as they slowly start to shut down. I sit on my suitcase at *binario* 10 with my face in my hands.

"*Un barca, signora?*" I look up into the shadow of a man who is blocking the sun.

"Yes, I need to get to Capri. Do you have a boat?"

"*Si, si, Signora.* I take you Capri."

"How much - *quanto costo*? I am surprised I remember any Italian at all.

"*Cinquanta euro.*"

"Fifty? That's too high."

"*Signora*, you miss last boat." He shrugs his shoulders and cocks his head to the side. He's right. I have to get there tonight. But where will I stay? Not now…I can't think about that now.

"*Si*, come." He takes me to the end of the pier to an old fishing boat that doesn't look sea worthy. Is it safe? It must be – has to be. The man sees the look in my eyes and says, "No, no. It's okay…good boat. I go Capri every week. I have delivery today."

I think for a moment that he is going there anyway and is charging me an exorbitant amount…the thought of bartering leaves my brain as that familiar mist permeates my thoughts and causes a disconnect. He pulls my suitcase and back-pack onto the boat and then throws me a life vest.

"For you. Put on." I sit down and feel as if I'm in a dream as my reality falls away. The water – the way it laps against the sides of the old boat, the color of the sea-foam green sea before me. I have never seen such colors….they are like something out of a picture book. My mind moves quickly from one thought to another, never finishing. I must be crazy to have come so quickly. I dropped everything in my life at the last minute and made this reservation within a month of the dream.

The dream - it came one night, out of nowhere. And then the internet…I tried to log on to mapquest.com, but instead…the *Isola de Capri* appeared on the screen… such a beautiful place… Will I get there tonight? Or will I end up at the bottom of the sea too tired to swim to the top. Would anyone see me and save me? I realize my eyes are closed.

Oh, did I fall asleep? How long was I out for? No worries…at least I am awake now. How strange that it happened in that way…Capri on my computer - no mistake….everything happens for a reason.

I gasp when I see what is on the horizon. There before me, an island appears, as Avalon did for Morgaine when the mists parted as she made her way across the lake. Capri - her shape is that of a woman lying on her back, her head at one end, her breasts and then her protruding abdomen as if she were about to give birth. What a beautiful sight! Home! I am coming home, at last!

The island is 6 kms by 3 kms with only 12,500 inhabitants…a small island. There are two villages, Capri down near the port and AnaCapri high above on the cliff-tops. I am being pulled there for some reason. It makes no sense to me…but sometimes life doesn't make any sense at all

– like this…all of this. All I know is that I have to follow the calling of my soul.

I wanted to come here – had to. I didn't need any prodding. As soon as I saw the photos, I knew I was supposed to be here…and my boys. I remember they are with their father. My heart smiles as I remember them telling me to go. They said it was time for me to give them their own lives to live and to find one of my own. There is more to life than being a mother, they said. They are no longer my little boys…

Mothering was the biggest role in my life and I loved it – lived for it. My sweet boys…I was so attached to them, doted on them. I treated them as if they were still five instead of the young men they now are. It had been painful breaking away from them these last few years. But now I can see their wisdom and I am proud of them. I know they will survive while I am gone.

I open my eyes to the sun and watch it move closer to the horizon. "*Vesuvio*," my boatman points toward the largest peak in the distance. It almost appears to have two peaks, and I know it is because the top has blown off. He points to a small island to its left and calls it Procida. To the left of Procida, he points to Ischia. Then, he smiles and nods toward our destination, "Capri." He has that dreamy look on his face, that of someone who knows it intimately.

"I make delivery in Marina Piccola. Then, I bring you Marina Grande." I have no idea Marina Piccola is on the opposite side of the island, so I sit quietly and look out over the water. The colors…how beautiful. The sea is almost aqua in places, even out here in open waters. It seems so calm…as if it were a dream…

I think about my life and how strange it has been lately, as if I am being guided by the gods to do unthinkable things. Not long ago, I had dreamed about leaving my career as a manager at a southern California manufacturing firm to paint full time and within two weeks, I had resigned. Many called it madness. They thought I had gone insane! Even if I might struggle financially in the beginning, it was something I had to do because of the dreams – always the dream…I realized after these episodes, I no longer had the passion for the work I had made a living by for the past thirty years. I knew that coming to Capri would give me clarity, and help me pick up the brush again. It has been so long…

The reoccurring dream …It is always the same - I see the same vista, high atop the cliffs of the island and I see myself standing watching the sea. I feel the presence of a great spirit beside me and I can feel his loving touch upon my shoulder – so sweet, so strong, so protective. He speaks to me.

"You belong here, you know. This is the home of your ancient ones. They are calling to you. Here, you will find what you have been searching for…" He laughs before he disappears as quickly as he had appeared. I am not startled, for I can feel his great love and guidance. I know he is a great protector of mine, although I do not know his name.

How can I get there except in this dream at night when I lie in my bed? I have responsibilities and my two sons…I have no extra money for travel, I think.

"Ah, silly human…" I can no longer see him but can feel his love. "Don't you know that you can have anything you desire in this lifetime? All you need to make it happen is a dream in your heart, focus within your mind, and the intention and knowingness that you are already there! This is all you need…remember the formula. You will be on this island - your homeland, sooner than you think. Remember me, for I will come to you often once you arrive."

I am about to ask him another question, but he is gone even before my lips part. Who is he? Although I am standing in the boat, I am still inside the dream standing on the island looking out to sea beneath the night sky that is blanketed with stars. Suddenly, while lost in thought, I am pulled back into the reality of the boat and the sea as the wind rises up and plays with my hair, teasingly, tossing it gently to and fro. The smell of the air…so sweet….it is that smell of fresh, sweet sea water...like perfume.

"I will come to you on the wind…." The voice…it is all around me, resounding in my ears. Where did it come from? I notice the dampness in the air as it catches my attention, the humidity on my bare skin, and the setting sun as it casts its orange glow across my new Italian seascape.

Again - back in the dream – walking the cliff tops - that smell, the flowers, they are all in bloom. And the sounds of the sea below, I can hear a distant boat horn. The air feels deliciously sensual on my bare shoulders. A sound brings me back to my reality, but once my conscious mind investigates and feels secure, I am back on Capri, walking the cliff tops, looking out to sea with a full heart.

Where am I…on the boat to Capri with this fisherman? Or am I inside my own thoughts, remembering how and why I was catapulted to take this trip? No, I think I am inside the dream, walking on Capri. My worlds are colliding now, all at once...I am short circuiting as I stand here on the boat with my eyes closed, giggling into the wind. I think I've gone mad!   Sparks can surely be seen dancing in the air around my head. Nothing makes sense.

I remember the night I changed my name to "Roxanna." It came to me as I walked along the cliffs, and I knew it to be mine, given by the gods themselves. When I gazed upward, it was as if the ancient ones or the rocks had sung it to me. I wasn't sure which, but I knew I was now Roxanna. It was a name of strength – a name of someone who could accomplish anything – a name to remind me of home…my home - Capri. I was no longer Deborah Allen of America.

I am drifting…in and out…this lazy fog. I hear the boatman, "*Signora*, we almost there." I open my eyes and see that the haze over the water has thickened a bit as the sun is setting into the sea. I smell the dampness, just like the dream. It is all so etheric. Then I hear them.

Their voices are so incredible that I am mesmerized, glued to the spot where I now stand. They are singing…two, no three? Angels…no, there is something so eerie yet so enticing about them, as if they are calling to me to come to them. They are louder than the sounds of the sea, louder than the sound of the motor or the water splashing against the sides of the boat. Louder and louder…so loud…it is all I can hear. So beautiful…it takes my breath away….so…....

CHAPTER 2

The boatman, Luca doesn't see me slumped on the floor like a rag doll until he turns to tell me he is pulling into Marina Piccola. He runs to my side and then confused, runs back to the helm to take control of the boat. We are in dangerous waters, as we have come close to the *Scoglio delle Sirene* - the "Rocks of the Sirens." It was believed that three sirens would sit on these rocks at night and call to the sailors and the pirates to come to them. And when they came closer, they would be trapped by these women of the sea - lost here forever, never to return to their homeland. The story of Ulysses and his men encountering them is told in the Odyssey. Could they have been at this very place…Capri?

I now imagine Luca running around the boat not knowing what to do. As my mind tries to swim upward toward consciousness, I can hear him calling out, *"Mama mia! Mama mia,"* as he docks the boat. His excited behavior catches the attention of his brother Mario who is waiting for the delivery of cheeses and wine from Napoli, and also another man who is walking along the pier. They both start running toward us.

When they see me lying on the deck of the boat, Mario clasps his head in his hands, *"Mama mia! No good….male, male…very bad!"* The stranger hops on the boat and is now bending down beside me. Mario and Luca's voices are elevated, as Luca tries to explain that he knows nothing of what happened. Neither wants to get the authorities involved, since it would not be a good thing that Luca has picked me up, a strange woman who is paying him to take her across to the island, and that he is also unofficially bringing in wine and cheese for Mario to sell.

The stranger is speaking to both men in Italian, but with a Swedish accent. Although I am out cold, I can see everything – hear everything as if I am fully awake. Someone is bending down close to my face as one of my eyes is being pried open as he looks at my pupil. Suddenly, I feel his mouth upon mine - mouth to mouth resuscitation.

Ah-h-h…I awaken. I am being kissed – two lips, and green-blue eyes, so beautiful. Are they real? I am dazed, stammering, "Oh, what happened?" All I can remember is the sound of the voices calling to me. "The singing….where is it coming from?"

"What singing?" The Swede asks in English.

"Can't you hear it? Oh, it has stopped. I know I heard it." I am alarmed now, feeling like a foolish girl; and I am still hypnotized by his eyes….so sleepy…I'm so tired. Nothing seems real. He smiles down at me.

"You must have heard the voices of the sirens. That is the Rock of the Sirens over there." He points toward a large mass that juts out into the water.

"No, I'm sure it was something else…women's voices…I know they were real."

He laughs and helps me sit up. "Are you all right?"

"Yes, yes. I'm fine. I'm sorry. I haven't slept in awhile – long trip." He gives me a drink of water from a bottle.

"Thank you." I try to collect myself as I strain to hear the voices again, but Luca and Mario are still arguing loudly. The singing fades and then disappears, only to be replaced by the sounds of chaos.

"Piano, piano"…easy, easy, the Swede waves his hand slowly, as he tries to quiet them down. I know he is explaining to them in Italian that I am okay.

"Where are you staying, *Signora*?" His eyes…

"I...I don't know. I don't have a room yet. Do you know where I might find one?"

Luca is now hesitant about taking me on to Marina Grande and wants to drop me here with the stranger with the green-blue eyes. He waits, but not patiently, muttering and pacing all the while.

"Hmmm…it's Easter weekend and it seems everyone has come to the island. I'm afraid that all the hotels are booked, but let me make a call and I will see what I can do."

"Sbrigati! Sbrigati!" Hurry! Hurry! Luca is impatiently yelling to us.

"I will take her from here. I have a car, says the stranger," as he lifts me from the boat. Within seconds, Luca has thrown my suitcase onto the dock; and just as we step off the boat, he and his brother motor quickly out to sea. They are still passionately discussing these events, as most Italians seem to do…I am never sure if they are actually arguing or just having a loud discussion.

"My name is Stephen," he says taking my hand.

"I'm Roxanna. Thank you for your kindness." The wind has suddenly whipped up my hair and once again it is dancing all around my face, making a nuisance of itself. No matter how hard I try to control it, it has a life of its own, dancing, escaping, whirling and twirling freely – like me on the island as I have seen in my dream…

He's so handsome. I feel myself blush, especially after the kiss…God, I could use a shower. When was my last one? I try to comprehend what he is saying on the telephone, but he is speaking Swedish.

"I have a place for you to stay for the night in AnaCapri. Can you walk?"

"Yes, I'm fine now."

"Come. I have a small car." I feel his arm around my shoulder, guiding me to his automobile. He opens the door, helps me in and fastens my seatbelt. All this closeness is making me dizzy. He gets in behind the wheel of this little Italian model that I know is probably made only for these small European towns and islands where the roads are so narrow.

"Thank you for your help, Stephen. I'm so grateful you came along."

"No problem. You would have been in trouble with those two! They would have dumped you on the dock if they had a chance." He laughs out loud. As we drive away from the marina, I keep holding my breath, straining to hear the singing, but I never hear it again. Much time goes by as I sit quietly looking at the scenery as the little car climbs the mountainous road. The houses are so beautiful with their whitewashed fronts and open air terraces. Later, the islanders would tell me proudly that the architecture is called "Caprese" style, which they are known for.

We climb the side of the mountain, a long narrow road with no guard rails, only small plants and little rocks along the edge. The vista is magnificent, even at this time of day when dusk is edging its way in. We are probably eight hundred meters above the sea, looking down at the Mediterranean and the lights from the little boats below. It takes my breath away and I feel as if I am in a dream. Maybe I am dreaming after all, because this is far more beautiful than anything or any place I have ever seen before.

"Ah, *bella signora.*" He points to the marina far below. "That is Marina Grande, the main port. Marina Piccola, where you came in, is never used anymore except by a few of the locals. It is now the main swimming beach for the islanders and tourists. Everyone comes to Capri by way of Marina Grande. This is where the hydrofoils to the mainland dock."

"What's the name of the hotel?" I am trying to make conversation in the long silence that follows, although I am incapable of it. Each time I want to ask a question, I forget what it is before I open my mouth…exhaustion…

"It's not a hotel. It is called the San Michele Villa. I manage the museum which is on the grounds of the villa, so I have connections. There is a room available there, so you may have it."

"No, no. I can't put you out like that."

"Oh, there is no problem. There are many who come to the island to do work for the foundation or who perform in our concerts, so they are there for those who need a place to stay."

My brain is misfiring once again as I think of asking about the foundation. But then the car bounces and Stephen slams on the brakes to allow a bus to pass that is coming toward us from the other direction.

"Don't be alarmed. We all know how to drive this road pretty well." I am now acutely aware of how narrow it is and how close we are to the edge.

"It's breathtaking."

"Yes, when most come to visit, they never want to leave. I think you will enjoy it here."

We pull into a small driveway and into a garage and then walk along a small street, *un poco strada* called *Traverse Capodimonte.* Stephen uses an electronic card to open the gate and we enter a circular courtyard that is filled with color. Even in the fading light I can see the flowers and I am assaulted by the scent of them as we move past. I close my eyes and breathe in the perfume of night jasmine mingled with geranium and rose.

"*Fiori*…the island is known for its flowers – especially at this time of year." He smiles. "This way." He holds the door for me and we walk through corridors and up a flight of stairs to the second level. It is quite a large villa with many hallways, terraces and stairways. We come to another terrace and another outside stairway to an apartment. The grounds are quite beautiful with sculptures and flowers everywhere and tall palm trees surrounded by a circular grassy area.

Stephen unlocks the door and gestures for me to enter. There before me is a double bed with linens that only the Italians are known for. I can already feel them on my skin, so clean and cool. He is speaking to me, telling me where everything is in the small apartment, but nothing registers. My brain is no longer working, only misfiring from lack of sleep; now it has gone unconscious. All I can see is the bed.

"I can see you are very tired. If you need anything at all, my rooms are at the front of the villa on the left as we entered. Just knock and I will come. Sleep well, Roxanna." He smiles and leaves me standing at the foot of the bed. I barely find my toothbrush, brush my teeth and wash my face before I fall onto the bed and into a restless sleep for the next twelve hours.

I am in and out of sleep all night, no longer in my familiar bed in California, but here, high atop the island where the Spirit has taken me to. I am walking around Capri, feeling the sea breeze upon my skin, as the wind plays with my hair, walking…. I come to an outlook, a portico where there is a great marble sphinx perched on the wall overlooking the sea.

"Lay your hands upon him and make a wish." The voice comes to me on the wind, and I know it to be his. I reach out and lay my hand on its back.

"I wish for the answers to all that I am searching for. I wish for freedom in my life and passion like I have never known before…I wish for a great love." This I whisper even more quietly than the rest as if it were a secret I don't want anyone to hear but the gods themselves. Every word that I speak is a surprise to me, as if someone else is speaking them.

"As you wish, Roxanna. You will have it all and more." He laughs. You are in for the ride of your life; so get in, sit down, and hold on. Your tiger awaits you…or should I say your sphinx! Ha! Ha! Ha!"

CHAPTER 3

The next day, I awaken disoriented and it takes me a few moments to remember where I am; and when I do, I am filled with glee. I've made it! I am finally here where I have dreamed of being for months! The dream...I start to remember it...pieces anyway, my conversation with the Great Spirit, the sphinx...I've never even seen a sphinx before. I try to remember what it looks like, but all I can remember is how massive it is. I don't see its face in the dream for it faces the sea and it sits far out on a ledge. He came to me again. He said he would. Who is he? His voice is so familiar to me as if I have known him before.

What did I ask for? Answers...freedom from my life...passion....and wait...did I say a great love? Where did that come from? I haven't thought about a lover for quite some time. My divorce happened ten years ago, and I have been in and out of relationships all these years. In the last year, my fiftieth, I had finally come to the conclusion that I might be alone for the rest of my life – not without men of course, but I didn't see myself with another husband. I had been happily dating for quite some time now.

And passion, what do I know of passion? I remember that feeling inside me, ignited like a fire in my belly that used to move me to express myself on canvas or paper. That was that place I used to paint from. It was a place so deep inside me, that it seemed ancient, as if it had been inside my soul since the beginning of time. I must have always painted in every other lifetime.

I felt it so deeply that at times, it took me over and drove me to do things like this – to come to this island on the other side of the world out in the middle of the sea. Most people don't even know where Capri is - often thinking it a Greek island instead of Italian. Of course it was in the beginning...

As I lay here, I feel the passion starting to rise inside me, the heat of it, and think about making love for the first time in ages. How long has it been? I try to remember. Years – two to be exact...How have I lived without love all that time? I haven't painted in two years either. Yes, now I remember...

It all started the year before I turned fifty. Every woman says it's a difficult thing to go through, but I said it wouldn't be for me. But as I look back, I guess I fell under the spell of that belief as well. I started to notice my body changing: my breasts were becoming smaller, inching down my chest. They weren't as full as they used to be as if they were shrinking. My skin was a bit dryer and my face showed my life as if it were a roadmap. Thank God I smile more than I frown! For my frown lines make me look older as time has etched them into my skin!

I never really believed that age mattered; but as a woman walking through the doorway to fifty, it really does. I was a twenty-year-old girl as I entered the portal, but once I stepped through to the other side (the fifty-mark), I became a middle-aged woman. I am no different than the rest. I am now the crone, older in physicality and wiser with life's experiences. But my passions still run deep. I can feel things that others don't - like the flowers and how they smell. They fill me up as if I am intoxicated. They move me so making my heart flutter. And when the sun sets, it takes my breath away. I can feel it inside me as if I am the sky giving it to the sea as a gift for the night.

With all this passion, will men still find me attractive? Will they see how I feel – know that I am still filled with the feelings of a young girl or a beautiful woman? Will I ever make love to a man again? Ah, the thought of it - the romance of it, the feelings of being swept away to the edge of the abyss where nothing matters except that place of love. How I yearn for it.

Suddenly, I feel the linens against my breasts as I roll over, and they make me stir inside. How I love the feel of them. My stomach growls…is this hunger? When was the last time I ate? It was in Munich twenty hours ago! I'm famished! All other thoughts of lovers or passion are gone now, for the hunger is far greater in these moments.

I take a quick bath since there is no shower, and throw on a pair of jeans, a linen shirt and sneakers. As I walk toward the front of the villa to knock on Stephen's door, I round a corner and bump into someone. My hands move out quickly in front to protect myself as I fall into Stephen's muscular and well-defined chest. He reaches out to grab me.

"Oh, I'm so sorry Stephen. Are you all right?"

"You just knocked the wind out of me a bit but I'm okay." I blush at our closeness.

"I was coming to thank you and to ask for your help in finding somewhere to stay for the next two weeks."

"I've already been making calls and I'm afraid you're out of luck. You'll have to stay here. I hope my apartment is acceptable."

I feel like a shy schoolgirl. "Thank you again. It seems you have been helping me since I stepped off the boat.....or before that even." We both laugh.

"Now you can help me. Would you like to have lunch with me? I know it's early by Italian standards, but not by American, and you must be hungry after your long trip."

He is looking at my hair which is pulled back in a loose barrette, wisps flying every which way. I am shy in these moments and I can feel my cheeks heat up. I see him looking into my eyes and I hope they are the aqua-blue that they become at times. I want to impress him, for he is a man and I a woman. Little do I know he is hypnotized by them.

"I would love to. I'm famished." We walk out of the villa and down the little walkway toward the main *piazza*. A little café called the Caprese sits on one corner and we choose an outside table. After ordering *panini* sandwiches, espresso and aqcua naturale with local lemon, Stephen talks about AnaCapri and how it came about that tourists started coming to the little village at the top of the island. I am now hypnotized by his eyes which are green at the moment.

"Around 1876, a young eighteen year old medical student named Axel Munthe was in the south of Italy and decided to visit Capri for the day. Once he arrived, he climbed the 770 stone stairs to the top and came to the little town of AnaCapri. He fell in love with it and its villagers and swore he'd come back and live here. Eventually, he bought the land that now houses the San Michele Hotel, the Villa, the gardens and the foundation. There's a lot more to it and it's quite an interesting story, but you'll have to read the book to get a feel for him and the story as he tells it. When he died, he left the villa, its grounds and all of its artifacts to the Swedish government. Other properties on the island which he had amassed over his lifetime were split between his family and the Italian government. I work for the foundation that was set up to manage the villa, and that's my story."

"So you live here year round?"

"Most of the time, but the tourists stop coming to the island in the autumn, so I usually go home to Sweden for a few months then. What about you, Roxanna? Where do you live and what do you do?"

"I live in a small town in southern California called Carlsbad. I have two sons who are seventeen and nineteen. And I'm divorced...have been for ten years. I left my job to come here and I'm not sure what I will do when I return to the States. Maybe a new career...maybe I'll paint and try to make a living doing that. I don't know yet..." A woman with long dark hair and dark eyes is walking toward us.

"Stephano, *ciao, bello.*" She bends over and kisses him on the lips. I know she is his lover. It's the way she holds herself and the way she approaches him – that dance of romance and intimacy. It is also that look they share - as if they are making love with their eyes.

"Rosa, this is Roxanna, a new guest at the villa. I was telling her about AnaCapri."

"*Ciao, bella*; nice to meet you." She is stunning, tall with a beautiful curvy Italian body. Her hair is long, thick, and dark, pulled back from her face by the sunglasses that are resting on top of her head. Her skin is smooth, dark and beautiful and she is dressed in a tight fitting pencil skirt and tight top, her breasts pressing against its fabric to be released. At the end of her long slender legs are open-toed, high-heeled sandals.

"Nice to meet you, too. Would you like to join us?"

"No, no, *grazie*. I must go." As she turns to leave, she smiles at Stephen, "See you tonight, *bello*. *Ciao.*" She blows him a kiss as she sashays through the *piazza*. She is very sexy. When I look back at Stephen, I do believe he is blushing.

"She is very beautiful. Did you meet her on the island?"

"Yes, yes, I did." That was it…the end of the discussion. Obviously, she is very important to him and they have a serious relationship between them.

"Where were we, Roxanna?" The conversation continues until lunch comes and into the next hour, and then we say our good-byes. After we part, I ride the *seggiovia* - the chairlift, up to the top of *Monte Solaro*. As it moves up along the side of the mountain, I look out over the sea and to the little town of AnaCapri below. This is the vista from my dreams! I have been here before! The hair is standing straight up on my bare arms and I shiver. It's not from the air, but from the fact that that I have only been here in a dream. My heart flutters.

Once at the top of the mountain, I look over the edge of the cliffs and see *I Faraglioni* – the two famous rocks that jut out of the sea. Sorrento sits in the distance with Amalfi at its backside. There is a small chapel at the top of the mount across the way, which I am guessing is somewhere in between the towns of Capri and AnaCapri. It looks as if the only way there is to hike down this mountain and up the next ridge since it is set so far out in between both areas of civilization. A small hamlet perhaps…I'll have to explore further at another time. Seagulls are flying half way between here and the sea far below. What a strange thing to be so far above the sky where the birds fly. I snap pictures from every viewpoint and then sit on the veranda sipping *acqua minerale*, contemplating my life.

Being a manager in corporate America had made me weary after twenty-five years. I had been responsible my whole life and needed a break so desperately, felt as if I was trapped in my life suddenly. Why? I keep turning it over in my mind but can't find any particular reason. Nothing had changed – except me. Painting was always a passion of mine, but I was so tired most days that I stopped painting for long spells, the last being two years. God, I miss the feel of the brush between my fingers…

When I painted, it was as if I was creating my own life, my own destiny. It didn't matter what the subject matter was, only that I was creating with brushes and paint. I smell the oils for a moment, taking me back to a memory of another time and place when I painted for a living…my heart sings as I remember. The passion rises up inside me and my body heats up as if I am making love in this moment. The heat is rising inside me now, taking me out of the memory and pulling me back to the present moment on the veranda, atop *Monte Solaro*.

I look around at the few tourists that have taken a chance vacationing here this time of year, so early in the season. Stephen had said that most days in early spring are still cool enough for a jacket and when the winds rise up, it is cold and damp. I am warm-blooded these days, so the weather doesn't bother me much. The flowers are in bloom everywhere – along the paths, in the fields along the mountain, and in the distance on the ridge in front of the little chapel half way to Capri. It is so quiet that I hear nothing, except my own breathing and the thoughts inside my head. There are no birds chirping, no sounds of the sea, no traffic, and no chatter. It is as if the world has no voice and silence is a way of life.

My mind is not used to sitting in this silence for long, so it hurries back to the life I have just left behind…my boys…Josh and Devon. They are hardly boys anymore. They have lived with me all these years, seen me work hard. They have known me as their rock, never faltering in life. When they had issues, those that teenagers have with life (friends, girlfriends, school), I was the one they would come to. In my arms, they could revert back to their childhood where their mommy would hold them, hug them, rub their hair and whisper that all the pain in their world would magically disappear and rainbows would appear. They felt safe with me, wrapped up in my love. They always came home to me when they were ill or needed a hug.

I love them as if they were my every breath - had a difficult time watching them grow and pull away as they started dating. I was no longer the one and only woman in their lives and that had been painful.

I found myself sitting with dinner on the table each night, waiting for them to come home. They would run through the door, grab something from the table and run in to change their clothes, only to leave again. After the tenth time, I stopped making dinner and started to ask when we could eat together. Once a week, we shared a meal and all the other nights left me alone to sit and contemplate my new role in their lives. They no longer needed a "mommy." They were grown men now who loved their mother still, but no longer relied on her for her wisdom and her love. I had already laid the foundation for them. They were men of the world and it was time to let them go out and be men. When I had talked about wanting to leave my job and take a break from life, they were the ones that told me to go.

"Mom, you have always been here for us. Now it's your turn. You need to go and have fun. Find whatever is inside you that inspires you to paint again. You're really good, you know."

Devon painted, too and loved to watch me when he was a child. We would paint in the backyard, him standing next to me, mimicking me, a small canvas resting on his little easel. He too had stopped. Was it because of me? No matter right now. He will pick it up again when the time is right – when he is more settled in his life; after all, the life of a teenager is a busy one.

It was as if they were pushing me out the door, although I knew they were not. They only wanted me to go and find a life. They knew I worked too hard, letting all other things fall away. Little did they know that the only reason I buried myself in my work was because I did not know what else to do. I had become a victim of my circumstances and allowed the end of my life as a mother, define my future.

No more! I decided to go and live – to find passion – to ride the back of the tiger! I am giggling out loud as I think about my choices. Here I am on top of the world with a new name and a spirit talking to me in my dreams, driving me to do strange things….igniting the passions inside me. I can't stop giggling and wrap my arms around myself like an excited little girl.

"*Scusi*, what is so funny, *signora*?" I am startled out of my thoughts as I feel him move closer to me. "Can you share your happiness with me?"

CHAPTER 4

I hesitate since he is a stranger, but he is beautiful to look at. His face is sculpted like one of those Greek statues, the perfect nose and the chiseled lips, the deep set eyes. He is tall and dark with perfectly bronzed skin as if he had been baking in the sun his whole life. His hair is thick, black and curly, glistening from some kind of gel that probably tames the wildness of his curls. He is smiling wide, his beautiful white teeth blinding against his bronzed skin.

"I was just thinking about something." I am uncomfortable. He takes my hand to shake it and introduces himself.

"I am Antonio."

"My name is Roxanna. Nice to meet you, Antonio. Do you live here on the island?" He is the most beautiful man in Italy - like a god…

"Yes, yes. I am born here. I am sorry my *Inglais* is not so good." "It's fine, Antonio. Would you like to sit?" He sits beside me.

"Are you alone, Roxanna?"

"Yes, I arrived last night." Is it safe to say so? I had heard stories about the Italian men and how they liked to pinch…and god knows what else.

"Then I will be your tour guide for the island. There are so many beautiful places you need to see. I will take you to all of them. I have a scooter."

"Thanks, Antonio. I'd like that."

"Would you like to go to Capri tomorrow afternoon, at about three o'clock? There is the Ruins of Tiberius called the Villa Jovais. He was a Roman emperor who built a castle and lived there. It is about an hour walk from Capri. I will take you down on my scooter and then we will walk from the town. I will bring picnic, yes?" I laugh because his accent is sexy.

"Yes, that sounds nice." We sit and chat for an hour, and then take the *seggiovia* down to AnaCapri. I blush as he kisses my cheeks in the Italian fashion, because I am not used to this custom that seems so intimate. How old must he be, I wonder as I walk back to my apartment…maybe twenty-five? Why would someone so young, so beautiful, be interested in spending time with someone twice his age?

My stomach growls and I realize I am hungry again. Directly in front of me on the small street is a stand; so I stop for a *panini* sandwich with tomatoes, mozzarella and basil called a *caprese*. Is everything called *caprese* here, I wonder? I think about eating and a long hot bath before crawling into bed with my book, for I still need to recover from my long trip.

The book is the "Birth of Venus," by Sarah Dunant, about the life of a young female painter Alessandra Gecchi, in the 15th century. I am excited to read it since I too am a woman who paints…or once painted. She, of course, is one of the first female painters recognized during the Renaissance.

As I lay with my book in hand, I find my eyes heavy with sleep after just five pages. And before I can even muster up a vision of Antonio and his statuesque features, I am gone from this world and into the next.

The next day after leaving the café at the *piazza*, I stroll down a small street with shops on both sides. I smile to myself for I remember Stephen telling me that the Italians called a little street *un poco strada*. I love the sound of this Italian phrase.

I walk on looking at the shops and the people as they work and everyone is smiling. *"Buongiorno, Bella"* or *"Buongiorno, Signora."* They are all so friendly. As I am buying water at the small kiosk where I purchased my panini the night before, I hear a familiar voice.

"Buongiorno, Roxanna."

"Stephen, *buongiorno*." His dark shades are covering his eyes, as mine are. Now, I can focus on his smile without being hypnotized by those eyes…

"What sights are you taking in today?" He asks.

"I don't know yet. I am just roaming the streets to see where they will take me."

"Well then, I have somewhere special I want to take you." We head down the walk toward the San Michele Villa Museum and grounds which is the original house that Dr. Axel Munthe had built. In his book, "The Story of San Michele" which I purchased yesterday at the little bookstore in AnaCapri, he writes, *"I built the house on my knees, like a temple to the sun, where I would seek knowledge and light from the radiant God whom I had worshipped all my life."* And, yes, he describes it perfectly. It is a temple to the sun. There are columns and porticos everywhere. The building is white, the pergola is open to the sunlight and it is decorated with the most divine statues and vases. There are ancient artifacts everywhere, many of which he had dug up from the gardens as he was building his house; and yet others are reproductions.

So many photographs to take…so many sacred spots to remember…It is all so familiar to me as if it is my own home. Each room, I remember as if I have lived here once long ago, in my past. I gasp…my sleeping quarters…I mean Munthe's…there in the corner – Kouros. He is six feet tall and bronzed, beautiful. He represents youth in Greek mythology. It reminds me of my own Kouros statue that sits in my bedroom in the States….what an uncanny coincidence…or is it? I had found it on Ebay and had to have it. I didn't even know who he was…only that I had to have it. And every night after, was like sleeping with the gods.

We leave the house, and are moving out into the Sculpture Loggia which is filled with Munthe's art collection. The arched loggia's flooring is of inlaid marble with a Cosmati table and a gold mosaics top. A life-size reproduction of *Mercury Resting*, a gift from the city of Naples, sits at the far end, with other sculptures lining the loggia: a *Helmeted Ulysses,* a bust of the *Emperor Tiberius,* a life-size bronze of *Artemis*, the bust of a beautiful woman and others. Outside the loggia is a courtyard where a replica of Verrocchio's fountain, *the Boy and the Dolfins* sits in its center reminding me of children laughing and playing.

We move through the grounds, the gardens, an open gallery and then come upon the pergola supported by thirty-seven columns that Munthe designed himself. I know he must have spent many hours out here each day: I feel his spirit all around me and the gooseflesh raises itself on my arms. It is as if he never left. Stephen tells me that Munthe wanted to build a house "open to the sun and the wind and voices of the sea, like a Greek temple, with light, light, light everywhere." Well he accomplished this and so much more. This is a place I do not want to leave…I want to stay and sit and just be here in the gardens all day.

"It is all so beautiful. It is *paradiso*…the gardens…the statues…the flowers…"

"I knew you'd like it." He is holding his sunglasses and I notice his eyes flash in the sunlight as we walk to the end of the pergola where we can see the Marina Grande port far below. "There…" he points. "…are the seven-hundred and seventy-seven Phoenician Steps that Munthe had walked up to arrive in AnaCapri that first day." I have to come back to paint all of this, I think to myself.

I feel desire rising up inside me once again, needing to be expressed. My body is tingling all over as if my blood was made of little champagne bubbles. I am overwhelmed with the beauty of the land and the seascape before me. I have never before seen anything – felt anything so beautiful in all my life! I want to live here forever, wake up here, walk here to bid good night to the stars and the sea before I retire. I feel like Munthe, as if I were a reincarnation of him. I feel his soul upon these grounds, his breath whispering in my ear, "Take care of my sacred site…." Then…it is gone, carried out to sea by the wind.

Stephen takes my hand as we walk on to *la scala* – the stone stairway leading up to yet another portico.

"Wait until you see the chapel and the 3200 year old Egyptian sphinx." My breath stops in my throat.

"A sphinx?" The dream…my feet are still moving one in front of the other, although I am frozen in time. There, sitting up on a ledge with its back to me, is the same great sphinx as the one in my dream. It is framed by an arched window with a view of the sea behind it.

"They say if you have a wish, stroke its back as you wish it and it will come true." I feel his hand upon mine as I place it on its left hind quarter, and in the next moment, the wish forms in my mind.

"I wish to feel passion every single day that I am here!" I whisper inside my own mind so that only the gods can hear me. And then I am finally forced to take a breath since it has been minutes.

"Are you all right, Roxanna?" Stephen sees the look of shock and wonderment on my face. My heart is beating rapidly and I know he feels my excitement.

"Roxanna, are you all right? I know it is a beautiful thing." I am embarrassed.

"I'm just surprised. I dreamt about this sphinx two nights ago."

"Then you were meant to stay at the San Michele Villa after all. It is your destiny." I pull my hand from his, self-conscious that we are sharing this intimate moment together.

"Axel Munthe also dreamt about the sphinx. In it, a spirit came to him and told him he would find it under the sea one day. And years later, when it was time, he had another dream, and this time the spirit told him where it would be. So he took his boat, sailed exactly to where he was told to go, found it, pulled it out of the sea and brought it back here."

Am I actually standing on this spot on this island, on the other side of the world, touching a 3200-year-old sphinx that I dreamed of?

"Come…one more important place for you to see." We arrive at the entrance of the San Michele Chapel and I can feel Stephen step back away from me. It is as if he is delivering me to Archangel Michael himself.

"Breathe…" I tell myself. "Don't forget to breathe, Roxanna"…. Tears of love escape me. I have always been close to him – always felt his presence in my life…such a sacred experience.

Stephen is talking to me, but my emotions have taken me out of this reality. "The little chapel was built during the Middle Ages, dedicated to Michael and everything inside is from the 13th to the 17th centuries." He points to sacred artifacts that are about the room, a wooden statue of San Michele, his carved eyes still shining with love, if that is at all possible. Statues of Joseph and Mary sit on the right wall and a baptismal font to the left. A 15th century crucifix and a 3000 year old statue of Horus the Egyptian God are also in the room. The floor is the same beautifully inlaid multi-colored marble as the *Sculpture Loggia,* and the room is roped off so that the tourists cannot enter, but Stephen has stepped forward to unlink the chain.

"You may enter." He motions for me to go inside. My heart is racing as I try to adjust to the energy all around me. The sacredness…my eyes fill with tears, my heart beats wildly.

"When Mr. Munthe came here and saw this chapel, he fell to his knees and knew he had to build his home right here on this very spot. He restored this place after it was burned down almost completely by Corsairs in 1535 led by the infamous Barbarossa, you know - the pirate? That's his castle up on top of that mountain." He points toward the window where I see a castle upon the hill.

I can no longer hear him speak…I've been transported to another time inside this holy place. I promise myself I will come here often while I am on the island.

"I think I have found heaven." He steps closer to me.

"I knew you would like it. It's pretty spectacular." We linger for awhile before leaving and I hope Stephen does not speak, for I need to recover. I know if I have to speak, I will weep instead.

We walk back down through the gardens, past the fountain of the boy with the dolphins and out the gate. I am recovered, finally.

"Well, I need to get to the office. We're having a concert here in the chapel on Friday night and I have a lot of work to do to make sure everything is in order." He takes my hand as if he is going to shake it, and then he kisses both my cheeks. I barely thank him because I am feeling too delicious as I float back down the street toward the villa. I am to meet Antonio in the *piazza* in one hour.

CHAPTER 5

"*Ciao, bella*. You are so beautiful, Roxanna." That smile…

"I have my scooter; is good?" That thick Napolitano accent…

"That's good. I have never been on a bike before." What am I getting myself into, I think to myself? Cars are not allowed on the streets in AnaCapri except the main road connecting AnaCapri to Capri below, so we walk to a parking lot at the edge of town. At the bike, he hands me a helmet and starts the scooter, and within minutes I am riding along the cliffs, holding on tightly to this beautiful twenty-five year old dark haired, dark-eyed *Italiano* with chiseled features who looks like Michelangelo's *David*; while my skirt is blowing in the island breeze, baring my legs. Diane Lane in "Under the Tuscan Sun" comes to mind.

At this, I laugh out loud and Antonio turns and says, "What makes you laugh, Roxanna?"

"Nothing, I just can't believe I'm doing this!"

"I will show you more of this, my sweetie!"

I can see his brilliant white smile as he turns his head. This is something to write home about! I feel that now familiar feeling inside my chest, probably my heart - those feelings of surprise, delight, excitement, and rapture….passion…that's what it is. Ah! I am so happy in these moments. I am feeling passion!

It takes fifteen minutes to get to our destination where Antonio parks his scooter and pulls out a sack filled with our dinner. The walk is long, an hour to get to the Villa Jovais, the home of the great Roman Emperor Tiberius, who had lived the last ten years of his life on Capri. As we walk along, I can't help but stop and smell the flowers, the *fiori* that Capri is so well known for; and since it is April, all are in full bloom.

"They are to die for!" I have never seen so many flowers in bloom at one time! So I dance around them filled with glee. I can't control myself! I try to bend down close enough to smell each one – become one with their intoxicating nectar. They are everywhere. Antonio stoops to pluck one from the earth.

"No! It will die. You should leave it there!"

"Oh, no, bella. You are so beautiful; they would be honored for you to hold them until they take their last breath. They have grown beautiful just for you." I feel myself melting and now I am putty in Antonio's hands. I keep laughing and my laughter turns to giggles for I am deliriously happy. I haven't giggled in years. When was the last time I felt like this? I am here on the other side of the world, on an island in the middle of the *Mediterraneo*, with this beautiful man who is picking flowers for me. How romantic is this?

By the time we reach the ruins, Antonio has gathered a large bouquet of spring flowers for me, and I accept them graciously. We walk to the very top of the ruins where there stands a ten foot tall monument, in black patina, of the crowned Madonna and child. I have never seen her in black. Is she the same Black Madonna that they speak of so lovingly in Sicily? The story I heard was that she was stolen from a church there by pirates and then came back to them unharmed. I didn't remember the whole story, but I do remember that the Sicilians believed she had magical powers and could make wishes come true, even healing anyone who was ailing.

So I stand before her in her shadow and close my eyes just in case. I wish to find clarity to what I am looking for in my life. I say a prayer and bless her and then walk toward Antonio.

He opens the sack filled with salad, bread, cheeses and Lemoncello, the famous lemon drink that Italy is so well known for.

"I have never had this before. What is it?"

"My grandmother makes it. She takes eight lemons and then takes the skin off of them…she uses only the skins. This is very important. She adds alcohol and then puts it in the freezer for twenty eight days…this is very important too, Roxanna….no less and no more." He is adamant that her recipe is the best and that her Lemoncello is far better than any other in all of Italy. This makes me smile.

"After twenty-eight days, she takes it out, puts it through a…how you say…filter, and then boils one cup of *sucra* – sugar. Then she puts the sugar and the alcohol in a jar in the freezer for twenty eight more days. Only then is it ready to drink! That's how you make Lemoncello. Try it. It is good, but be very careful, Roxanna….it is very powerful. You cannot drink too much." He looks at me as if I am a school girl and he is trying to protect me.

At first, it is too strong for me, but I sip slowly and eat the sandwich he has made. The magic of the hour of day when the sun comes to eye level in the sky, and the Lemoncello make me giddy, for I feel light, happy and intoxicated.

Antonio smiles at me, enamored with the fact that I am so giggly. So he plays the part of the suitor in a mating ritual, telling me stories of his manhood and his life, while I sit there in awe of the day – giggling at all he is saying. My smile is as wide as my face will allow. I giggle with each word, for his accent is so thick. Although he speaks English well, he slips into Italian if he forgets a word. I don't mind because I find it sexy. I finally ask.

"What does *Aspette*" mean?

"It means "wait.""

"What about *pero*?"

"That means 'but.' I will help you with your Italian, Roxanna, if you help me with my *Inglais...capisce*?"

"*Capisco*. I understand and I will help you." Oh, what fun...I am falling in love with the language....the romance of it...

On the walk back to the town of Capri, Antonio takes a turn in the opposite direction and we walk to the Natural Arch and the Grotto of Matermania, a naturally formed arch made of rock that has been hewn out by the wind and the sea. I think it should have been one of the "seven wonders of the world" – or is it the Lemoncello that makes me think so? Antonio tells me that during the Imperial Age, orgies took place here. I wonder what that must have been like...my mind is feeling amorous from the Lemoncello.

We sit and watch the sunset - a red fireball as it drops into the sea. I have never experienced a sunset quite like it – could it be the Lemoncello and the thoughts of orgiastic rituals that have taken place so long ago underneath this arch? Or is it the smell and the smile of Antonio?

Once we arrive in AnaCapri, Antonio walks me to the villa and asks me to dinner the next night.

"Can we do it the following day? I have plans, Antonio." I don't, but want some free time to explore the island alone. He agrees and as he moves toward me to kiss my cheeks – he surprises me and pulls my face toward his, kissing my lips. I am startled and pull away.

"I'm sorry, Roxanna. It's just a kiss." He shows his pearly whites, winks and says, "*Ciao*," as he walks back to his scooter with his hands in his pockets. I turn and walk through the gardens toward my room, not sure how I should take Antonio's kiss. Is he interested in me in that way? Or is it just the Italian way? I'm not sure.

The romance of the island makes everyone seem so appealing...I have not met one man that hasn't been beautiful in one way or another. As I turn the key in the lock, I think to myself, are all the men here really as beautiful as I think; or is it just my passion awakening inside me?

I fall asleep restlessly contemplating passion. My thoughts seep into my dreams and each time I awaken, it comes to me in whispers…not a peaceful night's sleep, but one instead filled with my own heightened senses…

Exploring the island the next morning, I drink *espresso* as I sit on a beautifully painted tile bench and watch the local shop keepers open their shops. Each day is a ritual for them. They sweep the streets or walkways in front of the stores and then wash the windows. Then all of their wares are carted outside for the tourists. Each day, it is the same. How hard they work, from early morning until late at night. Nevertheless, they are always smiling and happy, often singing.

The townspeople sing as they move through the streets or work in their gardens, for I often hear them as I walk through the village. Is it the magic of the island or just the way of the Italians? They surely don't sing in the corporate world I have come from. Life seems so simplistic. The people are real – they aren't afraid to express themselves.

When they talk with one another, they talk with their hands and use their faces, so full of expression - from talking with their children, telling them they love them, to praising the cooks in restaurants. They use all of themselves to express what they are feeling. That's it! They aren't trying to express what they are thinking, but what they are feeling. That's the difference between them and us! They are passionate about what they do – even their work, no matter what it is. Passion….they have what I am searching for…

And suddenly, it walks by me…

"*Ciao, bella. Como va?*" He is a very handsome young man who I have seen in the *piazza* yesterday, and he is smiling at me flirtatiously.

"*Ciao.*" I smile shyly.

"My name is Bruno. *Chiamo?*" He has stopped now. His eyes are a pale green, the color of opals and his hair is cut short like Caesar's. When he bows down to take my hand, I notice his eyelashes as they touch his skin, they are so long.

"Roxanna. Nice to meet you, Bruno."

"Roxanna, would you like to share a drink with me?" He is looking at me in a very flirtatious way and I am not quite comfortable with this…although he is beautiful and seems very sweet. I am attracted to his perfect well-toned physique and his smile…his opal colored eyes… But then I allow my common sense to take over.

"No, *grazie*." He pretends to be sad and looks at me through those lashes.

"Oh, *bella*. Maybe *domani* - tomorrow?" I can't help but giggle.

"*Ciao*, Bruno. Nice to meet you." He shrugs and walks away, smiling. It is getting hot now…is it the sun or Bruno?

Two hours go by…who knows the time since I have stopped wearing a watch. I giggle to myself. What does it matter? I am gleefully happy sitting in the clean, sweet island air, watching fathers hold their babies as they call them either *bello* or *bella*. One man holds his three year old son in his arms as he hugs and kisses him…what love. A little boy of about eight stoops down to look closely at a flower that has grown out of a crack in the cement.

"*Bello*," he says as he smiles. Do they come out of the womb romancing life…being so aware of the beauty of it?

Oh, these people – the way they express themselves. For hours, I sit and get lost in it, and I remember that at one time in my life, I was like them – demonstrative with my feelings, filled with expressions of love. But over the years, it dried up, broke into dust and blew away with the wind. Where had it gone? I want that life back –feeling passion in each and every moment – such love, that nothing else exists! I feel at home here as if I am one of them – that they are my family and we know each other intimately. I belong here!

A man sits with his little girl of about five. She is in his lap and continually reaches up to rub his balding head and pat the side of his face with her little palm, all the while lovingly calling him "Papa." The look in her eyes is of love and admiration. He lovingly kisses her hair and her cheek. Then, she falls asleep in his arms as he continues to caress her. She is cuddled up with her little head in the crook of his arm and he never stops caressing her all the while.

Is passion noticing the beauty of life around you? Is it expressing how you feel with your fingers, your lips, your heart? Is this what romancing your life is? Ah, *paradiso*…So lazy in the sun... intoxicated by all of this. I could sit here forever. Time to move; more to see.

Lazily, I walk further through the village and notice there are no supermarkets here – no one-stop-shops to hurry the process along, like in America. Here, shopping for necessities is like a meditation of sorts. Each item to be purchased has its own store. Chicken is purchased at the Macelleria Polla, the butcher for chicken. Fish is bought at *Sopori di Mare*, tobacco from the Tabacchi Shop, deodorant at the *Farmacia* and wine or beverages from the *Vini e Bibite*. All the shops close from 13:30

(1:30 p.m.) to 16:30 (4:30 p.m.) for their siesta time. I could never understand that concept until much later when I would feel the heat.

Over the next few weeks, in between my sight seeing with Antonio, I continue to walk through the village each day, meeting and greeting the locals and getting to know my new extended family. I roam down the little lanes or walkways that lead to the hidden villas. They are only wide enough for maybe one or two people to walk together as they weave intricately throughout the village causing me to lose my way quite often. The walls surrounding the homes are incredible - made by the hands of the men of the island. They are built of heavy, large rocks mortared together so perfectly – rough yet with a pattern.

For weeks, I watch a man building a wall in his garden. I know he works in the village. But still, he is out there each day at dawn and then again at dusk breaking rocks, laying them with mortar and setting them in place. I see others do the same. They take such pride in these walls as if they represent the strength of their families. They seem to be the strength of the island. It's all about the sea, the sky, the sun and the rocks; for Capri is an island built out of rock. There are no pebbles or sand on this island or upon its shores. No, it is all rock – Roxanna…I smile to myself as I mouth my name. How appropriate that my ancestors have named me so, "Roxanna" whispered from the voices of the rocks themselves.

I notice so much about life each day that I have never seen before. I watch the men and women tending their gardens as I walk into town. There are grapevines, fruit trees - apple, peach, kiwi, plum, apricot and lemon trees, and then there are raspberries, strawberries, fava beans, artichokes and tomatoes, and basil and other herbs. Each day they water and prune, and speak to the earth that birthed them. They touch the fruits and vegetables lovingly as if they are their children. Their yards are impeccable; and if they work in the shops in the town during the day, they are hard at work in their gardens late at night - singing all the while.

In America, I had forgotten to step outside my home, forgotten that the night air soothed the soul and that the stars and the moon infused energy into the body. But here in Capri, these people have always known and never forgotten.

The women are strong, caring for the children, helping care for the gardens, preparing meals and caring for their husbands. Each day, they walk to the market to bring home whatever is needed. They carry their bags the long distance to their villas since there are no automobiles. I notice how the men treat their wives, mothers and daughters with reverence. They care for the women as if they are all Santa Maria, who is everywhere in Italy. They put them on pedestals. It is their culture, passed down from father to son and even as young boys, they know their mother is special, hence all women are sacred.

I have fallen in love with this island and these people. How will I ever leave them when it is time? Can't think of this now...I push all thoughts of leaving out of my mind...

So many new friends...there is Nuncio and his sons at the family *ceramica* shop and Ciero, the man in the little stand on *il poco strada,* the little street from the main *piazza* to the San Michele Villa. Federico Salvatore, the great painter of the island plays his guitar for me when I stop by his studio. There is Alessandra from the Perfumeria, Franco and Vinnie from the Barbarossa Pizzaria upstairs overlooking the *piazza*, Danielle and Maria from Il Martino, and Carlo from the Lemoncello factory. I am falling in love with each and every one of them as if I am having a love affair. I am giddy with anticipation each morning when I awaken, excited at the thought of walking into town to see each of their faces and share kisses with them.

CHAPTER 6

During my two week stay at the San Michele Villa, Stephen is never to be seen. Is he traveling? I hope that I might run into him again, but I never do. Soon, it will be time to leave the little apartment that I have grown to love and call my home.

My days have been filled with Antonio. This night, we ride the scooter down the long narrow and winding roads that hug the edges of the cliffs to Marina Piccola. When we arrive at the water's edge, it is 18:00, six o'clock, the magical hour – that surreal time of day when the sun spills thousands of tiny diamonds on the ocean and then dances upon them. I like to live my life always looking for the brilliance of those diamonds in everything. I find their shimmering beauty in even the smallest of things, and this time of day here looking out to sea, reminds me to do so.

This night is so beautiful with the sunlight in that perfect place in the sky and the *Scoglio delle Sirene* before us. The water is like a vast pool of aquamarine set in liquid gold as the sun lowers itself – more vibrant with different shades of aqua than anywhere else on the island. And since there is no sand on Capri, the waters edge is strewn with bits of colored rocks and stones that have been polished by the salty sea. Mixed in with them are bits and pieces of colored glass and painted tiles. I imagine that the colored glass is from old pirate ships when pirates threw their bottles overboard after nights of intoxication. And the tiles…who knows? I have no idea how they arrived here. I have no need to guess, but just to enjoy them. No wonder the sirens loved this magical place.

Besides occupying my time, I find that Antonio is also occupying my heart and my mind. He is so passionate and romantic that I am always caught off guard by his many small gestures. He walks with me, holding me close to him, holding my hand often. He is always touching my face as he tells me in Italian how beautiful I am. And he is so protective of me when other men are around, as if he was my lover - which he is not. After spending much time with him followed by long hours of contemplation on the subject, I realize I am more intrigued with him than anything else. He is young - half my age and a gorgeous Roman god, and he thinks that I am beautiful. This is startling to me. I don't see myself as he does. No wonder I am dazed and confused with thoughts of fantasy and love!

"You know, you must have been so beautiful when you were younger, Roxanna, do you know what I mean?" He always says that, "…do you know what I mean..."

"Thanks Antonio. I feel ancient now!"

"No, no…you are still beautiful now, my sweetie," (something else he always calls me). "You are very beautiful, but I can imagine what you were like when you were my age… oh, so beautiful."

I giggle at this, something I do constantly since I have arrived on the island and whenever I am with him. There is a compliment in there somewhere, I think.

"Roxanna, when I go home to sleep at night, or when I sit outside with a glass of *vino* and look up at the stars, I often think of you. You are always on my mind; do you know what I mean? You are like my angel. You know, sweetie, when you laugh, you look like a little girl." So I continue to laugh and giggle because he makes my heart smile. It is all very innocent between us, although I seem to always be fending off his kisses.

One evening as the sun is low in the sky and the night air cool and damp, Antonio takes me to dinner to a little family restaurant at the edge of the island. Here, we eat on the *terrazzo* and watch the colors of the sky change and the sun set into the *Mediterraneo*….something I do every day from a different vantage point since coming here.

We are the only two in the restaurant this night as we share pasta and a bottle of *vino* and laugh for hours. Then we ride to *Il Faro* – the Lighthouse Beach to see the moon and the stars. Here under the moon, he kisses me. I am tipsy with the wine and the light from the heavens. So I let him do it. At one o'clock in the morning, we ride to the town of Capri to the Number Two Discoteca and dance until almost four in the morning. This is an intoxicating ritual that everyone does on the island when they come to visit – like the orgiastic rituals that were performed under the Natural Arch….

I am so enraptured, hypnotized by the music and the strobe lights, my passions rising up inside me. When he drops me off at my villa in the morning, he asks to come inside. I say no and hold my ground. So he relents and leaves quickly, smiling big with his dazzling smile that shines in the early morning light.

Upon awakening, I realize my foolishness at kissing him. I remind myself that I did not come to Italy to fall for a young boy, but instead to find my passions. So I take more time for myself over the next few weeks.

What shall I do now with all of my free time? I decide to visit a new place every day. And during my adventures, no matter where I am on the island, I find myself continually asking, what do I want to do with the remainder of my life since it is half over. I want to find my passions and live a life that I love since time is quickening – or so it seems. My god, fifty years…it has gone by so fast – only memories now. My childhood, my marriage, my youth, the childhood of my boys…here I am in the present moment wondering where it will lead me next.

What is my dream, I ask? How do I see my future? How do I want to live and where, for that matter?

By the end of the second week, I have decided I do not want to go back to America, but to stay on the island for another month. Every few days, I call my boys and my ex-husband to share my adventures. And in the last conversation, my sons tell me not to return until I am ready. Permission – although I don't really need it to make up my mind without the guilt. Nonetheless, it is welcome. I feel giddy with freedom – my life is a blank canvas, and now it is time to add color to it.

Thoughts of passion fill my head and Antonio's close companionship in this romantic setting has made me feel edgy for a physical relationship. Capri is such a beautiful and romantic place, especially with all of the attention I am getting from the men in the streets as I pass by. I am constantly reminded of my alone-ness at every turn. My passions rise up inside me and I am hardly able to contain them! I am walking around obsessed with thoughts of making love to beautiful Italian men with beautiful Italian hearts! *Mama mia*! Now I am thinking like an Italian man…

As I sit in the *Umberto Piazza* in the town of Capri contemplating making love to beautiful men, I notice Bruno walking by. He is looking at me seductively, again, as he has done twice before, this time winking. I have been coy with him, shy, always pulling my eyes away from his…but not on this day. Our eyes meet and I smile. He walks to a café and a few minutes later, comes back to me with two small glasses filled with Lemoncello….the liquid of the gods, I begin to call it.

"*Ciao, belissima, mio amore*…may I sit?" He hands me a Lemoncello.

"*Si, molto grazie*," I say. He clinks our glasses and we toast.

"*Salute! Alla vita* – to life!" I say in return. I taste the golden liquor and realize I love this taste more than anything. He drinks his down quickly and smiles into the sunlight. I sigh and take a deep breath for once again I am intoxicated by the light of day, the Lemoncello, and this beautiful man.

"You are so beautiful, *mio amore*." He takes my hand in his and brings it to his lips. He kisses me there and I can feel the moisture of his breath that is left upon it.

"There are many places on Capri that are more beautiful than this one. Would you like to go to one with me?" He still has my hand in his. He is very young – maybe thirty, I am guessing…an Italian god with light colored eyes. I am holding my breath as I gaze into them, trying to see what is inside, for they remind me of the sea.

I know that if I go with him, it will lead to something else – something I have dreamt about lately. Is this wrong? No. I don't believe so. I tell myself that if it manifests in the physical when I have been longing for it…praying for it…then it is meant to be…a gift.

"Yes, I would love to." He squeezes my hand and his eyes sparkle.

"You are *magnifico*, Roxanna. You are a gift to us on this island, so beautiful." I blush and eat it up like sweet honey. How should I respond to this? He looks into my eyes as if we are making love.

"Come walk with me." He pulls me up from the bench linking my arm in his.

"*Mio amore* - My love…" He leads me as if I am his. "I take you to *Il Farro*."

"I hear it is beautiful there." I go easily. This is a place on the island where the lighthouse sits, surrounded on three sides by sheer rock walls that look black against the night, all the while, a piercing light beam scanning the sky that is carpeted with the stars and the moon. In the sunlight, it changes from this surreal otherworldly place to an aqua pool of the sea, where one jumps off the rock floor into the warm salty sea, only to bob up and float like a buoy.

"We will go visit there…no, no…I change my mind," he says. He is smiling as we walk. "The *fortina*…yes, the *fortina*. This is a place I go to be alone. It is my special place. I take you there instead." He seems to have fond memories that he is recalling in this moment. His eyes the color of the *Mediterraneo*, flash in the sunlight and in them I can see that he is thinking sweet thoughts.

You are the most beautiful woman on the island, Roxanna." I feel he means it. I think of my age and his, but don't want to challenge him or ask if he is insane. The moment is too dreamy, but he breaks the dream by speaking.

"*Bella*, have you been to the *fortina*?" I shake my head no. "They are old ruins near the Faro Lighthouse Beach, and the view is *bello*. I have my scooter and will take you there." We arrive at his scooter. He places a helmet on my head and clasps it for me. Then he kisses my lips. Ah-h-h…I can feel the energy building in that sacred place that has been barren for so long. I wrap my arms around his waist as he takes off down the narrow street. I am holding him tightly so I won't fall off. He pulls both my hands together and clasps them at his naval, and I am acutely aware of his physicality, for I can feel the taught young muscles of his abdomen through his white linen shirt.

"Are you okay, Roxanna?" He asks as he turns his eyes from the road to catch a glimpse of me.

"Yes." I can barely get the words out; I am smiling into the wind and the sunlight.

"*Bene*. We are almost there."

He parks on the side of a quiet road, gently helps me from the scooter, and then unfastens my helmet. He takes my hand, intertwining our fingers and pulls me along the winding trail that leads to the fort. My heart is racing for this great adventure that I have embarked upon.

He tells me the history of the ruins as we walk, but I don't remember a thing now; for I am lost in the feeling of his hand in mine as I watch the wind push the linen fabric of his clothing tightly against his perfect body. I have never thought a walk in broad daylight could be the way a man romances a woman before making love to her – foreplay. He makes me feel like the only woman in all the world.

I am lifted up and placed on the walls of the fort so that I can see the view, then Bruno jumps up beside me. Ships pass by so far below that I can hardly make them out. It's as if we are standing on an airplane, we are so high above the sea. Except for the muted sounds below, it is silent – no birds, no cars, no noise. Time stands still as I am transported back to a delicious time of youth when I anticipated love.

My Italian god is standing behind me with his arms now wrapped about my waist, as he kisses my neck and breathes into my hair. He moves his fingers down along my bare arm, tracing my skin as he goes. Then he picks up my hand lacing his fingers into mine. He takes my index finger as if it is a pointer, and then he proceeds to point out the *Il Faro* to our left and the *Grotto Azzura* to the right. He turns me around to face him and kisses me with that passion that only the Italians have. They are the sweetest and most erotic kisses I have ever known, for he breathes in the entire time, his eyes wide open and fixed upon my face. He envelopes my mouth in his as if he is savoring a juicy plum that is over-ripened. I think I hear music…

My passions are boiling up inside me as he presses himself into me. I can feel all of him through his linen slacks and shirt. His body has such perfect physical definition, his waist indenting in to where his abdomen starts - his perfect abs. His chest is the final touch, creating the perfect V to his anatomy, muscular and well-defined. His hands are on the back of my neck as if he is holding me there in place as he speaks Italian to me in between his kisses. He is doing many things at the same time, breathing me in deeply as he kisses me, speaking to me, and holding me tightly all in the same moment.

"*Tu sei cosi bella* – you are so beautiful. *Dal giorno che ti ho incontrata io h sempre atteso questo momento* – since the first day I met you, I have been waiting for this moment. *Tu sei massimo magnifico donne alla Capri* – you are the most beautiful woman of Capri."

I feel as if I am in a romance novel. This is something I have never dreamed possible, standing here high above the *Mediterraneo* under the bluest of skies, standing on the wall of a two thousand year old ancient ruin with an Adonis half my age…and he is telling me that I am the most beautiful woman in all of Capri – in Italian! And in this moment, I AM!

All of my fears and my years melt into the rocks I am standing on, as I allow myself to be held and loved. He reaches for my breasts, his lips making a beeline to them. I cannot remember what happens next…except that my dress is pulled down below my breasts and up around my waist, and I am suddenly lying on the ancient rock wall, although I don't remember the moment I got that way. I allow him to have his way with me – to make the most profound and meaningful love to me, as I do to him.

He whispers to me in Italian - into my ear and into my mouth in between his own breathlessness. I can hear the faint sound of motor boats in the distance and a bird that passes by. The wind caresses my body everywhere that his hands are not – and that is not too many places.

"*Bellissima, bella* - oh, Roxanna…*ah, mio bella donna. Io le so che tu sei una donna di passione.* I can feel it – beautiful, beautiful Roxanna, ah, my beautiful woman. I know you are a passionate woman, for I can feel it."

Lost inside this magical world of letting go into bliss and romance, I do things that would make me blush any other time but this. I am no longer self conscious of my aging body. He makes me feel beautiful – tells me I am. I am the goddess Aphrodite and he Apollo. It is not the love making of two humans, but that of the gods. I wonder if they are looking down upon us with smiles upon their faces, clapping their hands ecstatically as they shout, "Yes! They have found freedom and ecstasy at last!"

Afterward, he continues to kiss me all over and whispers sweet words to me with his dreamy eyes gazing lovingly at my face.

"*Mio amore* – my love, you are far more beautiful than any twenty-year old. You have such *passione*." So I stand there naked, high atop the cliffs of Capri, with the confidence of Aphrodite, the Goddess of Beauty, letting the wind have its way with me now, after he is finished. He tells me I am magnificent and I know I am.

"My sweet Roxanna, I have been carrying this around since the first day I laid eyes upon you, with hope that you might spend time with me." He pulls a black velvet pouch from the pocket of his pants that have been lying on the ground beside him.

"I never dreamed you would be mine this way. You are like a young girl and oh, so beautiful." His accent is thick and his eyelashes close lazily as he speaks the words. "You have given me the most wonderful gift – the gift of you, and for that I want to give you something to remember me by." He is pulling something out of a velvet pouch – a gold cross lined with emerald stones.

"I think of you when I see this. It was meant for you. It told me." As he clasps it around my neck, he speaks again.

"It is a gift from me, Bruno of Capri and this island – to protect you and give you strength when I am not with you...I want to always know you are safe so I don't have to worry about you, *mio amore*." He smiles and kisses me on the place where the cross falls somewhere between my breasts.

"Bruno, it is beautiful." I am in love with his soul and all of the emotions of this moment. I reach for his face and bring it to me so I can kiss his lips once again. "Thank you. I will never forget you or this moment."

We continue the kiss as we become one with the sea and the sky and the ancient rocks beneath our human bodies. We fall into love-making again, hot and sweet, dripping with sensuality – in the sunlight and in the heat, as the Mediterranean sea air cools our nakedness. And afterwards, we lie together and doze, for we have found an opening in the universe, and slip through it into a sacred place where only love lives. And as the sun starts to move toward the earth, we awaken, realizing how hungry for food we are. While I dress myself, he still kisses me all over, all the while speaking Italian to me. I find myself giggling again…so many giggles have spilled out of me like little jewels of happiness.

"Thank you, Roxanna, for giving yourself to me." I know that he is a gift to me as well, and that I am the lucky one, for I no longer have to feel older than I feel inside my heart, for I have been transformed by this experience – beautiful and oh, so young once again. He holds my hand all the way back up the path to the scooter and as I wrap my arms around him, he clasps my hand tenderly in his.

We stop for pasta at a little family restaurant near *Il Faro* before returning to town. There, he looks into my eyes through the candlelight on the table as the family serves us – the only patrons in the restaurant. It seems as though we are the only two on earth, except for those that are tending to our needs at the moment. He kisses my hands and tells me he loves me – tells me I am so beautiful and that I have fallen from the sky for only him to catch and that I am his angel. It is as if we are meant to be together, and have been forever. This has been a moment in time that has etched itself in my memory and I will always refer back to it as a measure for all others after him.

And as the day ends and we say our good-byes at the edge of the *piazza*, I know I might never see him again – and still - all is perfect.

This night, I dream I am painting. There is a large canvas before me that covers one wall in my room and on it I am splashing brightly colored paints that become pictures of my life. The first is of the encounter with Love this very day. And when I awaken in the morning, I decide to buy paints and supplies. It is time…

The Caesar Augustus Hotel is perched high atop the cliffs of AnaCapri overlooking the sea and the town of Capri far below. This property is known for its vistas overlooking the islands of Ischia and Procida, and the Bay of Naples where *Monte Vesuvio* and Sorrento lay in the distance. The Farouk Suite sits on the top floor of this paradise, which is the best suite in the hotel.

I decide to treat myself to a night languishing here after my rebirth back into passion with Bruno for I have opened myself up to the fact that life is now my suitor and it has come knocking to romance me once again - only this time, it is in the Italian fashion which is so much more pleasurable.

My room is to die for…simple yet elegant. My bath is white marble with a large Jacuzzi tub, surrounded by windows to the sea; and there are candles placed all around the room. My bed is three times a normal size! Too big for me, but I will make due. I have a sitting area that overlooks the bay and from this height, I feel as if I am in heaven overlooking the kingdom of earth. My favorite part of the suite – besides all of this of course, is a very large picture window framed with an embellished and scrolled gold picture frame. It takes my breath away as I look into it thinking it is a picture of a seascape, but soon realize it is window to the Mediterranean!

I step out onto the loggia and weep, for I have never seen such beauty – even with all the places I have visited thus far on the island. Each one is more breathtaking than the last…but this…this is a place for a queen, in her castle - this exquisite palace high atop the world looking out over her empire. And it is a glorious one.

I am overcome with emotion and feel that familiar feeling of passion rising up inside my breast igniting my soul, moving up into my throat forcing it to close, pushing the tears upward and out through my eyes. So I stand on the loggia for almost an hour, riveted to the same spot, watching the sky change and the sea beneath me. I am in love with it – with myself – with my life. This is what I am here for – to find this place inside me. And if I die in my sleep this night, all will be well, for I have found what most never even touch in their lifetime.

The light in the sky has shifted and is so brilliant this time of day that the sea seems to be a mix of lavenders and blues with aqua trim at the edge of the shoreline far below. After pulling myself from this spot, I move inside to the marble tub. I run the water, and light candles and incense and lounge for awhile, and as I close my eyes, dreams come and go – dreams of living my life in this way. I realize I can create this if I want to. So I set my intent that I will live a life filled with all of this. I don't know how, but I know in my heart that it will be so.

I sleep in that semi-conscious state I was so familiar with in California, moving from sleep to awakening and back again. I walk from my bed out through the open doors of the loggia and back again, all night long. I don't know how many times I have the desire to gaze at the sky and the sea, but I think it is at least every hour. I have to go for I don't want to miss anything. The vista changes each time the light does, so it is new in every moment. First it is by starlight, then moonlight when the moon moves into the southwestern sky. Then it is that soft golden light just before dawn. My heart weeps each time I see the magnificence of this place where heaven and earth have merged.

At one point, I can't remember if I am awake on the loggia or if I am dreaming; but the Great Spirit is standing beside me as I look down at

Marina Grande. Beautiful music is playing somewhere down below and I can hear it floating upward toward me. I don't even know what time it is – don't even care.

"Come, I want to show you where you will live now." In an instant, I am somewhere else with him, on Capri, overlooking the sea; and the vista here is as beautiful as the one from the hotel. There are gardens everywhere and statues lining the *terrazzo* in front of a stone villa with patios all around.

"Just keep looking and you will find this place, Roxanna; and here, you will be inspired to paint!" He lovingly touches my arm, for I can feel his warmth there.

"How will I find it? And who are you?" But before I can finish my questions, he is gone and I am standing alone. I will myself to go over each word and each picture in my mind, for I don't want to forget a thing he has said or the vision of where I will live. I want to know it as soon as I come upon it. How silly of me…how could I ever forget it?

The clock reads five-thirty and I can no longer sleep, so I sit on the loggia contemplating the dawn's early light. I must stay another day, for I cannot move from this place. If I could live here, I would. So I wait for the eight o'clock hour to go down to the front desk and talk with the gentleman Enrico who is a sweet man with sparkling eyes. He is always smiling and cares for my needs as if I were the only one in the hotel. This is what I love about this country – another Italian who makes me feel as if I am the only one in the world besides him.

"How is your stay here, Roxanna? Is everything to your liking?"

"Oh, Enrico, it's wonderful. I have to stay another night…." My heart starts to weep and the tears come before I can stop them. "I'm so sorry. It's so breathtaking that I need to stay."

"I am sorry, Roxanna; all the rooms are booked. There is nothing available for this evening." He pats my hand lovingly. At this, I weep even harder and cannot stop.

"I must stay! I have to stay! Isn't there anything you can do?" I am almost delirious now.

"I will try and find you another hotel close by. This is the best I can do. You can sleep elsewhere and you can come here and enjoy our facilities. It will be as if you are staying here. Will that make it better?" He is still patting my hand, smiling at me, trying to comfort me. I am hoping someone will cancel their reservation for the night for I'm sure I am meant to stay in my room. After all, I am the queen and this is my kingdom! There was no reasoning with me. Is it the lack of sleep? I check my sanity.

"Anything you can do, Enrico. Thank you."

"I will call when I find something." I know I can trust him to do his best for me, so I cross the lobby and return to the Farouk suite and my loggia where I sit and wait looking out over my paradise.

Enrico finds me a room at the San Michele Hotel across the street and I spend only my sleeping hours there. The rest of the time, I live at the Caesar Augustus, lounging on the lower loggia, swimming in the infinity pool overlooking the sea, and dining in the patio restaurant surrounded by blooming night jasmine. And late at night, I walk the *terrazzo* while everyone else sleeps, and feel the magic of my life.

For three days and two nights…I live with my heart wide open and my soul singing.

CHAPTER 7

A week passes and I realize I have done so much but actually I have done nothing at all except sit for hours in the sunlight, just sitting – listening to the sounds of the island. Or should I say the quiet? There are no noises - only silence. There are no traffic noises, no honking horns, no televisions or radios, only the sounds of music and singing in the distance and that familiar sound of the scooters as they move through the outer streets. Their low humming is music to my ears, reminding me of my romantic liaison with Bruno at the fortina. Time has passed and I have not seen him once, nor do I care that I haven't. Our moment in time on that day was so special and so magical, that I am afraid if it happened again, it would take away from the enchantment of the first time. I would always remember it as my sweetest and most mystical liaison.

On this day, I ride the bus down the narrow winding road to the little town of Capri to explore the shops and restaurants. The Grand Hotel Quisisana is well-known for its famous patrons and its famous restaurant and I am into pampering myself these days. After all, I am a queen, right? I am seated at a table overlooking the water and Raffaello comes to my table.

"*Buonasera, Signora.*"

"*Buonasera.*" This means good evening in Italian and is only used after three o'clock in the afternoon.

Raffaello is a good looking man with dark hair, bits of silver running through it. I guess him to be my age. He has a strong nose, a beautiful face and I can see the love in his soul through his eyes. My soul knows his for I feel my heart flutter at the memory. Each time I look into his face, my heart races and my cells begin to move as if they are dancing.

We are friends immediately, the kind that are intimate. If you look at us when we are together, you would think we are sharing a secret. He waits on me as if I am the only one dining this night. God, I love Italy.

Although there are many patrons here, they all melt away each time he stands beside me. We are alone and time has stopped…standing still for the two of us. He requests a special meal from the chef, special desserts - an array of little pastries, cakes, cookies and chocolates…it goes on and on… It is all far too much for me and I have to beg him to stop!

From the moment I met him, I want to lie in his arms and feel his touch as he strokes my hair like the papa and his little girl I had seen in the *piazza*. When he looks at me that is the kind of love I feel from him. I have known him forever, loved him deeply, and we have just come upon each other again for the first time after lifetimes apart. I know it to be true, for I can feel it in the core of my being.

Oh, how sweet his face is…It is as if I am being romanced by him, although he is only doing his job – or is he? It seems so familiar to me, to be waited on and cared for by Raffaello. I feel as if he is my husband and I his wife – a silly thought. But my heart knows we were once together long ago in another lifetime.

We catch up on each others' lives like old friends who haven't seen one another in fifty years. He tells me he is married with a grown son and very much in love with his wife; but I know he feels the same about me for his eyes give him away. It is not that he is being flirtatious like some Italian men you hear about. He is different and this is a different kind of love. As he waits on others in the room, I see him steal glances; and in those moments, I see his heart swell each time he looks my way. My heart swells in response to his and my soul whispers his name. I feel intoxicated as if I have drunk three Lemoncellos!

I wish to sit and hold his hands, kiss his sweet face, the lines around his smile. I want him to put his arms around me as a husband does, so I can feel his strength envelop my body. But no. We do none of this except longingly look into each others eyes and smile.

"Please stay Roxanna. Please don't go. I bring you anything you wish." He pleads with me. If there was any more he could do for me, I would have stayed, but the evening is over. I have been sitting for three hours already, reconnecting with only our hearts through our eyes. He comes to me and I rise from the table.

"Roxanna, do you believe in reincarnation?" He is kissing my hands as if we are making love and they are the bare skin of my breasts - my face is flushed.

"Yes, I do. Do you?"

"Yes. You are my wife, Roxanna. We were married once before, and I am still yours. I will be yours forever." He laughs nervously. "You must think I am crazy!" He drops one of my hands and nervously runs his fingers through his hair, moving it back from where it has fallen upon his brow.

"No, I don't think you are crazy at all. I believe you, for I feel the same." I kiss his cheeks and he holds me close for a moment before releasing me. My heart starts to weep the moment his hands drop and he steps away. It is not easy for either of us to part, but we know he has to go back to his present wife and life.

"Please come again to see me. I will wait for you until then." I blow him a kiss and hope that he feels the love that has left my lips for him.

I walk the street to the outskirts of town where the bus will pick me up for the trip back up to the top of the island and my mind tries to understand what happened this night with Raffaello and the other night with Bruno. I think my soul is now driving my life instead of me driving it. And the rewards are me being open and aware enough to feel the love that is coming my way. I am a changed woman. I am no longer a fifty year old woman in search of anything. Making love to Bruno opened the door for me - the door to my passions. Connecting with Raffaello opened my heart so that I now welcome all the love that the universe has to offer me.

I know I am so loved. I no longer feel as if I am alone or lonely with no romance in my life. After Raffaello, I now feel as if I am a married woman who has a husband somewhere out there. I am happy and in love; and I am only traveling on holiday without him. Of course this marriage took place in another lifetime. I smile to myself.

Call me crazy – insane even. I can only try and explain the depth of my encounter with him, as if he is mine through eternity. No matter where I am in this world, I will always know that there is someone out there that loves me truly, madly, deeply, forever. I, Roxanna of Capri am so loved by this beautiful man, Raffaello whose heart was once mine.

That was the night I learned to make love without removing my clothing…

CHAPTER 8

The next few days are busy ones as I work with my new friend Enrico, to find a more permanent room where I might live for awhile. There is nothing available; the island is booked solid, for springtime is upon us and the *fiori* the flowers are in full bloom, their scent drawing everyone here. But he does have a small stone house on his property that he offers to me, the sweet man. He calls it an artist's studio but to me, it is a little villa. So, I prepare to move.

It is my last day at the San Michele Villa, so I stop at Stephen's door to thank him and say good-bye. He greets me with a smile and his green-blue eyes, which are green today, and they still captivate me.

"How are you, Roxanna? You have been busy?"

"Yes, I've been meeting so many new friends and I think I've seen all of Capri's secret spots that are so beautiful. How have you been, Stephen?"

"I have been well and busy, too. I actually took a holiday to Firenze last week. I love the museums there." I assume Rosa accompanied him.

"Yes, that's on my list of places to visit. Thank you for your hospitality and the gift of the apartment. I will never forget what you have done. This is for you." I hand him a bottle of "Brunello di Montalcino" from Toscana. He is surprised and pleased.

"You shouldn't have!"

"It is the least I can do. Thank you so much for putting me up here. You have been so kind and so generous." He smiles and holds the bottle out to look more closely at the label. "I hope you drink wine."

"I am in Italy, yes? You'd be crazy not to drink wine here of all places." He laughs as he looks at the bottle. "Brunello…it's a favorite of mine…and it's a "97." This is considered one of the best wines in the world! Thank you so much, Roxanna." He is clearly excited. "So are you leaving the island now?"

"No, I decided to stay another month or so. Enrico, the gentleman at the Caesar Augustus Hotel has a place on his property, a little studio that he has offered to me."

"Yes, I know him well. He is a very good man. Well, good luck. Maybe we will see each other again? Stop by one Friday evening to enjoy our concert."

"I will, Stephen." I kiss both of his cheeks, right cheek first as is the custom. "*Ciao*, Stephen and *molto grazie*."

"*Prego*," is his reply.

The walk to my new home is about a mile outside of the little village and I have to walk through a maze of tiny lanes, my luggage in tow. As I walk through the gate to the little stone cottage, the view takes my breath away for it is almost the same as the one from the Caesar Augustus Hotel. I continue to walk down a long path with beautiful rock walls that Enrico's family constructed. There are grapevines hanging overhead, lavender wisteria intertwined, and flowers and statues along the walkway. I recognize a few - Michelangelo's David, Venus, and Athena. At the edge of the property down toward the water is a replica of a sphinx perched on a wall. How appropriate…I take this as a sign that I am meant to be here.

I arrive at the studio and find it is actually a small stone cottage which I guess to be at least a hundred years old. It has glass walls and doors overlooking the sea, with one small bed, a writing table and a small kitchenette. Although it is sparse, it is incredibly romantic.

In front of the cottage, are two *terrazzos* with low wrought iron fences at the end of each lined with little potted plants, facing the sea. One patio off to the side has flooring of hand-painted tiles – plenty of places to paint if I choose to do so. There are three bas-reliefs cemented to the front wall of the cottage by the door. There is a stone bench and table made of inlaid tiles. Tables and chairs sit lazily in the sun here and there.

Enrico has instructed me to eat from the garden where there are numerous fruit trees - lemon, kiwi, peach, pear, mandarin orange, and apple. And he has also given me access to the gardens that are filled with tomatoes, beans, lettuce, broccoli, artichokes, fresh *basilico*, and other herbs and vegetables. I praise the gods for such gifts as these, including the gift of him.

After giving thanks, I unpack my suitcase that is now stuffed with the extra clothing I had to buy since I needed more than I had brought for my short two-week visit. There is a new light-weight black leather Italian jacket I had purchased to keep warm on those scooter rides about the island with Antonio. I also bought three pashmina scarves which are the rage on the island. All the Italian women wear them doubled over and tied about their necks to keep the chill off in the early spring mornings or late in the evening when the weather cools again. I feel as if I belong here when I wear them.

I also had to acquire a new pair of jeans because the ones I brought from America are now falling off my hips since I have lost the middle-aged spread I had carried around with me for the last few years. This, I attribute to my new diet of *olio d'olivia*, olive oil, salad and pasta. I am eating less and now, my choices consist of organic produce since all of the produce on the island is grown organically.

I, Roxanna, am now the proud woman of this land. This is my new home and it is beautiful. I explore the property taking pictures with my camera for I don't want to forget anything about it, this *paradiso* I have fallen so gently into the lap of. I want to paint, feel the passions rising up inside me like the rising tide of the ocean. Soon...I will know when... Right now, I just sit, enraptured with all of this...as little lizards lie about me basking in the sun while white butterflies fly about my head.

The sea beckons me to stare at its colors of purple and aqua set in gold as the late afternoon sunlight spills its diamonds upon it. I close my eyes and feel the warmth of the spring sun upon my face, feel it caress my skin. It reminds me of Antonio each time he teases me, his beautiful and seductive smile against his darkened skin. It reminds me of Bruno – I can almost feel his fingertips upon my neck as he positions the gold and emerald cross there. I feel Raffaello's lips upon my hands as he kissed them that night in the restaurant. Then, a gasp escapes from my lungs as I remember myself standing on the loggia of the Farouk Suite at the Caesar Augustus Hotel. The sounds of the birds chirping in the trees fall away for a moment as I am lost in these, my memories.

I close my eyes and think back to the distant life I once had. When was it....just a few weeks ago? The dream had prompted me so suddenly to get up and leave it all behind. It was as if I was in the midst of a mid-life crisis....whatever I choose to call it... thank you for coming into my life. I smile. Life is strange sometimes....and I have landed here in *paradiso*...gently fallen into the lap of God, because this is surely heaven.

What do I want now for myself and my life? I don't know yet. But I do know that in this moment, I can create anything I want.

Today is the first day of the rest of my life. I cannot see where I am going, but I can see how I want to feel each and every day from here on. I want to feel passion such as this. I don't ever want to forget the smell of the *fiori* or the aroma of a home-cooked Italian meal. I never want to be so busy that I don't hear the birds singing or the sounds of the night, or the wind as it moves through the trees or the sound of rain as it cascades down through the grapevines in the vineyard.

I want to laugh, make love again like I did high atop the cliffs with Bruno - kiss, hug, hold hands, dance, paint, and ride on the back of scooters in the night on Capri with beautiful Italian men. I smile to myself. I want to feel all of life, express how I feel and enjoy every moment. I want to feel my soul pulling me to Raffaello again. I want to feel free like the wind and wake up each morning with nothing to do but love! I want to be wild with passion like a wild steed in a pasture roaming free. I want that feeling of coming together with my lover after waiting so long that I am out of control, on fire - dancing with bliss! As if I had called forth the god called "anticipated passion," I feel my heart flutter - the cells in my body dancing. I take a breath so as not to drown in it quite yet, here alone at the villa! All these things - they are what I want for my life! This is what I want to create…a life filled with passion. I close my eyes…

Hours pass as I watch the light change. And when the sun finally sets into the sea, and the music of my life quiets inside my head and my heart, I rise from my seat to go inside and make dinner.

CHAPTER 9

Dawn comes early this morning in my new place. I lie in my bed of Italian linens and listen to the sounds of silence all around me…peace…quiet… solitude. The only things I can hear are the things that are the size of June bugs, buzzing in the flowers outside my window. I hear a few birds chirping, unlike the many that chirp in the springtime in California. But mostly, I hear only quiet. This is the sound of life on the island…and I am lost in the silence of it. I look around the room and see the bookcase against the wall. I notice the titles of the books – some in English, some in Italian and some in German. I look at the simple chair that is across the room and the lace curtains on the windowed doors.

I turned over onto my back, looking upward toward the thin lacey linen that is fastened to the ceiling. It drops into three sections reminding me of a material hanging on a clothesline as it billows in the breeze. Fresh - *fresco* as they say in Italy. I am lazy, lying languidly here with no thoughts swimming in my mind, only emptiness…only peace.

After an hour, or so it seems…I no longer track time …I am getting really good at tracking it by the light of the day – I remember that Antonio has promised to take me fishing today. He said we would go somewhere in AnaCapri and not down to the sea in Marina Grande or Marina Piccola. How can this be, I wonder? But then I realize that anything is possible on Capri, the isle of magic. What new surprise will I encounter today?

After walking the mile into town, I meet Antonio at Monument Square in front of *Il Martino*, the newspaper stand and internet point I visit daily, for this is the only access I have to the outside world.

"*Journo*, my sweetie. You are beautiful today."

"Good morning, Antonio." His black hair is glistening in the sunlight from the gel he dresses it with.

"Come. We will be there soon." He hands me the helmet and helps me fasten it; then we ride the scooter to the farthest point on the island, to one of the old ancient *fortinas*. This is not to be mistaken with the one Bruno and I made love on… The sun is brilliant in the sky so blue, as we climb down the rocks toward the fort. This one is a little smaller than the one I had visited previously. The sea seems so far below, probably 70 meters so how will we fish from here?

"Roxanna, you stay and sit in the sun. It is too dangerous for a woman down below. I bring you fish." He walks very carefully, each foot strategically placed in front of the other as he moves along the uneven volcanic rocks with their dangerously sharp tips and jagged edges.

"Roxanna!" He is half way down to the sea and I can hardly hear his voice. "You can take your clothes off, you know. No one comes here. *Ciao!*" His teeth sparkle in the sunlight.

Naked…I couldn't…or could I? Suppose someone comes and sees me?

"And?" The voice inside my head asks. I remember seeing women bathing topless at the little beach near Marina Grande. No one seemed to pay much notice to them.

"Go ahead!" It prods me. Although my encounter with Bruno has opened me up, I am still self-conscious of my aging body – just a little. I lie down on my towel and bask like a lizard in the noon day heat. It is hot, no movement is best. I can feel the beads of sweat collect on my skin and beneath my black swimsuit. What was I thinking…black in this heat? My justifying mind reminds me that women wear black to look thinner.

"Ha!" I laugh big and bold into the wind! "Roxanna, I do believe no one in southern California has made love like you – the goddess Athena herself! High atop the cliffs on some romantic isle in the middle of the sea on the other side of the world….in this fairy tale called YOUR LIFE!

I stand up on the cliffs and laugh into the air as it cools the rivulets of sweat that are now slowly moving down my neck, my face, and between my breasts, slithering like little snakes of heat.

Then, I espy Antonio far below and he turns, looks up at me, and blows me a kiss. *Mio amore*…life is *mio amore*!

I am restless…the heat, oh, so hot, on fire now. So I pull down my top, careful that Antonio does not see, hence he climb quickly up to catch a glimpse of a middle-aged American woman's breasts! I sit on my towel and feel the cool Mediterranean breeze brush seductively across my nipples and the dampness on my body. I gasp with anticipation – anticipation of what, I laugh out loud. Of whatever comes next, I tell myself!

I lay there for hours and dream of anything and everything that heightens the senses. I dream of the sounds of the sea down below. I think I barely hear a tour boat and the voice of a man on a speakerphone talking about the island. It drones on, no audible words, caressing me into a quiet mind. I think I hear a distant airplane, but I'm sure I am imagining it. I hear the Capri June bug as its wings flap as quickly as a hummingbird's. And I hear the twittering of a small bird. Then, I hear nothing else, for I have fallen asleep.

Upon awakening, I wonder what time it is and notice the sun has moved to that place in the sky telling me it is about five o'clock. The rocks beneath my body are hard and I can no longer tolerate the pain, so I reposition myself many times; but my physicality is finished with lying down, and my skin is finished with the sun.

My new lifestyle here - walking into town each day for my groceries, walking about during the daylight hours, and also sitting in the sun…has caused my skin to become the color of Antonio's, so I now look Italian. I am dark, but only my arms and legs that are bared to the air and not beneath my skirts and tops that I wear each day. Even my sandaled feet are tanned.

I have been lying here all day, so I suddenly stand up on the wall of the fort so that I can see Antonio's tiny head so far below. I think, please turn around, Antonio. I'm finished with lying here in this heat and I am so hungry. At that very moment, he turns to look up at me and holds up a string of ten little fish as he starts to make his way up the sharp rocks.

"Are you okay, sweetie?" He asks.

"Yes I am; but I'm tired of the sun. Can we go?"

"*Si, si*…I am finished. Look! Now I make you dinner, sweetie." He smiles proudly.

"That's so many, Antonio!"

"I know! *Aspete!* Wait until you taste them; they are the best you will ever have and you will never forget me after I cook for you!"

He comes to my villa and cooks a meal for me that is far more impressive than any five-star restaurant I have ever eaten in. I will always remember the smell and the taste. The fish are meaty and sweet - little silver ones that remind me of sardines although slightly larger - frying them in olive oil, herbs, salt and pepper until their skin is seared and crispy. As he prepares all of this in the little kitchen, I can smell the sea as if we are on it and I realize that it has come from the fish. I will remember this recipe so I can cook it myself, but know I will never taste fish this fresh again unless I catch them myself and cook them the same day.

"So what do you think, my sweetie?" I am speechless and cannot find the words to explain how it tastes.

"I have never had fish like this before," is all I can say.

"No? I am the best cook." He smiles proudly once again as he thumps his chest with his thumb.

"Yes, you are a good cook, but the fish…it smells and tastes like the sea, so sweet. It's so fresh." I realize he probably doesn't understand. After all, he has lived on this island his whole life and has eaten this fish many times. How could he possibly know what I am talking about?

"Ah, yes. The fish on Capri is the best! But I am the best cook, too." He laughs as he smokes his cigarette sitting across the little inlaid tiled table from me. We are looking at the night sky.

"Do you like my grandmother's *vino*? She makes it every year. I help her. You know, Roxanna, she lives with us. She makes the wine and the Lemoncello. She also prepares the tomatoes for the winter and makes olives and jams. I love my grandmother. She is very strong."

"And what of your grandfather, Antonio. Is he still alive?"

"No, he died ten years ago and my grandmother came to live with us then. My father goes to the villa and takes care of the grapes and the gardens every morning and every day after work." I knew his father was a shopkeeper in the *piazza*.

"And what about your family, Roxanna?"

"My father and mother live in San Diego and I see them almost every week. My ex-husband and my two sons are in San Diego, too."

"Why did you divorce, Roxanna?" He moves closer to the table, intently waiting for my response.

"My ex traveled so much that we hardly had a marriage any more. It just happened. But he is a good man; and he has been a good father to our sons. What about you, Antonio? Do you want to get married some day?" He has plenty of time ahead of him I think.

"Yes, someday…I want many babies and a son. But I have not found the right woman. I don't like the island girls. They are not right for me." He smiles seductively. "Maybe you are the one for me, baby."

"I am older than your mother, Antonio!" She is forty-six and I am fifty. "And you and I are great friends. I don't think of you in that way." He takes my hand from across the table.

"I can change your mind, you know. I cook for you and prepare your meals. I do anything you want and be a good husband." I laugh out loud but realize by the look on his face that he is serious.

"Antonio, no! I am too old to have babies and don't want to start another family. You need a beautiful young girl to marry – one that you love! This is not me."

"Think about it, my sweetie. I could be very happy with you; and you could learn to love me." He was looking at me seductively again.

"No, you are my friend and only my friend – no more than that." I am starting to feel uncomfortable with the conversation. We have been drinking wine and are now sipping his grandmother's Lemoncello. He is feeling amorous so I move from the table and start to clear the dishes when he comes to me and touches my arm.

"I am sorry, Roxanna. I make you feel uncomfortable. I hope you think about this and someday change your mind. I love you!" He walks into the kitchen and starts to sing. It's as if it's no big deal to say the words "I love you." *Mama mia*! The Italians!

I come into the kitchen with plates and he takes them away from me and swooshes me out of the kitchen.

"No, you sit! No help - I do dishes. This is your night, my sweetie." So I move back outside and sit looking at the dark sea and the lights twinkling across the bay. I think I hear music from here, but maybe it's my imagination, for it is too far away. Maybe the wind has carried it from somewhere else on the island.

There is singing coming from the kitchen as I hear dishes being washed and pans clanking in the sink. The air is starting to cool and I can feel the chill on my arms so I pull my pashmina closer to me but otherwise am too enraptured to move inside.

I am loving the day and loving the meal, still thinking about the smell of the *Mediterraneo* that we have brought to the villa in the fish. I think about Antonio's words, but push them away. I adore our friendship and love having my young Italian friend as my personal tour guide; but maybe it's time to venture out on my own. I think that whenever I am with him, it gives him the wrong impression.

I close my eyes and think about everything that is new to me and about the riches of life I had been too busy to notice in America. Then, I think about the wildflower bouquets that have been picked for me since I have set foot on the island.

Antonio had bent down and carefully picked the flowers himself. He put thought and feeling into each one as he spoke to them and smiled before he pulled them from the earth. Then, he found a strong blade of grass and tied them up in a bow to hold them in place. These have so much more meaning than the bouquets I have received from a florist. I remind myself that life is so busy and so very different in America that florists are the only way to get flowers most times... but the beauty of these precious hand-picked bunches so tightly wrapped in grass ribbons are unforgettable.

At dinner tonight, he had waited on me hand and foot – something I do not allow easily. It is my nature as a mother, a wife, and a woman to wait on everyone else because I believe a woman's natural instinct is to nurture. He has been singing in the kitchen all night long as he cooks and cleans. It is so spectacular and so very romantic. Having dinner made for me in this setting on the edge of heaven and earth in *paradiso* is far better than going to any restaurant!

"I vow that I will never be too busy to notice the little things in life that are so precious!" I lift my little glass of Lemoncello to the heavens. The script of my life is being rewritten since I have arrived in Capri. All my old conditioning and beliefs are falling away because there are no longer any reminders of how I should handle situations since all are new and different now.

"I am finished, sweetie." Antonio sits next to me on the bench seat and we look at the lights across the bay. He bends into me so quickly that I am caught off guard as his lips kiss mine.

"No! Antonio, no!" I rise quickly and move away from him. "It's time for you to go...we have had too much wine. Thank you for dinner." I am angry.

"Come on sweetie. It's just a kiss!" He tries to wrap his arms around me but I won't let him.

"Don't be afraid." I move away from him and say good night. "I will see you tomorrow in the *piazza*?" He smiles and leaves.

As I lie in bed, I think about how easy it was for me to be with Bruno but not allow myself a kiss from Antonio. "It's just a kiss…" I hear the words he mouthed said inside my head. Then I laugh out loud. It's not complicated at all. I am not interested in Antonio!

Smiling into my pillow, I roll over onto my stomach and feel the crisp linens brush against my body and I fall asleep thinking of Bruno and how his lips felt on my breasts.

CHAPTER 10

That next week at the cottage, I sleep long hours and sit on the *terrazzo* all day hardly moving from the grounds. A few times, I walk into the village for supplies, but those times are rare. I am loving my place – nesting, I suppose. I sit and soak in the air and the sunlight and watch the sea as if I'm waiting for something to rise up out of it, but it is always the same - so placid, so mesmerizing with its serenity and beauty.

I watch the colors change with the weather. If the sky is clear and blue, then the water is different shades of aqua. If there are clouds, then the sea changes to a deeper smoky purple and at dusk after the sunset, it changes once again; and with each change in the weather, the land masses change. Sometimes, I can see areas on the islands and mainland that I hadn't seen before; while other times, the landscape looks like numerous islands on the horizon. It isn't until this day that I have noticed the castle at the end of Procida and I make a mental note that I want to go there to explore….once I feel I can move from my nest.

Since it is springtime, I watch the flowers bloom each day, finding a new one that has come out to dance in the sunlight. There are butterflies everywhere and lizards with bright green stripes down their backs with long tails. Sometimes, I sit very still so they might come close and I can reach out to touch them; but each time I move my hands to pet them, they scurry away.

My days at the cottage are spent alone, and in the early evening, I head into town or out to explore. I am beginning to settle in to the life of an islander, even though I am not a native. No matter. I still feel as if this is my homeland and these are my people.

On one of my trips away from my paradise, I take the autobus to Capri, which is always an adventure. It's usually filled with tourists, everyone lined up holding on for dear life as the driver rounds the deadly corners. I too am standing, holding on to the handrails as we round the three hairpin turns along the cliffs. Many riders gasped with excitement and sometimes horror as the driver maneuvers his way around the other buses and taxis as they climbed the mountainous road heading toward us from the other direction. There are no guard rails or walls to stop the bus from plummeting over the side; and we are on the cliff's edge overlooking the Marina Grande port anywhere from six hundred to one thousand meters below, depending on which stretch of the road we are on.

Once we arrive in Capri, I walk to the Gardens of Augustus. Here, there are ancient statues of the gods dispersed throughout the gardens amongst the flower beds. Another inspiring place to paint, I think to myself.

A group of about twenty school children have come to the gardens for an outing and their teacher has asked me to take a photograph of them. As soon as the children see this, six of them come running, asking me to do the same with their own cameras. Laughter fills the garden as the children jockey for position in the front row of the photos, and the ones that speak English are calling to me.

"*Signora, chiamo*? What is your name?"

"Roxanna," I reply. But for some reason, they cannot get their tongues around it and proceed to call me "Caterina." How Caterina has come from Roxanna, I do not know. No mind. I'm having fun with the children. The name sticks and for the next fifteen minutes I am known to everyone as Caterina. They all shout "*Grazie*" and "*Ciao*, Caterina," as they leave.

Walking down the wisteria-lined path, I meander slowly, taking everything in for I don't want to miss a thing or hurry to get anywhere - I have nowhere to go. I am playing with what it is like to just be inside my day with no plans and nothing to do. I want to take mental photographs of every thing I see, every thing I pass, and every person that passes by me or that I encounter so that I can be here forever – even when I return to the States. God, I don't want to leave just yet! I'm not ready!

My thoughts are interrupted by a sign that reads *Toilettes*. I need to visit one, so I walk up the short path where an elderly gentleman is tending to the restrooms. He doesn't speak a word of English, but somehow manages to invite me in for a cup of *espresso*.

"*Espresso*?" He is a short man with a beret cocked to one side on his head of white hair and his name is Alberto.

"*Si, si.*" Why not, I think? So we sit and try to communicate through sign language and with what little Italian I know. The conversation is not a long one, for I think we both have grown weary of *si*, *no capisco* and *capisce*. But I linger for a few more minutes after I finish my coffee.

"*Grazie*," I speak as I get up to leave. He comes close for the customary kissing of the cheeks; but to my surprise, he grabs my face and kisses my lips.

"Alberto, no!" I am shocked for a moment and so is he for I can see the look of confusion on his face. Had he thought I would like it? How strange. Why do they think it is okay to kiss any woman – even a stranger? My heart beats anxiously.

He keeps apologizing and continues to do so as I turn to walk away. I am now down the path at the gardens once again, before I feel myself relax. Then I hear the voice inside my head saying, "Roxanna, it's just a kiss! Get over it! It's just their way." At this, I start to giggle uncontrollably. I have to sit and compose myself for a moment and I am still laughing as people walk by and look at me to see if I am senile and need assistance.

What a wild adventure here in the land of "love Italian style!" Every woman who is having any self-doubt about her beauty or her age should come here for an ego boost. Then she would know how beautiful she really is. Lost in this thought, I round a corner to the *Umberto Piazza* and hear my new name.

"Caterina! Caterina! *Buonasera!*" All the school children, my new friends are walking through the square, excitedly waving at me with smiles on their faces.

"*Buonasera, ciao...ciao!*" My heart swells as they leave the *piazza* for I am happy to have met them this day. I continue to walk and explore the village of Capri this night and wait for the setting of the sun so I may view it from here.

Capri is half way down the mountainous island and closer to the port town below, and the lights from the yachts and the sailboats are burning brightly. I can hear music as the wind carries it upward to where I am standing. Magic...I can feel it as I breathe in deeply and close my eyes. Mmmmm...*paradiso*... I want to stay here forever.

After the sun sets, I stroll through the town as the shop keepers are performing their evening rituals the same as those in AnaCapri do - each one, bringing in their wares from the sidewalk, closing their shops as the last of the tourists leave. I know they are going home for dinner, as I have walked by their houses on the shaded path to my little villa and seen their wives with open arms, greeting them, the smell of tomatoes and garlic wafting through the night air.

It is time to return to AnaCapri, so I walk to the edge of town where the bus comes to take me back to my perch up on the cliffs above.

I will have to return to Capri and spend more time in the streets of the town itself where the restaurants and the cafes are. This is where all the tourists come to dine and watch the rich and famous. Capri is a secret jewel in the Mediterranean – a magical destination for movie stars, entertainers and Italian designers. Everyone who is anyone comes here for holiday and I love to sit and watch them. *Domani*…tomorrow, I think to myself as I walk the last stretch to my villa.

Enrico comes by twice daily, early in the morning and just before sunset to water the gardens and flowers, and to prune the trees and the bushes. He always has a pair of cutting shears with him and sometimes when we walk he takes them out of his pocket and clips the branches or the flowers sculpting his garden as we go. It is the most beautiful garden I have ever seen, bushes, flowers and trees everywhere with rocks strategically placed creating little paths with vines and wisteria hanging overhead. While we stand on the *terrazzo* talking, he cocks his head to one side, takes out his cutting shears and nips a branch. His gardens and grounds are perfection at their finest, every form perfect.

Sometimes he stops to chat and have a cup of the wonderful tea that I have brought from the States which is a mixture of black teas with jasmine and rose. It soothes my soul when I drink it, reminding me of home and now it is part of my daily ritual in my new life as I sit and watch the world from this vantage point. On this day, we are sitting and drinking tea in the early evening, Enrico and I.

"Roxanna, I am moving you to a Bed and Breakfast for a week and then I will find something more permanent for you. I am sorry you have to move again but I have negotiated a very good rate for you."

"No problem, Enrico. I appreciate everything you have done for me. Where is it?"

"It is called *Maruzzella*. Do you know where the steps are that you go down to get here?" By now, I am used to getting these types of directions.

"Yes."

"You go down about half way to the trash cans. Do you know where they are?"

"Yes, I remember." I had passed them every day on my way to and from town, the row with three small green bins where the townspeople carry their small bags of trash each day to be collected. He continues.

"You go down those stairs and it is right there on your left. You cannot miss it. Take your things there tomorrow."

"What does *maruzzella* mean?" I am curiously learning new Italian words each day and this one seemed strange to me. It is pronounced "mar-**roo**-zella."

"It is the name of the little thing inside the round shells…like this." He draws a picture of a snail in the dirt.

"That's a snail." I wrinkle my nose and Enrico laughs.

"I don't know why, silly, eh? It means little snail." Somewhere new to sleep…a new adventure, I think after he leaves. Although I am not looking forward to leaving my little villa overlooking the sea, I know that I will be well taken care of as I have since I came to the island. I came here with nowhere to sleep and had met Stephen and stayed at the San Michele Villa. Then I had met Enrico who put me up here, so I now trusted him for my next place to live.

The sun blazes high above me as I carry my overstuffed suitcase and backpack to *Maruzella*. As I walk the long distance towing my luggage behind me, I think of how sad I am to leave the cottage; but as soon as I move into my new home, I am elated with my room and the grounds. I have been living like a gypsy moving from place to place thus far, some more rustic than others. But my room here is enclosed with screens – a luxury many don't have on the island - such as the cottage… The bugs and mosquitoes sleep with you even in *paradiso*. The bathroom has a modern enclosed shower, something I have not seen since I came here, except at the Caesar Augustus. Everything is white, bright and clean – "fresh" as the Italians say. That is the English word they use to describe it.

There are only three rooms available at the B & B and mine is the one closest to the main entrance - a locked wrought iron gate with a hand painted tile on the stone wall next to it reads, *Casetta Bettina*. Bettina is the name of the proprietor, a beautiful woman with bright eyes and a big smile - a friend of Enrico.

The building is stark white and over the *porta*, the gated entrance, grows a colorful bougainvillea flowering everywhere as if it were a beautiful painting. The walls inside the room are painted white and there are white linens on the bed and white tiles everywhere. There is a writing table, a chair and a large closet for my clothing. I unpack as if I will be staying forever, for this makes it feel like home even though it will only be for a short time. I have been away so long it seems, that all this moving is making me feel like a vagabond. Time stands still here – or moves so slowly that a month seems like a year, my old life falling away like faded memories.

The bed and breakfast is in the middle of a vineyard and the grapes are starting to take form hanging in little tiny bunches everywhere. There are *terrazzos* all around the house and a patio hidden in one of the gardens that has an ocean view. This day, I sit and sketch bunches of grapes that hang on their vines and of my new surroundings. My notebook is now becoming filled with sketches of places I have visited and scenes I have been inspired by.

It also contains snippets from my heart that have spilled out onto the paper…poetry, now an expression of my unleashed passions.

> *The wind and the sea whispers to me –*
> *"Come!"*
> *"I have love for you – as wet as my waters –*
> *as vast as my seas;*
> *and I will wrap you up*
> *inside my blue skies and soft breezes!"*
>
> *My soul cries out!*
> *"I am coming!"*

I sit all day, happily settling in to my surroundings…so peaceful and so quiet…a tabby cat moves lazily from patio to patio as I do, trying to out smart the sun as it moves across the sky. It is hot this day – so hot that I can feel the moisture on my arms and little beads of sweat running down the nape of my neck. But at six o'clock – or 18:00, the breeze rises up and starts to cool things a bit.

I am silent, listening to the sounds the wind gently makes as it blows through the vineyards, a sound that I have never heard before. It is louder than the wind blowing through the trees in a mountain forest – almost like an audience clapping hands. How intriguing…music to my ears, stopping me in my tracks. A sound such as this, I will never forget.

Inspired, I sketch and write poetry until sunset. Then, I feel the setting sun beckoning to me, calling me to come to it as it has every evening since I have been here. So I chase the sun in search of an opening to the sea and the sky - and then I find it…a covered patio at the edge of the vineyard in the middle of a little garden. It is canopied with grape vines, a small settee underneath. From here I can see the isle of Ischia as the sun starts to fall into it; and once again, I feel that now familiar elixir called passion rising up inside me.

"I have died and gone to heaven…my own *paradiso*."

CHAPTER 11

It has been so long since I remembered the dreams, for I am so busy with my new life. I have forgotten everything - except how I feel in each moment.

But today, I am focused on taking the hydrofoil to Napoli for shopping. But as I step onto the boat in Marina Grande, I look back at the sheer cliffs jutting up behind the little port town and start to weep. My heart feels heavy, and it is almost too painful to leave. Will I ever be able to leave here, I ask myself? Someday, I'll be ready. But what if I'm not? I will have to stay forever I think, and I sigh.

So, I continue my life as an islander, feeling more comfortable with the language and the people. My ritual these days is to awaken around eight o'clock and walk into town for tea. Then, I roam the little streets and visit the locals – my new friends and family. I stop by and say hello to Enrique, one of the shop keepers, a beautiful *Napolitani* with blue eyes and long eyelashes. Soon, I move on down the street to the next shop.

"Alessandra, *ciao. Como va?*" I have stopped by the *Carthusia, I Profumi di Capri* next and we chat for awhile.

"*Bene, bene*…and you, Roxanna? Where have you been? We have not seen you in awhile." She has light brown hair pulled back in a barrette. It is humid that day, but she looks fresh and unbothered by the heat and the dampness in the air.

"I am well. I have been busy." I try to think of what has taken up my time but can't think of anything.

We make small talk as the tourists stroll in and out of the shops looking for treasures to remind them of this place on the other side of the world. We talk about them as they walk by, trying to guess where they are from. Then the conversation turns to men and which cultures make for better husband.

"American men make the best husbands. That's what I am waiting for – a beautiful American man to come in to my shop and sweep me away!" She is smiling dreamily.

"No, the Italians," I say. "They love their women as if they are the Madonna herself." I am remembering Mother's Day on the island as I watched all the families strolling through the streets. The fathers were holding their babies and the hands of their wives. And if there were no babies, they walked with their arms around their women, holding them close. You could see their pride. I was also remembering the way Enrico had spoken about his wife and Mario about his. Mario is a friend of Enrico's who looks in on me occasionally, bringing me vegetables and sometimes home-cooked meals that he and his wife cook.

"I never think of the Italian men that way..." Alessandra wrinkles her nose. "They like to have lovers on the side. This is not a good thing!" She is adamantly shaking her head from one side to the other, frowning at the same time.

"But it is because they love all women so much – they don't know what to do with them and want them all! They are like little boys in a candy store!" We both laugh.

After hugging good-bye, I walk down to Federico's studio. He is a painter who often plays his guitar for me and sometimes sings.

Each morning at five a.m., he goes for a swim somewhere on the island and sketches, draws or paints. He often shares them with me and explains how the light was at that time of day and how he has captured it on the paper or the canvas we are looking at. He is my mentor. We talk about technique and sometimes I sit quietly beside him as he sketches the outline of one of the tourists who walks by.

"Roxanna, I want to see you paint! You must paint...let your *passione* fly free onto the canvas! You are keeping them all bottled up inside! *Mama mia*!" He brings his hands to his head as if he has a headache.

"You are wasting your life away not painting. It is a gift from God!" He begs me, his hands clasped together as if in prayer.

"Soon...soon Federico...I have been too busy!" It is an excuse, I know. But actually, I am afraid, I think. What if I can no longer paint...no longer have the talent? Or worse yet, what will I unleash inside me and can I live with all the emotions that will be stirred up? My heart skips a few beats.

"Would you like me to sing for you, *bella*?" Federico has already picked up his guitar and is tossing the strap over his shoulder. He starts to strum the strings making them sing a flamenco-like melody.

"*Si*." He ends the melody and starts to sing an American tune – "Love Me Tender." Eerily, he sounds like Elvis himself. He often plays classical music, Napolitano or flamenco; and these old Elvis tunes…so much talent in one man I think to myself.

Soon it's time to leave for I want to visit the San Michele Villa. I have to go…feel the pull. I have been dreaming about it, and it has been too long…I can no longer control the desire.

"Federico, it's time to go. I must leave." I rise from the little couch that sits in his studio and he rises at the same time."

"Oh, so soon, *bella?*" He hugs me and kisses both cheeks.

"Yes, I am on my way to the San Michele."

"Ah, *si,si.* I understand. It is pulling you, eh?" He smiles. "When you come again, we will have champagne. Okay? *Ciao, ciao.*"

"*Ciao,* Federico." I love the way the islanders say *ciao* twice. I feel special because it is so intimate and only for the closest of friends - *amici.* When friends greet each other in the evening, I hear them say *sera…* instead of the formal *buonosera,* or *journo* in the daytime instead of *buonjourno.* You are considered one of them when they greet you in this fashion. Federico, Alessandra and all the others I have met are intimate friends. I love sharing conversation with each one of them along with all of the hugs and kisses.

I walk the small street past the little stand where I had purchased the *caprise panini,* the sandwich from the sweet man my first day on the island. As I watch him waiting on tourists, I almost bump into Donata, a friend I met while sitting in the main *piazza* in AnaCapri. That first day, I watched her with her little boy, Luca as he played at her feet. He was three years old and his father was *Napolitano,* so baby Luca as we called him, has a very expressive face like the *Napolitani.* He is always scrunching it up when he is being inquisitive. He talks with his hands, and is also very demonstrative – all at the age of three.

To me, the *Napolitani* know life, feel it, express it with passion and live as I love to live. Baby Luca had come out of the womb with that type of expression – or so it seems to me. I fell in love with him instantly and with his mother, Donata. Her father would later tell me her name meant "gift from God." And she was a gift to me.

"Donata, *ciao! Como va?*"

"Roxanna, *ciao, ciao…bene, bene.* And you?" She has long blonde hair and big brown eyes and she is without Luca.

"I am good. Where are you going?" I ask.

"I have been for a long walk and to the market. And you, Roxanna?" Her sacks are filled with vegetables which are spilling out of the tops.

"I am going to the San Michele. Where is Luca?" I miss him…I haven't seen him in a week or so.

"He is with my mother. He is a handful so I cannot take him to the market when I do my shopping." We both laugh for we know how Luca can be. "Roxanna, why don't you come to dinner? We miss you and would love to see you."

"I would love to, Donata."

"*Bene, bene*. What about Wednesday?" That is two days from now.

"Yes, I will come."

"Come at 19:00 – you know, 7:00 o'clock p.m." My friends always note the time in both ways when they speak to me, just in case I can't figure it out. I smile. "Do you remember how to get there or should I send my husband to meet you?" Their house is at the end of the island – abut two miles - a long but beautiful walk. There are winding walkways and little paths laden with flowers all along the way. By the time I had reached her home for dinner the last time, I was intoxicated from their smell.

"I remember. I will call on my cell phone if I get lost."

"Good then. *Ciao, ciao*, Roxanna." We hug and kiss goodbye. I had dined with Donata and her family the first night we had met and we quickly became friends. She has been my teacher of all the customs and tradition on the island and she has also helped me with the language. I guess you could say she is my best friend in Capri.

As I continue toward the San Michele, I remember my first dinner with her family. Her husband, Marcello and her father, Mario – who is Enrico's friend…everyone is so close on the island… they had cooked pasta and fish as we women - Donata, her mother Lousia and I sat at the outdoor table on the patio and laughed and talked as the men poured us homemade sparkling wine. They kept refilling our glasses, enjoying the fact that we were all giggling and having so much fun.

Louisa is just a few years older than me, a small, petite woman. But she is strong like most of the women in Capri. I had seen her carry not only Luca but also sacks of groceries from the village market to their home. She has short, dark hair and dark eyes, and a beauty mark on her face, reminding me of Sophia Loren.

We had such fun that night and it was so easy to feel at home with them. They took me in as if I were one of them. And I was. They are my *famiglia* – my family here.

The gates of the San Michele bring me back to the present. I pay and walk through the *porta*, through the *museo* and into the villa. I never tire of this tour through each room for it is as if I am coming home to my own place and I am just walking through noticing all of my things. I had purchased Axel Munthe's book when I first arrived and have been reading it each night before I fall asleep. It is the strangest thing, as if I had been there with Dr. Munthe, as he walked the grounds with his dogs and his pet monkey, walking to the edge of the *pergola* each night as he lit his pipe in anticipation of the sunset. I can feel his spirit all around, in each room and I can almost see him at his writing table across from his bed. I'm inspired, as he must have been, by the picture of Apollo that hangs over it - and I also feel his love for Kouros as he stood over him while he slept. How similar we are…

Walking into the gardens, I feel his presence – almost see him surrounded by his animals. He was a great lover and protector of them, reminding me of San Francesco. Munthe was also a talented doctor who helped out tirelessly when the plague hit Napoli in the late 1800s. The more I read about him, the more I admire him and feel as if we are kindred spirits. Of course it's probably because I am as enraptured with AnaCapri as he was. We are both madly in love with this place, so simple, so untouched, so real.

I am elated with his description and detail of how he felt the first time he came here, walking up the 770 stone steps that Tiberius had built. He was almost delirious when he arrived at the top, the locals feeding him food and wine for strength, his description so dramatic. I wanted to get down on my knees and kiss the ground when I arrived on the rocky shore, but I was too busy swooning from the songs of the sirens, Stephen's kiss, and my lack of sleep.

So there is a bond between us, Munthe and I – and that is why I had come here in my dreams. It was my destiny; and when I am on the grounds of the villa, the connection intensifies. I walk lost in thought now, gazing at the flowers, looking to see which ones are new, trying to remember their names. I am lost in the flowers...everywhere all around me…different colors, and the green of the lush trees. He planted them all and they are still intact after all these years. So I continue to walk, to dream, to wish with my hand upon the sphinx, lingering here…

Where am I going? Where will I be in a month…in a year…who am I? I am now Roxanna and no longer Deborah. I feel my cells changing as if I am morphing into someone else…or maybe it is already done. My thoughts are interrupted as I feel a hand on my shoulder.

"Roxanna, this is your life. You are who you will always be now that you have found yourself. And you may go wherever your heart carries you, next month or next year. Whatever you wish for is yours!" I am startled and turn, but the Spirit is gone. I laugh at the insanity of all of it, and feel the tears that have welled up in my eyes. I am weeping with happiness, for I have found so much to be thankful for. This day, this moment, this life – is where I want to be.

The sounds of tourists bring me back as I realize how crowded it has become – a tour bus, I am sure. I look for Stephen in the hopes of running into him and I often wonder what he is doing, how he and Rosa are; but I never see him again after our parting.

I think of Raffaello again and realize I have not seen him either. I had visited the Grand Hotel Quisisana for dinner in the hopes of dining with him, but unfortunately, he was not there. Maybe it is best since he is married; I do think of him often - especially the first thing in the morning when I awaken and the last thing before I fall asleep at night. I think of his beautiful face and his eyes filled with love. I have never been looked at like that before, so sacred as if I had been looked upon by God himself. This is what inspires humanity to go on and know that they are not alone, but loved and supported. And with this sweet thought, I fall asleep each night.

The island is weaving its spell, working its magic upon my soul, and there is a new peace that blankets my life.

I have been here at *Maruzzella* for four days and I awaken this morning feeling blue. My sons have filled my dreams and now I miss them terribly. So, I lie here until noon, the darkness inside my mind keeping me company throughout the day. At 6:00 P.M. I call them. I try to sound cheerful, but they hear it differently.

"Mom, is everything all right? You sound funny." When I hear Josh's voice, I start to weep.

"I'm okay. I just miss you both so much." I am now laughing, trying to make light of it.

"Oh, it's okay. We're fine. We miss you too but everything is fine here. I have a new girlfriend!" I hear the excitement in his voice. "It's Mom!" I hear Devon asking who is on phone.

"What's her name? Where did you meet her?" I am starting to feel better, more connected to him.

Her name is Stephanie and she has blonde hair. She's pretty, Mom. I met her outside the movie theatre a few weeks ago."

"Mom!" Devon is on the other line. "How's it going? Got any stories?" He always loved my stories. It was like a game between us when he was a little boy. I am surprised that they are both home at this hour. How strange for teenagers, I think.

"Devon, I miss you both so much." I start to cry again.

"Mom, stop! We're fine. We're just chillin' with Dad tonight, hanging out watching a movie. What have you been doing?" I tell them about the island and my new friends and about how I spend my days. Devon has asked for a story, so I weave one about Axel Munthe and the San Michele Villa while Josh listens on the other line.

We talk about the photos I have been sending them and of Josh's new girlfriend. He is smitten, his first real girlfriend. The boys hand the phone to their father, and when I hear his voice, I break down and cry now feeling there is no familiarity in my life here in Capri. I think I must be crazy to have left all of this love behind…my family.

"Deborah, they are doing fine. They are happy here with me. Stop worrying. Yes of course they miss you but they've been pretty busy. It's their time away from you, too you know. They need to be dating and spending time with friends. Let them go a little."

He is the voice of reason. I did coddle them too much and now they are learning how to live life on their own.

"Maybe I should think of coming home, Ed…" He cuts me off.

"No, absolutely not! You need to stay through the summer. Enjoy yourself. Figure out what you want to do with the rest of your life. I'm envious. Look at you! I wish I was there instead of you; so don't do anything you'll regret. We'll expect you in September. In the meantime, I'm getting to know my boys again and frankly, I like it. I'm not quite ready to give them back yet." Josh is on the other line now.

"Mom, stay for the summer. Dad's taking us to Yosemite for vacation so we won't be here even if you do come home. Be strong, Mom! Love you." Devon is back on the line.

"Mom, stay for the summer. We want you to meet someone and fall in love!" He's laughing, teasing me and I'm now smiling.

"Are you both okay with this?" I need reassurance.

"Yes, we are. But you have to promise to send more pictures. We love you Mom." They are both talking into the phone at the same time. "Bye."

"I love you both. Bye."

"Deborah, I mean it. Stay. And if you need to talk, call me. I'll straighten you out." Ed is firm but supportive. He always had been, throughout our marriage and even our divorce. He's a good guy. I feel like the old Deborah in these moments and it's okay.

"Thanks, Ed. I couldn't do this if it wasn't for you. Bye."

"Bye, Deb; love you."

"Love you, too." He had always loved me and never wanted the divorce, and I guess I never stopped loving him either. He was a good man and a good father. I'm glad we have the relationship that we do and that he has found happiness again. Cynthia is a good step-mom and I couldn't have asked for a better one for my boys.

It's amazing how clear things become when you put yourself out there. Of course I still miss my boys, but I'm going to be okay. I remember their smell, their faces, their hugs. I remember Devon's sense of humor and Josh's wisdom.

"We are all going to be just fine." Now, my day has turned around.

And at the end of the day, I fall asleep with beautiful dreams of my sons and of my own mother. I am with Josh and Devon, as if they are on the island here with me, and they are telling me to stay and finish what I need to do. My mother is holding a place at home for me, baking cookies and just loving me from afar, and this is confirmation that I'm doing the right thing, a message sent from the heavens.

CHAPTER 12

When I awaken, I bolt from my bed without trepidation.

"Roxanna, it is now time to go and really explore the world! Let's go have an adventure!" My feet are dancing as soon as they hit the floor. "A whole summer! Yes!" I am giddy with anticipation, talking to myself. I ready myself and leave *Maruzella,* blowing kisses to the rock wall, the bougainvillea, the long stone walkway, the little lizards and the cat that comes to greet me. I am happy with everything once again. Time for tea and eggs before heading to the Marina Grande.

Trying to get down to the port this day is not easy because they are resurfacing the roads in AnaCapri. The bus service is slow and the tourists are lined up in the heat waiting for hours for transportation to both Capri and Marina Grande. I wait for thirty minutes and then decide to get on the autobus which is going only as far as Capri. From there, I can catch another that will take me to the port in a roundabout way, bypassing the crowds. It takes me two hours to get to the hydrofoil, but luckily, they are running every hour to Sorrento.

I stand at the rail of the Alascafi hydrofoil and feel the wind from the sea whip through my hair, my eyes affixed to the form of Capri and its cliffs. I want to make sure I memorize its shape. Yes, I can see her head as she lies on her back, her breasts and her belly. I close my eyes and feel the hot sun as it bleeds through the dampness of the sea air.

I am free at this moment…free from any thoughts, from missing my sons, or from feeling the need of having to be anywhere else. I hear the horn rousing me to open my eyes and I realize how crowded the boat has become. I move inside to take a seat and moments later, a young man sits next to me. He tells me he is from Sorrento and works on the island so he travels back and forth daily.

"You *bella*." He is smiling seductively. "I Rosario. You - me - Sorrento?" He makes the sign of walking and snapping photographs.

"No, *grazie*. I have *commissione*, errands to run." I am smiling to myself with this silly thought. He is staring at me intently. Does he think the smile is for him?

"You, me Prosecco...*domani a Capri?*" He is inviting me to meet him for champagne tomorrow and a big stick comes to mind. Although he is cute, he is also very young. They are everywhere, *Mama mia!*

"How old are you? *Come anni?*" I have to ask.

"I am *trenta,*" as he writes 30 in the air with his finger.

"I am *cinquanta*, fifty! No champagne, but *grazie.*"

"No...*pero you bene per cinquanta.*" He is telling me I looked good for fifty. He smiles as he moves his arm onto my lap and rests his hand on my knee. Should I remove it? This keeps happening, I think. I decide to wait just a few moments....but as I sit there holding my breath, his hand moves toward my legs and his fingers moved up and under my skirt!

"No, *fermata!*" This is one of the first Italian words I learned and it means to stop or halt and it has come in handy. I pull his hand away quickly before it roves any further, and I place it on his own lap.

"Oh, *bella.*" He rests his head on my shoulder as if he is my best friend! Quickly, he moves his face close to mine and tries to steal a kiss. I am firm with him and keep him at a distance for the rest of the ride, but not easily. Thank goodness, only fifteen more minutes on this twenty-five minute ride! It is like fending off someone with four arms instead of two! Finally! We are here.

"You...me...please?" He has turned to me and grabbed my arm as we both stand to leave.

"No." At that, he waves goodbye and walks far ahead, disappearing into the crowd, probably trying to catch the next available woman. As I walk from the port up the long street that leads into the city, I laugh out loud. I laugh so hard that I start giggling as people walk by wondering if I am okay. I soon collect myself.

As I walk through beautiful Sorrento, I realize I am lonely for love. I have encountered all of these beautiful men and had different experiences with each one of them, but there is still a void inside me. Does this mean I'm ready?

Two lovers pass by me holding hands - British tourists, probably newlyweds. Many travel to Sorrento and the Amalfi Coast for their honeymoon because it is one of the most romantic places in southern Italy. He is holding her hand as they walk and each time she stops to look at something in a shop window, his eyes are affixed on her and not what she is looking at. He has found the love of his life and is proud of this beautiful woman that is now his.

I see couples, both young and old everywhere. Everyone seems to be half of a pair or a set. I walk through the little alleyways where only the locals shop and if you are lucky enough as a tourist to find these hidden places, then you have found the romance of Sorrento. And even here…I am the only *solo* person. No mind…I am suddenly sidetracked by the man selling flowers.

"*Molto bella!*" He smiles and winks as I pass. I turn my head to see if it is me he is talking to or someone else behind me, but I see I am the only one within range. I smile back at him and say *grazie* as I pass. Now, what was I thinking about? I have forgotten…

The clouds dance across the sky giving the streets a much needed break from the sweltering sun and the damp humidity as I approach the *piazza* before the train station. A cool breeze rises up and blows my hair into my eyes and I carelessly push it back into my clip. I loved the way the wind always seems to play with me here.

A young man is standing in front of a restaurant, the tables behind him dressed in red and white checkerboard cloths.

"*Buonjourno, bella. Venire mangiare e bere.*" Am I hungry? There are little vases on the tables with one geranium in each of them. He smiles at me with shy eyes.

"*Si, grazie.*" He takes me to a table with a view of the *piazza* where I can watch the people as they pass by.

"*Prego.*" As I sit, I watch as people mill about or rest as they eat their gelato. Flowers are everywhere and the smell of the geraniums is soothing. As I sit sipping my *vino bianco*, I breathe in their sweetness and the smells of Sorrento. Then I close my eyes and savor the moment.

"Go to Rome, Roxanna…" I bolt upright in my chair and look around, but there's no one there…then I realize it is the voice I am now so familiar with. Rome…I have always wanted to go there, visit the Sistine Chapel, the Vatican, the Coliseum, and Palatine Hill. Why not? I can feel my excitement building! I'll leave in two days; after all, I have nothing pressing to attend to. My mouth curls into a smile.

As I finish my lunch, I dream of *Roma* and how I will conquer it. And these thoughts keep me company all the way back to Capri as I see the shape of her on the horizon. Once again, she has my full attention. Home…my home…a smile of contentment crosses my lips and my heart skips a beat. I can feel it calling to me like a lover, and my body responds.

"I am coming – wait for me." I whisper. I hope I can leave her – my own Capri - to visit Rome…

After changing my clothes, I ride the autobus to the town of Capri and buy a tour book of Rome. I am sipping a glass of local wine as I sit on the veranda of the La Palma Hotel to strategize my plan of attack. I will stay in the opera district, for someone in the States has recommended a boutique hotel there. It's quaint and quiet, and close enough to the train station for easy access to transportation. This way, I can carry my backpack to the hotel. The first day, I will visit the Borghese Villa, its museum and then the famous Tivoli Fountain and the Spanish Steps.

The next day, I'll go to the Vatican and the Sistine Chapel…and the Coliseum and Palatine Hill…well, maybe I'll see these on the third day! I'll stay until I have seen it all!

I'm giggling again – always giggling. They probably look at me here and say, "There is that giggling American woman again. Do you think she is crazy?" *Bucco* Antonio tells me. He says this is the Italian word for crazy, although I can't seem to find it in my dictionary. Another adventure….I can feel the skin on my arms as it starts to crawl with gooseflesh.

"Oh, this is a delicious sign!" What a life I am leading. I think back to the emails I have sent from the *Il Matino*, the internet café. I have a network of six girlfriends that are living vicariously through me so I email them every few days to tell them what I am doing, seeing and feeling. They live for those emails as they work their jobs, take care of their families and live their lives. A few even wish they were here with me living their dream as I live mine, while the others just want to hear my stories. What new adventure would I find in Rome to tell them about?

I am pulled out of my daydream as a crowd gathers on the small street in front of me, hovering around the doorway to Armani's. The crowd is starting to grow, drawing more people with curiosity as I sit watching for fifteen minutes. Many have their cell phones in their hands raised over their heads trying to snap photos of whoever is inside.

"Would you like anything else, *signora?*" The waiter is standing beside me now.

"No, *grazie*. Who are they waiting for?" I ask.

"It is Sophia Loren. She is very beautiful and very famous." I heard Donata say that she had seen her shopping in AnaCapri a few days ago. She said that she was so tiny and still as beautiful as she was forty years ago. I find myself as excited as the crowd is.

"She has a villa on the other side of the island – above Marina Piccola. It is the big white house, a compound." I pay the waiter.

"*Grazie, signora.*" I walk out to the street to wait with everyone else to catch a glimpse of this famous beauty. The stores across from the La

Palma are Georgio Armani, MASA – a male and female clothing store, and Snobberie – *bella* Italiano lingerie and undergarments, lacey g-strings and matching bras adorning the windows. These are the high-end shops in this part of Capri and they cater to the wealthy. The movie stars shop here and try to hide from the world when they come but they cannot escape, even here. The only saving grace is that this is *paradiso* and the crowds are a lot smaller.

I study the gorgeous Italian women as they walk by, amazed at their beauty. They are dressed in beaded tops or halter tops and have heavy necklaces of gold and gemstones draped around their necks. They either wear long flowing skirts, very short tight ones, or Capri pants of white linen – the choice fabric here on the island because of the heat and humidity.

I watch them with their long hair. Most wear it pulled back tightly in a ponytail, or pulled back in the Romanesque style with a clip or barrette gathering the top half only at the back of the head, the rest falling loosely around their shoulders. Capri is a magnet for the rich and famous, unlike AnaCapri which is more of a hidden treasure. If you don't know where to go, then you might not find it as interesting or as exciting as Capri. But I am now a local and know where the best restaurants, the best shopping, and the best hikes are off the beaten path. It is a village untouched by time, the people precious to me.

Paparazzi are lining up in front of Armani's now, and I look just in time to see Sophia walk out onto the street. She is radiant, glowing, and very petite, dressed in a floral dress that reaches mid-calf with strappy sandals on her feet. I wonder how she can walk on the uneven stone streets with these beautiful shoes with spiked heels but she is doing so gracefully. The skirt of her dress moves with her, flowing as if it has been orchestrated. Her breasts rise out of her top, and a sizable collar of gold leaves drapes around her neck, reminding me of something that Cleopatra would wear for Caesar.

She stops for a few moments and smiles at the crowd allowing her fans to snap photos. As she turns to leave, I can hear the men, both young and old say, "A*h, bella, molto bella…*"

"*Grazie, grazie mille…arrivederci!*" She raises her hand over her head signaling her departure, and smiles wide. Yes, she is small, but oh, she is larger than life. I walk on toward the edge of town and the autobuses. Another amazing day filled with adventure…

CHAPTER 13

ROMA

The walk to my hotel, at the Piazza della Opera in Rome is only four blocks and my backpack on wheels is light since the weather is warm and I am carrying less clothing in it. I have five thin skirts and tops and two dresses, a nightgown to sleep in and my swimsuit. My toiletries and hairdryer are the heaviest, but a necessity. Where would a girl be without them? I also have my sketchbook with me, for I know I will be inspired after visiting the museums. The uneven Roman stones on the sidewalk echo rat-tat-tat underneath the plastic wheels.

The smell of tomatoes, basil and garlic blended with geranium float through the air invading my senses…the perfume of Italia, and I can hear the musical sound of the language being spoken all around me along with the sounds of scooters as they move through the busy city. Little cafes and shops are tucked in between the hotels – there are so many…and as I walk by one of them, I hear that old so familiar phrase.

"Molto bella…" The Romans are very expressive and vocal about what or who is beautiful to them, just as they are in the south of Italy. I wonder if it's the same all throughout the country. I smile each time I hear these words for I am flattered and feel more beautiful while here in Italy than anywhere else.

My hotel is easy to find and I check in and am in my room within thirty minutes of leaving the train. I immediately throw open the shutters to the window and take in the view. The skyline is filled with old buildings, the kind you would expect in Rome. How old are they, I wonder? The windows are large - many of them open - so I have a view inside. I espy a man walking around in his room bare-chested. He is on the telephone talking with his free hand, moving it with each word as if it helps him make a point to the person on the other end of the line.

A pretty dark-haired woman in the building directly across from me is bending over the sill hanging clothes on a line.

"Aspette! Aspette! Wait, wait!" Frustrated, she calls to her little ones who I can hear speaking to her, although I cannot see them. A sudden breeze comes out of nowhere…unusual because of the heat, and

picks up the edge of the linen sheet she is hanging and carries it upward on the air.

I look down the street to my left and see a great church sitting in the distance…I know it to be the Santa Maria Maggiore, the basilica from my tour book. I'll visit it tomorrow. The Opera House sits across the street from the hotel with its large *piazza* and I can see children chasing pigeons as their mothers sit talking with each other. It's breathtaking! I'm here in Rome! My heart is full and I know I will fall in love with this city too, for I already have, just from reading the tour book!

"Let's see what new adventure awaits me in the Eternal City!" Smiling, I move from the window and start to ready myself for my trip to the Vatican.

It's noon before I arrive and the sun is beating down on the city as if it were punishing it. It's a sweltering heat with so much dampness that it takes getting used to. I am able to stay cool by moving slowly and dressing in the light weight linens which I have purchased in Capri.

I arrive in Vatican City and see thousands of people milling about. Hundreds are standing in the scorching summer sunlight waiting to get into the museums. Hundreds more are just walking throughout the small city, and the rest are milling about inside the *Piazza della San Pietro* where the Bernini Fountains stand before *San Pietro's Basilica*. I walk in through the columned portico, and stare at the beauty of the place.

The fountains – so perfect and so large sit on either side of a great obelisk which is actually set further back in the distance – an optical illusion. The *piazza* is huge and even beyond the obelisk, are the steps to Saint Peter's. It is vast, opulent, sacred…

I walk out toward the fountains and my heart races, for I have never seen anything quite like this before. I can feel the history here and I am suddenly flooded with love. I let it rush into me as I hold back the tears and try to breathe. It's as if I can feel all those who have walked here - prayed here before me - for I feel their spirit.

After a time, I move toward one of the fountains and put my fingers in the water, bringing them to my lips. I want to fall into it, be blessed by it, but I know it is forbidden. So I stand still until the feelings pass. I remember to breathe as I snap pictures with my camera, snapping them from every angle; and just when I think I have captured everything that is beautiful, I look upward and see the statues of all of the saints lining the roof of the colonnade that circled the *piazza* – over a hundred, it seems.

I sit to rest in its shade and am quiet for a long time with no thoughts, only emotion. I know I have been here before. When? Not in this lifetime for sure...another perhaps? I see myself walking with books in my hands, underneath this same portico and my clothing is that of a nun's. As I walk, I can feel the love and devotion in my heart. Whatever I am carrying in my hands is sacred to me, for I feel how closely I am holding it against my breast. What is it...a book maybe? I cannot see and the vision is lost...the sounds of children's laughter bringing me back to the present. I rise from where I am sitting and move toward Saint Peter's Basilica.

My eyes adjust to the dimness as I enter and walk through the interior. Bernini's *Balducchino*, his sculptured bronze tabernacle containing St. Peter's throne and tomb sit before me in the distance. High above it, I see the stained glass window with its colors of golden tones and white. It is surrounded by two large angels, a sky filled with clouds and a dove. There is a gigantic hood with four colossal spiraling columns beneath it, decorated with olive branches and vines, and statues in each corner. Each time I think one great work of art is the most brilliant I see another just as majestic and as brilliant.

I have to pull myself away to move toward the first chapel where I find Michelangelo's *Pieta*. It takes my breath away and makes the tears rise up from deep within me; and I weep openly as everyone else does around me. He was only twenty-four when he sculpted this. What amazing talent. The Madonna's face is so beautiful, I want to kiss it. I think to myself how much he must have loved her to create such beauty with his fingers and the palms of his hands as he smoothed her skin and sculpted her delicate features. I can almost see him creating her...

He has captured not only her youth and her sweetness, but also her strength...the way her dress drapes over her lap and the way it falls to the floor. The look of love and compassion for her son is apparent in the Mother's eyes. The body of Crist, his skin clinging to his ribs, the way his lifeless limbs fall by his sides as his arms hang resting on her lap...This is the most beautiful work of art I have ever laid eyes upon. I have to pull myself away to continue on...

The wooden bench beneath me is hard as I sit in quiet contemplation. I feel the need to pray after seeing the *Pieta*, even though I have not been a practicing Catholic since I was twenty. Since I've come to Italy, I have found Santa Maria everywhere. That is what the Italians call her, so I too call her this, because I love the feel of it on my tongue and the way it sounds.

If there is a grotto in the rocks or on a mountainside, it becomes a home to a Madonna statue. Everyone has her displayed outside of their villa. They build little alcoves in the walls near their doorways, which they adorn with candles and fresh flowers for her.

As I sit, I pray to her with thanks for the gifts and miracles I have received since arriving in Italy. I tell her I love her and honor her for her life, her strength and her undying love. Then I linger in silence for quite awhile.

Slowly, I move deeper into the interior where I come upon four huge pilasters containing four colossal statues each representing the crucial moments of *Christ's Passion* - St. Longinus, St. Helen, St. Veronica and St. Andrew all sculpted by Bernini. I look at the fine lines and their detail, and I am mesmerized by their size. I move through each room taking it all in and then walk out into the brilliant sunlight. What I have seen is emblazoned upon my mind… the beauty of it all, the passion…the romance…the talent.

The Vatican Museums are next and I am able to walk right in without standing in line as if the sky has opened up for me only. Another miracle…I move through each gallery, each room, each hall, and make note of everything I see. In the *Pinacoteca*, the picture gallery, there are paintings and portraits lining the walls. In Room VIII, I find Raphael's *Trasfigurazione, Transformation* painted in oil on wood, and I can feel the reverence he was trying to convey. In this same room is his *Madonna of Foligno*…the colors of the paint, the context, the emotion…my heart flutters with each one.

In Room XII, I stand before Caravaggio's *Deposition*, his startling portrayal of emotion. It is brilliant! Then, I come upon the entrance to *Capella Sistina,* the Sistine Chapel. As I walk through the portal, my eyes take in every inch of every wall, the floors, the tables, the ceilings. Each one is frescoed, painted, sculpted, or inlaid with ornate tile. Every inch is a work of art in and of itself. Housed here are works by Pinturicchio, Boticelli, Rosselli, and Ghirlandaio who is Michelangelo's master. Then, of course, there is Raphael and Michelangelo, two of my greatest loves – my mentors.

I feel the need to paint as I trace the lines of each painting with my fingers in the air. I can do this, too. I know I can…I have…

I feel insane…it looks so easy. I move closer and see the heavy layering of the paint, their technique. Such time and effort…such attention to detail...

Then the ceiling…I had seen pictures, but this…this…I have no words for. I know it had taken him, Michelangelo almost five years to finish. And he has covered every square inch with paint, sculpture or architecture...but I am not prepared for what is before me. Breathtaking...keep breathing, Roxanna... overwhelming...my senses are on overload...immense...the masterpiece of the world...scene after scene across the entire ceiling. I cannot tell if it is painted tromp l'oeil, architectured columns, or scroll work - It is all so real...so perfect.

All nine panels depicting the *Episodes from Genesis* are here... *Separation of Light and Dark, Creation of the Sun and Moon, Creation of Trees and Plants, Creation of Adam, Creation of Eve, Fall Follow, Noah's Sacrifice, the Flood,* and *the Drunkenness of Noah.* Then, there are the Prophets and the Sybils, Jesus' Forefathers, and *Episodes from the Old Testament.*

In the scene of *The Fall* - Adam and Eve are being forced out of the garden, the serpent as his body wraps around the tree of knowledge...Sybil, her beauty captured...her pose. The *Creation of Adam,* the finger of God reaching out to touch Adam's. I had seen the likeness so many times before, but now that I see the original before me, I realize the power...the look in Adam's eye.

The *Last Judgment* is on the wall behind the altar. For more than an hour, I stand looking upward and all around me, with my heart. I take it all in, breathe it in, live it, and love them all - every blessed scene. It's as if Michelangelo has just left moments before my arrival, for I can feel his heart, his soul, his energy.

As I walk back to my hotel from the train station, I realize how overwhelmed and filled with awe and passion I am and have the need to lie down to quiet my mind and body. And as I lie here on my bed in Rome, I also realize that although I came for adventure, what I have found instead is a passion for the art, for history, for the paint - and I promise myself I will paint before I leave this city.

To live in a city such as this, I would surely spend every moment with these masters and their creations. I know now why Rome is called the eternal city, for I can feel everyone who has come before me, their souls in these great masterpieces that I have seen and touched today.

CHAPTER 14

After a two-hour nap, I bathe, washing away the excess energy that is left over from the day. I am more exhausted than I realize…my senses on overload. I must be taking in too much for my mental and emotional bodies to handle, my mind trying to process without success. But now, after the nap and the bath, I feel alive again.

I dress in my thin, black, flowered Italian dress which has bits of lace at the hem. I purchased it especially for this trip. It was my dream dress that I had tried on and fallen in love with because it reminded me of promises of love in *Italia*. I am so silly I think, as I stand looking at the reflection in the mirror before me. But I still giggle, for the woman who looks back is sexy and beautiful. I have lost much weight.

"*Alla olio d'olivia*! To olive oil," I shout! Once again, I am giggling as I walk down the hall and enter the little elevator that is only big enough for one body. I feel as if I have an invisible lover at my side; so with him, I leave in search of food in this magical city.

The smells again…I am intoxicated as if I have drunk wine. Maybe I am still exhausted from all that I have seen today. No matter. I'll get something to eat, walk a bit afterward and get a good night's sleep. I have become accustomed to sleeping long hours here with no work schedule and I am getting used to it. Will I ever have to go back to that lifestyle? I wonder…

I love roaming these streets, watching everyone. A beautiful middle-aged woman walks toward me, her arm intertwined with a handsome Italian man. They both have the dark hair and the chiseled Romanesque features. She is in a dress that reminds me of Sophia Loren and he is dressed in a dark suit as many men are in the city this time of year. I wonder if he is sweating under it. But they never are; they are all so cool and unaffected by the humidity.

I watch her walk, sauntering beside him. She has his full attention; he only has eyes for her. He smiles as she speaks to him as if they are flirting with each other. Are they lovers? Three elderly men sit at a table on the corner next to a café. Two of them have hats on, the kind that breathe with the heat. They are swapping stories, but stop to gaze at the beautiful woman.

"*Molto bella,*" I hear one say. And they all sit in silence until she turns the corner; and once again they start talking. I walk to the fountain near the train station and then to the church, but it is closed for the night. I'll come back in the morning I tell myself.

I head back toward the opera district, but via a different street and on the corner, I find an old building that is part of the original wall that had once protected the city in ancient times. It has to be thousands of years old. I touch the brick with the palm of my hand and rest it there in hopes of communicating with the past. How silly of me, I think. If these walls could talk, what stories would they tell?

The restaurant inside is named *Il Forte*. I walk inside and wait to be seated. A young Roman takes me to the rooftop where there are six tables, candles as their centerpiece, and a decorative wrought iron fence with potted plants hanging from it that borders the patio. Bougainvillea grows up the sides and covers any view of the street…the effect is pure romance. There is a young man with a beard and long hair playing Italian folk music on an acoustic guitar and I listen as I am seated at a table and given a menu.

"*Sera, bella.*"

"*Sera, grazie.*" I am so happy to have found this place, and am watching the groups of people laughing, singing and clapping their hands to the music – in between their eating I find myself also singing and laughing as if I am part of them.

"You are very beautiful, *signora.*" My young waiter's eyes are affixed upon me.

"*Grazie.*" I feel shy suddenly, for he is gorgeous. He is not quite Roman looking; I think he looks more French with his short hair and beautiful light colored eyes. He has a thin nose like the French and high cheekbones but speaks Italian like a native.

"May I recommend the Chianti, *signora*? It is *molto bene.*" He kisses the tip of his index finger and thumb as they are pressed together. I giggle at his expression and his passion.

"*Si, grazie.*"

"*Chiamo Natale.* You?" His name is pronounced "Nah-**tah**-lay."

"I am Roxanna…nice to meet you, Natale." His eyes are looking deeply into mine as if he is searching for something and he makes my heart flutter.

"I will take good care of you tonight, Rossana. I be back *un minuto*." He smiles and bows slightly before backing away. This is going to be a very romantic night, I can feel it.

"*Amo l'Italia,* I love Italy…" I whisper to myself so only I can hear. He has dimples in both his cheeks and a face you want to cover with kisses. He is well built, thin, but solid and strong and I guess him to be in his late thirties. There is laughter and singing all around me and I am so taken in by all of it that I forget I am alone. Natale returns with a carafe of *chianti*.

"For you, *bella*." He pours and I taste and it is excellent.

"*Molto bene…perfecto, grazie*." I smile.

"May I recommend the *pesce*? It is sautéed in Italian herbs and *limone*."

"*Si*, I would like the fish."

"I will bring you *insalata e pasta*. Yes?" With each word, he looks intensely into me as if he is making love to me and I feel naked. I know I am blushing. I can feel myself doing so. But he only continues to see into me with those soulful eyes. After he leaves me, I catch my breath and realize that to go to a restaurant in Italy, to be waited on, to order food and then to eat - is to make love with the food and the waiter. I am flushed and this is only the foreplay!

I wonder if he looks at every woman with those eyes…it's almost haunting the way he uses them on me…assault weapons! I giggle as I sip my *chianti*.

I sit for hours being entertained by Zuchero the guitar player, the waiters and the patrons. Two women and a man are sitting at the table next to me, laughing and singing along with Zuchero. They turn to me and invite me to their table to join them where I learn they are from Germany here on holiday. We laugh and tell stories through dessert. It seems so sudden that the music has stopped and Zuchero is saying "*arrivederci*," but I realized it is 11:30 p.m. Where has the time gone?

"*Bella*, stay and have drink. Please wait for me." Natale has brought over a bottle of Lemoncello and glasses for all of us. Remembering how potent the Lemoncello is, I sip it slowly. It reminds me of the controversial Absinthe, the emerald green liqueur I had heard so much about, that is now banned everywhere except the Czech Republic, for it makes you do and feel strange things. Natale returns.

"You stay for me?"

"No, no, I am so tired, Natale. I have to go to sleep. *Sonnolento*, I am sleepy."

"No, *bella*. Please. I have scooter. I take you to see Roma by night! You will not be disappointed." He is looking into my eyes intently and I cannot resist…the Lemoncello…the magic of Roma…

"I will wait for you." He grins wide and starts to leave.

"I will hurry! *Mi affretterò! Mezzanotte*, midnight, I will be finished." He is gone.

"We are leaving now, Roxanna. It was nice to meet you. Enjoy Rome." My new friends kiss my cheeks in the Italian way and I watch as they depart. I am now alone but only have a few minutes to sip my Lemoncello and think, what am I doing…am I out of my mind? But Natale is back in a flash, interrupting my doubting thoughts.

"I am ready, Rossana. I have so many places to take you. Have you ever been to Roma before?" He is excited. I wonder how many times he takes female patrons on this "Roma by Night" tour on the back of his scooter.

"This is my first time." We arrive at his scooter which is parked down the street from the restaurant. He helps me onto the back and then jumps on himself.

"Hold me tight, *bella*. I will show you things you will never forget. You will always remember me this night." I am sure that I will…

He pulls my hands together at his waist and drives off. I love scooters…I love the brr-rr-r-r-r- sound of the engines, for they remind me of Italia. It is soothing to me somehow - helps me relax, lulling me into a soft, safe peacefulness. I close my eyes and enjoy the feel of him against me. I hear the sounds of the eternal city – the little automobiles, the sounds of scooters and the sound of a water fountain. I open my eyes and we are at the Trevi Fountain! That's it…I've died while my eyes were closed and gone to heaven! As I open them, I see the most famous and the most fabulous fountain in the world. It is huge, just as I have seen in the movies, yet larger and more beautiful.

"This the *Fontana de Trevi*." He stops the scooter and pulls me by the hand. "Here, you stand. I take *foto*." Natale poses me as if I am a model. He says smile and snaps the picture with my camera. Then he shows me the photo on the digital screen. "*Molto bene*…you are so beautiful, Rossana." He is rolling my name around in his mouth as if I am a sweet hard candy.

It is dark as night, but he thinks it's beautiful none the less. Natale pulls two coins from his pants pocket and hands one to me.

"We throw coins…is good luck. Wish for something good to your heart, Rossana." I smile, and as I stand with my back facing the fountain, my eyes closed, I remember my wish for love, passion, and romance -

and I ask for it. All I can hear are the sounds of the water rushing over the statues and back into itself, and the sound of a mandolin playing a romantic tune close by.

"Come. We go now." He holds my hand, guides me to the scooter and we ride off into the night and toward the Vatican. I have a smile on my face that I cannot remove and my teeth are dry from the wind, but this thought makes me even giddier.

"This, *Vaticano*." We arrive at the Vatican and walk into the *piazza*. I remember it from daylight and see Saint Peter's before me. The saints on top of the colonnade are lighted making the scene more beautiful by night than by day. I can hear the sound of pigeons flurrying into the air as we move toward the fountains - Natale is holding my hand and is whispering in my ear that this is his sacred place, the place he comes to when he is troubled. We walk to the fountain on the left and dip our fingers into the water and with his own, he blesses himself out of respect, and then he dips them again and blesses me.

"You are my gift from God." He bends into me and kisses me on the lips. It is a gentle kiss...a long kiss...his lips pressing into mine with firm sweetness. It is a purposeful kiss...one that means he likes me, thinks of me as someone special. He moves his chest into me so that his touches mine. Then he takes both my hands and clasps them so they are inside his as if for safe keeping. After his lips leave mine, he brings each of my hands up to them and kisses them gently, seriousness filling his eyes.

"*Mio amore*...you make Roma magic for me." I am speechless and have no words, or jokes for him. I am content just to be here. We leave and ride over the Sant'Angelo Bridge to the castle, the lights lining the sides of it as if we are in a fairy tale riding to our palace to live happily ever after.

Next, we drive to the Forum, Palatine Hill, and the Coliseum which are spectacular with the lights. Then we move to the Victor Emmanuel Monument which is more massive than anything I have ever seen. He holds my hand, pulling me to each perfect spot for *fotos*; and each time we leave the scooter, he moves closer to me - so close that I can feel his breath on my face and my neck.

I am deliriously happy as I hold on to him while we ride through the Italian night...feeling as if I am on the back of the great steed of King Victore Emannuell, the first emperor of Italy, riding across *il suo citti*, his city – the city he has been left in charge of. Natale squeezes my hand.

"Rossana, you are so beautiful," he says with his thick accent that I will never tire of hearing.

"And, Natale, you are so sweet!" I giggle. I feel safe with him, as if he is my boyfriend and I am a girl of fifteen. He is a man, not as young as the others I have met so far. He stops the scooter in front of my hotel at three a.m. and lifts me from it as if it were a horse and I the rider.

"I have enjoyed you, Rossana. Thank you for showing me Roma by night. I have never seen it through your eyes before. You have beautiful eyes, you know." I feel myself swoon over his sweetness, his words, and his dimpled face. It is beautiful to gaze upon – strong, and his deep eyes take my breath away when he looks into me. He kisses me long and hard but with such gentility, all the while holding my face in both of his hands while he lovingly plays with my lips. His tongue moves all over them, licking my mouth inside and out - the hottest kiss I have ever received. I gasp for a moment from the heat of it, and pull my head back a bit.

"Please come home with me tonight, Rossana; I want to make love to you."

"Natale, not tonight. Thank you. It is late."

"My heart feels sorrow here." He takes my hand and places my palm over his heart where I can feel his slender, muscular chest underneath and wonder if he is built like this all over.

"Maybe tomorrow - *domani*?" What am I saying? I am shocked at my response, but can't help myself!

"*Allora…domani*. I will count the hours on the clock until I see you again." He pulls out a pen and a card and writes his number on it for me. "Call if you change your mind tonight. If not, *domani* under the stars *a mezzanotte*, at midnight after work. Wait for me by the *ristorante, Rossana*." With that, he smiles and blows me a kiss goodnight.

Romance, *fantastico*….I will never be the same…

The next day, I awaken after dreaming of him. I dream he is my lover and we are sitting on a grassy Roman hill in the countryside and I am draped across him, my head resting upon his chest. He's brushing my hair with his fingers and whispering words of love to me. I feel twenty and I feel the passion inside me as I awaken and wish I had asked him to spend the night. I pretend he is my pillow as I roll over on top of it, pressing myself into him. God! The Italians stir me so! I breathe in and out until these feelings subside…tonight, I think…tonight…

I tour around Rome all day with Natale in my thoughts every moment. But the ruins of the Roman Forum and Palatine Hill steal them away. I imagine what it must have been like to live here long ago and visualize Nero standing on the portico of his house and Caesar walking in the forum, his white toga flowing in the breeze, his diadem - the wreath of laurel upon his head.

I imagine seeing the vestal virgins standing in the atrium of the temple, and I remember how before Caesar was assassinated, he had delivered his last will and testament, in secret to them for safe-keeping. I envision Marc Antony stealing it away to deliver it to Caesar's wife Cleopatra after his death; and I envision her running to the forum to see her husband lying on the steps on the Ides of March, that last day in his history…the last time she would lay eyes upon the man she loved.

Augustus, when he was emperor, made his imperial residence here, as well as Tiberius, Caligola, Flavii, and others. Octavian, Caesar's successor walked here and young Caesarion, the son of Cleopatra came here as a young teenager in disguise after his father's death, for he wanted to learn about his heritage but must not be found out or he, too would have been assassinated.

This had been the cradle of Rome once upon a time and I can feel them all as if they have just left here…the Eternal City…

After hours of walking through the ruins, then resting beneath the shade of the arch, I walk to the Coliseum which had taken eight years to build around 80 A.D. Gladiators were trained to fight to death here against other men and wild beasts, and Christians were fed to the lions, for all to watch. Although I am in awe of its size, I feel sick in my stomach and have to leave. I never understood all of the fighting and the violence throughout the course of history…what for? Wealth…greed…power…what about love? I think…I would never understand any of it, and do not care to try, for I am a romantic and always will be.

Instead of pondering it too much, I leave and walk the hill to *Vittoriano*, the Victor Emmanuel II Monument which I had seen last night in the dark. It seems to spread out over city blocks and is so massive that I cannot capture it in one single photo. It will take many that I will have to place side-by-side to see an expanded view – to capture all of it.

The king sits upon a steed at the entrance to the monument with massive steps behind him leading up to the colonnade. There are colossal Winged Victories with carved wings standing at each end. The building is of bright, white marble and the structure is covered with bas-reliefs too numerous to count. In the center of all of this is the *Altar of the Fatherland,* and at its base lies the Tomb of the Unknown Soldier watched at all times by two guards. I walk up the long flight of stairs to the colonnade and through the halls viewing the frescoes on the ceiling.

This too is another overwhelmingly incredible wonder of Rome and I wonder just how many more there are to see. Has anyone ever counted them?

As the day comes to an end, I walk back to the hotel to bathe and rest before dinner and the midnight hour. I am anxious to see Natale, his intense eyes, his dimpled face and his smile. At 22:00, ten o'clock, I walk to the restaurant and the streets are filled with people coming and going to and from dinner. They eat so late in Italy and life does not stop at midnight, but instead comes alive continuing into the wee hours of the morning. The cafes are filled with patrons. There is music floating through the air intermingled with the scent of Roma's romance – food and *fiori*, the flowers – tomatoes, basil and garlic, night jasmine and geranium. I want to dine with Natale as he works, so I walk inside and ask to be seated on the rooftop. He is surprised but happy that I have come.

"I am so happy you come again. You no order...I bring you specialty of the house!" He leaves quickly, only to return in a moment with *vino* and sparkling water.

"Enjoy, Rossana." The place is full once again and Zuchero is singing as he did the night before. He nods and smiles remembering me. Is it possible to recreate a beautiful moment in time? I think so, for I feel the same as last evening. Natale walks toward him to whisper a request in his ear and Zuchero nods toward me.

"*Per amare! Per* Rossana..." I realize that Natale has requested a song for me and my heart flutters. Natale delivers my meal, a pasta dish with *frutti di mare* laid upon it; and as the music plays in the background, he winks at me. Another night of romance, I think...ahhhhh...I could stay here and live lost in Roma forever...if I hadn't fallen in love with Capri.

"*Dolce* - dessert, Rossana? I make special for you."

"No, no...I am full. I can't eat anymore."

"Okay. *Allora, aspete*...wait...sit and listen to the music." Soon, it is *mezzanotte*, midnight. The patrons have left the restaurant and I sit sipping Lemoncello while Natale finishes his shift.

CHAPTER 15

"I show you some place, Rossana." I am sitting on the back of his scooter, arms wrapped around his waist clasped in front, all the while, aware of the heat between us. He holds his hand over mine and moves his fingers back and forth across my skin caressing my fingers. We ride quickly through Rome and out to the edge of the city where we climb a hill that leads to a park overlooking the city. There, he pulls me gently to a belvedere where busts of great heroes from history sit upon Roman columns at its edge.

"It's incredible here!" Stretched out before me lies the city of Rome dressed in white lights that sparkle with the moonlight. He tells me the name of the park, but then he kisses me and I choose to remember the kiss instead of its name. I feel as if I am in a dream, standing high atop a mountain park overlooking where we have just come from, and am being kissed by my prince.

He moves his fingers over my face as if he is reading Braille; then he moves them down my neck feeling every inch of my skin there. It's as if he is making love to all of me in these moments. He slowly moves his hands down my back, feeling every line, every muscle, moving on to that place where it curves into my lower spine, then down to my bottom, outlining every inch with his fingers.

He rests both hands there, and pulls me closer. I can feel his loins and his upper thighs. His abdomen is touching mine, and his masculinity touching that place of pleasure in me. I hold my breath…and swoon. The blackness of passion in the night has enveloped me like a welcome mist, removing all thoughts. And he continues to kiss me so sweetly, so carefully as if I am a porcelain doll. It's a dance of sorts - he masterfully making me want him more. I take a deep breath while he is still kissing my open mouth, and I almost buckle from the expansion that I feel, for it is as if I have breathed all of him into me.

I begin to reach out to pull him closer, become more aggressive wanting him…he stops and steps back. What? I am stunned… and notice the feeling that has welled up inside me, that sexual tension that is screaming for release….and I don't know what to do with it now. But I don't say a word, just stand there waiting for what will come next. He takes my face in his hands again and touches his forehead to mine, all the while looking intensely into my eyes.

"*Mio amore*…kissing you is like kissing Venus herself. Where did you come from? You come all the way from America for me…" I still have not recovered from his kisses and caresses…my body tingling, charged with that electricity that short-circuits everything it comes in contact with it. I don't laugh or giggle this time, but only smile as I try and breathe. Again, he breaks the silence.

"Come, I take *foto!*" He positions me next to the bust of Caesar, with the lights of Rome in the background.

"Smile, *Bella*." We sit on a bench afterward, his arm draped over my shoulder, the other resting in my lap as he holds my hand.

"I come here often to see the night. *Molto bello*. Roma is very romantic place, you know."

"Yes, Natale…I know."

"Come!" He takes me to the bridge of Sant'Angelo that connects the castle to Vatican City again, the second time in two days. I am now officially in love with Rome and want to live here. We walk, talk, kiss and giggle for hours, he nuzzling into me speaking Italian all the while, which drives me insane. It is three a.m. when we reach the hotel and as he did the night before, he lifts me off the scooter and kisses me.

Only this time is different from the last, for this is the kiss that never ends. It is long - very long and I forget my name in that moment! I also forget his name as well and how to tie my shoes…as a matter of fact I forget everything about my life. The only thing I remember is how he feels and how he makes me feel.

Somehow, we make it to my room; although later when I try to picture those moments, I cannot recall them except that I was lost in the abyss of his kisses. Once in the room, he throws open the shutters so we can hear the sounds of Rome by night…the last human thing I remember.

He makes love as if he is sculpting a statue with his bare hands, his fingers the tools. I feel delicious. He is a skillful lover who keeps me in that etheric place where I touch God - nothing else exists but the two of us as we merge. And we remain there until the evening ends and the swallows come out to feast at dawn.

This is the first thing I notice in the morning - the sound of them singing as they circled the *piazza* below feeding on the insects and mosquitos in the air…a sound only heard in Rome. Natale is still kissing me as I lay with a sheet draped over my bare breasts and torso, my legs lying languidly outside the thin covers.

"You have the most beautiful legs, *bella*. Your breasts…I think I am in love with you." I laugh tiredly and roll over to kiss his cheek. He smiles as I touch his dimple.

"You make me smile, Natale. You are a sweet man…*uomo dolce*." At that, he rolls over and starts kissing me all over again…first my face, then my neck. I squirm with delight. "No!"

He speaks Italian as I try to get away from him; but he continues to pursue me, covering me with kisses, trying to get to my breasts, my mound of Venus. Oh how I love this cat and mouse game. I finally relent and for the fourth time this day and night, we make love. I am powerless with his passions, but I don't care. I care only about this…I feel young and vibrant, my passions have been unleashed and let loose to run wild and free. I want to feel like this forever and never know them to go to sleep again.

At some point - some hour after he takes me to heaven this last time, we come back to earth and fall asleep in each others arms. At noon, I awaken to him watching me. How long has he been here like this? I can see in his eyes that he feels I am beautiful.

"I thought last night was a dream and you were not real, but you are." He kisses the palm of my hand and fingers, the skin there as if he is testing its texture. "Rossana, what you do to me…I love this. I have not felt this way for many times."

"You mean for a long time?" I laugh.

"Sorry, my Inglais is no good sometimes."

"Natale, you can speak to me in Italian anytime."

"I am so hungry, *Bella*, I could eat all of you." He comes at me with his mouth as if he were trying to eat me.

"No!" I shriek playfully pushing him away. "I need to eat real food or I will pass out. I'm famished!"

"Me, too…food for our …how you say *forza*?" I try to understand what he means but don't have a clue until he sits up and flexes the muscle in his arm.

"You mean strength!" He pulls me close to him once again and kisses me gently before we both rise from the *il letto di passione* - the bed of passion, as he has called it.

We spend that day together and the one after that and the next one as well. On these days, Natale calls into work for time off so he can be with me and time is lost for us, for we don't care to keep track. Only the light of day and the coming of each night, reminds us that we have lost more time dancing inside love.

We sleep together, make love together, eat together and even sit quietly together. We watch the sun set over Rome, its glorious colors kissing the horizon, and we kiss each other as it goes down behind the city. He reads the newspaper to me in Italian and tells me stories while I linger in this quiet soft space with him.

We stay at his apartment in the center of the city and ride his scooter to see more sights. I have never smiled and laughed so much as I have now on my whirlwind adventure. He takes me to St. Peter in Chains and the Santa Maria Majorie Basilicas where I have a religious experience. The Mother comes to me as I sit for hours in bliss. Natale understands because he too is in love with Santa Maria as all Italian men are.

Saint Peter in Chains Basilica's belfry is the tallest in Rome, built in Romanesque style. It holds Fuga's *Great Canopy* and Sangallo's golden gilded ceiling filled with mosaics, all reproductions of scenes from the *Old Testament.* There is marble and gold everywhere on the high altar and in the chapels. At the altar, I fall in love with a bas-relief by Bernini called the *Assumption* held up by four columns. I think the basilica is as opulent, and as beautiful as the St. Peter's Cathedral is at the Vatican.

We visit Bernini's *Fountain of the Tritons* and then head to the oldest street in Rome, the *Appian Way* where tombs and catacombs of the patrician families of Rome lay. Then, we are off to the Baths of Caracalla, museums and galleries, including the famous *Borghese Villa and Gallery.* Housed here are masterpieces by Bernini, Caravaggio, Domenichino, Rubens, Raphael, Canova, Messina, and Leonardo da Vinci. I think that everyone who ever painted or sculpted might be here and I fall in love with the grounds and the art. To me, it is so romantic, and having Natale as my guide makes it even more so.

We see two bas-reliefs by Michelangelo: *Prometheus Bound* and *Leda and the Swan*, also Bernini's *Apollo and Daphne* and his *David.* Then there is Canova's *Statue of Paolina Borghese*, in the pose of Venus Vetrix resting lazily on a chaise, her head resting on one arm, the other on her hip and her long slender legs out before her. When we leave the museum and walk across the lawns to the lake, there sits a marble bench which Natale pulls me toward.

"My sweetheart, lay here like Venus, like Paolina. I take *foto.*" Those eyes...filled with admiration and love...I have never felt this before. How can I resist him? So I pose once again for another photo, and this time, I feel like a *regina*, a queen. When I am in his presence, this is how he treats me. Would it go on forever like this if I chose to stay here with him? Would it eventually stop when he had grown tired of me, the newness worn off like a dull coin...or when the romance faded, extinguished by the wind, an old relationship once the flame has gone out?

Over these next few days in Rome, Natale takes me to many places in Rome that only the locals know exist. I see ruins that aren't on any map and churches I have never heard of. They are decorated with ancient frescoes and paintings. I finally check out of the hotel and move into his apartment on the third floor, near the Trevi Fountain where we make love day and night and he cooks Italian meals, that we eat by candlelight. He says it is the only way to eat when you are in love.

I am being romanced and I am falling in love, for he is the most beautiful man I have ever known. I flutter each time he comes near me and my heart short circuits when he touches me, my soul whispering his name as I sleep. It is as if I am under a magical spell – a spell of love.

Every day before breakfast, Natale walks to the little bakery and brings back pastries and flowers for me. Oh, how I love those flowers and their sweetness. Every day, he kisses my hands, holds my face as if it is precious, looks deeply into my eyes and tells me how beautiful I am. He also tells me he loves me at least ten times a day.

CHAPTER 16

On the fourth day that I am in Rome, I awaken from a dream in which I am painting. I am standing in a Roman market in olden days, and I am painting the light of the fading day as it washes over the city. I can smell the oils - feel the brush in between my fingers. I am hurrying to complete it before darkness sets in and I cannot see the colors on my palette. I am looking at the architecture of the Forum before me and its likeness that I have just created upon my canvas, and I'm proud of it because it is near perfect. I know I'm good at what I do in my dream, for I can feel it.

I lay in bed, Natale still sleeping beside me. His face is that of an angel's, and I want to paint him. "I will start today," I whisper excitedly to myself. I've been nervous about painting up until now, feel that I might have forgotten how. To paint a portrait might be too much for my first in two years, but I want to try. "And if it's not so good?" I ask myself. "How can it not be with a face such as this as my model?" I can feel the need and the desire rise up inside me and I need to unleash its power. I have to empty it onto a canvas. I can lie here no longer and rise to take a bath so that I will be ready to shop for paint supplies as soon as Natale awakens. So I steal from the bed, quiet as a mouse.

I lie in the tub and close my eyes, reflecting on how my life has changed. I wonder for a moment how my friends and business associates are doing in America and whether or not they are fulfilled in their lives. I imagine some are, living their dreams of being mothers and wives and friends. Not everyone is like me. I have always had this desire to have more - live more - see more. I've always wanted to feel life and to move through it in ecstasy until insanity sets in. It was so long ago…was I in my twenties when I last lived like this?

I sink further down into the water, feeling its warmth now tickle my breasts and my shoulders. I look around at the tiled bathroom, the yellow walls and the white towels that are hanging on their hooks from the night before. The mirror is outlined in old Murano glass made to look like flowers…some of them have long since been broken. This is the only decorative thing in this room.

It's sparse but neat and clean. I like the way Natale lives, so impeccably, so cleanly and simply. Everything has its place - an orderly life which makes me feel safe when I am with him. And his cooking…who would have thought Italian men could cook so well? I love his pasta and the fish he fries for me, squeezing the lemon over it at the very last moment, a ritual he talks me through, telling me how important the timing is, everything prepared with love.

"*Mio amore*, why are you awake so soon? I miss you. When I wake up, I think you have gone." I'm startled out of my thoughts and jump, splashing water everywhere. He sits on the edge of the tub and I look at his well-defined chest and the hair that covers it. I love that chest and reach out to touch it.

"Now, you get me wet! I fix it!" Before I can blink, he steps into the bathtub and is now kneeling over me.

"E-e-hhh!" I shriek with surprise. It's a tight fit for two, but he manages to maneuver himself into position so that now he is on the bottom and I am lying across him. Of course he is more in the water than I am.

"I'm cold now, Natale."

"I warm you…mmmmmmm, *mio amore*." He playfully cups his hands, filling them with water to wet me, which somehow helps. His arms encircle me and he wraps his legs around mine. It never ceases to amaze me that with each touch, I become aroused. Most times it's sexual; but sometimes, it's simply that my senses are heightened.

"Natale, can you take me to buy paints today? I want to start painting."

"I did not know you painted. What do you paint, sweetheart?"

"I used to paint scenery and landscapes, and sometimes portraits; although it has been so long…years in fact." I think back to the last portrait I had done of the boys when they were eight and nine. It had hung in my living room all these years.

"I want to paint you, Natale." I turn my head, removing it from his shoulder. I take my finger and outline his cheekbones and the dimple that indents the moment he starts to smile. "I want to capture these dimples…" He grabs my face with both hands and envelops my mouth with his and I fall into him and let him take me.

"Rossana, I love you. Will you marry me?" I giggle nervously and squeeze his chest lovingly.

"Natale! I've only known you for what…five days?" I joke.

"*Sono nell'amore con lei,* I love you…" He looks at me like a lovesick puppy. I move from him, stand up and step out of the tub.

"Come, the water is cold now. I will make you breakfast. It's my turn today." For a moment, I think I glimpse pain in his eyes, but I want to divert the conversation to something else, for I'm not prepared to talk about our relationship - where we are in it, or where it's going. I'm nervous, because I care for him deeply and am fearful of it because of that fact. I don't know whether I belong here in Italy or in America…can't think about that now…

We dress and then make breakfast and Natale never brings up the subject of marriage again. He takes me to an art store near the Spanish Steps so I can purchase supplies. I choose two soft-haired sable brushes for detail work and one stiff one, a palette and knife, and oils in eight different colors. I also purchase poppy oil over linseed oil for the under-painting because it dries faster and doesn't yellow. This is important since I will be using lighter colors for the face. Then there is the stretched canvas, the thinner, primer and the alcohol that I will use to clean away layers of paint that I don't want. I am so lost in thought and the feeling of painting that I never think about how long I will stay in Rome. I only have the need to paint this beautiful face that I have fallen in love with.

We drive the scooter directly to the apartment - my only thoughts are how to hold on to my bags filled with supplies and the small canvas as we move through the busy streets. It is hot and damp with humidity, and the air hangs thick but I welcome it for it is the Rome of my dreams and I love it here. Would I love it if it were not for Natale, I wonder? Maybe it would be a little less romantic…still I would love it nonetheless–

The light in the airy apartment is bright, the windows facing the south west. Natale chooses to sit on his balcony and watch the people pass by as I sketch him. I have to practice, to make sure I can capture each detail of his face before I even touch the canvas. We sit for hours as I trace his nose, the curve of his lips, his eyelashes.

"*Ho bisogno di mangiare*, I need food to eat, Rossana. Can we rest now?" He takes my sketch pad and studies his image.

"This is me." He seems surprised. "Is my nose like that? I like to see it. It is nice." He grins and his dimples pop out. I suddenly have an idea.

"Natale, I want you to smile so I can paint you with those dimples."

"I cannot smile forever, sweetheart." I decide to snap pictures with my digital camera and then use them to sketch from. This is not my ideal way to paint, but I want more than anything to capture his smile – not just for the dimples, but for the look in his eyes as well. I want to always remember him with this face that shines with pure happiness.

"Wait…*aspete!*" I laugh proudly each time I am able to squeeze my favorite word into a conversation, for I love the way it sounds coming from my mouth. I leave briefly and come back with my camera snapping pictures as I go.

"You make me smile, Rossana; you are …comical." I giggle at the use of the word. He comes to me as I back away trying to get his face from every angle, and as I do, he chases me through the apartment as I continue to dodge him, moving carefully between each piece of furniture and through each doorway. I keep snapping pictures all the while. I end up in the bedroom and fall onto the bed laughing, my sides aching from it. He comes to me and pins my hands over my head and starts to growl like a dog.

I become excited and from my excitement, he becomes aroused. We move over each other touching every inch…I tear at his thin tee-shirt to get to his skin and the hair on his chest. Our love-making is heated and passionate - thoughts of food are now long forgotten.

"Do you think we will last forever like this, *mio amore?*" We are now laying together, his arms embracing me as he studies my face. I am captured and cannot escape so I have to face him.

"I don't know, Natale." I move my fingers over his face as I tell myself that it's time to be honest with him. I'm struggling to find the words and afraid he will be hurt… but I start anyway.

"Natale, I went to Capri in search of something. I was unhappy in my life. I didn't know what I was looking for or what I would find there, but I knew I had to go. I still have my boys in America…you know, we talked about them." He kisses my forehead.

"I know you miss them."

"Yes, I do, and I miss Capri. But I love Rome…and I think I have fallen in love with you." There I said it. It came out of my mouth and it is the truth. He kisses my lips gently and I can see the pleasure and relief in his eyes. I continue because it is quiet in the room.

"I'm so confused, Natale. I came to find myself…my passion… something that died in me long ago. I never expected this - you." I can feel his chest swell and his arms tighten around me. He pulls me into him and kisses my hair and in that moment, I want to stay forever here in his arms, protected by him, loved by him. I want this man to be my husband, I think with my heart.

We speak no more but instead, lay in the quiet of what has just been spoken. And I float in between that semi-conscious dream state where the sounds of the city from the open window blow in and blend with the thoughtlessness that is in my head. And it creates a dream…I dream that

I am walking the streets of Rome in my new life. Alone, with a flower filled basket in hand. I can feel the love that fills my heart so completely – that feeling I felt the first moment I awoke with Natale in my bed.

The telephone rings and Natale answers it, and when he turns back to face me, he tells me he has to go into work.

"They need me, sweetheart. You be okay while I work tonight?"

"Yes, I'll sketch." Although I'll miss him, it will be nice to have this break. It's been six days and six nights and I'm beginning to lose myself and my own thoughts. All I can feel is him…and who am I now? Am I changed forever by all of this or is it just a dream - an intoxication?

After he leaves, I transfer the photos to my laptop and pull them up to view and then I sit for hours sketching. I stop every hour or so to take a break and watch the colors of the city change. Everything I see from my vantage point, I want to paint. I feel as though I am now the painter I have always been…so filled with passion for the brush and the smell of the oils…I can think of nothing else. I feel like an old master having a love affair with the art…almost as if it were sexual…

I think of Natale, the man I am in love with and I'm not sure if it's the wine or the smell of the oils, or even fear…but I grow dizzy and have to lie down; and I fall into sleep – at least I think I do…

"Roxanna." I am standing at the Forum with the Great Spirit beside me. "You cannot linger here too long. You are not finished yet. You have so much more to do. You can come back here if you wish, but now is not your time." I feel my heart weep in my dreams…

"I think I love him…am I crazy?"

"No, sweet woman…you are intoxicated with life and love and all that it offers you." He laughs as he touches my shoulder lovingly.

"You have only touched the tip of all of this. Welcome to your new life!" I am stunned and speechless – cannot think of a word to say - for I have so many questions. His hand leaves my shoulder.

"Stay as long as you like, but soon, you must leave here to move on…" His voice disappears as my logical mind struggles to awaken. I want to debate him about why I should leave and what it would mean. Would my lover wait for me if I leave him for awhile? Would he understand? Does he love me enough? Do I love him enough that if I am gone for months or even a year, the memories of my heart will not fade and the pull will be just as strong as it is this day?

I suddenly feel sick and barely make it to the bathroom before I retch. All thoughts leave me then…except my feelings of confusion. I am too tired now to think anymore and my fear keeps me from doing so.

I toss and turn on the bed until I can stand it no longer and the pull of Natale's face leads me back to my sketch pad. If I can only perfect those smiling eyes, I will be able to transfer my sketch to the canvas and start…

"Sweetheart, you wait awake for me." Natale has come back and is kissing me. It's after 1:00 o'clock in the morning and I have been fully engrossed in my sketchbook.

"Was it a good night?"

"*Si*, but it is better now that I am here."

"You have to work while I'm here. How will you eat?" I try to make light of it, but my mood is dark.

"I don't need food when I am with you…" He tries to play with me, but senses something is wrong as I pull away from him.

"What is wrong, Rossana?" I don't want to talk about any of this…I need to think. Maybe soon, it will be time to leave him.

"Sorry…I'm just so tired…"

"Then we will go to sleep. Come." I can't…I am afraid he might want to make love again and I'd be lost inside him and this fairytale – held captive by my own heart.

"No, I want to sit here for awhile. You go. I'll come to bed soon."

"I sit with you and have a drink of Lemoncello." He moves to the freezer and pulls the bottle with two little glasses. The cool lemon taste soothes my throat.

"Is something wrong, Rossana?" His eyes are serious as if ready for a deep conversation and I am uncomfortable with the moment. I know I will have to speak up soon.

"Natale, I am so confused. My time here in Rome has been wonderful. It's been all that I have ever dreamed of with the man that I love. But I'm so afraid."

"What are you afraid of?" He asks, his eyes searching mine beseechingly. He is now holding my hands, kneeling down in front of me as I sit on the chair. He reaches for my face and gently brushes the hair away from it. Then he rubs my cheek from top to bottom with the side of his thumb as if he is feeling a smooth surface.

"I am afraid of the power of this and how I feel about you…it's all so cloudy. I don't know what is real and what isn't. I don't know how I feel. I'm confused. I feel pressured to make some kind of decision here. I just left my boys to go to Capri and I love it there. I don't know if the timing is right for me to be in love…this is all so confusing." My sobbing is coming from deep within and Natale is trying to console me.

"Here drink…drink all down now." He is handing me a full glass of the lemon drink. So I drink it. It stops me from crying, for I have to breathe as it slides down my throat into my belly. The heat of it on my insides soothes me...my Italian grandmother... He has pulled the other chair over and is sitting in front of me now as he reaches for my hands and holds them.

"*Mio amore*...you don't have to make any decisions about us now. I am sorry to pressure you. I know you were not looking for love when you came to Roma. I was here and you were sent to me by Santa Maria. She knew it was time for us to meet and you came all the way across the ocean to me. I know she sent you to me...*il forza di amore*." He is smiling weakly and I know he is trying to comfort me. He looks down and his eyes close as he kisses each of my hands – and I see his lashes touch his face. They are long and dark and I want to kiss them but I cannot move. He is so beautiful to look at...

But this is not why I have fallen in love with him. My soul calls to him and wants to feel his heart. It wants to feel his touch upon my skin, to connect with him and feel the heat and electricity between us when we come together. He is part of me and if I leave him now, some of me will be lost out in the world and I don't know if I will be able to recover. Would all the energy and the life force I have now leave my body?

"Sweetheart, you take the time you need. I will wait for you, my love. I have never found someone like you. You are the one for me."

"I love you," is all I can say. We reach for one another, and our embrace is of only our faces and arms because of the distance the chairs have created between us. We rise and move to the balcony and sit to watch the sky. No more words are spoken this night, for there is no need for them. Everything has been said.

We move through the next day as if we have left part of ourselves behind in the conversation the night before; but we are closer still, or so it seems if that makes sense. We understand each other. But underneath, I am churning inside, not knowing where I shall go or if I should leave at all. I have hit a speed bump and my world has been turned upside down in the eternal city.

CHAPTER 17

Over the next two days, I finish my sketch on the canvas and it is a perfect likeness of Natale. When I show it to him, he is excited.

"Rossana, this is *molto bello…magnifico*! I love my face! I have never seen it like this." He hugs me tightly. "*Mio artista*…I am proud of you."

But I cannot bring myself to start the paint, for I know if I do, I will have to stay in Rome until it is finished - and the longer I stay, the more confused I will become. A dark cloud has settled over me as I continue to churn inside.

This night, we are sitting on the patio. Natale has my hand in his and he is kissing it as he fingers the rim of his glass with the other.

"Rossana, please stay with me. I take care of you.   I don't want you ever leave."

I only have silence for him. His eyes darken as I see the look of pain on his face; I can feel the aching inside him as if we are one and the same. It's time to make a decision - it is no longer right for me to hold his future in my hands.

"Natale, I love you…but I can't stay here with you. I've got to finish what I started before I can make any decisions. I reach for his hands now that he has withdrawn into himself. "Please. I need some time. I have to leave tomorrow but I will see you again, I promise."   There, my lips have spoken before my mind and heart can falter.

He rises from the chair and walks inside.   I follow him as he paces the floor all the while running his hands through his hair. He doesn't speak, only paces and I try to reason with him.

"Natale, do you understand? I need to get clear on some things. I came here for a reason and I need to find myself – find what I want to do in my life – find out who I am.   Do you understand that? *Pensare…capisce?*"

He reaches for me and holds me tightly with his strong arms, and I can feel his chest heaving softly for he is crying. My heart breaks.

"I am so sorry, Natale. I love you." I think that if only I can hold him tighter his pain will disappear; so I try harder. But it doesn't.

"I have to go, but I promise I'll be back. I'll write you, email you, call you. I promise...I love you."

He does not speak, but the look in his eyes is one of a desperate man. He pulls me to him and holds my face for a long time looking intensely into my eyes before kissing me.

With Natale, each kiss is different – each has different meaning – especially this one. This one means it is the last kiss...the last time. It is the kiss of a desperate man who is about to die. It's longer than the one we shared that first night, and a more serious one.

I pull him slowly to the bedroom this time, and together we make sweet love to each other. He is slow and gentle, me feeling as if I am the aggressor. I don't want it to end. I caress him and touch him with my fingertips...every inch of him so that I will remember and never forget. I want these moments to be seared into my heart as if they were made with a branding iron, the scar always there to remind me of how deep this love is.

I keep my eyes open so that nothing escapes me, so that I will remember the expression on his face when he loses his mind with pleasure, shuddering into that abyss of passion. I hold him tightly as I enter through that precious gateway with him, digging my nails into his back, leaving my mark. If it is painful, maybe it will be felt more deeply...more intensely...and maybe it will mean more to both of us. He doesn't seem to mind.

We crawl inside each other in these moments, not wanting the other to escape or to be left behind. And then we fall asleep, wrapped up in each others bodies as if we are one. We are. There is no ending to me or beginning to him. He awakens with the breeze from the window blowing through the thin curtains, at that special time of day when the sun is spent after making love to the earth all day....just as we have done to each other. It isn't quite sunset, but an hour away. His gaze upon me is filled with both love and pain. I think he knows I might not come back to him.

"*Mio amore*," he whispers. "*Ho cadato a amore con questo donne*, I have fallen in love with this woman." He lingers over the bed as he reaches for my cheek and caresses it.

"I know you are different than other women. You go. Do what you need. Please, come back to me..." He kisses me good bye and leaves the apartment for work. He never asks if I will be here when he returns, and for that I am relieved, for I cannot promise I will be.

I lie here with a twisted heart, and weep for hours. Crazy thoughts whirl through my mind like a hurricane. I have found such passion with Natale and in Rome, to depths and breadths and heights that I never knew existed. So why must I leave? The other me - the voice of reason that I hate to listen to says, "Roxanna, you need to go now. Move forward. Go back to Capri and finish what you set out to do. Once you know what you are looking for and have put all the pieces together, than you can come back to him."

I lie here on the bed – the sheets half covering my naked body, the breeze blowing softy across my skin…and cry some more.

I leave a note for him, my love, with my scent of geranium and patchouli on the paper, for I don't want him to forget me. On it, I write:

My sweet love,

Please understand why I had to go. I will see you again…soon.
Time will move swiftly like the blink of an eye.
You forever have my heart.

Baci grandi e l'amore,

Roxanna

CHAPTER 18

ASISSI

I am at the station a short time after midnight awaiting a train out of Rome. I know Natale has found the letter on his pillow, for I feel him. I envision him reading it as he sits on the bed, his head in his hands, and I see him weep into the paper. My soul hears him cry out, "Rossana…" but it is lost in the sound of the whistle calling me to board.

I have decided to go to Assisi to the home of San Francesco to grieve and to heal. He was my saint when I was a child. I loved him for loving the animals. As I grew older, I felt him everywhere around me. Yes, Assisi is the perfect place to go to with my broken heart.

I find my seat and am alone in the car. I sit and weep yet again until my face and eyelids are swollen and pink. Why does love have to hurt so? I stop crying and then start again, gasping for air in between. The shooting pains to my heart are as real as if I were being stabbed with a knife. Have I done the right thing by leaving? What have I done…allowing myself to fall in love…allowing myself to break his heart? Yes, I am guilty of causing him much pain…and my own pain…God help me…

I am angry at the part of me that told me to leave him this night…I want to pound on her chest and tell her I hate her. I want to go back to Rome, to be in his arms, him holding me closely and making me feel safe and secure. I miss his lips, his face, the way he touches me. I miss all of him and the life we shared for the days that have stretched into forever, both of us losing track of time.

What of the calling of Capri? Has it faded from my memory? Has it seeped so deeply into the back of my mind that it is now covered over by the recent memories with my lover, hidden away from my reasoning? I can no longer feel its pull.

I feel insane in these moments on the train when I think of him; and he is always with me so I cannot help but think of him. He is like a drug to me, so soothing and sweet…an elixir that makes life so much easier…so romantic, so passionate.

"Am I wrong to want this all the time…to be in love with life…the laughter every day, every waking moment? Why can't I have it?" When in Rome, I felt like I was living a life of passion. Isn't that what this is all about? Wasn't that my quest…my holy grail?

I fall asleep around the town of Terni from sheer exhaustion, and dream of the Great Spirit. We are standing on the cliffs of Monte Solaro in AnaCapri and once again, his hand is resting on my shoulder.

"Roxanna, why be so hard on yourself? He has called you forth just as you have called for him. You are not responsible for broken hearts or this sadness you think you have created. This is a beautiful thing and both of you agreed to come together and let your souls drive as you both enjoyed the ride. Forgive yourself. The love will not die and will always be there. Hearts don't break – only egos do. You will never forget this great love you shared and why don't you sit back and see where you are guided to next? Remember – let your soul do the driving."

Before I can open my mouth to ask a question, he is gone. Then, from this reality, I hear the next stop…"Foligno"…the stop for Assisi. I need to change trains.

It is 6:30 a.m. when I arrive in Assisi and the countryside is still sleeping. Only the birds have risen with the sun and they are starting to sing to the day. I hear them from the most distant point and then like a blanket across the hills and valleys as they chirp to each other and to anyone that will listen. It is an orchestra of sound and it soothes me.

By now, I am numb, feeling no pain…nothing at all. I am spent and I barely have the energy to find a taxi but know I must. I pray the taxi driver can help find a room for me with little effort. Sleep. I need sleep.

"Tassi." As soon as I raise my arm he pulls to the curb.

"Buonjourno, signora."

"Buonjourno. I have no reservation, but need a place to stay. Do you know of somewhere?" He is a very big man with a gentle face.

"Si. I take you to San Francesco." We hardly speak. He does not ask me where I have come from and I am happy with that. I don't want to talk for each word brings pain. We soon arrive at a pensionne next to the Basilica de San Francesco and luck is on my side as they have a room available and allow me to check in at this ungodly hour. I am thankful to San Francesco...

My heart weeps again before I fall into a restless sleep filled with Natale, he begging me to come back to him. When I finally awaken, it is mid-afternoon. I bathe, not wanting to leave the tub and its water, but need to eat.

There is a small café attached to the pensionne that overlooks the rooftops and out into the Umbrian valley. It is lush and green and wispy clouds are moving lazily across the sky leaving their shadowy imprint upon the land as they go. It's so peaceful here – the perfect place to heal.

The memories are starting to fade and I can no longer feel the daggers in my heart. Now, it only feels like a wound that is starting to scar over. If I move or think about it too much, I can feel its pull. But if I sit with no thoughts, it is numb.

Food is necessary for my body, although I cannot eat. I have soup and a piece of bread, leaving most of it behind. But what I do eat soothes my stomach and nurtures me. As I think of Natale and the last meal he cooked for me, my eyes start to well up again and I have to blink the tears away.

"San Francesco, I ask for the strength to get through this and to take my pain away." I say this quick prayer, and then walk the hill to his church. It is more than a church – a giant basilica, the largest I have ever seen and it is built into the hillside, an upper church and then a lower one beneath it. I had read that after his death, his followers had continued to build it, as if it would bring him back to life. I sit quietly in a pew – the only one here. Is it the time of day I wonder? Where are all of the touristas? It's as if this silence and aloneness is a gift to me…solitude. So I sit alone with him and close my eyes.

Saint Francis had spoken to me in the past - you know the way spirits do sometimes. His voice would come to me when I was confused or troubled. It started when I was four years old…when I could hear all the ones from the other side. I communicated with them as if they were right beside me in the physical, and maybe they were, only a thin veil called time separating us. But I knew I could not share this with anyone, for they would think I was a child, lying about something they did not understand.

I felt that I had lived and walked with him during his life. And that would surely explain my attachment and love for Italy – and my love for him. I try to piece together how it must have been if it were true…I knew he was born in a stable somewhere in the early 1100s, just as Jesus had been. And throughout his life, he had been so in love with God that he denounced all earthly possessions to imitate Christ and travel with only his message that all men were brothers, no matter what walk of life they came from.

The incense has thickened the air as it always does inside a church. There is nothing inside my head – not a thought, problem or idea. My pain has melted away and in its place is gratefulness for the gift of Natale.

It's as if I have left the human level and moved to a higher place, outside and above my pain; and from this place, I can see the great gift I have been given. Rome was no mistake. It was meant to be. I smile to myself as I think how funny life is, to travel to the other side of the world and walk into a restaurant to eat a meal and meet the man of your dreams…the man you might spend the rest of your life with.

Or would I? No worries. Whether I do or not, at least from this sacred place that I have come to, either decision would be the perfect one. I do not have to figure it out or worry about it, but just let it be for now. If he waits and I choose to go to him, then that's okay, too. If he does not wait and I change my mind and realize it is just a silly whim, then so be it, too. I am mystified as I sit here. Nothing matters for I am feeling no pain.

All that is in my heart and my mind is the deepest love and compassion I have ever felt, and it is more powerful than the love I have shared with Natale, or with any other human being. It is a knowingness, a wisdom that is felt instead of read and it is understood – that all is right in the world. All is perfect.

Just then, I feel him come and sit down beside me, and we talk as old friends do.

"Shall I call you Roxanna now, woman of many names?" It is he, Francesco. I laugh. It is good that no one is in the church with me as I sit alone, laughing out loud.

"Yes, Roxanna, the name I shall take to my grave this time."

"Then Roxanna it is. It has been a long time since we have spoken like this. Were you twelve then?" I remember. I had started to question it and told my best friend at the time. She laughed at me and called me crazy, then told others. The children were cruel - the ridicule, too great for a twelve-year old. So I denied it and lost the ability to talk with spirit.

"Yes, I was twelve." I lower my head and am filled with sadness with the memory.

"It is all right. It happens to all of us. But you are here with me now. Are you not?" I nod. "Then we shall sit together." So we do. After awhile, he speaks again.

"Roxanna, enjoy your life. There is so much living to do. Go and fly free like the birds that I love so much. Bathe in the sea of time and drench yourself in all of it, for it will be over in a flash! Love, live, laugh…be happy. Give...give of yourself. Teach love and compassion by being you…teach others to have it all by being you. You be the example and the gift to you will be your fulfilled life! You have not lost anything, for it will come back to you. Do you understand?" I am weeping for my heart is full.

"Or as they say in this part of the world, *capisce*?" I laugh now, even though a tear has slid down my cheek, giving me away.

"Si, *capisco*."

"Good then. You know you are so loved. Life is perfect for you in every way. You have so much love in your heart and so much to give, that it would be wrong to not share it. You are on the right path. I remember you and I hold you so deeply in my heart. Go with my love." I know he will leave me soon and I don't want him to.

"I want to walk where we walked together, sweet friend." I say beseechingly.

"Ah, so you do. Go to the Piazza Umberto – there we were together and spent much time. It is a beautiful island you know…you have many ties there."

"Yes, in Capri."

"Go and sit in the piazza and our memories will come back to you." His voice starts to fade away into the echoes of the basilica and all I can hear are the voices of the pilgrims that are filing into the structure. I sit, bathed in his love, my heart open, my soul singing. I am happy again, healed I guess you could say.

Eventually, I take my leave, and as I exit, I notice the door to the other level, so I enter and am now inside the room that holds his tomb. I walk past piles of sacred candles that are there for a small donation and pick up two. I move forward toward a large room and there lies his body surrounded by fields of flowers. I have no tears, only a smile for he is still alive to me…I have just spoken with him. All I feel in these moments is the energy emanating from the center of the room – from his casket.

A woman prostrates herself across it as she weeps uncontrollably. I feel her grief and want to tell her he is standing behind her with his hand on her back, but I don't. Instead, I move back through the door and out into the Umbrian sunlight.

I have been changed once again by yet another new experience. How many changes have I gone through since coming to this land? How many adventures have I had? Too many to count…and I realize the longer I linger here in the middle of this new life of mine, the more unrecognizable I become.

Life is never as it seems. Once you think you've climbed to the top of the mountain, reach the peak and looked out over the horizon, there lies before you, a thousand more peaks – all to be climbed by you. The art of climbing those mountains is in the mastering of each step – mastering the journey.

I had journeyed well with Natale and now, in place of the tears and the pain in my heart, lay a deeper feeling of love and understanding. I sit on the hill at the back of the church and close my eyes. The heat of the sun feels hot upon my face and I remember the word sun-kissed. That is what it feels like…as if I have been kissed by the sun. Or have I been kissed by something more divine? I smile up into it.

A healing of the heart and a soothing of the soul…that is what I have gotten here – such a gift. And as I sit here in the sun in Assisi in the Umbrian countryside, I make a promise to myself. I promise that I will journey on until I know I am finished, and then return to Natale - whether it be forever or just to walk with him again one last time. That promise will hold me together throughout my journey, for I know there will be a treasure at the end.

Tonight, I dine next to the basilica because I want to stay as close to it as I can. After all, my only reason for coming here was to be with Francesco…and of course, the restaurant's name is San Francesco, as well. Instead of a meal, I order hors d'ourves of shrimp in lemon with a light sauce of mayonnaise, parsley, pepper, celery, lemon bits and other spices, the local bread, and a salad of fennel, greens, and tomatoes with little tiny slivers of lemon and lemon peel throughout. I also enjoy a glass of the local Umbrian wine which is delicious. And as I sit overlooking the massive but simplistic church, I know life is as it should be. I am happy again, and have found my center.

After dinner, I walk through the ancient town which is enclosed by a ring of old walls that protected the city during the Middle Ages. I learn that Saint Clare, a great follower and love of San Franceso also has a church erected at the opposite end of Assisi, but I will not have time to visit as I have decided to leave first thing in the morning.

It is time for me to move on to Venice. My soul is calling to take me there and I will follow. I have learned to let it drive me, hopeful that if I follow it, my pain will never return, leaving happiness in its place instead. I have received what I have come to Assisi for and it is now time to depart. After Venice, I will go back to Capri for a while and maybe then, I will remember why I fell in love with the place, and maybe then, I will find clarity for my feelings and my future with or without Natale.

My room is sparse and simple but comforting as I return to it late this night. In it is only a bed with simple Italian linens, a closet, a writing table and a chair. There is no television or telephone or anything else for that matter. The building is so old and medieval, that the windows are round portals in both the bath and the bedroom, adorned with simple white linen curtain panels. Both rooms are completely tiled – walls and floor. I love this about Italy - perfect and beautiful, but simplistic.

I sit at the little table in a contemplative mood, reflecting on my life these last few weeks and realize that my journey has finally led me to passion and romance. It is not the passion and romance you feel when you have a lover, but the kind you feel when you take your own soul as your lover.

As I sit, once again, I feel it rising up inside me, singing, dancing to the music called life as I contemplate the next place I will be led to. My soul had decided, "We are going to Assisi," when I had originally thought it was my idea. I know now, that I needed to experience this healing, so my soul led me there.

My sleep is peaceful, a soft breeze wafting through the tiny open portal of a window all night. At dawn, I am awakened by thousands of tiny voices, little birds chirping, singing me awake all across Umbria. I run to the window and look out and there in the distance, I see a lush, green countryside, trees hither and yon, and the sunrise in the sky dripping shades of gold and salmon everywhere. And cast over it all is a sheer veil of mist adding to the glorious vista before me. I am enraptured. What a magnificent way to be called awake…I know this is a gift from San Francesco.

CHAPTER 19

VENEZIA

The Eurail ride from Assisi to Venezia is quiet and uneventful. I arrive at the Santa Lucia Station at 15:00, three o'clock, and take a water taxi into Venice. I am delighted with the view as I am shuttled down the Grande Canal, the buildings along the waterfront indescribable. The taxi driver directs me to a *pensionne* that is through a small alleyway off the canal and very close to the Rialto Bridge.

My room is three floors up with a single bed and a very small bath, but the centerpiece of the room is a large and opulent mirror boarded with Murano glass flowers and stems in a pale fluorescent pink. Some would think it gaudy, but I love it because I know it is hand blown Italian glass from a little island near here, and it reminds me of the one in Natale's bathroom.

I immediately clean up and leave the hotel for an adventure. I try to acclimate to the layout of the city by walking along the Grande Canal. I venture out into the inner city only slightly for I have a penchant for getting turned around and lost. I can get lost anywhere and it's a running joke between me and my sons. My hotel is two alleyways from the famous Rialto Bridge, so that will be my marker - the bridge that reminds me of one of my favorite movies, "Dangerous Beauty" about a 15th century Venetian courtesan who leads a very romantic life.

Venezia - Queen of the Adriatic - I remember this from college. I had read that the architectural styles here are a mix of Byzantine, Romanesque, Gothic and Renaissance, making each building so different and very interesting. I can't wait to explore; my passion for architecture is almost as great as my passion for art and sculpture. I look at my map book and see that the Grande Canal is shaped like an "S" running through the city. As I look around, I begin to notice brightly colored buildings and stone palaces flanking the canal, each from a different period in time.

Musicians, writers, poets and lovers come to Venice and never want to leave because they are so inspired here. I can feel it already, for I feel the inspiration starting to bubble up inside me. It is a city for lovers and I wish that Natale was here with me. I am remembering his kiss and how it felt, the feel of his hand in mine, his strong chest against mine.

I roam aimlessly, and come to San Marco's Piazza. My head is lowered, for I have been overtaken once again by emotion. I am lost in thoughts of him…missing him…tears blinding my vision. I only look at the stone beneath my feet as I move them one in front of the other, mindlessly – not wanting to lose the feeling of him touching me. I don't want anything to interfere with this love – not even Venice.

I must be a fool for leaving him. Am I crazy? And this spirit that keeps coming to me…what does he know of love? Why should I listen to him? I only want Natale here beside me…maybe I should call him and have him come to me…

Thoughts of making love with him and exploring this romantic city together fill my head. I remember how he made me laugh…I stand here brooding and have not even looked up to see where I am.

I hear singing and the voice pulls me from my misery. I look up to find its source and see a beautiful woman in a long black gown holding a champagne glass in her hand. She has blonde hair - big hair, and her dress is strapless, only her large breasts are holding it up. She is dancing in circles, twirling, singing in Italian with her glass upward as if she were toasting the heavens.

She reminds me of Anita Ekberg in Fellini's "La Dolce Vita" – only there is no fountain. Instead, she is barefoot in the middle of the *piazza* with a thousand pigeons scurrying about her feet. She seems out of place and I look around to see if they are filming a movie, she the star. But she is alone. I am mesmerized by her song and her beautiful voice. Although she is blonde, I know she is Italian for she has all of the features and I would guess her to be about sixty years of age.

She stops to sip her champagne and then starts up again. I have forgotten about Natale and my dismal mood and am fully in the present moment trying to figure out why she is here. Is she drunk on champagne or life? People are standing around her in a circle and some are singing with her. When she finishes the song, she takes another sip from her glass but realizes it is empty. So she stops and moves out of the circle as the crowd claps.

"*Bravo! Bravo! Bellissima!*" Shouts from the crowd…and a few men even whistle. As she walks away, I move to a table at a small café and sit.

"*Signora?*" A waiter asks me for my order. I am thinking and decide to order *aqua minerale* with lemon.

"*Si, grazie signora.*" I look for the woman in the evening gown but cannot find her in the crowd that has now filled up the square. Just then, the waiter comes back and sets a glass of champagne in front of me.

"No, please. I ordered mineral water." I lift the glass to him so he can remove it, but instead, he bows.

"No *signora.* You need champagne like her. She is happy. You are sad. *Male*...not good...please. It is on me." I smile at him for his thoughtfulness and concern.

"*Molto grazie.*" I lift my glass and toast to him as he smiles and walks away. I must look pathetic, I think to myself. So I sit and look out over the *piazza* and the happiness it is filled with. People are laughing and smiling and everyone seems to be feeding the birds. Because of all of the food, the pigeons are landing everywhere – even on the heads, shoulders and arms of those holding the food. Little ones are giggling and I find myself caught up in the magic of it all.

I have only taken three sips of the golden Prosecco which the Italians call their own champagne but already I feel its affect...or is it the magic of this place? Saint Mark's Basilica - the Cathedral of Venice stands before me in all its glory and it is the most opulent, grandiose, beautiful building I have seen thus far. It is so big and there is so much to take in that it will not fit in one photo...even from this distance across the *piazza*.

So much detail...I know it was built a thousand years ago...so old...and every architectural style is represented in its façade - Byzantine, Gothic, Islamic, and Renaissance, with Moorish and Oriental flares and Greek crosses on its roof.

"*Scuzi, signora*, may I sit with you?" My thoughts are interrupted by the woman in the dress. Close up, she is beautiful, porcelain skinned with a beautiful Italian nose and her eyes - the color of the Grand Canal, an emerald green.

"Yes, please." I am taken aback, not sure why she has chosen me to sit with but it's as if she has read my thoughts.

"I see you alone drinking champagne and know you are like me. You know how to enjoy life. *Tostato*...a toast...*alla vita!*"

"*Alla vita* – to life!" We take a sip. Her English is as good as her Italian. "You sing well."

"*Grazie*. I used to sing for a living here in Venezia, my home..." I see a dreamy look in her eyes. "Yes, those were the days...My name is Elana...yours?" I realize how beautiful she is as she smiles at me. Her dress is expensive and tailored as if it were made for her, her breasts holding it perfectly in place. Men must adore her, I think.

"My name is Roxanna, nice to meet you, Elana."

"Roxanna," she says perfectly. "What brings you here and are you alone?"

"Yes, I am alone. I was in Rome and decided to stop and see the Venice that everyone speaks about."

"Then you must be a writer, a painter, a musician or a lover; for these are the only ones that Venezia calls to, to come to her shores." She laughs and sips her champagne.

"I paint…or I used to. I am just getting started again."

"Ah, Italia…everyone paints here and if you're not from here, then when you leave here you know how to paint." She is intoxicated, happy. "Are you in love, Roxanna?" I am startled by the question.

"Yes, I am." I think of Natale guiltily because I had forgotten him for a moment…

"Then why is he not here with you?" She asks innocently.

"It's a long painful story, Elana…one not to speak of on such a beautiful day." I try to change the subject.

"Ah, *amore*…such ecstasy…such pain…someone once said that the greatest journey is the distance between two lovers…" I wait for more, but she says nothing else. So I think about this in the silence that she soon breaks.

"I am in love as well. He is a beautiful man who loves me like I have never been loved before…" She has that dreamy look in her eyes again and she starts to stand and dance in a circle with her eyes closed, all the while humming to her own memories. "La-lala-la de-dah…hmm..hmm-hmm…."

She is lost in thoughts of him and I can feel what she feels. I am consciously aware that everyone might be looking at us but then I realize that they are anyway. So what? Her long blonde hair is beautifully styled and her voluptuousness is swaying in all its glory. She has bright red lipstick on her lips and her emerald eyes are sparking.

I am mesmerized watching her as the waiter comes to the table with two more glasses of Prosecco.

"On the house, *signoras*." He smiles as if he is enjoying this. They must know her. She grabs her glass and toasts to him.

"Salute! Per amare!"

"To love!" I find myself getting caught up in her passion. She starts to sing a beautiful love song again and with champagne glass in hand, she is once again making her way out into the middle of the *piazza*, tourists surrounding her as she sings. I am smiling, supporting her efforts. She is beautiful and talented and they love her, and at the end of her song, I find myself clapping.

"*Bravo…bravo! Belissima*!" She comes back to my table.

"Now this is living life to its fullest. Roxanna, do not let anyone tell you how to live your life. Just follow your heart. Remember this…for it could be gone in an instant!" She snaps her fingers together creating a clicking sound and I see the look in her eyes…

A man is playing a mandolin now in the *piazza* and everyone has turned to him. We are alone at the table and the waiter has brought bread, olives, meats and cheeses. I think he is lusting after Elana…We sit enjoying the food and conversation, getting to know one another. I find her interesting as she tells romantic tales of her life. However, she is careful not to reveal too much, making it somewhat mysterious.

No matter what she is talking about – even if she is describing a tourist in the *piazza*, she describes them in a romantic light. "Look at the way he is gazing at his lover, oh, he is so loving…*bello*…" Or "Look at this one. She is *bella*, so beautiful…look at the men. They are tripping all over themselves." She laughs. The woman she is describing is actually quite plain, but she has this air about her and Elana sees it and knows it as if it were her own.

It's as if she has this filter that she sees everything through and that filter is a sheer veil of soft, sweet sexiness. It is undulating and luscious…intoxicating…and if you are enveloped in it, it stops your breath and blurs your vision so you cannot see for a moment – only feel. Then ah! It's over and you feel as if you've been hit by a MACK truck.

I want to see through her eyes, live like her – free spirited, exuding sensuality. So I continue to sit with her, and drink Prosecco after Prosecco until I am woozy and need to go to bed.

"Roxanna, it was a pleasure spending time with you. Remember, life is like a tiny soap bubble floating in the air before you. You have to reach for it in order to feel its magic and only then will you have found happiness." She laughs, saying "I have no idea what I just said! Ha! Ha! Ha!" We are both walking precariously as we leave the table, arm in arm and we make our way toward the Grand Canal. I hope I can find my hotel.

"Elana, please point me in the direction of the Rialto Bridge. I think I have had too much to drink!" We giggle loudly, bumping into each other and I almost step on her bare toes. "Oops! So sorry!" I giggle again.

"It's nothing…come, I will take you to the bridge." We arrive and I am still feeling tipsy but find my bearings.

"*Ciao,* and *grazie*, Elana."

The pleasure is all mine, Roxanna. This town thinks I am a loon, but what they don't know is that I am just enjoying my life more than they are their own. It could be gone so fast, you know…" she has that look again.

"Can we meet again before I leave Venice?" I want to spend more time with her - see life through her eyes once more…

"You can find me all over Venezia. We will see each other soon. *Ciao, bella.*" She laughs loudly and twirls past the bridge down the Grand Canal in her black dress, shoeless, singing as she goes. The street light shines down on her golden hair and her breasts as she twirls. And me – I find my hotel and fall into bed, feeling rosy from delicious Italian Prosecco…

I think of Elana the next morning with hopes of running into her. I walk the streets trying to get lost on purpose just to see where I will end up. From my guidebook, I learn that there are 70,000 people living here and 120 churches…for 70,000 people! Then I read how the wealthy commissioned talented artists and sculptors to do work for them in their own personal chapels which would later become the churches of Venice…120 of them…all on this small landmass. How many can I see while I'm here?

So I roam the streets in search of them, walking for hours, entering each one I come upon. As I come through one of the alleyways, I find myself in the Piazza de San Marco the same as the day before. But this time, there is no beautiful Elana amidst thousands of pigeons…only thousands of *touristas*.

Now, my complete focus is on the architecture of the *basilica* and its majesty. Every inch of its façade is covered with detailed design work, gigantic arches, statues, and colorful mosaics or Romanesque bas-reliefs. The upper portion of the structure is an elaborate Italian Gothic sculptural composition that is indescribable and above the portal is a 12th century angel, the one who had appeared to Mark. As I walk into the glowing atrium, I realize the walls are marble and the mantle gold mosaic. There are domes and portals throughout the *basilica,* too many to describe; and the one that stands out is a three-part dome named the *Genesis Dome* with scenes of the *Creation of the World.*

The marble mosaics on the floors and walls and the frescoes throughout the building are detailed, intricate and beautiful. There are five chapels: The Chapel of the Mascoli, of Isidore, of Madonna Nicopela, of Saint Peter, and Saint Clement, each one designed beautifully and filled with extraordinary works of art. The main altar is mounted by a tribune resting on four columns of oriental alabaster and covered with reliefs depicting scenes from the lives of Christ and Mary.

There are bronze sculptures of the evangelists and of the fathers of the church, including the famous *Pala d'Oro*, by the Venetian master, Giampaolo Boninsegna. It is ten feet long by five feet tall, embellished with gold and enamels, brought to Venice after the Crusades, and then set with gemstones. It contains eighty enamel plaques illustrating scenes from the lives of Christ, the Virgin, Saint Mark, and other figures such as angels, prophets, Oriental emperors, and evangelists. I had seen it in books but wasn't prepared for it in person...this jewel of Venice...breathtaking...

I don't know where to sit because the church is so large; so I choose the Chapel of the Madonna Nicopeia, the Virgin Victorious since the Venetians consider Mary their city's protectress. A hush comes over me. I close my eyes and say a prayer of gratitude; then all of my thoughts leave. I have been sitting for quite some time in this quiet chapel which seems to be off the beaten path, for all the tourists milling through the building don't seem to notice it. Suddenly I hear weeping.

I don't open my eyes but sit as the weeping continues. The woman is distraught it seems, crying openly now. So I turn and see Elana not too far behind me, her head in her hands, a black lace veil pulled over her soft blonde hair - a far different woman than I had seen the night before.

I wonder why she is crying, what could have happened. So I sit waiting for her to stop, hoping her anguish will subside; but it doesn't. I leave my pew and move to hers, sitting beside her. She has a hankie in her hand and is wiping her tears. I take her other hand in mine and squeeze it to let her know I am here, but her reaction to me is that she starts to cry louder. So I sit with her for as long as she needs comfort...an hour or so, and I, too feel her pain, her sorrow, and her grief.

The incense is thick like a mist in the chapel and I hear singing somewhere... beautiful angelic male voices. It is somehow soothing and I can see why she doesn't want to leave. It's like being wrapped up in the arms of the Divine – comforted by the angels and God himself.

I think of Natale and how much I miss him. I think of his pain and hope he is not feeling it as deeply as I am. Was it a dream? Was it real? Maybe I made the whole thing up...maybe he's not thinking of me as I am of him, the pain in my breast too hard to bear. Nonsense, I try and tell myself. It was real – very real.

Elana releases her hand from mine and moves out of the pew. She waits for me to catch up and we walk through the main part of the *basilica* where the ceilings seem to be one hundred feet high. There are priests chanting and the pews are filled with people, the lighting softened gold and surreal. When we reach the street, Elana removes her veil and wipes her eyes one last time before putting her sunglasses on which are large and in vogue, making her look as if she is a movie star.

"Come, Roxanna. I have a special place to take you." We move through the city down alleyways, weaving in and out, past hundreds of shops selling mostly gold and jewelry, baubles from Venice, and masks that the Venetians are known for. There are kiosks everywhere in the streets selling food, scarves, sandals, wares…it is a shopping mecca, but we don't stop here. We walk down the *Riva Degli Schiavoni* from the *Ponte della Paglia* along the *Canale di San Marco*, to the *Giardini di Castello* - the Castle Gardens. There along the promenade, Elana takes me to a little café.

"Giovanni, *ciao; como va?*" She is smiling, her old self back as a short man kisses her cheeks and embraces her.

"*Bene, bene…mio bella* Elana." He is clearly happy to see her. He takes us to an outside table and snaps his fingers ordering two young waiters to jump to attention and bring bread, olives, cheeses and Prosecco to the table.

"This is my home – where I come when I need to feel loved." She raises her glass to me. "*Salute,*" then sips the golden liquid. After a few minutes of silence, the Elana I first met is back, no longer any signs of her sadness and grief from the church.

"Roxanna, tell me about your love. Now we have nothing but time to talk." She smiles and clinks her glass against mine. I am hesitant, not sure I want to open this door, but then I realize I would like to talk with someone about my confused heart.

"His name is Natale and I met him in Rome last week. We spent a whirlwind week together and I fell in love with him. I know he's in love with me. He asked me to marry him, but I left him there – didn't even say good bye. I knew if I did he would have talked me out of going, so I left when he was at work."

"Elana, I'm so confused, not sure if it was the right thing to do. I think I'm insane and my whole life is a lie. What the hell am I doing here? Two months ago, I was living and working in America and my two boys were with me. I worked all day and watched television at night. Now, I think I'm this worldly person who is romancing life and I don't know a damned thing!" My heart is beating wildly but I get it all out.

"Oh, sweetheart, it's okay. You are confused. That's all. Let me tell you a story." The waiter refills our glasses.

"There once was a young woman…quite beautiful actually…tall, voluptuous, beautiful hair. She actually had to chase men away - they trailed her like they were the hunters and she the prize!" She throws her head back and laughs that beautiful laugh as if she is remembering.

"She had big dreams, wanted to sing her way to stardom. She was actually quite talented, you know. So she went to London in hopes of finding fame. Yes, she sang in clubs and made a good living. But she was never happy enough with what she had or where she was…always wanted more." She takes another sip.

"There was a beautiful bartender – from France, Jean Pierre. He had come to London to work there and he was in love with her. They dated and then she moved in with him, lived with him for years. No one ever loved her like he did." She has that dreamy look in her eyes that I had seen in the *piazza* the day before.

"He had brown eyes you could get lost in and make you forget your name - a square jaw, beautiful hair…and his chest…mmmm…God he was gorgeous…and he loved to make love. Those Frenchmen…" She stops to catch her breath and then picks an olive off the plate, playing with it before putting it in her mouth. Then she plays with it with her teeth and her tongue before chewing and swallowing it. It's as if she is making love to it, as she remembers how he made love to her.

"He was a beautiful man – but she left him for someone who promised her a record deal, someone from London - William." She drinks her whole glass in one gulp. "William, a lover of women with his flashy car and expensive suits…he bedded more beauties that long year - every woman he crossed paths with, and she was left night after night – alone to contemplate her mistake and her broken heart. Once she realized she had left the only man she had ever loved, it was too late. More champagne," she calls to the waiter.

"Stupid girl…by the time she realized what she had done and gone looking for Jean Pierre, he was back in France married to a beautiful French woman. That was thirty years ago, Roxanna." She grabs my arm and squeezes it hard to get my full attention.

"If you love this man, then go to him before it's too late. Or you will end up a lonely old woman with nothing but romantic notions – like me." Now I see the real Elana as she looks at me with her sunglasses off, her eyes filled with old memories and lost dreams.

"I am so sorry, Elana." I try and think of something more to say but cannot find the words.

"It's all right, Roxanna. I am doing well after all these years. If I had it to do again, I hope that I would have the sense to make the right choice. This is what I would wish for. And in my old age, I am settled in my life, living each day as if I am with him, my Jean Pierre. I sing and dance and dream that we are still together and I am always in his arms." She has her eyes closed and is breathing as if she can smell him, her face turned upward toward the sunlight.

"I am old yes, but I do not fear death, for I have known love. He read those words to me once, you know. He always read to me, said he didn't trust his own words to describe his feelings for me. Damned French…so damned romantic…they do that on purpose, you know, so that you'll fall in love with them. Their words are like foreplay for chrissake…" She turns to the waiter who hands her another glass.

"*Un sigaretta, per favore*." He pulls one from his vest and lights it for her. "*Prego*. Enough about my history, Roxanna…what are you thinking?"

"I'm thinking that I should go back to Rome but I'm afraid. I came to Italy and to Capri because it was calling to me. It's so crazy…" I thought of telling her about the spirit but decided against it for fear she'd think me insane.

"Nothing is crazy. Except if you don't follow love. Life is too short not to. But if your heart calls you to another place, then go there, but go back to him before too much time passes. *Capisce*?"

"*Capisco*." Now I am the one lost in thought. So we sit quietly, Elana puffing her cigarette and me lost in memories of Natale's touch and his whisperings of love, while the sound of a distant mandolin caresses the day. We sit for hours talking and laughing now, a little closer like women get after undressing their souls for each other.

Tonight, we walk back along the Grand Canal laughing and flirting with the waiters as they stand in front of their cafes and restaurants trying to entice us to come in and eat. Elana is at her usual best, bewitching them as she moves. The Prosecco has cast a soft glow over both of us.

"It is time to retire, Roxanna, so I bid you farewell." We are standing in front of the Rialto Bridge not far from my hotel.

"Will I see you tomorrow?" I ask.

"No, I have business in Milano so I will be leaving early on the train; but here is my phone number and address in case you ever find yourself back in Venice." She writes the information on a piece of paper she has in her bag. "It was a pleasure, Roxanna. I enjoyed your company, and *mille grazie* for being there today." She smiles sweetly and kisses both my cheeks before embracing me.

"Elana, I will miss you, but I am so happy to have met you. Here, my email address and cell phone number. If you are in Capri or even in the south, please call me and I will meet you." I don't want to say goodbye to my new friend. "I will write you and let you know where I am."

"Yes, and remember to follow your heart." She blows me a kiss and then leaves me on the promenade.

I fall asleep quickly I am sure because of the Prosecco we have drunk so much of.....

CHAPTER 20

When I awaken, I can think of nothing but Natale. He is in my every breath, as if he were thinking about me in these same moments and I remember Elana's words. So I dial him even before I get out of bed. He picks up the phone.

"*Pronto*." He sounds as if I have awoken him from sleep and realize it is only nine o'clock. My heart is beating wildly.

"Natale, it's me, Roxanna." I await a response, but instead I hear him taking a deep breath as if he is trying to settle himself.

"Rossana…where are you?" His voice is solemn.

"After leaving Rome, I went to Assisi and I'm now in Venice." I am rambling on. "I am so sorry for leaving the way I did, but knew that if I waited to say good bye, I would never have left at all." There is only silence on the other end.

"Natale, please say something. I'm sorry. I love you, you know." I hear his heart flutter, or maybe I just imagine it. "Please." I am begging for forgiveness now, beseeching him.

"Rossana, you broke my heart. What do you want me to say? I come home and you are gone…only a note. I cannot sleep, I cannot eat without you. You have turned me upside down." I think he means inside out, but no mind.

"It has been hard for me, too." I start to cry on the phone. "I am confused about a lot of things in my life, Natale; but I am not confused about my love for you. I am just confused about the timing of it." I can't say anymore.

"Then go and do what you need to do, Rossana. I cannot guarantee I will be here when you finish. I don't know…don't know. I need to think." There is quiet on the other end and I picture him with his head in his hands, his fingers moving through his hair.

"I know. I understand. I just wanted to call and tell you I love you and that I am thinking about you." There is more silence. "Can I call you sometime just to talk, check on you?"

"*Si*." He sounds resigned to the fact that I would probably not come back but would haunt him for the rest of his days with quick phone calls from wherever I was. I feel his distance and his silence.

"Natale, are you there?"

"*Si,* I am here. Good luck, Rossana. I hope you find what you are looking for. If you want to call me on the *telefono*, you can. I wish you happiness. *Ciao*." That was the end of the conversation. I put the phone down and weep into my pillow, wishing it was him I was hugging. What did I expect? That he would be happy for me? I am even more confused now. I lay in bed until I have no more tears inside me.

Natale is sitting on the edge of the bed now, his head in his hands. His heart is beating fast and he is angry. He wants to go to her, to get on the next train to Venezia. But he knows if he does, he could push her further away by cornering her. She has to fly free like a bird. She made that clear to him.

"*No capisco!*" His thoughts are confused and running wild. Why does she need freedom from me?

"*Merda…*shit!" With his hand, he wipes the table clean next to his bed, sweeping everything on it onto the floor. "Good bye, Rossana." He moves to the bathroom with his heavy heart.

I expected that once I moved out into the sunlight, my mood would change, but it has not. No sunlight, or walk along the Canal, or the romance of Venice can change my mood. I am doomed to a day of brooding for my loss. I think of Elana….what would she do? Then I hear her say, "Follow your heart, Roxanna. It will tell you what to do next." So I walk on trying not to get caught up in my sadness but to instead focus on what is before me today. Time…I am willing to give myself time no matter how long it takes.

I walk slowly, through the streets and through the alleys, over the Bridge of Sighs, through the maze of shops, in search of things that stir my soul so that it will shift. Maybe then I can find clarity on what to do next.

I am back in the Piazza de San Marco and have decided to visit the Doges' Palace and its museum. Since art is a passion of mine, it will surely take me outside of myself. I find myself praying to the old masters for their assistance.

The palace is the home of the Doges, the supreme heads of state as they reigned over Venice in their time. It is an unusual building, appearing to be a delicate pink and white in color; its façade is decorated in the flamboyant Gothic style, with statues and depictions of scenes everywhere – Adam and Eve in the Garden, the *Judgment of Solomon*, the statue of Venus and the *Robes of Justice*, the Doge Andrea Gritti before the *Symbol of Venice*.

There before me is the *Staircase of the Giants*, with two colossal statues of Neptune and Mars on either side of the landing, the staircase once used for the official crowning ceremonies of the new Doges. I walk toward another building, the Procuratie Nuove which means the New Magistrature, once the residence of the Procuratori di San Marco which now houses the cultural institute and the Archeological Museums. The top portion of this neo-classically designed building is covered with statues of Roman emperors, and mythological and allegorical scenes.

Inside, its twenty rooms are filled with marble and bronze archeological finds and other antiquities from Rome and Greece - Roman portraits, Greek and Roman reliefs and statues such as Venus and Apollo, a Roman sarcophagus, ceramics, and the 4th century headless Athena, all of which have inspired me and I am now feeling better…

By the time I leave, it is three in the afternoon. I walk toward the closest waterway at the end of the *piazza* behind Saint Mark's where I see the church of Santa Maria della Salute on the far side of the canal. The scene before me is like a postcard, the marble church with a great dome at the top, set upon a series of curlicue braces, four columns in the front portal, statues about the roof and bas-reliefs in the façade and a staircase leading up to the front door of the church. The waters of the canal are shimmering in the afternoon sun and a line of gondolas covered with brightly covered blue and yellow tarps are sitting along both sides of the canal in the forefront of the scene. I snap a photo to sketch from later.

As I walk, I notice that all of the little cafes have beautifully embroidered linen tablecloths on the tables and it reminds me of the Italian linens on all of the beds that I have slept in since coming to Italy. Then I vow that I will always have them no matter where I am living.

The Grand Canal stands before me so I find a café along its edge to eat an early dinner since my stomach seems to be reminding me that I have eaten nothing today. I am served local fish and salad as I watch the gondolas go by carrying lovers; and again, I think of Natale and how much I love him, but I am feeling a bit more settled – not so insane at this moment.

My attention is pulled to the music I hear all around me. People are smiling; children are laughing and chasing each other. A man has come to sit on the sidewalk in front of the café and is playing his accordion. I am enjoying watching the people who are enjoying Venice, and once again, I am enraptured by its magic. I decide to take a gondola ride through the canals.

I soon approach three men that are sitting together, waiting for patrons who all smile and say in unison, "*Bella.*"

"You want ride, sig*nora*?"

"*Quanto costa?*" I have heard they are expensive.

"*Cento euro per un ora.*" One hundred per hour!

"*Molto caro!*" Too expensive.

"*Signora*, we work hard. It is one hour. For you, *ottanta*?" Eighty.

"*Si*, okay."

"Please get in. I will help." I sit with my back to him on a red velvet cushioned seat. The gondola is black, lacquered, adorned and embellished with gold statues and scroll work. It is beautiful…

"*Molto bella* gondola." To this, the boatman is pleased. He smiles and nods his head in agreement. He is a good looking man of about thirty-five with gigantic forearms which I assume are from moving the oar through the water all day. His shirt is black and white striped and his pants are black, and he has a red scarf tied tightly around his neck. His skin is tanned from the beating sun.

"*Grazie, solo?*" This is the Italian word for single or alone.

"*Si, io solo.*" He smiles at me.

"*Molto bella.*" I think I see him wink, but the sun is in my eyes. It is low in the sky this time of day creating that shimmering diamond pattern on the water; but here in Venice it is different then the reflection on the sea. Here, the sunlight dances on the top of the murky water that is being turned up from the oar, creating almost an emerald green color. The shimmering is upon the facades of the buildings, changing their colors.

"I take you somewhere special…somewhere we live…no *touristas* see *mio Venezia.*" He moves his oar in the water moving us out of the main waterway and into a smaller canal. Once inside, he pulls up to a building and jumps from the gondola.

"*Aspete*…wait." He disappears inside the building. I forget my heart and slip into the surroundings of the here and now in this gondola in Venice and suddenly feel like a princess.

The boat is gently tapping against the side of the cement wall. Three men, who are walking by, stop and keep watch, moving the front of the gondola out into the water each time it moves too close to the building, so that the banging does not damage it. For ten minutes they stay – to watch over a stranger's boat - how noble and caring of them. And after that time, he emerges with two glasses and an open bottle of *vino*. He pours and hands me a glass, then fills his own and makes a toast, all the while maneuvering the boat with his oar using his free hand. The muscles in his arms are bulging as he moves the oar.

"*Salute*!"

"*Alla Vita*! What is your name? *Si chiama*?"

"Marco. You?"

"Mine is Roxanna. Nice to meet you." He tilts his glass to me and bows slightly, saluting me. Another gondola passes us and the boatman is singing and we all smile. Venice, this is the stuff that painters paint…I will always remember Venice...

"Ah, Venezia." He breathes in proudly, puffing up his chest like a peacock. We float through tiny canals lined with charming houses and little squares with small gardens. The thousand year old houses and their windows are adorned with terracotta planters holding geraniums, reminding me of pictures I have seen in the art galleries in America.

There are bridges in between the streets and cafes which are everywhere. Each café has brightly colored awnings and planter boxes attached to the wrought iron fences at their edges. Clothes are hanging from lines along the buildings. A grandfather stoops over his small grandson who is looking down into the water. In his broken English, Marco tells me that the canal we are on at that moment is where the "Italian Job," the movie was filmed. I sit and listen to the sounds of the day and of the water as he guides the gondola gently through each passage.

Marco gives me a guided tour, telling me about each house – who used to live there, and what each building is named. With the sun slowly hanging just above the ancient buildings, the city seems dreamy, shimmering.

Just then, we ride under a small bridge. As I look upward, I see the sunlight reflecting from the water onto its underside…dancing light.

"*Molto bella*! Look, Marco!"

"*Si, luce del sole*- the light of the sun. *Bella*, quick, *foto*!" I am caught in the awe of the shimmering light for a moment, holding my breath, but pull my camera out just in time to snap a photo. Before I know it, we are back in the Grande Canal moving closer to the dock. We are done too soon I think…but I am so happy with the ride that I give him *cento deici*, one hundred and ten euro.

"Grazie, Roxanna. You come back later? Midnight I finish. *Si*?"

"Oh, that's so late, but *grazie*." I know I will be sleeping by then and want to be alone.

"Okay. But if you change mind" – he points to himself. "Come. I am here." He smiles at me and bows his head and says, "*Sera*."

Okay, I think to myself. I am now feeling the romance of this place…I find myself almost dancing down the promenade and think of

Elana. The Rialto Bridge is before me. I look past it just in time to see the sunlight reflecting off the top halves of the buildings along the canal. I want more photos, so I chase the sun, snapping along the way, until I realize I am in the middle of Marco's neighborhood where the locals live and the tourists never go. I roam the streets and alleyways looking for more photo opportunities and find many.

Every inch of every building, every *piazzetta*, and every bridge is exquisitely architectured. I come upon the *Piazza de San Paolo*, where there are three or four cafes, one at each end of the *piazzetta*. There are tables and chairs all around, all filled with families eating their dinner. I sit at a table and order something to drink as I watch them all happily eating and laughing….the sounds of life…

The little ones are laughing and giggling as if they know secrets the adults don't know. The adults are talking in that Italian way, you know when they are so passionate with every word, every phrase, speaking in raised tones, talking with their hands and their bodies as if they were musical instruments.

I can smell the fresh fish that has been caught today as it waits to be grilled with lemon, Italian herbs, spices and olive oil reminding me of that smell of the fish Antonio had caught and prepared for our dinner. It is the sweet smell of the sea. Mixed with this, the garlic, basil, tomatoes and vino is like an incense, intoxicating the senses.

Once again, as I move through this journey called my life, I feel my breath leave my body. Take it away forever, I beg! I could die here and be happy! I think about all the moments these past five weeks that have caused this reaction in me. Then, I whiff the scent of lemons, reminding me of Capri. They are so sweet, that you can eat them like oranges. I had watched Enrico in his garden, tending to the lemon trees under the black netting that protects them from the sun. He took care in pruning the trees, watering each night, nurturing them, and talking to them as if they were his children. Only great things grow with such love.

My memories are interrupted as two beautiful Venetian men jog past my table and I breathe in deeply in hopes of smelling them. I want to know their smell intimately as I have known the other smells of this Venetian night…

Upon returning to my room, I am inspired to sketch the Santa Maria della Salute Cathedral with the gondolas along the canal, so I download my photos onto my laptop and start sketching. I also throw open the shutters, and hear the sounds of the canal and the alleyway below as people pass by. After an hour or so, I am sleepy, so I turn down my bed and crawl in, forgetting to shut off my computer. As I lay here, I can hear the sounds of voices far below. Oh, how I love the language…my favorite words... *"Piano, piano…pero…aspette…allora…."*

Poesia - poetry…and this is how I fall asleep.

CHAPTER 21

L'ISOLA DI CAPRI

I miss Capri so much that I leave the Queen of the Adriatic, this emerald colony of Venice, at noon. While on the train, I try and reach Enrico by cell phone but cannot get through. *Italia* and telephones! *Mama mia!* It's not an easy feat. I have no place to stay when I return to AnaCapri since I had moved my things to storage offered by Enrico. He said to call when I return because he might have a nice place for me by then.

As I stand on the deck of the hydrofoil approaching Capri, I feel that familiar flutter in my heart as it begins to open to the island. Ah, this is love. Now I remember how much this place means to me. I look up along the rocky cliffs and make out the faint outline of the bright white San Michele Chapel and Villa and the yellow colored Caesar Augustus Hotel. My home...I love this place...I am here...once again I can hear it calling to me.

I splurge on a taxi to take me to the top of the island instead of the autobus. I will need to conserve my energy for the long walk once I get to town since I don't know where I'll be hanging my clothes this time and may have to tote my luggage a mile or more. *Mama mia*...the life of a gypsy is not easy!

As soon as I walk into the cool, marble lobby of the Caesar Augustus Hotel, Enrico is standing there in his blue suit with a wide smile as if he has been expecting me. He is always dressed superbly, looking so fresh and well-groomed.

"Roxanna! You are back...welcome! Did you have a nice trip?" I kiss his cheeks.

"Yes, Enrico, it was wonderful. I need a place to stay. Is there anywhere available?"

"Yes, yes. I am glad you are here now because the people, they leave today. I will tell you how to get there. Take your luggage and walk into town. You know where the *tabacchi* shop is on the corner?"

"Yes."

"You will see a little alleyway there. Go there and walk down the steps. Keep walking all the way down until you come to the trash bins…you know the ones…and then go right. Follow the path past all the villas. Keep going until you get to the end. There is a gate there that says *"Mio Paradiso"* – My Paradise. That's where you will stay. The key is in the door, and it is open. I will be down later to check on you. *Capisce?* Good to have you back, Roxanna."

"*Grazie, grazie.* Thank you so much, Enrico. See you later; *ciao.*" I wave good bye to him and leave, walking the distance to town with my luggage in tow. The heat and humidity, even at this hour, is like a wet blanket on my skin. I can feel the familiar dampness start to accumulate at my hairline and on my neck. AnaCapri is not an easy place to get to. It is not for the faint of heart, mind, or body, especially this time of year. I am tired of living out of a suitcase and I am yearning for somewhere to call home.

"Okay. I'm tired and hungry right now and have no idea where I'm going…it's hot out and I'm sweating!" I wish in this moment, that I am naked, with cool water running down my body like the cold showers I used to take at the cottage…so delicious…

I hear laughter in the ethers and suddenly, my bags feel light in my hands as if they are being lifted by unseen forces. I stop and start to giggle, and at this very moment, a soft breeze picks up and cools me…I smile toward the sky. Welcome, I think to myself. Who would believe me?

I arrive in town and decide to eat before the mile walk to the little villa. I arrive at Barbarossa's in the *piazza* where I am greeted by Vinnie who kisses my face.

"Roxanna, welcome back. How were your travels?" He has a big smile for me as usual.

"Wonderful, Vinnie. It's good to be back, though. I'll have a mixed green salad, grilled chicken and *acqua minerale.*" I never seem to get used to eating pasta…it's usually too heavy for me…

"*Si, grazie*…the same as you always order." He smiles. I finally cool down before the meal comes and am able to enjoy being surrounded by familiar faces and the food, in this familiar restaurant. Vinnie brings a Lemoncello after the meal. This is now my favorite drink which makes me feel as though my new Italian grandmother has made me hot cocoa and wrapped me in a warm blanket full of love. See what Lemoncello does to the senses?

By the time I leave and walk the distance to my new home, the sun is setting behind the Isola de Ischia. I find the gate to *"Mio Paradiso,"* open it and step inside; and what I see before me takes my breath away.

There is a long *terrazzo* as long as a football field. There are flowers, shrubbery and trees everywhere. The entire property has a view, just like the Caesar Augustus. Ischia is to the left, the tiny island of Precido is next on the horizon, then the mainland and then Monte Vesuvio and Sorrento are to the far right…breathtaking. There are statues lining the walkway and half way down the path, I see a little stone villa with a portico along its front with hand painted green tiled flooring. The stone villa, I would learn later, was the home of Enrico's ancestors and is three hundred years old; and the attached building, a kitchen with another portico, was built maybe one hundred years ago by his family.

Herbs, night jasmine, geraniums, roses, and numerous types of flowers I don't recognize line the outer *terrazzo*. There are three stone benches built into the wall underneath the flowers, and olive trees and grape vines are scattered about. There are plum trees, lemon trees, apple trees, peach trees, and orange trees. There are strawberry plants, basil, arugula, rosemary bushes and gardens that are filled with broccoli, fava beans, lettuce, tomatoes, and artichokes. Everything smells so sweet. It's as if the gardens and the land are welcoming me home.

I set my backpack down in front of the villa and sit to watch the setting sun and sky as it fills with different shades of salmon and pink. Life is to die for in these moments so of course I weep.

The dream…I remember the dream…"Come, I want to show you where you will live…you will be inspired to paint here…" This is it - the place he showed me – the vision – the *terrazzo,* the flowers and the view of the Mediterranean. I am in awe of it all…the dream has become my reality.

My own *paradiso*…

Over the next few days, I only leave the villa to buy food. Getting to the village is a bit of an ordeal but I get used to it quickly. Carrying my sacks filled with food and water takes some practice but soon I am strong enough and my arms no longer feel as if they will fall off. I now have the utmost respect for the islanders and what they do to support their households and families.

I settle in nicely, nesting in my new home and my new surroundings. Each morning, I sit with the lizards and the birds, welcoming the new day. I watch the colors of the sea and the sky change with each new wind and each new weather pattern. Enrico comes by to visit daily to water and nurture his gardens and he describes all of the flowers and plants to me, telling me each ones' name. He tells me the winds come from nine different directions on the island, sometimes creating wild storms that blow like a hurricane. I wonder if I will be all right out here by myself.

Well, I don't have to wonder too long, for tonight it storms so hard that I shiver. I hear the lightening strike all around the villa with such force, and then the rumbling of the thunder that goes on and on. It never seems to stop and I know that this means the storm is directly overhead and hardly moving at all. The rains come down, monsoon-like, so I am unable to sleep. But since I have nowhere to go except under my blankets, I lounge in bed in that state between sleepiness and wakefulness listening to the weather.

When daybreak finally comes, I rise to the sun and a layer of clouds on the horizon, and I sit at one of the little tables on the *terrazzo* with my tea – my morning ritual. A huge bumble bee flies about my head. The gigantic June bugs are playing in the flower blossoms and the lizards are basking in the sun, inches from me. I try to stay very still…I have never seen such brilliant greens on a reptile. There is a large one, who is maybe the mama and a young baby. They don't seem afraid of me so I sit so still, hardly breathing, watching them live and play.

Enrico's wife Bettina who speaks very little English has come by to introduce herself. She is a beautiful woman, always smiling and singing as she works in the gardens for I have seen her on the grounds. I am amazed at her energy and her hard body, which is lean and muscular from her life of physical work. She pushes wheel barrels filled with tile and rock, or grass, branches, and dirt from one end of the property to the other. She is amazing! And she is beautiful. Enrico and Bettina have a daughter, Maria who lives on the other side of the property with her husband and their two daughters, beautiful little girls. I often hear them laughing and giggling throughout the day.

Maria, who is also beautiful like her mother, speaks very good English. She brings me homemade tomato sauce and wine from the cellars and I thank her for her kindness. It's nice to know her family is just on the other side of the gate if I should need anything – especially if another storm should blow through like last night.

This night, Santa Maria comes to me in my dream with her powerful, loving and compassionate presence. She never speaks to me in the dream, but she reaches for my hand and brings it up to her heart and holds it there. I feel her love and know that she is my protectress on this strange journey.

After two weeks of spending most of my days and nights at the villa, I start to feel the craziness inside my head. I toss and turn in bed all night, thinking about Natale and how much I miss him, wondering what he is doing. I obsess about him every moment that there are no other thoughts in my head. Then I wonder about my boys that I have left behind in America. Am I crazy for living in this paradise without them? Should I be working? Should I go home? Or should I go to Rome?

The guilt rises up inside of me like a demon that has come to take my soul like the craziness that pulls people kicking and screaming, back into their reality that they are trying to escape.

After all this time spent being alone, I have my validation and yes, I am surely insane. No worries…who will know but me, right? I decide right now, that it's time to leave this playmate inside my head and go out and be with people.

This night, I walk into town and have dinner at a small family restaurant where no one speaks English. The owner is Patricia who has short, thick, curly hair and big brown eyes. She takes special care of me and we communicate as best we can as she asks me where I have come from and what I am doing. Another new friend to see when I am in the village…I smile to myself as I dine on roasted chicken which no one can make like they do in this country! It is superb…something else to fall in love with…

As I walk back to the villa in the wind and the rain, I feel alive…happy…in love with life. I crawl in between my linen sheets and I smile up at Santa Maria as I say, "Thank you..." She has become my guardian, my mother, and my friend - always watching over me. I can feel her spirit and her hand on my heart as I walk through these strange days where I know not where I am going.

CHAPTER 22

The storms have finally blown through, and the summer heat has arrived. The temperatures are now between 35o and 40o C, 92o – 104o F. *Mama mia*! I have learned to walk into town early in the morning to avoid the worst of it. I always stop to see Federico, Nunzio, Ciero, Allesandra and my other new friends.

I cherish these meetings, chatting with them and seeing their smiling faces. Sometimes I stop for tea in Alessandro's restaurant or visit the Il Martino to visit Danielle and Maria and to use the internet, or stop by to see Bruno, my friend from Rome who is now working as bar manager at the Caesar Augustus. He has helped me with my Italian since the first day I met him.

"Roxanna, you must speak Italian daily if you are ever to know the language well, *capisce*?" He then prods me with Italian for the next five minutes until I get used to using it. Since he is from Rome, his enunciation is different then those in the south where their speech is a little smoother and a little lazier – like poetry. The Romans speak perfectly in my opinion and it is easier for me to follow them.

On the nights I visit Bruno, I also chat with his assistant Enrico and listen to Adriano play the piano as I watch the incredible sunsets. He is so talented I don't understand why he isn't composing or writing concertos instead of playing night after night in a hotel.

Other nights, I visit the Capri Palace. I say hello to Gino, and listen to the singers that perform there. Yes, I have found all of the hidden places in AnaCapri.

Most nights though, I stay at the villa and dance under the stars, blowing kisses to the sea below and the sky above. After the sun goes down, there is a quietness that takes over the island. I can hear the sound of a scooter in the far off distance and I can hear children laughing. Sometimes there is music wafting through the air from someone's villa – always music in Capri.

This night, it is dusk and I am saying thank you again for another day. I hear one or two small boats motoring on the sea and the soft sound of a far off hydrofoil traveling to one of the other islands. I can hear crickets and the sounds of cats and dogs, muffled by the distance. But mostly, I hear the silence and this is the most beautiful sound of all.

After another extended period of time alone, I decide it's time for another adventure; so I travel to Tuscany on the train to see the countryside and to visit a few of the cities. I want to see the architecture and the museums – more inspiration for my art. I want to go to Florence, the seat of the Renaissance…where the great masters painted and sculpted and left their mark.

I decide to email my friends in the States to let them know there is another adventure on the horizon. One of them writes back that she hopes I will find a villa there like Diane Lane in "Under the Tuscan Sun." She even calls me Diane in our emails, but she has no idea that my adventure is far different from hers. I email her back. "Thank you very much, but I am having my own dream in the south of Italy and there is nothing similar about us at all!" Then I smile remembering lovemaking with Bruno at the fort and connecting with my soul mate Raffaello. I remember sweet Natale and our time in Rome. I remember San Francesco and Santa Maria coming to me and I remember the Great Spirit. And, oh, I almost forgot Elana. There is nothing similar about Diane's and my adventure…except maybe the scooter ride. So I write another email before I leave to tell them all of this.

I am in Pisa for the day and walk across the *Ponte Solferino*, over the Arno Fiume, the canal – which reminds me of Venice at first sight. The water is the same color – that emerald green - and the ancient buildings lay sleepily along its edge bathed in the golden sunlight of the afternoon. On one bank stands the *Church of Santa Maria Della Spina,* which is Pisan Gothic style with carved spires and pinnacles decorating its top. Pisan architecture is beautiful, but very busy…almost too much for my senses. I think that if I stay here long enough, only then will I get used to these intricately beautiful architectural delights.

I walk through the city to the great *Piazza del Duomo* where there are four major buildings of interest. I think I should be able to see them by now, but cannot until I round the corner of a building. Then, it is before me...too overwhelming a vista to take in. The Cathedral, the *Baptistry*, the *Camposanto* and the leaning *Tower of Pisa* are all standing in a row. They are surrounded by the *piazza* with its stone walkways and lawns of green grass. All the buildings are true Pisan Gothic style and I am dizzy by how much work has gone into the facades of each of them. They are architectural masterpieces.

The Cathedral is made of different colored marble with seven arcades or portals in front. There are arches and columns as the eye moves further up the structure, topped off by statues with the *Virgin and Child* in the center at the highest point. The bronze doors are reliefs done by Bonanno depicting the *Life of Christ.*

I enter the church to find works by Pisanno, Camaino, Cimabue and Sarto.

The *Baptistry* is as beautiful as the *Cathedral*, designed by Nicola and Giovanna Pisanno. This Pisan family is who the Pisan Gothic style was named after and whose work is everywhere here. It – the *Baptistry* - also has blind arcading, columns, gable shaped cusps, and pinnacles adorned with statues and reliefs; and at the top, the dome consists of sculpted marble ribbing, topped off with a statue of Saint John the Baptist. See what I mean about its busyness?

I learn that the leaning *Tower of Pisa* was where Galileo had performed his great experiments on gravity and falling masses in the 16th century. This strange looking round building is the backdrop for the other three...all built in a row. It stands 179 feet tall on the north side and only 177 feet on the south side. I also learned that it is leaning because when it was being built, the ground was sinking. It was centuries before it was finished and the Pisanno family were the ones who restarted the project – hence the architectural style.

From Pisa, I ride through the countryside toward Florence, stopping next in Lucca, the place where Caesar, Crasso and Pompey met in 56 B.C. This is a unique circular town enclosed by a wall that was built for protection at some point in its history. Many of the houses are made to look like towers with green tufts of trees and bushes on the tops. They are all tightly packed together with alleys or small streets running between them. Large villas and palaces that date back to the 1400s are hidden throughout. It is a quiet town like AnaCapri and Capri where the automobiles and scooters run mostly on the outer streets.

Here, I stay in a *pensionne* that reminds me of an Italian grandmother's house. It has a big bed with a white linen bedspread. There is a crucifix hanging on the wall and white linen curtains on the window – but they will not be blowing in the breeze tonight, for it is stiflingly hot and the air is thick...and I will be sleeping with the mosquitoes! *Mama mia!*

In the morning, after hugs and kisses from the husband and wife who run the place, and from the young woman who serves me breakfast, I take the bus to Florence, and we stop in a few of the little towns along the way. As I ride through this dramatic and colorful countryside in romantic *Toscano*, I think of Natale. I want to stop in Rome to see him on the way back to Capri, be with him, make love with him…but know if I do, I won't leave. This time, I would be swallowed up inside this big love.

Will it ever be time? I want to call him but know if I do it will only hurt more and I will be torturing him as well. I sit on the bus looking at the countryside through blurry eyes from the tears. I thought they had all dried up inside me, but I was wrong. I hold my hand over my heart and rub it there in hopes of healing the pain that I am feeling once again. Why do hearts hurt so when lovers break up?

I find the countryside soothing somehow… there are fields of sunflowers tossed here and there throughout the land, and rolling hills with old castles and villas hidden everywhere. I ride through a quaint little town called Pescia known for its flower markets, and then on to Montecatini. Pistoia is next sitting at the base of the Apennines, and it is surrounded by the Medici Wall.

Then there is Prato where we stop and tour its beautiful 12th century Romanesque *Cathedral of Santo Stefano.* We ride by the *Bishop's Palace*, the *Praetorial Palace*, and the famous *Emperor's Palace* ordered by Frederick II of Swabia in the 13th century. You know how beautiful a place is when everyone through history builds their palaces there.

CHAPTER 23

FIRENZE

We have arrived in Florence.

One only has to visit Firenze, to know they have fallen in love. Like Venice calls writers and poets to her, Florence calls artists and sculptors. She lies before them spread out, like a lover waiting to be taken. Her skyline with its ancient tiled roofs on top of multicolored medieval buildings paint the horizon like no other place in the world. The turrets, the towers, the *basilicas* and their facades, the famous *Duomo of Santa Maria Del Fiore* – all a mixture of Florentine Gothic, Baroque and Romanesque styles. Every artist, sculptor and architect who has come here before me has left their mark, not only in the museums and palaces, but also in the outer structures of the buildings – the facades, and the *piazzas*.

I fall in love with the city the moment I arrive. I am now sitting in my hotel room overlooking the *Arno Fiume* – the river. I can hear the sounds of the night on the water and in the streets below. I can smell life as it wafts up to me in the breeze that has come to cool the day. Firenze is what it has promised to be – a great lover.

Arriving just before dusk, I check in to my hotel room and get settled in time to watch the night sky. I never thought it would be like this, as romantic as Venezia was…my heart is humming now that I am here.

I hardly sleep, waiting for dawn so I can go out to explore. Finally, it breaks and I can feel the light upon my eyelids as they rest…waiting. It's six a.m. and I rise to ready myself. As I walk the streets and alleyways in search of *espresso*, I smell the morning air. The slight dampness from the night waits for the heat and humidity of the day to rise up. There are a few people going to work, but the tourists haven't risen yet so I feel as though I have the city to myself – as if it is waiting just for me.

I walk over the *Ponte Vecchio*, the old bridge, through the *Piazza della Signoria* containing the *Palazzo Vecchio* and Arnolfo's Tower. I am awestruck as I enter the *Loggia dei Lanzi*. The building is divine, Gothic, with its round arches, soaring clustered columns and a crowning decoration of trefoil arches. There are colossal works here, such as Giambologna's *The Rape of the Sabines* and the *Perseus* by Cellini. I also see a copy of the *David* (Michelanglo's) and *Hercules* and *Cacus* by Bandinelli. On my far left, is the *Fountain of Neptune* by Ammannati, a large figure of the sea-god Neptune with three tritons on a light chariot drawn by four horses. All of this is out of doors in the sunlight…

Everywhere I walk there is a structure with an amazingly decorative façade, a statue, a monument, a *basilica*, a *duomo*, a *piazza* – everywhere there is a work of art. Someone at some time between the 8th century B.C. and the 20th century A.D. – either a passionate painter, sculptor or architect, left their mark upon Florence, sealing the city with a kiss of his or her own love….even women. I searched the internet before I left to see if I could find female painters from the Renaissance, and found two - Alessandra Gecchi and Artemisia Gentileschi. I hope to find their work here. Florence…one of the most beautiful cities in the world, the seat of the masterpieces of the art world…being here is like going back in time.

Of course Florence has a history of conflict and battles but the streets are quiet now filled only with lovers and artists. It has survived barbarian invasions, the time of revolutions from the 13th through the 16th centuries, a revolt due to Spain's presence, and French domination, and so much more.

In spite of all of this, art flourished here. In the 13th century, Gothic style structures were built such as the *Duomo* and the *Palazzo Vecchio.* In the 14th century, this work continued and the *Ponte Vecchio, Giotto's Campanile, Orsanmichele* and the *Loggia del Bigallo* were constructed. The Pitti and Medici families came into wealth and power in the 15th century and numerous *palazzos* – palaces were built as well as other monuments. During the 16th through the 18th centuries, many libraries, museums and other important buildings were built including the Uffizi Museum, the Boboli Gardens, and the *Mercato Nuovo* to name a few.

I can feel the masters who have left their mark here as I walk through the streets, the buildings, and the gardens that house their works. I can hear them whisper to me, feel their fingertips upon my soul as I pass by - Brunellschi, Lippi, Botticelli, Donatello, Leonardo, Michelangelo, Zuccari, Bandini, Fabris, Cambio, Giotto, Caravaggio, Reni, Sanzio, Rossi, Lorenzetti, Buoninsegna, Fabriano, Raphael, Titian, Bartolomeo, Bonaiuto, Cellini, Cimabue, Fiorentino, Verrochio, Ghiberti, Vasari, Michelozzo, Poggi, Parigi, Gentileschi, Gecchi, Alberti...too many to mention. These are only a few of the many who came to kiss Florence….I feel my passion rise up inside me again, pressing me to paint, for I am so moved by these, my mentors.

For the last few days, my mind has been swimming, my breath caught in my throat in that place between rationality and pleasure, as I walk the streets, the *piazzas*, the *palazzos*, the museums, and the galleries. With my digital camera in hand, I try to capture all of it, knowing I cannot possibly for you have to be here to experience this and one photo does not do it justice.

I walk to the *Piazza del Duomo* which is considered the religious heart of the city, all green, pink and white marble. It contains the famous *Duomo* - the dome of *Santa Maria Del Fiore* - the great cathedral, *Giotto's Campanile,* and the *Basilica of San Lorenzo*. So much holiness in one place…another cathedral masterpiece, I smile to myself. Its façade is so busy that they say it took almost a thousand years to plan it, build it and then rebuild it again. It is opulent - every inch of it decorated, carved, frescoed, and containing mosaics bas-reliefs, pilasters, and niches with statues.

The *Campanile*, or bell tower stands next to the *Duomo,* also green, white and pink. Its corners are reinforced with octagonal pilasters and there are two rows of bas-reliefs at the bottom, one above the other. The lower is hexagonal and the upper row lozenge-shaped. There are pilaster strips and sixteen Gothic niches; and above, there are airy arched windows in the top three stories. Then, on top of all of this, the building is crowned by a cornice and balustrade resting on consoles and trefoil arches similar to the cathedral. I could stand here for hours and still not really see all of it.

I love, love, love Firenze…I roam the city and wonder what they call Florence if Rome is the "Eternal City." Would this be the "City of the Masters?" How appropriate, I think. This is what I shall name it!

I eat in the cafe and watch people walk by, both tourists and locals. I listen to them and hear the difference in the dialects of the Florentines from the north and the Napolitani from the south of Italy. I can understand those here in the north because their words are more crisp…sharper I guess you could say.

I notice that many of the women have dark hair and dark brows and lashes but light colored eyes. They are dressed beautifully and fashionably, their clothing and shoes from fashion magazines. I roam the alleyways and small streets looking at the old medieval buildings and then move to the open air markets, and it is here that I purchase pashminas, a tapestry of Florence's *Piazza del Duomo* and a leather coat. The prices are at least half of what I would pay in the States!

My first day has been full enough to make me dream of painting this night…but I don't…not yet…

It's Tuesday and the sun sits high in the sky as I walk across the *arno* toward the *Palazzo Pitti.* I thought the heat and humidity were only relentless in the south but now realize how wrong I was. I walk slowly and fan myself with the decorative fan I bought from a street vendor. I have learned to be comfortable with dewy skin since I arrived here. Maybe this is the reason I appear to look younger? I laugh out loud.

I arrive at the palace on the slopes of Boboli Hill which was built for one of the members of the Medici family and it was their residence for six generations. The gardens are magnificent, framed by flights of steps that lead to the upper hill, a fountain and a small museum. The gardens below contain a large granite basin in the center, originally from the *Baths of Caracalla* in Rome, and an Egyptian obelisk from the *Temple of Amon* in Thebes. There are flowerbeds, trees hedges and fountains, and statues from famous 16th and 17th century artists lining the outer edges.

The great Italian masters await me as I enter the royal quarters, the *Galleria Palatina.* There are many halls or rooms, each having their own name - Allegories Room, Room of Fine Arts, Hercules Room, Psyche Room, Music Room, Flora Room, Illiad Room, Apollo Room, Venus Room, etc. Then there are the Royal Apartments which are broken up into the Green Room, Throne Room, Blue Room, Chapel, Queen's Apartment, King's Apartment, etc. So many…and they are not small either…each one a museum in and of itself.

The ceilings are decorated with frescoes, bas-reliefs, trompe l'oeil, and sculpture. Sienese yellow columns or those of alabaster or marble decorate the halls as well. And if this is not enough for the senses, there are masterpieces hanging on every wall, and sculptures or ornate tables of bronze gilded malachite, or decorated marble all about.

The first room contains a collection of pen and ink drawings. Black or red sanguine pencil was used by each artist, then a brown wash, creating a highlighted or colored effect, giving the drawing the look of a completed work. The colors are brilliant I think, as I study each one…like this one…the *Council of Ephesus* by Giuseppe Nicola Nasini. Amazing definition and shadow were created with pen and black ink with a brown wash in *The Last Supper* by Giuseppe Cades. Such exquisite detail in Baldassarre Peruzzi's *Adoration of the Holy Child,* as he has used a brush, brown ink, and then highlights with black pencil which brings light to the drawing. I have ideas for sketching after studying these.

In the apartment of the Grand Duchess, the entire room is filled with incredible trompe l'oeil by Castognoli. The Music Room, *Sala della Musica* is filled with marble columns, detailed bas-reliefs on the walls, and tromp l'oeil and frescoes covering the ceiling. In the *Galleria del Pocetti,* the bottom half of the walls are covered in frescoes while paintings cover the upper halves.

Then, I come upon the masters I have been waiting to see – the ones that make my heart thump against my breast. Raphael...I breathe heavy as I view his works. *The Veiled Woman, Madonna of the Grand Duke, The Vision of Ezechiel* and then finally his *Madonna of the Chair - Madonna della Seggiola*...this brings tears to my eyes. Her face is so young, so serene, so detailed. Her eyes, her lips, her ears, her nose...all so perfect... She holds her child so close to her showing such intimacy, and the Christ child's face is the most precious I have ever seen. He is beautiful. And the intensity of his colors...

Of course there are others that make me shiver – Caravaggio's *Sleeping Cupid,* Andrea del Sarto's *St. John the Baptist*, Titian's *The Magdalen* and his *Portrait of a Man.* But then wait...here is Artemisia Gentileschi's *Judith.* She – Artemisia - was the young female painter during the Renaissance who had a profound influence on Florentine painting and one of the first artists to show true, deep emotion in the faces of women on canvas. Their faces...the details of their hair...their clothing...the scarf around the head... the flesh on the bodies...profound...

I see many works by Boticelli, but three hold my attention for quite awhile - *Adorate il Bambino* – Adoration of the Child, *Madonna del Mare* – Virgin of the Sea, and *Madonna col Bambino* – Virgin with Child. In the later two, the Madonna's face is that of an angel herself, so young like a schoolgirl, with soft pale skin. In one, her eyes are lowered, gazing downward toward her child, and in the other they are looking outward as if she is dreaming. The colors of the fabrics, the detail, the lace about her face, the thin golden halo around her head...and in the *Madonna del Mare*, there is a beautiful star that he has painted upon the shoulder of her robe. These, I have fallen in love with.

Although I have seen so much of Florence this day that I am dizzy, I don't want to stop. I want to see it all. I walk back over the *Ponte Vecchio* above the *arno* toward the Piazza San Marco where the *Galleria dell' Accademia* is, the great museum that holds the original Michelangelo's *David*. It also holds the famous statue by Giambalogna, the *Rape of the Sabine Women* which is exquisite. The museum is small and I take my time as I come upon the four *Captives* of "the David." This is what this piece is called – "The David" as if he is a god. You do not refer to the statue as "David," but "The David" as if it has power.

When I move out into the great Tribune at the end of the hall of the Accademia, I come face to face with this god that has been created from someone's heart and soul - *The David* - Michelangelo's masterpiece – the symbol of the entire Renaissance and of Florence.

Once again, tears fill my eyes; I can feel my heart pressing against my breast and my breath as it catches in my throat. I have no thoughts, only emotions and I am filled with passion, for I can feel it coming from the David - his strength, his youth, and his beauty. Suddenly, I feel a presence so close to me that I can feel his breath like a light breeze upon my damp neck. A young man is speaking Italian to me so softly that I can barely hear him.

CHAPTER 24

"*Scusi?*" I turn to face him. He is a god himself, with long hair parted in the middle, hanging loosely to his shoulders. He has dark eyes that are deep and expressive, and I notice light stubble on his chin covering his translucently, smooth skin. I also notice his build through his thin black silk tee and think he has the chest of David...or am I dreaming? He speaks to me.

"Oh, you are *Americano* – I thought you are *Italiano*. I was saying that there is a theory that this was a likeness taken of him after he slew Goliath. You see his face as he looks out into the distance as if he were contemplating, meditating almost? He is lost in thought. There is no...how you say, cockiness – no ego about him that he has won the battle. One arm is lazily hanging to his side and the other has his bow slung loosely over his shoulder. You see?" He smiles; all the while his eyes are transfixed upon the David. His accent is thick but his English is near perfect.

"I have never heard that theory," I whisper still breathless. "But I see what you mean."

"Yes....oh, please allow me to introduce myself. My name is Valentino. Valentino Lorenzo. And your name is...?" He reaches for my hand and kisses it.

"Roxanna." I am charmed by him.

"Rossana...that is how we say it in Italian." We stand in quiet for a few moments, me not knowing what to say, if anything at all. Finally, he breaks the silence.

"I come here often to look at his proportions. See how his feet and his hands are so much larger? It gives the piece such perspective. Look at the muscles in his legs and the way they are slightly bent at the knees. His rib cage and his collar bone...you can almost reach out and touch them. Do you see how he created the veins in his arms and hands? Such glorious detail...*perfecto*."

I can see that Valentino is clearly breathless and it feels good to know that someone else feels the art as deeply as I.

"You view art as if you too are a sculptor."

"*Si.* I come from a long line of sculptors, a descendent of the great Ghiberti Lorenzo. Have you ever heard of him? He was a great Florentine sculptor, painter and architect responsible for the Baptistery of San Giovanni in the *Piazza del Duomo*? Do you know this place?"

"Yes, I just visited there. Was he the architect that designed the structure?" I am excited that here, standing before me, is a descendent of someone with such creativity, talent and passion. We both start to walk toward the exit as we continue our conversation.

"He actually designed and built two of the great bronze doors – the one on the north side and then the one on the east side. Michelangelo called the one on the east side the *Porta del Paradiso* - the Gate of Paradise and that is what it is called to this day. It took him almost thirty years to finish this work in 1452. It is a group of panels with twenty-four niches and bas-reliefs representing stories from the Old Testament, and full length statues of biblical figures. It is *magnifico.*" There is a fire in his eyes as he talks about the doors.

"Of course they moved the original panels to the *Museo dell' Opera del Duomo*. They move everything here in Florence, you know…for safe keeping? Anyway, it is a masterpiece. You should go and see the original." He smiles in the sunlight, and I can see those eyes, still contemplative but bright now, for they are filled with pride.

"That's quite a heritage."

"He also produced work for the *Duomo* and the Church of Orsanmichele."

"You must be proud – and talented."

"Proud, yes; but no, I do not have the talent he had in his little finger." Valentino lowers his head in reverence. "Each time I sculpt, I always say a prayer to San Lorenzo and to Ghiberti before I start." He makes the sign of the cross upon his own skin and then kisses the small golden cross that is hanging around his neck on a thick gold chain.

"Well, Rossana. It is time for *espresso.* Would you like to come?" It is almost 17:00 (five in the afternoon).

"*Si, grazie*, Valentino." I like to say his name, for it makes me feel as if I am in a romance novel. We walk the *piazza* toward a bar, enter and he orders two *espressos*, which is the custom in Italy at this time of day. This is their pick-me-upper that holds them until dinner in the later hours. I never understood why they eat so late in this country.

"So, Rossana, are you *solo?*"

"Yes, I have come to see the art in Florence. Do you live in the city?"

"*Si*, I live in an apartment near the *Duomo*. It has been in my family for the last two hundred years. The buildings are very old here, no?"

I am enjoying the conversation and his company as we sit at an outside table talking about Valentino's family. He tells me that his work is shown on *Via de Vecchietti*, a street filled with art close to the *Duomo*. His pieces are half-life and full-life sculptures, pretty large. He tells me he has sculpted copies of the gods but has not yet attempted *the David*; although he comes to study him every week and says he will know when it is time to begin.

"My favorite pieces are those of women, but I have to feel them to be able to create their likeness. If I cannot feel them, then it is too bad."

"Do you sell many, Valentino?"

"Enough to buy food and clothing. My family supports me so I am okay. How do you make a living, Rossana?" His eyes are contemplating me, as if he is trying to look into my soul. He is sizing me up, looking at my face, my cheekbones, my nose, the curve of my lips. I can feel him in all of those places as if he were preparing to make love to me…it is unsettling!

"I am not working right now but I am a painter." Funny, how I can call myself this when I haven't picked up a brush in years. No matter…I know I am a painter…I feel it in my being. I laugh nervously.

"When painting like sculpture, you have to have the sight. You have to become what you are creating, get inside it…feel it. Is that what you do when you paint, Rossana?"

"Yes, sometimes I get lost in my characters and I have to remember to eat and sleep."

"When I am creating, I stay inside my studio for months; sometimes I see no one. I don't sleep for days and sometimes forget to eat. You see?" He pulled his tee shirt up exposing his abdomen. Although he is tall and of medium build, his stomach seems to almost indent there and I can see he works out because of the well-defined abdominal muscles. I look away for I can feel myself blushing.

"I see." I think he is flirting with me.

"Sometimes, I feel crazy inside my head…you know? No one understands what it is like to be filled with a love for something so deep…I cannot explain it." His eyes change now, becoming even darker – that look…

"I understand, Valentino. I do that when I paint, too. Sometimes, I don't know if I am the character I am painting or if I am me – Roxanna."

"You do understand me." He reaches for my hand and brings it to his lips, kissing the back of it. Now, his eyes are smiling. Ah, companions. We are so blessed in this life, are we not? Rossana, would you please have dinner with me tonight?"

I look away for a moment, thinking about Natale, and Valentino senses there is someone else, for he feels my love leave my body and go elsewhere. "No, no. I know you have someone. It is just dinner…nothing else. I enjoy your company. I will meet you at the restaurant. There is a place not far from here, in between *Santa Maria Novella* and the *Duomo* on *Via dei Panzani*. It is called *Ristorante Giglio Rosso*, half way down the street. Will you meet me there at nine o'clock?"

Just dinner…so I accept and say *ciao* until then.

He is outside the restaurant when I arrive, and this time, half his hair is pulled back at the top of his head in a pony tail while the rest hangs straight. Now he truly looks like an *artista*.

"Ah, *bella donna*…now you truly look like a Roman goddess with your hair and that dress." He kisses both my cheeks and then my hands.

"*Grazie*, Valentino." The owner, a friend of his, ushers us to the best table in the house. Valentino asks for a bottle of Chianti Classico 2000 which is smooth, bold, and full-bodied. "This is so good, Valentino. Is it from Tuscany?"

"*Si,* it is from the *Castello di Querceto* in Chianti. It is 95% of the Sangiovese grape and 5% of another grape that is grown in this region called Canaiolo. Then, it must sit in the barrel for three years before it can be poured. This is why it is so good. No one can label their wine as the Chianti Classico unless the grapes are grown in this region, the Chianti region. It is a law of the wine makers and it is a well respected one."

"How do you know so much about wine?" I am curious. He hesitates a little.

"Actually, the winery belongs to my family. I grew up working the vineyards and in the tasting room. It is a beautiful place. Do you know that it used to be the summer house of the Pitti family in Florence?"

"You mean of the Medicis and the Pitti Palace family…that family?"

"*Si.* Now, it has been in my family for the last century. It is in the Chianti countryside not too far from here. I will take you tomorrow and you can taste some of the other wines if you like."

He has been a perfect gentleman and I feel safe, so I accept his offer. We dine on special foods chosen by the owner, each one a delicious Tuscan or Florentine dish. The first course or the *primi patti* is *panzanella*. It is a cold summer dish made with moistened bread crumbs and onions, tomatoes and basil topped with oil and vinegar. The *secondi patti* is *ossobuco alla fiorentina,* slices of veal stewed in tomatoes, with garlic, rosemary, sage and lemon. The salad is fresh arugula and gorgonzola cheese with lemon and olive oil and salt. Mmmm…the tastes in my mouth…

For dessert, they bring *panna cotta*, a pudding made of crème, eggs and lemon served with a chocolate sauce and then the traditional *tiramisu,* a truffle with lady fingers dipped in liquor and dusted with cocoa. Tonight is like making love with food...

"Valentino, this is one of the best meals I have ever tasted."

"I knew you would love it, Rossana. The best for you only." We talk all the way through dinner, getting to know each other - our lives, my children, his family, and the fact that he cannot keep a girlfriend because he hasn't been able to commit to anything other than his art, his first love…and I understand him.

Walking me back to the hotel, he leaves me at the door, the gentleman that he is, and only kisses my cheeks. "I will come by for you on my scooter tomorrow at 13:00. *Arrivederci*, Rossana."

I open the shutters in my room and gaze out over the Florentine skyline and its rooftops. The city is still alive and once again I hear music somewhere in the distance. What a magical place and a perfect day it has been.

"Ciao, bella!" Valentino arrives right on time and off we go south of the city and into the Chianti countryside. The landscape is painted with vineyards and olive groves, and there are woods filled with cypress and oak trees. Scattered throughout the countryside are Romanesque churches, farmhouses, villas and castles. There are ancient hamlets, medieval villages, and large estates on top of the hillsides hidden by the trees. The landscape is rolling out before us like a magical carpet. Once again, I am on the back of a scooter with my arms wrapped around an Italian sculptor, the likes of *the David.*

"Rossana, do you see all the beauty? I live in *paradiso!*" He laughs from deep inside himself, full and hardy as he looks up into the sky. I am enjoying the ride, lost in the ecstasy of the wind upon my face, the sun in my eyes, and the feel of the sculpture that I am holding onto as we maneuver the turns in the road. He takes them with ease as if he and the bike are one with the road – as if he has driven it a thousand times before. I feel my body tingling with life, filled up like a glass of champagne with all of the bubbles trying to escape.

Valentino has turned onto a long tree-lined driveway which leads to a castle where the entire property, as far as the eye can see, is filled with vineyards and olive groves. There are gardens and grassy areas surrounding the building. There is a lily pond and there are two peacocks roaming the grounds - one with blue and green feathers and the other an albino. How strange, I think…peacocks in Italy… This is like a fairy tale or a dream and once again, I feel like a princess.

We dismount and walk through the side door into a large marble foyer with a winding staircase. There before me is a parlor or drawing room at the far end of the hall. The marble floors are covered with beautiful carpets as heavy draperies cover the windows.

"Do you like it? It is *grande,* eh Rossana?" An elderly man comes out of one of the doors in the large hallway and throws his arms around Valentino hugging and kissing him.

"*Mio nipote e bello! Si, si*! My beautiful grandson." He continues to hug him as they both speak their native tongue. Valentino introduces me to his grandfather, Dante Lorenzo. He says, "*Benvenuto, bella, bella!*" He is so happy to see us.

"My grandfather says welcome and that it is good to see you. He says you are very beautiful."

"*Grazie, grazie,*" I turn to him and smile. Valentino and Dante exchange a few more words and then his grandfather leaves us.

"He is leaving today for a long trip, a week. He is going to Roma, Firenze, Milano and Napoli on business – the vino, you know, but he wants us to stay and enjoy the house, so I will show you around."

I am being led from one room to another while Valentino tells me the stories of his childhood. There is the room he slept in and the enormous music room where there is a grand piano set in the center. He sits down to play an Italian tune for me and sings. Not only can he sculpt, but he is also a musician. Is everyone in Italy talented, I ask myself? Then, we walk out toward the olive groves.

"We make our own olive oil here, you see? One tree gives us one liter of *olio d'oliva.* We have to hand-pick the olives when they are young, not at the end of the season, because they will not be as fresh and not have as much oil. Then, we process them within twenty-four hours so we can call it *extra virgin.* The olives have a very different, very spicy taste in this region you know. I will make food for you later and I will show you the difference in the taste and the color."

I love his accent and think, I am on my own personal guided tour in Tuscany's Chianti region, and my guide is a beautiful, passionate sculptor whose family owns a castle and a vineyard. Did I just fall from the sky into an Italian dream? We have entered the vineyards and Valentino checks the grapes. He says he is making sure none are diseased and that they are growing perfectly.

"Rossana, do you see how perfect and how firm they are even though they are so very young? You see, the picking season is not until late September or early October."

"My grandfather taught me how to make perfect *vino* at a very young age. He said 'Lorenzo, you treat them as if they are your children. You come and talk sweetly to them every day. You touch them, caress them and love them. You sit and tell them stories before they go to sleep at night – stories about the *vino* they will make someday. You make sure they are not thirsty and that they have the love of the sun on their skin as they grow, just like babies. Then, when it is time, they will give you all of the love back that you have given to them. That is what makes *il migliore*, the best Chianti Classico. This is all you need to know, *mio nipote*.' My grandfather is the best winemaker in the region…"

"Valentino, have you ever thought of going into your family business? You know so much and have so much to give."

"And give up my art? Never! I have no time to give. *Morto*!" I see his brown eyes darken. Obviously, I have hit a nerve that has been poked at by his family.

Within seconds, the darkness is gone and he is walking through the rows of vines, talking to the leaves and the babies that are basking in the sunlight. He grabs my hand and pulls me back toward the castle.

"Come. I will take you to the wine cellars in the *castello*." Once inside, I feel the coolness of the air on my skin which is good since it is extremely hot in the vineyards with the intense Tuscan sun beating down upon us.

"Here we have only the best barrels in the world which we buy from France and America. You see?" He points out insignia carvings on the barrels and shows me the biancos – the whites, the Rosso Bianco which is a mixture of the Sangiovese grape and the Trebbiano white grape from the region. Then he takes me to the Chianti rooms where there are hundreds and hundreds of bottles of red table wines, Chiantis and the Chianti Classicos.

"Here, taste." He uncorks a dusty bottle of Chianti Classico and pours a glass for each of us. After swirling it in his glass, sniffing it and then sipping it slowly, he closes his eyes and moves his head back, "Ah, *la dolce vita, la dolce vino*."

"This is heavenly, Valentino. This is like no other wine I have ever tasted." I take another sip breathing it in as it moves into my mouth.

"The reason is my *famiglia.* They are the best." He says proudly, as he slaps his chest. "My grandfather, my father and my brothers love the grapes like I do. This is why it is the best. Come. We take this *vino* to the kitchen and make something to eat and enjoy it together. This way."

CHAPTER 25

I am now feeling a little intoxicated from the wine, or maybe it's my imagination since I have only tasted a half glass. Or maybe it's just because of where I am and who I am with. Why is it that when you are in Italy and you are with someone, you are with their ancestors as well? This is how I feel when I'm with Valentino as if we are somewhere else in time and the year is not 2006 but maybe 1406 instead.

He leads me out and up to the next level where we walk through two halls and two rooms before reaching the kitchen. The stove is *antico*, very old and very beautiful. There is a large wooden table off to one side where I imagine the servants used to eat hundreds of years ago.

"*Aspete*…I go into the garden for some fresh vegetables. Would you like *insalata*, bread and cheese?"

"That sounds good but can I help you?"

"No, no…sit...rest. It is hot – *molto caldo*. Enjoy the Chianti. I be right back." As I sit, I notice the stone floors and the leaded windows which run from the floor to the ceiling. There are pots and pans hanging over the stove and *ceramica* hanging from hooks on the stone wall…to live in a house as grand as this…a real castle.

I think back to the conversation in the vineyard and how Valentino had stiffened when I asked why he didn't go into the family business. I now understand how serious he is about his work as a sculptor. It isn't about selling his pieces, but about putting his heart and soul into whatever he is doing every day. I can see why people think artists are crazy. It's because they do it for the love of it even if sometimes there is no money to be made. Most well renowned painters and sculptors have to die before they are worth anything.

We dine on the *terrazzo* on fresh greens from the garden, fresh cheeses, olives, and homemade bread, topped off with the olive oil and a bottle of Chianti Classico…a delicious meal. "Now, can you smell the *olio* d'*oliva*? Does it not smell like fresh olives, *si*?" I am amazed at the scent of it. All this food I have been fed – like tasting perfume off of someone's body. I close my eyes and breathe it in. He drips some oil on a plate and breaks off a piece of bread for me.

"*Ora* - now, taste this."

As I bite into it, the oil drips down my chin. "Mmmm…this is wonderful." Valentino takes his finger and wipes it from my lower lip and chin and I blush. I should be used to this by now…Italian men waiting on me, feeding me, wiping my face, kissing me…

"You know, Rosanna, you are very beautiful. Your eyes are very different than anyone else's in Firenze and your skin…it is *porcellana*." I move my face away from his and looked downward, embarrassed.

"No, look at me," he says this so intensely that I am startled. He reaches for my chin and pulls me toward him studying my face all the while. "Look…your cheekbones"…he runs his fingers along my face. "Your nose, it is so different, and look, here…" He touches that place beneath my nose that connects to my lips. "This place is so well defined. These are the places I love most to create. Your lips are *bella*."

I sit patiently, trusting him, but at the same time, not feeling comfortable with this intimacy. He runs his fingers down my throat to the collar bone… "here…" He takes my hand in his and studies it, then traces the outline from my fingers all the way up past my wrist. "So delicate…so perfect. Give me your foot."

"Valentino…"

"Please, I have to see it." He kneels on the floor in front of me and before I can protest further, removes my sandal. His face is so close that I think he will kiss it; but instead, he uses his fingers to outline every inch of it - my toes, the top, the bottom, my arch, and my ankle. Then he pulls my leg out in front of him so it is inches away from his face. He extends it to the side to get a better view, and I sit quietly, speechless…I feel as if I am under a looking glass.

"Ah, *belissima*. You have the most beautiful legs." He moves his fingers and then his hands up my legs until he reaches my skirt - then my thigh; all the while, I am watching the look in his eyes. I can tell he is starting to become aroused.

"Stop! Valentino!" I grab his hands and push him away. "No, please."

"But Rossana, you are so beautiful. I want to feel you – touch you – make love to you. I will be gentle, I promise." Standing now, I walk quickly to the end of the *terrazzo*.

"I am not interested in making love to you. Take me back to the hotel now." He stops, realizing I am not amused.

"I am sorry, but I was lost for a moment. I want to feel you so I can sculpt you. May I, please?" He starts to walk toward me now, reaching out to me.

"Valentino, I have someone who is very special to me and I don't want to be with anyone else right now. Do you know what that feels like? My heart is elsewhere."

"Oh, *bella*. I am sorry. *Capisco.*" He gently embraces me now. "I am so sorry. Please forgive me. Sometimes I can't think of anything else except how you will look in marble." He hugs me and rubs my back while removing the hair that is now in my face.

"Thank you, Valentino, for respecting my wishes." He kisses my forehead.

"Rossana, I would like to sculpt you – may I?"

"What does that mean? Do I have to pose naked," I ask nervously?

"*Si.* That would be good."

"I can't do that, Valentino." I know it would be too dangerous with his passionate nature and the fact that he is a man – an Italian one no less.

"Rossana, the naked body of a woman is a beautiful thing! It is okay."

"No. I cannot and will not pose for you naked so I guess you will have to find someone else to sculpt."

"But there is no one like you." After a few moments of pacing, he relents. "Okay. You keep your clothes on and I will do your face, your arms, your wrists, your legs and feet…and the rest, well I will have to find someone else… but it won't truly be you, Rossana."

I start to giggle - partly from the wine and partly because I feel like I am negotiating for my clothing. At this, his intensity shifts and he starts laughing, too. His eyes are suddenly smiling and I know then that I can trust him. Now, the air around us has softened.

"Oh well. It is of no importance to me then, but think about it." So we sit at the table finishing our meal and our wine and we talk easily. "Tell me about him, Rossana." He is fingering the rim of his glass like he fingers everything, giving away the fact that he is a sculptor.

"I met Natale in Rome. I left him to travel; but I am confused about him. I think I'm in love with him…but I have to be sure before I go back." I move my eyes to the hills and the olive groves as I remember his touches. I also don't want to look Valentino in the eye.

"You have the look of love; I know it well. Unfortunately, I cannot hold onto a woman. They are all jealous of my work, because I never give them enough time. They always want more of me. When I go into my studio and do not come out to call them or be with them, they get angry. You know Italian women are very jealous. What they don't know is sometimes I take my marble slabs as my lover even sleeping with them. I love to feel their coolness on my skin." He laughs at himself but

I can tell he is unsettled about this, too. He is very passionate about everything - the way he fingers the rim of his glass, or smells each sip before it reaches his lips, the way he eats his food, breathing it in with each bite.

"Come, I will show you my studio." I am happy for the break from this talk. We walk down the stone stairway and through the gardens to the back of the property where his studio is. Once inside, the room is as big as my small villa on Capri. The ceilings are two stories high and there is light coming in from a windowed wall. There are blocks of marble everywhere, many half finished and there are sketches lying about as if he were a madman trying to perfect a vision. A long bench holds a half built armature and a few clay models of male figures. Marble dust covers the entire floor…

"My room…" His eyes glaze over. "This is the place I love most in this world." By the way his eyes light up, I can feel the presence of his heritage and all those who have sculpted here before him emanating from his soul.

"Let me show you how it feels to have marble touch you." He walks me over to a four foot high block sitting on a stone table. "Here." He places a tool, a chisel of sorts in one of my hands and a hammer in the other. Then, he stands behind me. "Hold it like this." He takes both of my hands in his, guiding them around the tool. Slowly, he starts to whittle away at the hard stone. I can feel him breathing hard as he presses up against me - not because of me, but because of the marble he is starting to merge with as if he were making love.

I can feel his passion rise up inside him and take hold of him like a wild steed in the wind. I know what it's like to feel this kind of pleasure, for I, too can feel it between my fingers. Fifteen minutes pass, then thirty before he stops, never speaking all the while…only chiseling away. I now see the arm we are working on beginning to take form. I think of young Michelangelo carving the face of the fawn and the intensity in his eyes. It is the same look Valentino now has when I turn to face him, as if he is possessed by the marble.

"I see what you mean. It's almost a sacred thing to be able to cut something so incredibly hard and strong and create form." He doesn't say a word but quickly finds his sketch paper and pencil. He moves me to the chaise at the far end of the room and sets me down. He is silent as he starts to study me and sketch my face. He is sitting close enough that every few minutes he rearranges my position so he can see me from every angle. He studies my nose and my lips, and then touches them. It seems he needs to feel them to draw them as if he were a blind man. I sit for an hour before I can take it no longer.

"Valentino, I have to use the bathroom and I am stiff from sitting here."

"Go. I will show you." I follow him to the back of the house where I use the bathroom and stretch my back and when I come out, his mood seems lighter and he is less intense.

"It is 18:00 now; should we head back to Florence?" I know he would be happy to do this all night, but I cannot. He takes my hands.

"Can I not change your mind about making love?" He brings my hands together up to his face, pressing them to his lips. I think to myself, my hands have been kissed more on this trip than any other part of my anatomy since I have been on Italian soil.

"No, I'm afraid not, Valentino. You have been a true gentleman and I will never forget this day."

"Rossana, I will take you to your hotel now if you will promise me your company to the *museo* tomorrow and then I want to continue sketching you. Please? I would be honored."

"Of course..."

"I will show you the sketches when I am done with all of them, yes?"

We leave and reach Florence at that magical hour when the light of the sun changes the color of the *Arno Fiume* to an emerald green color. Before retiring, I sit in my window day dreaming that I am in the 15th century and a great sculptor is sculpting my likeness in marble.

The Great Spirit comes to me in my dreams this night, and instead of walking with me along the cliffs of Capri, this time, we are in the Boboli Gardens at the *Pitti Palazzo* in Florence.

"Are you enjoying yourself, Roxanna?" He is laughing as I nod yes. "Good! This is why you are here. This Valentino has the blood of Ghiberti inside him. They are one and the same, you know. He is not of this world, but a gift from the gods for a very short time here. You would honor him by allowing him to sculpt you – all of you. And you will truly honor yourself, as you were a great lover of Ghiberti's when he was alive. Human flesh is nothing but an overcoat for the soul where the real beauty lies. He is feeling your soul, not your flesh."

"The flesh is only a covering that protects us from the winds of time. It is only flesh and blood, Roxanna. Be naked and be free and drop the puritan attitude that you have lived with from your homeland. You are in Italy now and everyone wants to paint and sculpt! Go for it! Live life!

Love! Let your form be created to last through eternity! Go down in history with him this time when he passes from this earth!"

Within the blink of an eye, he is gone and I am left alone in my bed, wide awake and it is four a.m. I forget how crazy it must seem that I have just been talking with someone from the spirit world and instead start ruminating about my nakedness. Being naked with a man other than someone you are about to make love to is something that I have never thought of doing. It just doesn't seem right.

My head swims trying to figure it all out and I finally drift back to sleep with these last thoughts, *"Human flesh is nothing but an overcoat for the soul where the real beauty lies. He is feeling your soul, not your flesh. The flesh is only a covering that protects us from the winds of time…It is only flesh and blood, Roxanna…"*

Another hot, steamy day in Firenze, the "City of the Masters…" The weather here is relentless and all throughout Europe for that matter. It is all over the news and everyone everywhere is whispering, *"molto caldo"*…too hot…But I have grown used to it now, just as the Italians have.

Valentino is waiting for me at the *Museo Nazionale del Bargello*, to view of course, sculptures. This is where he wants to take me – his special place where he comes to study the art and also to think. On the ground floor, we visit the Room of Michelangelo and his 16th century sculptures: *Brutus* and *Apollo* which is one of his biggest achievements, a work that was commissioned by Cosimo de' Medici. Then there is *Bacchus,* his first large scale free-standing sculpture.

This room contains not only Michelangelo's works, but also those of Sansovino, the *Bacchus*, Bandinelli's *Bust of Cosimo I*, numerous pieces by Cellini including his famous *Bust of Cosimo I*, and *Hermes* by Giambologna. Valentino walks through each room as if he is seeing them for the first time but I know he has been here a thousand times before because he said so.

We move through the Room of Medieval Sculptures and then into the Room of Donatello where we find Luca della Robbia's *Madonna and Child with Two Angels*, and *Madonna of the Rose-Garden.*

Valentino stops before two panels, one by Brunelleschi and the other by Ghiberti, and here he whispers with reverence, "This, he created for the competition for the Baptistery in 1401. It is called the *Sacrifice of Isaac.* Look at it. Look at the detail." Valentino smiles and outlines the relief in the air, as he cannot touch it. He outlines it with his eyes closed, too, for he has done it a thousand times before. Maybe the Great Spirit was correct when he said that he was the reincarnation of Ghiberti. After all, he knows this piece as if he had created it himself. "From this, he was awarded the pane work on the Baptistery - the *Gate of Paradise.*" He is blessing himself now, the sign of the cross.

I can see the love, honor and respect in his eyes for Ghiberti, so we linger until he is ready. As we walk the *Piazza Santa Croce*, we talk about all that we have seen. Valentino tells me about the differences in styles between all of the sculptors, and how Michelangelo was the best in his opinion, because his bodies were so anatomically correct, as if he had studied them long and hard. He speaks about Sansovino's *Bacchus* and how it stands up to the works of Michelangelo and that it is so detailed and also anatomically correct – just like the David.

We walk through the *Piazza Signoria* and are standing in front of the Fountain of Neptune, admiring it. "I have decided that I will pose nude for you for your statue." There – I have gotten the words out.

"Oh, Rossana, I am so happy. Thank you, *grazie, grazie.*" He kisses my hands and bows down before me. "You will be so happy! And so will I!" He starts to dance around the fountain.

I giggle and say, "Well, I am still a little nervous about taking my clothes off in front of you…you have to know it's not natural for me…after all, I am *Americano*!" I lower my eyes and do not look at him for fear that he might truly see the depth of my feelings.

"Rossana, you are a sacred thing of beauty to me, I will honor you and respect you. I promise you this."

"But why me, Valentino? I have seen the women of Florence on the street and how beautiful each of them is. They are far more beautiful and far younger than I. Why me?" I am curious – always curious that the young men in Italy find me attractive when I am decades older than them. It seems that there is no age in Italy. He is deep in thought for a few moments before answering and then comes to me and embraces me.

"I don't know, Rossana. My soul wants to feel your soul and to place it into marble for all eternity to see. In my eyes, you are more beautiful than the rest." I have no response. He embraces me and I rub his back as he does so.

CHAPTER 26

So once again, I travel to the castle. I see the sign on its façade, *Castello di Querceto*, and feel as if I have come home. Although I don't know Valentino very well, I feel safe and comfortable with him as if he is my protector. I trust that if I say no to him, he will relent as he did yesterday. So I have no trepidations about being here with him – except being nude… Why am I so self-conscious about this? I feel my heart fluttering with anxiety at the thought of it and wonder if he will help calm my nerves before I have to disrobe.

"Tonight, I will start with your face, but I need you to remove your clothing and lay on the chaise in the same pose I will carve you in. For now, I will give you a robe so you can drape it over yourself until you feel more comfortable." He hands me a crimson robe which I guess is his, for it smells like him. I like this fact; as it soothes me… so familiar…

After I sit, he piles my hair high on my head letting some of the curls fall loosely. Then, he moves me about until I am sitting in the correct position, as if he has done it before. One hand drapes lazily over my hip, the other rests on a pillow on top of the chaise while my head rests upon my arm.

I giggle…always giggling these days, "I feel like Canova's *Paolina Borghese*."

"Yes, this is my intention, but you will not have the fabric covering those beautiful legs." Now, look in the direction of your feet but look up. I want to see the curve of your neck. That's right…*si, si*." He is lost in thought, now the intense sculptor.

"Think of something beautiful, Rossana. Think of the sea or of the mountains. Think of the vineyards and how they smell at night. Think of a bouquet of beautiful flowers...or think of your Natale…"

This does it for me. I am now far away from here, lost in thoughts and feelings that have been evoked just by hearing his name.

"Yes…that is the look. You have captured it, now don't move your face…hold it…Ah!" He is like a madman obsessed, working so quickly. Every few moments, he completes a drawing and starts another, tossing the finished sheet over his head into a pile on the floor behind him. He comes over to me in between each one to touch my nose, my lips, the curve of my face. It's as if he has to feel me, merge with me to capture my likeness on paper.

Tonight, he finishes my head, my face, and all of the features on it. Then he starts on the outline of my body. He sees that I am starting to fidget, nervous that I might have to remove the robe and he becomes impatient.

"We are finished tonight. Tomorrow, we will capture the outline of your form. *Capisce?*" His voice is loud and firm, almost not his own and I know he is tired.

"*Capisco.* I will be ready tomorrow." I am happy that it is not tonight.

"Rossana, will you stay tonight?" His voice has softened and he is a bit more relaxed now. "I can begin in the morning when the light is the best. I fix you a room and you be safe here. Please stay tonight."

I think about my things, my toothbrush, staying in the same place with Valentino…would I truly be safe? I have to go back to Capri soon, I think…random thought…

"Yes, I'll stay. But I don't have a toothbrush."

"Is okay. I have two." He smiles tiredly. "Come. I will show you where you will sleep." We move to the second floor where he opens the door to a large bedroom with high ceilings which is fully decorated with lace curtains and a canopy bed. Obviously it is a woman's room.

"Whose room is this?"

"It is my sister's when she is here. Now, you can stay tonight and be very comfortable. Do you need something before you sleep? Food?"

"No, just sleepy…I am happy to be staying instead of the long ride back. It's almost midnight." He pulls me to him and holds me tightly. Then he kisses my cheeks and my hands…always the hands…

"Rossana, I don't know what it is about you that I have to have…this sculpture – this…I don't know." He seems puzzled, confused. "Thank you for the wonderful gift you are giving me, Rossana. You are a sweet angel to me. I will never forget this, and you will be pleased. *Buonanotte, e dolce sogni-* good night and sweet dreams…"

"Sweet dreams to you too, Valentino. Good night." Before I get into bed, I fill the bathtub and am just stepping into it when I hear a knock.

"Rossana, your toothbrush. I will leave it on the table near the door. If you need anything, I will be in my studio." He politely steps out without looking toward the bathroom.

After calling out thank you, I sink into the tub, too tired to think of anything except the water. The thought of Valentino's mood changing when he sketches so intensely crosses my mind, but I am not uncomfortable by it; as a matter of fact, I feel safe - as if he is someone else at these times when he is obsessively working.

I dream that I am lying on the chaise being sketched by Valentino, and as he comes closer to me, his face changes; and at that very moment, he tells me he loves me. In the dream, he is bending down over me, kissing me and I do not protest. As a matter of fact, I feel familiar feelings in my heart, as if I too love him. Before I awaken from this dream, he tells me he will "finish it this time." A knock on the door arouses me from my sleep and this strange dream…

"Rossana, are you awake? It is early I know, but the light, the light. It is perfect. Can you come please?"

"Valentino, give me a few minutes. Do you have *espresso*?" I didn't realize how intense this would be.

"*Si.* Come." I quickly dress and go to his studio where he is already deep in thought, head hung over a sketch. "There." He points to the stone table that holds the slab of marble, without even looking up. There is a cup of *espresso* ready for me with sugar. Mmmmm…I drink standing up as I look over his shoulder admiring his work.

"You have captured me for sure. My nose…I never realized it was that big before and I've never seen it quite from that angle."

"We never really see ourselves, Rossana. Now, I make a few changes, but we have accomplished much. Sit." He is already in that mode, so I try for the same pose as yesterday while he adjusts me a bit and fixes my hair.

"You *bella*, no make-up. I like you this way." Although he is talking about my skin, I feel completely naked - every blemish and imperfection showing, but I have no choice except to be who I am in this moment…unprepared and without the aid of powder or lipstick.

I am bare-skinned underneath this robe and I feel its coolness as I wonder what I truly look like through his eyes. I am fifty and he is possibly late thirties? He is a beautiful young man with half his hair pulled up in a pony tail today; and in his world here in Florence, he is surrounded by gorgeous Italian women with dark skin and flowing thick hair, curls falling everywhere. This is the land of Italian goddesses and he has chosen me to sculpt – he finds beauty in me – Roxanna. The thought brings shivers to my body and I move a bit.

"Be still!" Valentino is on a mission and is now that other person. He walks over to me and removes the robe, pulling it from me roughly with no warning. Now I am horrified, completely naked. He doesn't look at me, only turns his back to me and walks back to his paper. After a few minutes, I relax against the back of the chaise. This isn't so bad, I think. He has barely noticed that my body is bare…

And as I lay here, sensations of sunbathing topless in Capri come back to me. I close my eyes and imagine the wind on my breasts and my nipples, and I feel free. For almost two hours, I stay in this pose, the thoughts of the wind and the sea washing over me – keeping me company.

I am almost in a meditative state now, flowing with each of his movements on paper and I can almost feel the strokes of the pencil upon my skin, as if he is drawing on my body…every line, as if they were his fingertips. I can feel him even when my eyes are closed – how odd. We - he and I - are a part of each other somehow. I sense this great love and admiration from him, the artist, not knowing why, but I still feel it deeply.

He comes to me and with his fingers, starts to draw upon my skin. From my neck and then down over the curve of my shoulder, running his finger the length of my arm to the curvature of my wrist…he then moves it to the space between my underarm and to that area where my torso and hip are connected. I shiver, not knowing what to expect next. As I hold my breath, he runs his fingertips ever so lightly around the underside of my left breast and then up to its nipple.

"You are so beautiful, Rossana…your skin, your breasts, your legs, your face. You will go down in history with me." I am still holding my breath when he places his lips ever so gently upon mine and kisses me. He gathers me up in his arms and holds me to him as if I am a doll, and I can feel his breath in my hair. His face is buried in my neck but I can feel him weeping. I try to comfort him, yet I know not why. I only know it is the right thing to do – the natural thing to do - so I do it by wrapping my arms around him and holding him. Has he changed again? Is he Valentino or Ghiberti? We stay this way for quite some time. When he finally pulls away from me, I grab the robe and hold it tightly to my breasts to cover myself, as if he is a stranger.

"I am sorry, Rossana. I don't know what happened to me. Please forgive me." He moves away, retreating back to his papers.

"Valentino, I need to stretch and take a break, please?"

"*Si, si*…how thoughtless of me…go." He is a different person now; how strange this whole experience. One minute, he is the beautiful Valentino, the next he is this intense artist, sculptor who is so focused.

Then, he becomes this other being who has such deep love for me. My head is swimming as I walk out onto the lower *terrazzo* and look out over the vineyards.

Valentino has come out and is standing behind me now. He pulls me close and holds me there, wrapping his arms around me.

"I am sorry for kissing you, Rossana. I promised you I would respect you and I have…I mean I do. I don't know what came over me."

"I understand, Valentino," for I do. "You lose yourself in your work and sometimes don't know who you are. I understand."

"Thank you. Would you like something to eat? I make you something…come." We move to the kitchen where he makes eggs, juice, and fried bread with jam.

"You're good in the kitchen. Have you always cooked?"

He laughs. "Out of necessity…because women don't love me." He smiles as if he is joking. "I have learned to take care of myself." We eat and go back to the studio until early afternoon then he takes me back to Florence to my hotel. It has been days since we started this project, but it is all good and I wouldn't have missed this for anything.

I check out of the hotel and he takes me to *Castello di Querceto* where I will sleep for the next few nights. He has made much progress and feels confident that he can finish without me present.

He has chosen a beautiful white marble because of its slight surface translucency that is comparable to that of human skin; and this translucency gives a sculpture visual depth beyond its surface, evoking a certain realism when used for figurative works. He tells me that this marble is relatively soft and easy to work with. It is refined, and polished, and it proves itself as he quickly chisels it with his tools.

I look over the drawings that are strewn all over the studio floor. "These are very good, Valentino, *molto bene*." I am lost in thought as I see myself on paper. How odd it is to see your self like this…this face, is it mine? This shape…is this really how my body looks? I have aged, I realize as I look at my image, always feeling as if I am thirty years younger than I appear before a mirror. I am all of my fifty years, yes; but now I finally see my beauty. My breasts hang lower than I remember, softened by the birth of my sons and the years. They no longer point toward the horizon but instead point downward; but they are beautiful none the less. And, although I am no longer muscular and lean, the years look well on me. My stomach is slightly rounded but my waist accentuates my feminine shape. "So this is Roxanna…" I say out loud.

"You are a beautiful woman, Rossana and you are far more beautiful than Paolina. Wait when I finish. You will see."

"I love that you see my beauty. It has been a great gift to me. Thank you." I reach up and kiss his neck and he embraces me.

"Please have dinner with me tonight in Firenze before you leave? I have been so busy with my work that I have not treated you well. I want to make it up to you, *mio amore*."

"Yes, I would love to have dinner with you one last time."

When afternoon comes, I nap and dream of Ghiberti. I see him in his studio working on a marble relief, his tools in his hands. He stands over it half stooped with an intense look on his face, the same look I have seen in Valentino when he is engrossed in his work. In the dream, I am standing watching him as he works and I can feel my heart swell. I have a deep love for him that goes beyond anything I have ever felt before and at this moment, I realize I have been with him before – I am his lover.

It also comes to me in this dream as if it is part of my memories - the days I spent with him in that lifetime, that his first love was always his work and I was always left alone, loving him from afar. He never looked up, never acknowledged me in the dream. This was a feeling I always carried with me in that lifetime – that he never acknowledged me, even when I was in the room.

When I awaken, I contemplate it and know it is a past life dream remembering what the Great Spirit said to me. The answer comes to me then. The spirit of Ghiberti has returned from the year of 1393 when he was forty-five years old, to finish what he had promised me he would do. He never completed the sculpture of me - the only woman he had ever really loved, because of his other commitments. When the panels came along, the *Porta del Paradiso*, it took thirty years of his life, so he never gave me the gift he promised – the gift of his heart in marble. I died before him, at the age of sixty-seven, ten years before he left this earth. And for those ten years, his broken heart suffered so. He continually punished himself, never forgiving himself for breaking his promise to me. I was the only one he loved in that lifetime - except his art that possessed him.

I sit in my room for awhile digesting it all. I'm sure Valentino has no idea the part he has played in all of this. Or does he? Nothing is as it seems, I think. Now I'm very happy I have posed for him, for I have given something of my heart and my self back to Ghiberti.

At dinner we talk about him. "Valentino, do you know anything about his life? Was he ever married?"

"Ah, no…he is like me. He was married to his work…could not keep any woman… He was in love once they say, and she was the only one that had his heart. I understand she died before him, and he mourned her death for the rest of his days. He was never the same…feeling guilty probably…like me." His eyes grow dark as if he is remembering himself, so I quickly change the subject.

"I am so happy with the work you have done."

"I couldn't have done it without you, *bella*." His eyes brighten. "I am so pleased with how far we have come. I wish you could stay longer and see it to completion, Rossana."

"I would love to, but I too, have work to do. I haven't done anything since I arrived over a week ago; but I'm so happy we had a chance to spend time together. You are truly a gentleman, Valentino, and I will never forget you." He reaches for my hand but says nothing, lost in the gratitude. He runs his fingers along the tops of them, tracing the veins and the tiny scar on my wrist. Then he turns both over and fingers each line.

"These are hands of beauty, *bella*. These are hands filled with life lived and with much love." Then he reaches for my face, rubbing it with the palm of his hand. "*Porcellana…bella…*you have the eyes of the sea, the *Mediterraneo*. They change color like it does, for you belong to it – there is no one else with these eyes on this earth, so yes, you are a goddess." He kisses both of my hands so sweetly then lifts them to his face so he can feel them upon his cheeks. He is now the Valentino I met a few days before.

We share *espresso* and *dolci* – sweet desserts, before leaving the restaurant for my last night at the castle.

When we arrive, he walks me up the staircase and down the long hallway to my room; and as I turn to embrace him and thank him, he grabs me and kisses me hard on the lips while pulling me into him. His hands are everywhere rubbing my hair, my face, my back, breathing me in all the while. He intertwines his fingers with mine and with that knot that is holding them together, he pulls me into him as if he wants to merge with me. I can feel every inch of him – his abs against my stomach, his chest against mine, his thigh pressing into me…but mostly his heart reaching out to mine.

I relent for only a moment for it seems the right thing to do. I allow him to move into me – not physically – but as if skin and bone does not separate us. We become one in this moment, standing here outside my door.

"*Mio bella* Rossana, my angel…I want to make love to you; I love you, *mio amore*." I hold him closer to me, as if I could get any closer, before I respond.

"Sweet Valentino, I would love to, but my heart says no…I am in love with…" He finishes…

"Yes, Natale…" He is holding me even tighter now and then he pulls away. "I understand your heart when it speaks. I will never forget you, Rossana. I will write you and let you know when I have completed you. Maybe you can come back to see it?

Ti amo, arrivederci."

The next day as we ride to the train station in Florence, I hold on to him tightly – not to feel him beneath my hands or because I am afraid of the turns in the road; but because I feel love for him and know it might be the last time I ever see him again.

After our good byes, he turns and leaves me at the station, as if he had never come – a ghost in time. He blew into my life with such intimate force and left just as quickly. And now, it's as if it was a dream…

CHAPTER 27

As the train moves through the poppy fields in the countryside, I review all that has happened in the last week - the art, the sculptures, Valentino, the spirit of Ghiberti, the castle, the words the Great Spirit spoke. It is but a memory now, as if it had never happened, but I can feel the imprint it has left upon my soul. It has to be true, for I know it to be – all of it.

I think about my time in Tuscany and about the differences between the north and the south of Italy and how endearing the people are. The food, the wine, the way they interact with each other…I have enjoyed *Toscano* so much, but miss the *Napolitani* and the Sicilians that always speak so passionately and so expressively with their hands. I miss the way their language rolls off of their tongues like honey.

I feel more beautiful in the south – if that's possible after being sculpted by the gorgeous Valentino - Is it the sun and the water on my skin… the way it changes the color of my eyes? I feel as if I have risen from the sea, been birthed from there…that I am somehow invincible. It's as if I've been transformed by the Sea God Neptune himself –as if I am Cinderella of the Sea…I smile at my fairytale notions.

As I depart from the taxi at the port in Napoli, the hot, moist air hits me like a warm, wet blanket that has been wrapped around me and I think of my Italian grandmother and Lemoncello and this silly thought makes me smile. I have come home.

I can smell the humidity, feel it on my arms. Some might think it unpleasant; but not me, child of the sea and of the rock in the middle of the Mediterranean. I am the Sea Goddess, Roxanna, who has come back to her own Mount Olympus.

Standing on the boat as the sea rocks beneath me, I feel as if I am being held in the arms of my mother, loved like never before; and as the memories of the past week fade away, so does the shore of Napoli and Mount Vesuvio which are now on the horizon in the distance.

I'm going home to my village and to my people. They are the life I love more than anything right now, as if I have been transformed into someone else, no longer having the same wants and desires as the old

Deborah Allen of America. Where will the Great Spirit guide me to next? I hope it won't be too soon, for I want to bask in the sun of the island and swim in *Marina Piccola* and the *Grotto Azzurra*, have dinner at Ciero's family restaurant - *Il Saraceno Ristorante*. Ciero always has a warm smile for me and the last time I was there, he brought out his new batch of lemon peels soaking in alcohol and explained to me how he made his own Lemoncello – a slightly different recipe than Antonio's grandmother.

I want to see Enrico's sweet face and his smile, watch him as he prunes his garden, so peacefully and happily. I make a note to have dinner with Mario, his wife, Donatella, Marcello and baby Luca. They had taken me in as one of their own. I am so happy with these delicious memories that I cannot stop smiling the entire boat trip. I want to dance and clap my hands and tell everyone that I am going home to Capri, but stay quiet instead.

"*Ciao*, Roxanna! *Ciao, ciao!*"

"Mario! *Ciao! Grazie* for meeting me!"

"*No problema.*" He welcomes me with open arms, kisses me and carries my bag. Then he drives me up the mountain, back to the village of AnaCapri where he parks in a lot on the outside of town. From there, we walk to the villa, he pulling my back pack behind him. There is some conversation between us, as he speaks Italian and I answer with a lot of "*sis*"..."*capiscos?*" "*no capiscos*"…

It is 40o C today - 104o F and his wife has come to greet us. She has baby Luca with her and he is running her in circles.

"*Ciao, Lousia..como va?*"

"*Bene, Bene*, Rossana. You trip nice?" Her English is slightly better than Mario's, but not by much.

"*Si, molto bene, divertimento*"…she knows what I am trying to say and she smiles.

"*Bene, bene…*" I wipe away the moisture that has accumulated on my skin and she sees this.

"*Aspete…aspete…*wait, wait." She is walking toward the gate where on the other side of the property, she and Mario live. Moments later, she returns with two cool cotton shifts, dresses like she wears and hands them to me. "*Regalo…*you." A gift. I am honored that she has thought of me.

"*Grazie, grazie.*" I kiss her and hug her warmly…so giving, so hospitable. I have fallen in love with them – my family. And I remember that besides them, the entire island of Capri is like this. They say that once you come here, you are intoxicated, bewitched and you never want to leave. People that have never come, think you are either hypnotized by the sirens or have gone mad and should stay here locked away from the rest of the world. So be it! I am insane with love on Capri and will stay here forever!

I sit with Louisa while Mario wanders off through the gardens only to return with baskets of vegetables for my kitchen.

"*Per tu.*" He places them on my outside table and says, "*Sera*...Louisa..." He is calling her to come with him and take their leave so I might be alone. I kiss Luca and make him giggle and then kiss the two of them. It's nice to be here wrapped up in the arms of my island.

After they leave, I walk from flower to flower, from bush to bush and from tree to tree, talking to them all, saying hello and checking on them like a mother who has been gone and has just returned. I think of Valentino and his grapes and smile as I squeeze one tenderly. This is my vineyard here along these cliffs and I wonder what I will be birthing in this place...

CHAPTER 28

LE REGIONI DI BASILICATA E COMPAGNI

Days pass and I busily visit everyone I know on the island for I have missed them. I want to make sure I see all of them - kiss them and laugh with them. And I do. And at night, I stay at *Mio Paradiso* and enjoy my serenity. I have missed being on this spot when the sun says good night to the day.

"Roxanna, *journo*."

"*Journo*, Mario." He has stopped by and is asking me something intently and I am trying to understand all of the words. I understand *domani… basilica….* Sorrento… *amico*, Giuseppe…and he points to himself. He is asking me to accompany him and his friend Giuseppe to a *basilica* in the south of Sorrento tomorrow. See, I tell myself…I am getting pretty good at understanding the language. I even understand the time when he tells me he will pick me up at 6:00 to go to the port.

"*Grazie*, Mario, *ciao, ciao...domani.*" I wave good-bye to him thinking I finally understand and am fluent in Italian. Am I in for a surprise…

The next morning, we walk the mile to the outskirts of town where we meet Giuseppe waiting in his automobile. He is a very tall man, a big man with thick curly hair and sparkling eyes as if knows a secret but can't tell even though he wants to. He talks like he belongs in the movie the "Godfather," so I imagine he is Sicilian, although he tells me he is Napolitano. We drive to the town of Capri for a quick shot of *espresso* and I belly up to the bar with them and drink it like a local. Then we drive to the port, Marina Grande for the boat which will take the car and us over to Sorrento.

Once on the mainland, I listen to them talking in Italian for hours, laughing like old friends; all the while, I hear a lot of *"capisce?" "No. No capisco"*….which means they don't understand each other very well sometimes. This Italian is such a strange language. When you move from one region to the next, the dialect is different, the pronunciation is different, and sometimes they don't understand each other at all. With their thick accents, their passion and the way they talk with their hands, I can't help but laugh and get caught up in this scene taking place in the front seat.

It's about 105o today in the south of Italy and everyone is sweating profusely. Mario turns around every fifteen minutes or so and says, "Roxanna…*molto caldo*" as he smiles and wipes the beads of sweat from his brow with a damp, white handkerchief. The traffic is so heavy, it seems to take forever to get there; but I am enjoying watching all of the families and couples in their cars driving with their windows open since they don't have air conditioning, all the while, listening to their Italian music.

The countryside is beautiful reminding me of Tuscany at times. There are rolling hills with trees here and there dotting the horizon. Sometimes I see little hamlets or a castle, and there are many vineyards as well. Mario says they make *bene vino bianco*, good white wines in this, the Compania region in the south. It is all so beautiful and so close to the sea.

After four hours, we arrive in Padula and drive to the *Chartreuse* of *Padula* - the *Monastary of San Lorenzo* which stands beneath the Appenine Mountains and the little city of Montesano which rests high above Padula on the side of a mountain. After Florence, Pisa, Rome, Venice and every other gorgeous city I have visited, I think it will be just another church - that it will not live up to all that I have seen so far; but I am so wrong.

Have you ever been a lover of books, walked into a bookstore, and had so many to choose from that you were dumb founded, not knowing which one to take because you loved them all? Then, one falls off the shelf and hits you, so you pick it up and try to read it, but never really see the words that are written there. It's all a blur - except for the fact that you need this book, have to have it – You can't release it back to where it came from – you have to own it, take it home and sleep with it.

Not until you get it home do you realize that you have a secret gift that was only meant for you. It isn't so much the book itself, but it's the way it makes you feel when you hold it in your hands. Your eyes are glazed over and you cannot see what you are looking at, but you can feel the contents with your heart as if it – your heart has fingers, moving across the pages like reading Braille and they pluck a cord in you that you never knew existed.

This is how I feel as I walk through the gate of the monastery. Everything is in Italian so I have no idea what I am looking at except that it is a very old and beautiful monastery. I don't even know the name of it at first. All I feel are the stringlets of my heart being plucked like a fine musical instrument as it stirs when I walk through the outer courtyard, into the church, from one room to another, through the great cloister, out into the park and through the cemetery. I only know how I feel. San Michele is here, and I can feel him whispering to me everywhere I step. I want to stay here for the night, ask for a room…I want to sit and meditate, to pray to all those who have been here before me, loving God and San Michele as I do. But I know I cannot. I know I have to go back with Mario and Giuseppe. So I hide my face and my tears of deep love and walk quietly behind them.

It is only later when my heart settles that I learn the history of the place. It was founded in 1306 by Tommaso Sandeverino, Count of Marsico and given over to the Carthusian order of monks, which was established by San Bruno in 1084. Throughout its history, the church of San Lorenzo was also given to the order and eventually the inner cloister was rebuilt and enlarged becoming the *Great Cloister*.

It is said that the *divino* Michelangelo – as they call him in this part of Italy - authored the *Fountain of the Dolphins*, a precious ivory crucifix, and also the *Great Cloister;* although it has never been proven except for the sketches of these things that were amongst his possessions when he died. Its bronze panels represent scenes from the *Passion of the Christ.* They say that of all the monasteries of the Carthusian order, this is the most beautiful one, and I believe it to be so because I am standing here inside it.

I am reminded of the Italians and their stone work as I walk through the outer courtyard, the cloister and the gardens. As I move through the Prior's Apartment and all its rooms, I come upon the Chapel of Archangel Michael, the patron of Padula. It takes my breath away and once again, my eyes and heart are filled for I can feel him surrounding me. His presence is everywhere and I can feel his love, truth, protection, and compassion. How can he be in so many places at once I wonder, and who is he?

I stay as long as I can, trying to be silent as if I too am a monk; but soon it is time to leave. We drive up to Montesano half way up the mountain and visit yet another great cathedral, the Cathedral di Sant'Anna – Saint Anne. It's not a large church, but it has spires that seem to climb up to the sky. It is Byzantine in structure with three great arches on the front façade and sculpted walls. I realize how incredibly beautiful the churches are here in the south, and the sacredness of each of

them. Then I feel as if I am experiencing a first communion of sorts –
some type of ceremony or rite of passage. I feel as if I am being guided
on this sacred pilgrimage by San Michele, and Mario and Giuseppe are
his angels that are holding my hands along the way.

What a great gift for Mario and Giuseppe to bring me here – one my
private driver, and the other my tour guide - to show me the "Seat of the
Sacred" – the south of *Italia*. This is my new name for this part of Italy.

We stop at an *albergo*, a hotel, and I realize that I am in for a
surprise. Mario of course knows the owner of the hotel who is an old
friend he hasn't seen in many years. After greetings of hugs and kisses,
he asks to see a room. Giuseppe is waiting in the car as we talk with the
owner. I am confused and trying to understand why we need a hotel
room. What is he thinking and what does he have in store for me?
Aren't we going back to Capri now? My female antenna shoots straight
up out of my head as I remember that I am in romantic *Italia* where the
men love all women.

Of course the owner doesn't speak a word of English nor Mario, so
no one can explain to me why we are looking for hotel rooms in the
middle of the afternoon. I take out my dictionary and try to communicate
with them but Mario is speaking rapidly and I can't understand a word.
He tries to speak more slowly when I ask questions, but my mind has
blocked out all language and reasoning. I realize I am a woman alone
with two Italian men…why didn't I think of this before…and alarms are
going off in my head, disconnecting my neurotransmitters from any
understanding or translation.

I think I am in America and say, "*No grazie*," to the manager, ask for
a business card and walk to the car, Mario trailing behind me trying to
keep up while mumbling to himself…"*Mama mia…*" as he slaps his
forehead.

There is nothing to do at this point but go to lunch. So Giuseppe
drives on. We find a small restaurant called *Agriturismo Macchiapiede
di Vespoli Michele*. It's an organic sort of compound where they grow
their own produce and serve healthy meals; and it's also a Bed &
Breakfast of sorts. Mario orders for all of us and we enjoy the traditional
local fare and drink *vino rosso* with *acqua minerale*. As Mario is
ordering, I have my dictionary out and am writing down sentences so I
can ask him why we need a hotel room.

We try and communicate like this for thirty minutes without much
headway. Meanwhile, the wine has come, the bread has come and then
the food. And I am now nervously sipping in between my sentences,
trying to figure out how to get out of this predicament I think I am in.

Mario and Giuseppe are talking with each other and then agreeing on new words to try and help me understand. No one in the south speaks English so no one can help. The whole time, Mario is slapping his forehead and saying, "*Mama mia…*" and "*capise?*" a thousand times, as if this will help.

Then for some strange reason, or maybe it's the amount of the wine I have nervously consumed – I start to understand what they are saying to me. It is a three to four hour drive back to the port in Sorrento to catch the boat to Capri and the last one leaves at 17:30 (5:30 p.m.). We cannot possibly make it so we will have to stay. Did we know this when we started out so I could have been more prepared? Now I start to say, "*Mama mia!*"

After I resign myself to the fact that I have only the dress I am wearing which I have been sweating in all day…and that I have no toothbrush, we all start to relax and enjoy the food. And before I know it, I understand every word they are saying to me. Giuseppe tells me he is my age – fifty – and Mario says he is not yet fifty, although they both look older to me. I wonder if they are teasing me. We talk about where we will go after we eat and then discuss the plan for the next day. Maybe when you purchase an Italian-English dictionary, a bottle of *vino* should accompany it? I think I am having a wonderful time.

Our next destination after lunch is the *Grotto di Pertosa,* an underground grotto with natural caverns that were discovered five hundred years ago by a monk from Balogna. I think the monks lived everywhere in Italy and wonder where they all are now. Inside are caves, stalactites and stalagmites, beautiful waterways and rock formations. An altar stands in one of the caves but I don't know why until Mario explains to the guide that I speak only English and asks if he can give me the tour in English. He pulls me to the front of the line – there are about ten other people with us. He speaks to me in English first, then goes back to the group and does his tour in Italian. All the while, I feel like royalty due to my special treatment and also due to the fact that he is young, dark and beautiful in the way that the men are in this part of the world.

My guide, Gino explains that from the archeological findings in the cave, and from the sizes of the stalactites and stalagmites, the caves are estimated to be 35 million years old. He also says the water is sacred. He tells me he has been a tour guide at the Grotto for the last ten years and that this place pulls at him so much so that he just can't seem to leave it. I tell him I sense it too, that it feels so peaceful, so quiet, and so sacred. I am not a fan of dark caves and never thought I would feel as if I wanted to live in one, but here, I do. He tells me the monks used to live here and they would build little altars so they could pray.

Half way through the tour I ask, "Gino, what does the name mean *Grotto Dell'Angelo?*"

"These are the C*aves of the Angels of Archangel Michael. He is everywhere. Excuse me. I have to explain in Italian now."* He moves back toward the crowd and leaves me standing here and I think I hear the most beautiful music. I look forward into the darkness, letting the tears of my soul spill down my cheeks and onto my breast, flowing like a waterfall. They don't want to stop and I have no control over them. I feel his power beside me and his hand on my shoulder like the Great Spirit's and I am suddenly overwhelmed with love and compassion as if I have been infused with light - a blessing.

In this moment, I know he and the Great Spirit are one and the same and that is what he is revealing to me. I now turn and see his face, his golden hair and his blue eyes as they look into mine.

"You will never be alone, Roxanna, for I am with you always. Ask for anything you want and you shall have it; and remember to always follow the calling of your soul, for this is the road to happiness." I feel a puff of warm air as if someone has blown in my face so I blink for a moment and when I open my eyes, he is gone. So I stand here for what seems like five minutes as I collect myself. The tears suddenly stop, for I am no longer filled with emotion that I cannot contain, but instead giddiness and laughter are left in its place.

I am three feet off the ground for the rest of the tour and each time Gino guides me in English, I nod as if I hear and understand him. But I do not. My mind is lost in thought, my heart lost in memories as if I have been kissed and still caught in the rapture of it. My life flashes before me and I remember how as a child I was so close to the angels – to spirit. My relationship with them had no boundaries. I felt as though I belonged to all of them and knew the house of prayers.

The Cave of the Angels of San Michele…the entire trip was for this…so now it has been revealed to me that they are one and the same, the Great Spirit and San Michele. This is why I am so drawn to Ana Capri – the San Michele Villa and his gardens. He is everywhere there and he has guided me to come and be with him, to see his place of respite, the place he loves to hang out. No wonder the Italians have the word *paradiso* in their language to define both heaven and paradise.

I am quiet for the rest of the tour and even in the car as we drive deeper into the countryside toward another adventure.

"Roxanna, *L'acqua de Santa Stefano, naturale acquedotto,* spring...*bene. Tu vene.*" Guiseppe has driven down a long dirt road somewhere near Pertosa while I have been lost in thought. I am instructed to take my water bottle with me, and we move down a trail to a flowing spring.

"*Vedo...si.*" Giuseppe smiles as we move toward the spring, and when we arrive, he and Mario bless themselves by making the sign of the cross on their bodies. We wash our faces with the cool water as if we are being baptized and then fill our bottles, drinking all the while. My head is spinning with all of this so I am not sure what is real and what is not. Are these really sacred waters? Will they heal anything? I decide I am officially having a religious experience and this day will now be called the *Festiva de San Michele* by me...my own personal holy day and holiday. As I walk back to the car, both my driver and my guide are having their own religious experience as well. We are all drunk, intoxicated by the holy water.

My senses cannot take anymore and I realize this is probably why some Italians drink wine with their meals. All of the saints hang out in Italy and if you pay attention, you could run into one at any given moment. This is a staggering event that makes you want to sip Lemoncello or *vino.* So what do you do when they leave? You drink something to shake off the ecstatic stupor you are in and come back to earth. I smile at the thought of my visit.

There is no talk as we head back to town and a *farmacia* in search of toothbrushes. Of course no one speaks English, so I use the little words I know like *capella* - hair and *lavare* - to wash, for shampoo. I don't know the word for toothbrush so I make the motion with my hands as if I am brushing my teeth. They are more than happy to help me and probably happier with themselves that they understand, so I am given all sorts of toiletries *gratis*, free...a free hairbrush and natural conditioner, and a free toothbrush as well. I am surrounded by angels today, I think, as I leave with my things. People in the south of Italy are wonderful...

I have *venti minuti*, twenty minutes before I am to meet Mario and Giuseppe in the lobby of our hotel, so there is no time to rest. Lunch was so delicious that we will go back for dinner, and when we arrive, they remember us as if we are part of their family, greeting us with kisses as if we have been gone for a long time and are just returning. Vincenze and his wife Simone and their new *bambino* are there to greet us and they graciously feed us the specialties of the evening, an outstanding meal at an outside table. We dine on *fungo crostini* and homemade pastas followed by grappa and Lemoncello. All throughout dinner, Mario, Guiseppe and I talk and laugh in Italian and I communicate well and understand everything, until the Lemoncello, when my *cervello* becomes *stanco* – my brain becomes tired. I open my dictionary that I carry everywhere like a bible and tell them why I no longer *capisco*, understand, and they laugh saying, "*Si, si.*"

Since the heat has been so intense all day, I have to wash my three pieces of clothing in the sink – my bra, panties and my linen dress. How will I iron it? Do they have irons here? Will it dry? How will I dry my hair without my hardware and what on earth will I look like? All of these civilized American female thoughts race through my mind as I brush my teeth.

Am I in for a surprise, because the windows have thick metal grates over them to keep the cold and heat out and they have little tiny holes in them to let some air in…along with those little nasty creatures called "no-see-ums"… I lay awake almost all night, too hot to sleep, swatting invisible little creatures away from my skin. I move from the bed four times to soak the linen face towel with cold water, draping it across my body as I lay on my back. Do you know that the heat is so intense in the room that the towel dries within an hour every time? So of course, my dress and under-things are dry and wrinkle-free by morning…more so than me…

CHAPTER 29

At seven o'clock, the second half of my sojourn begins for we do not go directly back to Sorrento. First, we stop for a quick *espresso* at a café on the side of the road. Funny how Americans have such a fast paced society and sit with their coffee in the morning, but the Italians in the south that I have met, enjoy a slower paced life but drink their *espresso* quickly while standing. Who can figure this out?

After our quick and energetic meal of *espresso* and *connetti*, the pastries we eat for breakfast, we leave in search of the *Monte de San Michele* which is somewhere close to *Sala Consilina*, the town where our hotel is, and within fifteen minutes, we find it. Six hundred meters above the town, stands the Mountain of Saint Michael. It is difficult to tell how old the structure is because the plaque on the building has it dedicated in the 16th, 17th and 18th centuries; but Mario says it is a thousand years old. It looks like it is two thousand years old to me.

Walking through this church is like walking through the monastery the day before, old frescoes adorning the walls, sacred objects of antiquity everywhere. I am filled with the same feelings as then, so I take them outside and stand overlooking the *Vallo di Diano* below. This is the vast green valley where Polla, Pertosa, Padula, Montesano, Buonabitacolo and the other small towns and cities lie. I have no busy thoughts inside my head, only the quiet that you feel when you are praying. I stand there on the *Monte* overlooking the landscape with no need for anything - no wants, no desires. I just stand here in the moment, with my heart full and my mind empty. Life is everything I could ever dream it to be before I was born, if that is in fact what I did.

The next leg of the trip is three hours as we drive in a northeast direction toward a town called Matera which Mario pronounces **Mee**-tra. I don't realize until we arrive that this is the town where Mel Gibson filmed *Passion of the Christ.* On the drive, I sit in the back seat watching the countryside change as it reminds me of Tuscany with its hillsides filled with olive trees and vineyard; but each time I look over another hill the scenery changes. As we travel through Potenza and out into the Basilicata region, there are *boscoes* - forests with trees and running rivers.

I ask my companions the types of trees that are lining the hills, and think they say *pioppi* and *faggio*, poplar and beech trees. There are wheat fields everywhere, the grains a soft golden color, cut and rolled lazily lying about on the landscape.

Occasionally, old towns and hamlets dot the scenery and a castle rises up in the distance. There are sheep and goats grazing everywhere in the sunshine and the buildings in all of the towns are so old. I think that in ancient times, all the settlements were built high atop the ridges and mountains for protection.

As I look out the window, I can hear Mario and Guiseppe speaking in their native tongues. Oftentimes, they speed up and start to talk faster, and it is at these times that I think Giuseppe reminds me of Marlon Brando in the Godfather, with his deep throated low voice, his words rolling into one another like marbles rolling across a floor.

As we move closer to Matera, the landscape changes into a more arid and rocky terrain with rock formations that look as if they are made of soft stone. There are cacti everywhere reminding me of Arizona, although the hillsides and mountain ridges are still scattered with ancient castles, hamlets and small towns.

At some point in the morning, we stop at yet another monastery, *Santa Maria di Orsoleo in Sant'Archangelo*. It dates back to 1192…so ancient…and still standing with its beautiful tile and marble work and frescoes - one in particular of the Madonna.

Back in the car, it's another hour to Matera but I am enjoying this continuation of my *Festiva de San Michele*. We stop along the roadsides and fill our water bottles with water from old fountains which are scattered throughout the country the same as they are throughout Tuscany and Umbria. Mario tells me this is the best water… *l'acqua è buona.* He's right, for it is cool and refreshing and tasted like the springs of San Stefano. As I look up, I notice a crate of nectarines sitting beside the fountain.

"*Perche, loro ecco? Non nene…male?*" I try to ask why these have been left here. Are they bad?

Mario understands and says, "*No, bene,*" as he hands me three nectarines. As I bite into one, it is white on the inside and melts in my mouth, my senses overtaken by the sweet perfume that it contains. It fills my mouth and my nostrils and I feel myself flutter. This is the most delicious fruit I have ever tasted and I savor every last bite, for I know I will never taste another piece of fruit this sweet again.

In a small town, we stop at a place with the word *Panifico* over the door, and purchase homemade bread made with grains fresh from the fields…so fresh that I can smell the sweetness of the earth in it or so I imagine. It is sweeter than any I have ever tasted or am I just intoxicated again? I think that since I have landed on Italian soil, I have been continually intoxicated…

Finally, we arrive in Matera, the town of the *Sassi*. *Sasso* means stone and there are stones - no boulders - everywhere as if the town grew out of them. They say Matera means "Mother Earth." There are tufa rocks everywhere, and the churches and homes have been cut out of them creating cave-like dwellings. The town reminds me of Bethlehem, all of the buildings white in color, the same color as the rocks themselves.

Although Matera dates back to the Paleolithic Period, the rock hewn churches were dug out by monks between the 8th and 12th centuries. More monks, I think…

We walk through the two lower districts of the town stopping inside each rock hewn church…and there are twelve, where we find religious artifacts and frescoes. They are so simple – I can hardly believe people actually lived in them - yet so sacred. I am amazed at how they have survived time and weather.

We climb to the top of the hill that leads to the piano district where more churches and castles are, built in the 16th and 17th centuries. I realize how unusual it is to see a town like Bethlehem below and then this district up here with Gothic, Baroque and Renaissance structures. There are numerous churches and a castle - the *Aragonese Castle* of Count Tramontano. What a stark contrast - noble buildings with their loggias, borders and *freizes* above and then the cave dwellings that were homes and churches below.

In the piano district, we try to visit a few of the churches, but there are so many and the heat must be about 115o. It is an effort to hike around here in the blazing sun, and the water we are drinking is not helping. We do manage to visit the town's cathedral built in 1270 which is at the highest point in the city, a statue of Archangel Michael standing watch over it from the front façade.

We also walk through San Francesco's and Santa Chiara - Saint Claire's churches, but the heat holds us back from pressing on. So we stand in the shadow of a building comparing our map to the architectural-scape where we point out San Domenico's Church, La Palomba the Church of the Holy Spirit, and Santa Lucia alla Malve. San Michele is everywhere looking downward, guarding each and every church from its own facade. This has been by far, the most sacred journey since I have hit Italy.

Soon, we are in the car driving the long distance back to Sorrento and back to the port where we just barely make the boat. Although it has only been thirty-six hours since I left my villa, it feels like seven days – yes, seven days with San Michele, the Guardian of Truth and the Keeper of the Veil. A lot has been revealed to me on this sojourn and I need time to process it all.

Il tramonto - the sunset awaits me as I return to my villa, not setting until I have taken my place on the *terrazzo*. My heart is full and my soul is singing after my recent travels. This day, I am now wise enough to know that if I pay attention to the signs and listen to my inner voice, they will guide me through much happiness and the world will open up for me. And as I rest my head on my pillow and fall asleep, I am at peace with myself.

CHAPTER 30

Life is sweet on the island of lemons, Lemoncello and Caprese salads as I wander around watching the tourists. I carry my sketchbook everywhere, my thoughts spilling out of my heart as if they have been waiting for me to open the gate for a lifetime. I have decided that I want to sketch everyone on the island…a novel of sketches, of sorts.

I left my paints with Natale in Rome along with the canvas I had sketched his likeness on. Hopefully, I will be back to paint it. For now, I cannot bring myself to buy paints or even start to paint here on Capri, for somehow it reminds me of him. After all, he was the one who opened my heart and mind to it again.

This day, I am lounging at my villa sketching the lizards as they play and the grapes as they grow round and robust, and I notice the weather is changing before my eyes. The high temperature and humidity have gone and even the mosquitoes seem to have gone to sleep.

I am bathing in the light, the sounds and the wind of the sea and the air around me as I sit…just sitting paying no mind to anything but at the same time, relaxing into all of it. Where does the time go, I wonder? What a delicious feeling when I can play hooky from life, shun all responsibilities and only pay attention to my own wants and needs…how decadent…

When Donata, Mario's daughter calls to invite me to dinner with her family, I say yes, and she is very happy. I move inside to change my clothes and put my sketch pad away. The walk will take me about one hour but it is the most glorious walk.

"My angel…where have you been? I am so happy to see you!" Antonio has stepped out of a gate and sees me. He embraces me and is kissing me all over.

"Antonio, how have you been? It has been a very long time since I have seen you." I am happy to have run into him and he looks well.

"Oh, you know. I have been around the island. I met a girl, you know. She is from Florida and was here on vacation for two weeks. She asked me to come live with her there. I am going to work in a restaurant and then I will take care of her."

"Oh, Antonio, I am so happy for you." I've known that he has wanted to move to America since we met. He looks good with his big smile and his darkened skin from the summer sun.

"Where have you been, Roxanna? I come to visit you often, but you are never there. I thought you left the island, but Enrico said you were traveling."

"I have been traveling all over Italy, Antonio..."

"Good, good for you. Soon, I will be in America and maybe then I can come see you there!"

"Yes, email me, Antonio. I hope you enjoy your new life there. Keep in touch."

"I will, *bella. Ciao*." I give him a big hug, glad to have seen him and happy that he is happy.

"*Ciao, bello*." I smile and blow him a kiss good bye. As I walk on down the lane, I think of the days we spent hiking and sight seeing and I miss those times with him. I think of the black Madonna and the Lemoncello and how he made me laugh. Life is good, I say to myself.

When I arrive, Louisa and Mario greet me in the garden, and Donata's husband Marcello and their two-year old son, Luca invite me inside.

"*Sera*, Roxanna, *benvenuto*, come in, please."

"*Grazie*, Marcello. *Como va?*"

"*Bene, bene.* Life is good, no?"

"Yes, yes." We are all smiling wide as we greet one another. "Luca...Luca, come here." He is hiding behind his papa's pants, pulling on them. His cheeks are rosy and his eyes are shining brightly, and although he is shy, he is happy to see me. He is a beautiful little Italian boy who will grow up into a beautiful Italian man.

"*Regalo...per* Luca." He forgets his shyness and comes to take the candy from my hand. Then he kisses my cheek. Louisa hugs me and sees that I am wearing one of the dresses that she has given me and she looks on with pride. Although we are closer in age than her daughter and me, she is very motherly to me.

"Roxanna, *bella...bene, bene*." She likes the bright orange cotton shift which looks very tropical to me.

"*Grazie*, fresh...*fresco*." We move to the outside patio where we sit for hours, the men tonight waiting on all of us women. They have an outdoor fire pit where they cook and a long family table set underneath a linen tent of sorts that protects us from the sunlight during the day. There are torches lit all around and Marcello is playing tunes from Napoli - a

CD he has made for me as a gift. He is very good to me, treating me like a princess. I love the way the men treat me here and never want to leave because of it…especially after drinking Prosecco…

We are giggling and sharing stories about life with one another as we sip the homemade champagne that Marcello's family has made. It is quite delicious and intoxicating. Mario and Marcello are refilling our glasses as if we need it, and it has made the world a more beautiful place, if you can imagine that on Capri.

"*Grazie, grazie*," we keep saying as they pour and pour. Then we giggle after each pour because we feel like we have little champagne bubbles running through our blood by now – and I am sure we do. As we laugh and share, the men barbeque chicken and shrimp together.

Once they have served us, they join us and the Italian dining experience begins. We laugh and eat as they push more food onto each others' plates as if it is a love ritual. The more food they offer you, the more they love you. But you finally have to say "No, stop! *Fermata! Troppo pieno col cibo*, I am too full!"

The sun has finally gone to sleep and the air has cooled a bit, but the mosquitoes have come out to feed. The citronella candles that are placed around the tented table help quite a bit and the Prosecco relaxes me so much that I don't seem to care and they don't seem to bother me after all. The Italians tell me it is because of the olive oil in their diet. The more you eat, the less they like the taste of you.

The food is delicious and of course there is way too much. There is fruit first, melon with prosciutto, then cheese and olives. There is chicken and big shrimp - so sweet - then there is pasta that Louisa has made the best… and then the salad I brought from the garden is served. It is fresh arugula and gorgonzola cheese with lemon, salt and olive oil like I had in Umbria, and they love it. Next is the gelato and then sweets that are served with Lemoncello – my Italian grandmother who has come to join us…

How do they stay so slim? I feel as if I will explode! I say no to another Lemoncello because I feel that I will not be able to squeeze another thing into my body – not even a tiny sip.

"Roxanna, *si, si*…Lemoncello helps you digest. It is good for you when you eat too much." Donata is trying to assure me that it is a good thing and will help like an alka seltzer. I am skeptical but trust them and take another sip. Maybe they are right. Or maybe it is the relaxing conversation with *famiglia* that helps me digest as I sit with them and feel warm and cozy, wrapped up in the love of the island and my loved ones. I have never felt like I belonged anywhere in the world really, until here.

Soon, the night has to end, but I am so sleepy and afraid I will not be able to find my way home in the dark. There are no street lights on the island and I have to use my cell phone to light the way. Of course Mario and Marcello offer to walk me back as if it is no big deal and Donata and Louisa are offering their husbands for my safety but I say no that I am all right and can find my way. The hugging and kissing good bye takes ten minutes at least and then I am off, finding my way back to the villa with no problem. There is nothing to fear here because there are no coyotes or strange animals to jump out at you at night…only cats and dogs and Italian men. I giggle as I sway, sashaying my way down the walkway to my villa and then I remember Elana and smile.

My sleep is immediate, my belly full, for I am happy and content with love. I think of Natale and wish he were here with me. I hug my pillow tightly to my breast pretending it is him, and instantly, I am dreaming.

The dream - I am awakened by San Michele and we are standing on the *terrazzo* looking out over the coastline from Napoli to Sorrento.

"So now you know who I am, sweet woman. I have always been with you – you just never noticed. Life is easy when you pay attention to the signs." I am weeping because my heart is full and I am so happy. He places his hands upon my shoulders and faces me, looking at me lovingly.

"You paid attention to the signs that brought you here to your homeland, didn't you? Don't ever be frightened of anything in your life for you can change anything in a flash. Nothing is permanent. And you are never alone. We are all here. Your trip to the Basilicata region was a sacred journey and everyone you met along the way was an angel to insure that you got there safely – especially these two." He was referring to Guiseppe and Mario.

"And now you have also found a long lost family that was once yours in another lifetime here on Capri. So welcome home." I am without my voice, for I am weeping tears of love. I am so filled up in these moments – filled with the realization of everything that is.

"Now, it is time for you to go on another great adventure. Go to Greece. You will know where…." He kisses the top of my head and leaves me standing there at the edge of the sea. I know I somehow return to my bed and sleep, but don't know how, for I don't remember. I fall deeper into slumber erasing it all from my consciousness.

Mindful awakening….I roll over onto my side and feel my body as it moves between the sheets…it is all here, all in tact, feeling good. I can hear the silence of the morning, no noise, nothing to awaken my mind too soon. I breathe in a breath of the coolness that has come over the island in the last few days, taking all of the relentless heat away; and as I breathe, I feel the shadows fall behind my eyelids, a reflection of the early morning sunlight as it slips behind a wandering cloud.

I have found this space in my bed – this space of nothingness, of whiteness and purity, so I lie here under the sheet and hear the breeze outside my window as it whispers through the grape leaves, moving them gently as it passes. This is the only sound. I feel the peace and the cleanness, the smoothness of my awakening into this place of nothingness...mindful awakening.

Can I ever bring this back to the States? Or is it something that only occurs here on Capri – the place of peace and joy, of dreams…like a vision of white linens hanging on a clothesline to dry in the sun, with a breeze blowing them outward…no sound, only the vision. That is how I awaken each day – in this place of freshness and emptiness - this place of peace that I have called for throughout my life, always wanting that vacation from my mind's coming and goings…its busy thoughts and obsessions.

Fully awake, Italian words start to come to mind that I have learned from my friends…*fresco*, fresh…fresh and clean, and *piano, piano*, easy, easy…smooth and easy. This is my description in my new language that describes my awakening; and as the sleep wears off and I lie here wondering what I might do this day, I suddenly remember San Michele.

The dream! I remember the dream. I feel his love and his guidance and know I would be forever watched over and protected. Then I remember Greece. Why not? I have wanted to go for years…dreamt about it. When Capri came up, I put Greece on the back burner because Capri was a priority but I am still intrigued with Greece…the beginning of life…the seat of civilization…

I move quickly from the bed to start my day and my tea ritual so I can go to the bookstore in Capri to purchase yet another tour book.

CHAPTER 31

ATHENA, GRECIA

Mythology, thought to be a collection of imaginary stories, is one of the cornerstones of ancient Greek civilization. It has always been a belief that the Athenians were descendents of the gods. Hesiod, a great poet from 700 B.C. wrote about the *Creation of the World*. He believed that the beginning of creation started with Chaos, Gaia and Eros. Eros and Night were born from Chaos, and Ouranos and Okeanos were born from Gaia. Ouranos coupled with Gaia and they became the first gods to rule the world.

They bore twelve children known as the Titans: Okeanos, Koios, Kreios, Hyperion, Iapetos, Kronos, Theia, Rhea, Themis, Mnemosyne, Phoibe, and Tethys. They also bore the three Kyklopes: Brontes, Steropes, and Arges; and also the Giant with the three hundred-hands: Kottos, Gyges and Briares.

Their father, Ouranos, decided he didn't want to lose his power or become dethroned when his children became of age, so he made his wife hide them deep within her bowels. Chaos, his wife plotted to take away her husband's strength to achieve the goal of freeing her children, and armed her son Kronos with a sickle to cut off his father's genitals. When Ouranos's seed fell into the sea, Aphrodite was born; and when his blood was spilled onto the earth, the Fates, the Giants and the Meliai Nymphs were born.

Kronos succeeded his father and took his sister Rhea for his wife, and then freed the rest of his brothers and sisters. Unfortunately, he eventually was consumed by the same fears his father had and so he swallowed all of his and Rhea's children: Hestia, Demeter, Hera, Hades, Posiedon and Zeus.

Rhea fooled her husband by wrapping a stone in cloth instead of Zeus who was taken to Mount Dikte to be raised by the Nymphs; and Kronos swallowed the stone without knowing her secret. Eventually, Zeus grew to manhood and dethroned his father and saved the rest of his siblings.

Not everyone accepted Zeus in power; Gaia talked the Titans, the brothers of Kronos into revolting against Zeus, known as the *Battle of the Titans*. Zeus and other members of the Olympic pantheon sought refuge at Mount Olympus and finally managed to defeat the Titans, only after winning over the other children of Gaia and Ouranos, the Kyklopes, and the three hundred-handed giants.

Gaia refused to be reconciled and next went to the Giants, thus causing the *Battle of the Giants*. They were savage monsters who had human bodies with serpent heads or serpent tails instead of legs. This battle changed the course of rivers, and moved mountains and islands. Zeus and the other gods were finally successful but only after great damage was done.

From that point on, the twelve Olympian Gods: Zeus and his brothers and sisters, Poseidon, Demeter, Apollo, Aphrodite, Dionysos, Athena, Hera, and Hephaistos ruled from Mount Olympus democratically. The ancient Greeks also gave their gods human weaknesses as well; thus the stories or myths were woven around their jealousies, infidelities, loss, grief, love, etc. Mankind was then created by the gods who made them from a basic compound of earth and fire, and then added whatever other materials they could mix together.

Aside from the twelve who ruled, there were also many other deities who determined the fate of man. Helios the *Sun*, Selene the *Moon*, and Eos the *Dawn*, were the children of two of the Titans: Hyperion and Theia. Every morning, Helios rises from the ocean in the east and rides his chariot pulled by his four horses, through the sky to descend to the earth at night. When he completes his journey, Selene bathes in the sea and then dresses herself, finally ascending into the heavens. The following daybreak is brought by Eos, and once again, Helios sets out on his journey.

Some don't believe that these stories of the gods and these myths are true; but if they are not, then why are there temples and buildings built everywhere for them? And why was Greece one of the most powerful civilizations in ancient history? It seemed to be the seat of the world - that from which other countries were birthed. The story goes that the Olympian Gods awarded the city of Athens - Athena as it is called - to Athena herself, the Goddess of Wisdom, as a prize over Poseidon, both having fought over the beautiful city. Athena became the leading city of Greece, everyone wanting to own it as its history shows. It was home to the likes of great philosophers such as Socrates, Plato and Aristotle, and great poets like Aeschylus, Sophocles, and Euripid.

I have arrived here in Athena – and I am looking upward toward the ruins sitting high atop the limestone rock which overlooks the city. What an ancient site…I have to get there…so I walk up toward the complex. With my book as my tour guide, I walk and read at the same time finally approaching the *Propylae*. I am enamored with the history of the city and the myths, for I truly believe the Gods and Goddesses of Olympus existed. I scour the books looking for proof, but find none.

I come upon the *Parthenon* and am awestruck by its structure, one of the most beautiful ruins in the world. The highest structure on the site, it is the temple of the Virgin Athena, erected in 500 B.C. It had survived fully in tact for two thousand years until a few centuries ago in 1687 when a bomb was thrown into it during the war, turning it into a ruin.

A smaller building, the *Temple of the Wingless Victory*, stands on the southern part of the Acropolis Hill, built for the *Goddess Nike* or *Victory*. Although it had been demolished in 1679, Greece rebuilt her. The *Erechtheum*, is the most ancient sanctuary of the Acropolis, housing three temples: the *Temple of Athena Polias*, the *Temple of Erechtheus* and the *Temple of the Nymph* or *Maiden Pandrosus*. The southern portico to this building holds six statues of virgins used as columns to support its roof; they still look beautiful, most of their features still visible.

I roam for hours, looking at every angle, every corner, every facade. Those that I can lay my hands on, I do. How incredible that they have survived time, mostly in tact. As I walk through the museum, I am amazed at the collection of sculptures I come upon. In spite of the destruction by the Persians in 480 B.C., most have been miraculously preserved. There are pieces from the *Temple of Athena*, the *Frieze of Victory*, and the unique *Kourai maidens* thought to be Athena's high priestesses. There is a bas-relief of Athena leaning on her lance and fragments from the *Frieze of the Parthenon*, horsemen from the north side and the Gods: Poseidon, Apollo, and Artemis from the east side.

There is a statue of Nike loosening her sandal and so much more. Of course I am drawn to the large statue of Kouros. He is magnificent. I know I must have known him at one time… Everywhere I go on this side of the world, he is there as if he is trying to remind me of something.

There was an eight-foot tall statue of him at the Athens Airport where I wrapped my arms around him and kissed his chest as a stranger took my photo. He is perfect in every way as if he represents the perfect Greek man but he actually represents youth in all of its nakedness and raw form…so exquisite.

As I walk toward the southern slope of the Acropolis, I see the *Odean of Herodes Atticus*. This is the 5000 seat theatre that was carved out of the rocks in 161 A.D. as a memorial to Herodes' wife, Regilla. Herod was a friend to the Emperor Hadrian. This was also the place where Yanni played when he played the Acropolis with the lights from the buildings on top of the hill shining so beautifully behind him.

This is the place I have dreamed of coming for years…I am here walking through the ancient ruins…how old the world is. My love for sculpture, architecture and ancient history will be fed here, for I can already feel its effects on my psyche. I find Greece to be so different from Italy – I guess I shouldn't be surprised. After all, they are two different countries. But it is so much older here, as if I have been transported back to the beginning of time.

I spend most of the day in the museum at the Acropolis walking around the complex looking down at Athens – so much larger than I had thought. The taxi driver that drove me from the train station told me that since the Olympics in Athens last year, they had built a new freeway and numerous buildings and the stadium; and as I looked out the window, the city seemed to sprawl out in all directions meeting the horizon.

Making my way down the big hill is a challenge as I walk in between the raindrops. Blue sky tries to peak through the dark, leaden clouds that are crowding it out, but the sun finds a way to peak its head in every few minutes. Luckily, there is no downpour as I find myself in the Plaka, the oldest district in Athens.

Here, there are narrow streets that wind around through shops, taverns, restaurants, night clubs and bars and I hear Greek music carried upon the air as I lazily window shop and people-watch. In Capri, I was told the Greeks loved to celebrate all night long and that the Plaka was the place where everyone went to do it. I would have to come back here and enjoy the night life and since it is crowded with shops and people, I feel safe enough to come alone even if I don't know the language.

Each time I pass a restaurant or café, I notice the waiters standing outside giving away their business cards trying to entice the passing tourists to come inside and eat. As I walk by each of them, and there are so many, they all smile at me and ask me the same.

"No, thank you. I'm not hungry right now." I don't know any Greek and I can't seem to get my mind around the words – not even please or thank you. My first instinct is to speak Italian which is wrong.

"Please come back later then," as he writes his name on the back of the card and hands it to me. He speaks very good English. He has dark hair and a strong Greek nose that I am so fond of.

"Maybe later." I am being polite. I walk on and the same thing happens at the next café, the smile, the business card, my response. I stop looking at the restaurants finally so no one catches my eye, or I theirs. A small boy of about eight with the most soulful black eyes and thick curly hair is playing a mandolin at a small café on a corner and I stand in front of him to watch. As soon as I give him a handful of coins, he smiles wide, thanks me in Greek and then scoots off. I decide this is the perfect café.

Inside giant vertical rotisseries are hanging, filled with lamb and chicken as the men slice the meat from them for the patrons. There is music all around and everyone is drinking beer or Greek wine.

I am seated outside and soon served *souvlakia,* Greek salad, rice and olives. But as soon as the waiter comes, the skies open up like waterfalls falling from the heavens, dumping onto the awning, dropping heavily all around. Everyone has stopped where they are as if they are frozen in time, waiting…

The waiter immediately picks up my plate and motions for me to come inside with him where he clears the people who have run in for cover, from the middle of the floor, snaps his fingers and soon a table and chair are delivered and set up. I am seated now in the middle of the deli area with people standing all around looking at me, probably wondering who I am that I am the only patron from the patio who has been brought in and set up to eat inside as the others are huddled together outside still. I am also wondering who I am to be treated so well… Of course I am laughing at this quick change of events and find myself talking soon with the others who are standing all around drinking beer and are now singing.

Two young women from Australia ask if they can sit and share my table and of course I say yes relishing their company. They have just come from the islands.

"Where will you go next?" They ask me after we introduce ourselves and talk about our travels. One is petite and blonde and the other has dark hair and green eyes. They have been traveling throughout Italy and Greece and are now heading to Turkey and Istanbul, a continuation of their month-long holiday.

"I'm going to Mykonos next and then Santorini. My friends in Italy tell me Mykonos is fun and Santorini is beautiful. So I'll start there. Who knows after that."

"Good choices. They're both so different. Mykonos is filled with nightlife. People never sleep there! You'll be up all night and the action doesn't start until midnight." I can tell that Rebecca loved Mykonos.

"But Santorini, you will absolutely fall in love with." The dark haired woman, Wanda's eyes light up at the thought of Santorini. "It's indescribable. You'll have to see it for yourself. We loved it there…we were able to rest since we never slept in Mykonos. You've decided well enough by going to Mykonos before Santorini." They both nod in unison and laugh as they rise to leave.

"Have a wonderful time on your holiday. Oh, when you are on Mykonos, don't forget to go to Paradise and Super Paradise…you'll have to see it for yourself. "

"You, too; it was nice to meet you." Now I am excited and intrigued about Mykonos. Since I'm alone, I won't be going to any clubs, but it sounds like a fun place to be.

I pay my bill and leave a tip for the waiter who was so gracious. Shop owners are starting to pull their wares back out or uncover them by removing the tarps they had secured over them for protection from the rain, and all is back to normal.

I try to find my way to the hotel which is somewhere just outside the Plaka; but I am lost anyway. I should write a book titled "Lost in Paradise." I am laughing at myself again. I had decided back in Florence that I was going to get lost anyway, so why worry about it? It was inevitable and I had nothing but time…I still have nothing but time here in Greece. If it takes me a week to get back to the hotel, so what…no worries.

"Excuse me, could you please tell me how to get to the Olympic Palace Hotel?" I stop at yet another restaurant at the edge of the Plaka to ask directions. The dark-haired man standing outside the restaurant is smiling at me. "I can help you. I am Stavros." He puts his hand out to me to shake mine. "And you?"

"Nice to meet you, Stavros. I'm Roxanna. Am I going in the right direction to get back to the hotel?" Silly question…I should know by now it's in the opposite direction from my sense of where I think I should go.

"No, it is where you came from." See, I knew it…He is pointing behind me and he sees me frowning so he speaks very slowly since he wants to help. "Follow this road all the way to the end and then you can only go left or right. Go right. Then it will turn a few times like this." He makes a snake like motion with his hand. "You see? Then, when you get here, you go right. No problem. You will be outside the Plaka and your hotel is one street up from there." I think to myself, I hope I can follow his directions…seems simple enough, since I am so used to these types of directions in this part of the world.

"Thanks for your help."

"Roxanna, please come back for dinner. Here is my card." He writes his name on the back of it as the ritual goes. "We have Greek dancing here at night and you will have a good time. Remember the name, Mourayio's Restaurant. If you can't find us, ask. Everyone knows us. And remember my name, Stavros."

"Thank you, Stavros. I will think about it." I hadn't thought that far ahead, but being in a strange city, I wasn't sure I wanted to venture too far from the hotel.

As I head back up the street, I turn and catch his eye as he is watching me. He winks and waves. Are Greek men like Italians, I wonder? Before I have too much time to contemplate this, my hotel comes into view.

My bath is warm and bubbly and I enjoy it, as I lounge lazily. Why not go back to the Plaka? I can always come back to the hotel if I decide to. So after asking directions three times, I find myself at Mourayio's. Stavros is standing outside soliciting the tourists as they walk by. He looks up and sees me, remembering me – and I am surprised. Then I think, of course he would remember me, for I think I am memorable.

"Roxanna, so happy you are here. Come." He takes me to a table inside, close to the floor where the musicians are already playing.

"Do you work all day and night, Stavros?"

"I have a break before dinner, but I am afraid, yes…we work very hard when the tourists come, but we take a long holiday in the winter. The dancing will start in one hour. I will get you someone." He walks away and signals for a waiter to come with a menu. The ambience is wonderful and the food is very good and I am having a good time sitting here in the midst of all the action, watching the musicians. Just as I finish my last bite of baklava, four men dressed in traditional Greek garb start to dance. They change costumes three times in between sets and I am amazed at their clothing that seems so strange to me. Most are colorful tunic types, belted at the waist. Their shoes seem bigger than their feet with big black bumps on the front of them.

When the musicians leave the stage, I think the show has ended; but after a short break, they come back to play more and four men come out onto the dance floor dressed in modern black pants and black button down shirts with high collars. To my surprise, one of them is Stavros. I laugh and clap as he dances in line with the others, their hands on each others shoulders as they move their legs in unison, kicking one out before them and then the other. They continue to do other dances that I have not seen before, my favorite where they take turns doing their own dance in the center while the others clap around them.

When it is Stavros's turn, he crosses his arms and dances slowly, inching down toward the floor with his shoulders, as he bends his knees further each time. Eventually, he is in a position that I would have doubted a human being could shape himself into. His back is literally one foot from the floor and he is still on his feet being supported by his legs as he moves to the music. In between his upward and downward motions, he thumps his hands behind him on the floor, then brings them in front of himself clapping them once to the music, and the dance repeats itself. All the while, the patrons, mostly tourists are going crazy clapping and yelling and the Greek men are shouting "*opah!*"

One of the other dancers brings over a shot glass and places it on his forehead very ceremoniously for this auspicious dance and ritual that he is performing.

The shot glass is filled with what looks like Ouzo, and as they clap louder cheering him on, he keeps the rhythm of his movement. Suddenly, he claps one last time and with a final loud thump to the floor with both of his hands he manages to maneuver the shot glass so that it flips in the air. When it comes backs down, the liquid has fallen into his mouth and he catches the glass with his teeth!

The crowd goes wild and the screams bring people in from the streets to see what is happening. I am also screeching with delight, for I have never seen anything like it before. The men on the dance floor pick up Stavros and lift him high over their heads, parading him around the room as if this is a ceremony for a male who has reached manhood by passing this special test. And I agree wholeheartedly for the body movements he has been able to perform.

"I can't believe you did that! How did you do it? You must be so strong to put that kind of pressure on your legs! I can't believe you can bend like that!" He has come to my table with two shots of Ouzo, one for me and one for himself and I am breathless as I drill him. He laughs at me, but I can see how proud of his performance he is.

"It is nothing." He lowers his eyes as if he is shy. "My father taught me to do it. It was a game when we were little."

"Is it a traditional Greek dance like the others?"

"No, we do it to entertain the tourists. They think it's Greek but it's not…only something we made up. You like?" His English is a bit broken.

"Yes, yes I do." I'm still excited and the energy in the room is that of one big party now.

"Good. There is more. Stay and have more Ouzo. It is good. If it is too strong, then put water in it." He smiles at me and walks back to the dance floor where the other men are starting to gather. The music begins and they are pulling women from the tables to dance. Of course, Stavros comes back to me and tries to pull me from my chair.

"I can't dance like that!" I am fighting him all the way, nervous, afraid to go up.

"I teach you. Don't be afraid." He has a good grip on my hand and won't let it go. "Come!" I love the way the men on this side of the world always said, "Come," as if you will because they are in charge. Finally I relent and let him lead me to the dance floor. He holds me and walks me through the steps of one of the traditional dances and finally I think I've got it. In fact, I catch on so quickly that the patrons start clapping for us and the others clear the floor.

Of course I am mortified, but having the time of my life. We dance for quite some time until the belly dancer comes out. She too has pulled me to the dance floor. Now, I am belly dancing with a scarf around my waist and little golden bells strung through my fingers – in Athens, Greece…oh, joy…what a life! I am ecstatic.

After the Ouzo I shared with Stavros, I find myself quite confident. So I dance the night away with the confidence of Athena herself - once again in a far off land with Stavros and this beautiful Greek woman.

After my performance, he comes and sits with me for awhile and we talk about his dancing and my vacation and travels; and before I know it, the restaurant is closing and it is three a.m. My god, I think…now I know how easy it is for the Greeks to stay up all night…they drink Ouzo, dance and lose track of time!

"Come. I walk you to your hotel." I am concerned a bit, but more concerned with getting lost trying to find my way out of the Plaka at this hour. At the hotel, we stop outside to say good night.

"Thank you, Stavros." I give him my hand to shake, but instead, he leans in and steals a quick kiss. I think I should be pretty good at dodging them by now, but obviously, I need more practice.

"No. I…I don't know you." I move away uneasily.

"It is just a kiss." He smiles at me but moves back to a safe distance to assure me his intentions are good.

I smile at this and bend toward him and kiss him gently on both cheeks in the Italian way.

"Thank you, Roxanna; you are very beautiful you know. Do you want me to come in with you?"

"Stavros, I don't know you very well and I am leaving in a few hours…at seven a.m." He pulls me to him, embracing me and then kisses my lips gently again. I think of Natale and pull away from him.

"Good bye, Roxanna. It was nice to meet you." He turns and walks back toward the Plaka. Well he didn't bite me, I think to myself, and it was just a kiss…everyone kisses here. Tiredly, I walk in to the hotel and fall into bed for the few hours I have left before leaving for the airport to Mykonos.

CHAPTER 32

MYKONOS

According to mythology, Mykonos took its name from the son of Anios who was a descendant of the god Apollo and the nymph, Roio. The large stones that lay everywhere on the island are believed to be the petrified giants that Heracles – their spelling for Hercules - once defeated. It is also believed that the body of Ajax Locros was buried here after his ship sank.

In ancient times, the Egyptians, Phonecians, Cretans, Ionians and the Romans all took their turn inhabiting the island. Long ago, Barbarossa captured and ravaged it, and the Venetians ruled off and on for over five hundred years. But in 1822, Mykonos finally belonged to Greece.

It is far different than Athens. As I take the short taxi ride from the airport, the terrain reminds me of south western Mexico. It is arid with lots of brush and small trees. Even the houses remind me of Mexico. Each house on the outskirts of the port town has a dove-cote, an interesting little structure which was brought to the island by the Venetian nobles who raised pigeons for their meat. I espy a row of pure white windmills with conical wooden roofs decorating the edge of the town.

As we arrive in Mykonos, I notice the houses are cubical and pure white, very simple. The unique thing is that they are all white-washed and sparkling, and each one is decorated with a bright blue door, a porch and stairway. Sometimes I see one decorated in red or yellow, but most are a beautiful cobalt blue – the color I call Greek blue. They sit amongst each other on narrow spiraling alleyways of white-washed flagstone between shops, restaurants and art galleries. There are flower boxes everywhere filled with colorful plants, and bougainvillea hangs lazily from the rooftops and down the walls and staircases. Every now and then, I catch sight of one of the churches, many with blue or brownish red domes - some with small arched spires. Greek crosses sit on top of the spires, and bells hang inside the archways.

I check into a quaint two-story hotel in the middle of town, the Hotel Philippi. It is white with blue framed windows and doors and beautiful gardens all around. As I walk toward my door, I realize there is a small patio painted blue, and a sundeck where I can sunbathe if I choose to, which overlooks the art gallery across the narrow whitewashed street.

The sun is hot, as hot as Capri on a summer day, but much drier. I leave my room in search of mineral water and somewhere to sit to continue to read my guide book. There are 500 churches on the island, mostly Greek Orthodox and I see a few as I walk the winding lanes. I had read on the plane that most were built by the islanders when they were at sea in treacherous moments. They found religion and promised that if they were saved, they'd build a church. So they did. As I look inside a few, I notice they are very simple and modest, unlike the churches throughout Italy.

In the distance, I see the *Paraportiani*, one of the most photographed churches in the world, and walk toward it. It was originally a complex of five churches – four on the ground and one on the roof that were built between the 16th and 17th centuries. But time has eroded their structures, giving them the appearance of having melted down into themselves, all five buildings sort of melding together into one. Nevertheless, the Mykonians have continued its upkeep and painting of the outside with that beautiful white sparkling paint. I think it is the most beautiful church here.

The port is lined with small cafes. I choose one to sit in and watch the old boats come in with their catch for the day. It is serene here, very peaceful and the air is soft. The fishermen are coming off of their boats and meet their wives who wait patiently for the fish. This is the daily ritual where the wives sell the wares as the men sit together and tell stories of the sea. I watch them for awhile and notice that one seems to be the elder and all are listening intently as he puffs on a cigarette and weaves his tale.

I yawn and realize my eyelids are heavy for sleep, and then I remember I only slept three hours the night before. I am too tired for the nightlife here already, so I return to the hotel for a nap.

When I awaken at seven p.m., I realize most of my first day is gone. The shower is hot and it feels good upon my skin. I can't help but think of Natale who is always on my mind, seeping into every thought. The water has aroused my senses and I remember the showers and baths we used to take together. One afternoon when it was so hot in Rome and the air was unmoving and heavy with moisture, he bathed me and poured water over my body to cool me down as I lay in the tub.

I remember him singing to me all the while as he stared into my eyes with such profound depth. When he was finished, he toweled me off. Then he rubbed my feet and my legs with lotion as he continued to sing to me, his deep eyes sparkling with delight as if I was a new Lamborghini he was washing and waxing. Such care, he took of me…

I wonder where he is tonight? I move from the shower and dress with memories of him still with me as if he was right beside me… I want to call him, tell him to come; but I do not and will not… for I can't hurt him anymore by pulling on his heartstrings if my intention is not to return to Rome with him. I sigh and hope I know what I'm doing. I am gambling everything, I know; but I have to finish this journey first. The voice inside my head says, "And what if he is not there when you are finished? What if he falls in love with another? What will you do then, Roxanna?"

"I don't know…I don't know," I absently say aloud as I turn the key in the door. "I don't know what I will do." Maybe it is just a faded memory that is nothing but an illusion, and maybe these feelings never existed between us this strongly. Maybe my heart embellished the memorial of him because I have been living this part of my life like Elana lives her life – so romantically…everything is romance.

I hate it when I get heady!

Little Venice or the Venetia of Greece is where I find myself as I walk with these thoughts still clouding my mind. Thank the gods that I am suddenly distracted enough to release the guilt I am feeling. As I come to my senses, I feel as if I have stepped through a mirror and am now in Venice, Italy. The buildings are close together and the Adriatic is gently lapping against their facades. Some have cement walkways or sidewalks between them and the sea, but many don't.

There is a combination of those that are painted a dazzling white with their bright porches and window frames like the ones in town, and others that are built of wood with enclosed porches. The buildings that house the restaurants and bars have cement *terrazzos* built on their backsides so people can eat or drink outside. It is breathtaking as the sun lowers itself in the sky for the setting.

As I snap away, trying to recapture the beauty of this island so that I never forget these moments, I hear beautiful music as if an angel is calling to me. I follow the sound, moving down the lane past restaurants and bars where I am drawn to the second floor of a building and the origin of the singing. On the second level, there is a lounge called the Veranda Bar. People are sitting out on an enclosed patio enjoying cocktails and watching the sun hover over the sea as Sarah Brighton sings a celestial tune. I never realized how beautiful her voice was until this moment. I sit on a cushioned bench at a small table on the patio outside to bathe my ears in the sounds of her melodic voice.

"May I help you?" He is about twenty with those strong Greek features and beautiful eyes, a tray in one hand.

"Do you have a drink menu?" I am not sure what to order, but Ouzo it is not. After perusing the menu, I decide on a "Greek Passion" – just because of its name - which is a mixture of juices and two different kinds of alcohol. The sun gently slips into the Adriatic as Sarah lulls it to sleep with her angelic tune; and in its place are shades of oranges, pinks and yellow-golds. I am sitting, just sitting, watching the colors of the sky change and am reminded of my days at the villa. Yes, I am so happy right now. Yanni plays on the air as I dream I am on holiday in a far off location…oh! But I am…

The music stirs my soul, pushing me to dream of possibilities, tugging at me, whispering my name to come and follow. I am enchanted as I sit finishing my drink, gazing out over the darkened sea and the fading sky; and I smell the change in the air that comes at this time of day. I let my breath out, I feel the energy shift in the room as someone comes up behind me.

"Excuse me, is anyone sitting here?" He is clearly Greek but speaks as though he has been schooled in America and he is pointing to the empty seat across from me.

"No, there's no one."

"I'm sorry to hear that. You shouldn't be alone on an island such as this." Blushing, I turn my gaze away from him to look out at the water one last time before leaving in search of food. He orders his drink from the waiter – a glass of champagne. He doesn't seem very Greek, I think, or he would be ordering something more exotic and ethnic than champagne…like Ouzo or Grappa.

"Even though I am back in my homeland, I still love the taste of good champagne to toast Helios on his journey. It is a miracle each day that the sun rises in the east and sets over the western sea here – each day that we breathe, each day that he is successful in his journey. This man has my attention with his eloquent and poetic speech and his mythological ideals.

"Yes, I agree. Are you from here?"

"No, no. I grew up in Kalamata where the olive trees grow on the hillsides overlooking the sea. But I now have a home here as well. I have always loved this little village and its people." He lifts his glass and savors a small sip.

"You cannot find a people better than those on Mykonos. Once they get to know you, they will treat you with kindness and love and then take you into their hearts as well as their homes. That's what happened to me and that's why I am here. They are the family I always come back to when I return from America each year."

"Where do you live in America?" He is an attractive man who reminds me of a Greek Omar Shariff.

"I live in Cambridge, Massachusetts for most of the year. Every spring or early summer, I come here to see family, to rest, and to pay homage to the sun God Helios." He smiles with reverence as he looks out over the now darkened sky. "You know the skies are usually gray there most of the time – summer or winter…it does not matter." His face is sweet, the face of someone who has known love, compassion and life intimately. His eyes are dark and his hair is graying and there are two deep dimples in his cheeks and a cleft in his chin. Although his face is rugged, it is filled with warmth and makes me want to smile when I look into it.

"I have never been to Boston, but I know the weather. I need the sun every day or I feel blue." As the conversation continues, he flags the waiter over for another glass of champagne and motions for another of whatever I am drinking. I think about dinner, but want to stay and talk with him a little longer. It's as if he is a male counterpart of Elana.

"No, please. I'll have what he's having."

"Excellent choice; it is Veuve Clicquot, a French champagne. No one can beat the French in the making of champagne, you know." He extends his hand to me and introduces himself. My name is Cristos; but you may call me Chris as everyone does in the States."

"I am Roxanna." We politely shake hands.

"Where are you from, Roxanna?" He seems so pleasant and well-bred with his beige linen suit and woven leather shoes.

"I'm from California, a small town near San Diego."

"I travel to San Diego a few times every year. What is the name of the town?"

"Carlsbad."

"Yes, I have been through there. You are not traveling alone, Roxanna, are you?"

I think before answering the truth and feel safe enough to do so.

"Yes, I'm traveling alone. A little vacation I guess you could say." We talk for an hour or so and finish our champagne. I learn he has a wife, an American woman who is a professor at Boston University and three boys, all now in college. I enjoy talking to this man with the sweet face and a wonderful outlook on life. Everything is poetry and music to him. Nothing gets by him without notice and he explains in detail, everything he is thinking and experiencing. I ask him if he is a writer, a poet or a painter, but he says he is simply a businessman. Soon, I find myself telling him about my wild journey and how I have left my life in search of romance, passion and adventure, as the music sets the scene.

"Have you found what you are looking for yet, Roxanna?" I am taken aback by the question and he sees that I am startled. "I apologize. I did not mean to pry."

"No, no…don't apologize. I haven't thought about it. I've had so many adventures so far and have found romance…and passion within myself. I want to paint again and feel life always, each and every day, every moment, since I've come here."

"Excellent, then…I am guessing your journey is almost complete?" Again I feel as if a jolt of electricity has entered my fingertips and gone straight to my heart and I have no response for him.

"While you are contemplating your life and your next move, I think that I should feed you so you will have the strength to do so!" His laugh is big and hearty and I am caught off guard by it, so naturally, I am laughing too, which releases some of the tension that has come with these questions. We rise and he takes my arm in his as we walk out of the Veranda and down into the street in search of a restaurant. We round a corner in Little Venice and arrive at Nico's Tavern.

"Will this do for you, Roxanna? It has the best seafood on the island, caught fresh every day."

"Yes, this is perfect." I have been quiet, deep in thought as Cristos talks on and on about this shop that we have just passed, or the owner of that one, or this man's family, or the weather. I shake my head to tell him I am listening, but I am not. I'm thinking about whether I'm finished traveling or not…is it time to go back home? But home to where? To America? To Capri? To Rome?

A man approaches and speaks to Cristos in Greek, hugging and kissing him in greeting. They are laughing and happy to see each other again, and then he takes us to a table overlooking the square where we can watch everyone as they pass by. Cristos orders fresh fish for both of us and the owner takes him outside to the fish case to choose our meal from the fresh catch of the day.

We are served Greek wine, *spanachorizo* – spinach and rice, *kolakothopita* – zucchini pie, the fresh grilled fish and Greek salad. As we eat, the local pelican named Petros, the island's mascot has arrived at the front of the restaurant causing quite a stir. He is three feet tall – a big one, trying to nose his way into the case of fresh fish at the door, and the owner is talking loudly but lovingly to him to move away, as if he were a small child. His hand is on the pelican's long beak as he steers him away from the restaurant. Everyone is laughing at this funny site, the pelican looking as if he is the one in control while the owner looks like a crazy Greek talking loudly with his hands.

"Petros is the local celebrity, you know. Everyone loves him, but he is like a child always into everything. He has been tormenting poor Niko since I have been coming here all these years." He laughs and I see the roadmap of his life etched upon his sweet face in the candlelight. I have to ask him.

"Cristos, why is your wife not with you on this trip?"

"Ah, my beautiful Teresa…" He has this dreamy look on his face when he speaks her name. "She likes to go to the Cape - you know, Cape Cod every summer. She is not one to travel the world like me. She prefers the sounds of the same ocean lulling her to sleep at night while I prefer to roam the world in search of many different sounds. I am always up for an adventure." He winks at me and his dimples deepen.

"Where do you go? What are some of your favorite places?" I am intrigued by this unique human being who sees light in all things and beauty in every breath he takes.

"I have a home in Kalamata of course, Mykonos, in Cambridge and also in Falmouth on Cape Cod. I would have homes all over the world if I could, but these are my favorite places. My beautiful wife allows me to travel to Greece whenever it calls to me as long as it takes me home to her when I am finished having my soul soothed. So I travel the world and return to her when I am done." He eats in between the conversation.

"She is very beautiful, you know. I fell in love with her the first moment I saw her. She was a student, as I was at Northeastern University many years ago. She had blonde hair, which we Greek men love…I was no different than them. We fall in love with everything you know." He laughs out loud at his own joke; then he continues.

"I asked her out many times, but she was never interested in someone as rough looking as me. She told me so…spicy that one. She has never been afraid to tell me what she thinks."

"I was a young man in love, pining away for her for many, many months before she finally did me the honor of going to dinner with me. Well you can guess that I brought her flowers and we celebrated with champagne. After that first night, she was mine and what a prize she was. She knows I cherish her but she lets me run free."

"She's a very lucky woman, Cristos. You are very unique as I am sure she is as well. Relationships like yours don't happen every day."

"Thank you for the compliment, Roxanna. And you, what is your experience with love?" His question is profound and unexpected. I think about my life thusfar - my ex-husband and then all of the men I have loved as they quickly flit through my mind. Then, I think of Natale. A warm shiver creeps across my heart and spills out onto my face in the shape of a smile. I am thinking about the way his breath feels upon my skin like moist words when he speaks to me, so close that his lips are almost touching me. Then I remember his dimples and the way he cups my face in his hands as he kisses me.

"I have known love before, Cristos. I have someone waiting for me in Rome, but before I go back to him, I have to make sure this is what I truly want. I met him when I was searching and I want to make sure I am not just trying to fill that empty place in my heart. I want to make sure it's real."

"What is real, Roxanna? Nothing is real...everything is. What you felt when you were with him is the only real thing there is. There is nothing out there anywhere else in the world that is better than that place you felt then. I know. I am much older and wiser than you." He laughs that deep, hearty laugh again and I can see his chest rising and falling with each guffaw. "Enough talk of life now; let's enjoy the food and wine!"

I am relieved to change the subject for I know I will spend much time pondering it as I try to sleep later. The night is coming to an end and Cristos is walking me back to my hotel as we walk arm in arm.

"Roxanna, I am here for another day and I am going to the island of Delos tomorrow to pay homage to Apollo. It is not too far from here. Would you like to go there with me? I will show you Delos like no one else can. It is a very sacred place – his and his sister's birthplace."

"Yes; where shall I meet you, and at what time?" We set a time and say good night and as I ready myself for bed, I think of Cristos and wonder if all Greeks have the depth that he does.

CHAPTER 33

DELOS

"You see the land mass there? It is not actually all of Delos but two separate islands connected by that narrow strait." We are on a boat motoring to the island. "This one, the smallest, is Delos. It's where we are going. That one over there used to be called the Great Delos because it is three times bigger; but it is actually Reneia." He continues.

"History goes back to at least 400 B.C. when the Athenians ordered the purification of Delos. They thought it to be sacred because it was the birthplace of Apollo and Artemis. They moved all women who were about to give birth and all those who were on the verge of death, to the island of Reneia in order to keep Delos pure. Have you heard the story, Roxanna?" I had read about it but wanted to hear him tell it.

"No."

"The story goes that Zeus loved beautiful women – goddesses that is. He was married to Hera, but had a love affair with Leto, and his wife was so enraged because of all of his infidelities, that she sent out an order that no place in the world was to receive Leto and allow her to give birth there. Zeus went to Poseidon and asked for his help; and he then struck the sea and many islands appeared – now called the Cyclades."

"This island Delos appeared, flat, rocky and barren…treeless, with no mountains – except for that small one, the Sacred Mount Kynthos." He points to a small rise in the earth before us and then continues.

"Because of the landscape, it appeared it was always bathed in sunlight, a place that the god Helios blessed daily. They say it draws the light into itself and reflects it back to the one who is looking down upon it, and that is how Zeus and Leto saw it when they chose this place." I am enjoying his tale as I close my eyes and feel the sun bathe my skin. The air is hot and dry, but when a small sea breeze blows off of the water, I am cooled.

"Leto, being persecuted because of Hera's wrath, took refuge on the island and brought Apollo and Artemis into the world here. There is a museum on Athens – the national Archeological Museum…did you visit there, Roxanna?"

"No, I am afraid I ran out of time."

"You must go back and visit this place. It has many mythological artifacts that you will enjoy. Anyway, there is a figure of her dated 370 B.C. in which she is sitting holding on to a palm tree, as she gives birth. She is surrounded by Athena, Aphrodite and a few others. It is most beautiful." He looks out toward Delos as he recalls the image in his mind.

"Now I have to go back and see it. I love Greek Mythology, Cristos. I really believe the Greeks were the first to inhabit the earth and from them, humanity was born." He laughs full and hardy.

"Yes, I do, too. The world is divided on that one, but at least the Greeks are on your side." We step off the boat and walk along a dry sandy path as the lizards scurry from our sight.

"Tell me more. I love to hear your stories, Cristos." He takes my hand and places it inside his arm like old friends do when they walk together.

"So you like my stories, eh? Let's see…they say the island is held in place by diamond columns that no one can see but the gods. Once Apollo was birthed here, it became a very sacred place. Do you know about Apollo, Roxanna?"

"I know that he is the God of Music."

"Ah, but he is so much more than that – although they say no one played the lyre as well as him. He is also famous for his skills in archery - and medicine, for he held the secrets to healing people. But what many don't know about him is that he was a prophet of sorts. He is the one who found Delphi for his sacred temple where the priestess or Pythia communicated his prophecies to the world. You see, he wanted the world to know and understand his father Zeus; hence the oracle of Delphi and the temple."

"I read that many traveled far to go to the temple to seek answers to their problems…many kings and emperors."

"Yes, you are correct; even Alexander the Great traveled there, for he thought he was the incarnation of Achilles. He traveled to Apollo's Temple and took the great bronze, tin, and silver armor and the helmet with its triple crest that belonged to Achilles. The priests were holding it for safe keeping in the temple because it was considered a sacred object, and when Alexander saw it, he knew it should be his, so he took it. He was, after all, a descendent and heir to Achilles; but in his mind, he also thought he was his reincarnation. Who knows…maybe he was." Maybe…

"Did you hear these stories as a child?" I am curious.

214

"They were our history here growing up. And yes, I loved them. My grandfather used to tell me stories of the great gods and goddesses every day of my life as we worked in the fields. These are my fondest memories of Kalamata." He has a far off look in his eyes as we walk through the ruins, past the Avenue of the Lions that used to guard the Sacred Lake that has since dried up.

"Around 400 B.C. there was a great plague on Delos which people thought was the wrath of Apollo, which is why they decided to move all the pregnant women and the dying to Reneia. After that, no one was allowed to be born or to die on this sacred island. It is one of my favorite places because I am very fond of Apollo. To me, he is the god of light, the healing arts, music and all that is important in life."

We continue to walk through the ruins as Cristos fills me with its history, pointing out all of the temples, the agoras, and the houses. I am amazed at how many temples are here. There are the Houses of Cleopatra, Dionysos and Trident, the House of Masks, and the House of the Dolphins, the Temple of Serapis, and finally the Temple of Apollo. Everything is built from marble with mosaic floors, some still beautifully preserved. Most of the original statues have been removed although a few are still standing. The now headless statues of Cleopatra and Dioskouridis remain and there are other partial statues throughout the city. Many of the columns have been put back together and stand tall so one can envision what the buildings must have looked like in their time.

There is even a place called the Terrace of the Foreign Gods below Mount Kynthos where lie the ruins of the sanctuary of the Egyptian Gods and the ruins of the Heraion, an old temple of Hera's. The mosaics on the floors of the homes are superb, but the one that stands out to me is in the House of Dionysos. I try to take photos of it and hope they come out in the bright and almost blinding sunlight, for there beneath my feet is a statue of Dionysos himself dressed in robes of gold and white sitting on the back of a panther. The panther's head is turned upward toward him and his eyes are wide, his teeth bared and his huge talons out as he looks at the spear in Dionysos's hand. It doesn't seem thousands of years old for it is still mostly in tact and the colors are sill vibrant and beautiful.

"Roxanna, each year when I come here, I go to the mountain to pay homage to the gods. Would you like to walk to the summit with me?"

I consider it for a moment but want to sit alone amongst the ruins and feel the place. "No, thanks. I think I'll just sit here. I'll wait for you, you go."

So I sit on a marble seat outside Apollo's sanctuary feeling the heat of the sun upon my face and eyelids. I now understand what they mean when they say that Delos is flooded with the light of the sun…so bright. As I open my eyes and look at the ruins around me, I see the blurriness and iridescence that comes with intense heat and light when you are looking out toward a horizon. It seems as if the ground is boiling in the distance. I close my eyes again to protect them from the dryness of the heat.

In this moment, I feel the presence of someone standing before me so I open my eyes but am mistaken, for there is no one. I wait, so familiar with the energy of the spirit world when it appears. I now feel the radiance of light envelop me as if I am being bathed by light instead of water. Then I hear a voice speaking to me.

"I am Helios, the God of Light and of the Sun. You have come to my sacred place to connect with the light and with Apollo. Know that he and I are one and the same. If you look closely at our faces on many of the statues that mankind has sculpted, you will see our resemblance. I assisted in creating this place for him for it was also a place for me. When you bow to Apollo, you bow to me. You see, the light heals all that ails humankind and Apollo knew this but no one would listen. Did you not know that when you go out into the sunlight, it rids the body of disease?" He laughs.

I am so enraptured with the light I am bathed in and the luminescence of the being that is standing before me. Although he comes to me without form, only light, his voice is strong and his power great. I am speechless and cannot speak a word.

"Do not be afraid, as I am here in love. You were meant to come here to connect with me, Roxanna, for I am a friend of the one they call Mih-**kyle**-rah, the Lord of Truth. Bask in the sunlight here and heal yourself, for once you feel me, you will yearn for me upon your body every day. That is why you love Capri, the place that worships the sun and the light." I open my eyes, but he has already left.

My head is spinning and I feel drunk and dizzy. Mih-**kyle**-rah is my name for San Michele. He loves Capri – said it was his place - Helios is connected with Apollo - okay… I understand that, but how is Michael connected with them? My head is swimming and I need a drink of water.

"Roxanna, are you all right? You look confused?" It is Cristos who is walking toward me from the mountain. "You are in the sun too long I fear."

"I'm fine, but I need some water."

"Let's walk toward the museum. There is a place to buy something to drink there." He holds my arm in his once again as we walk in between the hot sun and the baked earth.

"What do you know of Apollo and Helios? Are they connected in any way?" I am curious but don't want to tell him anything.

"Ah, Helios…some believe that Apollo and Helios are one and the same – that Apollo is a reincarnation of Helios. They say that Helios was not content with only the power of making the sun rise and set each day, with bringing light to the earth. He also wanted to make people aware of the power of the light and its healing properties; so the only way he could do this was to be reborn into Apollo, the Great Healer. They also believe that even then, he wasn't satisfied that he had touched enough of the world so he chose to reincarnate again and again." We reach the concession area and I excuse myself for the ladies room. I need a few moments alone to process all of this.

So if Helios is Apollo, is he also Michael? He has always been with me in my times of darkness, holding my hand…and the times when I was ill… He is the bringer of light and truth. The bringer of light… everything is running together in my mind now, like melting snow.

"Yes, yes, they are one and the same…" I hear the voices as if they are those of the sirens.

Cristos has been standing outside the restroom waiting with a bottle of water. "Are you feeling better?"

"Yes, thank you." I have finally collected myself, I think.

All of the artifacts from the city have been moved to the museum so we visit the place and walk through room after room of ancient sculptures and bas-reliefs. Most are in good condition and some have been cemented back together. There are many of Apollo, Artemis, Athena, even Kouros and other Greek gods and goddesses. When we return to the boat, it is mid-afternoon and I am sorry to be leaving this sacred island. I promise myself that I will be back.

"Roxanna, I would like to take you to a beach at the end of the island that you have not yet seen, Paradise Beach." I nod my head yes. "Good! Then we will leave from the port."

CHAPTER 34

When we arrive back on Mykonos, we walk to Cristos' scooter which is parked on the outskirts of town. I hop on and hold on tightly for the three mile ride to Paradise Beach. When we arrive, I am surprised by the difference between here and the port town. I can see immediately that this is a place of decadence. The beach is lined with bars offering fancy drinks and exotic music, the kind that is sort of Euro-disco. It has a gyrating beat that makes you feel sexy, makes you feel that anything is possible.

There are cabanas and chairs everywhere overlooking the beautiful expansive coastline, and a sandbar half a mile out where a young man in a pink speedo is standing. As I look more closely, I realize almost everyone is nude. It's a nude beach! Cristos laughs when he sees the look of surprise on my face.

"Yes, yes…they are nude. Anything goes here. But pay no mind. It is old news for everyone here, for it is a way of life." He takes me to the back of one of the bars called Nirvana where there is a small harem room filled with beds topped off with colorfully stuffed pillows, and a small pool of water in the center. I can imagine what goes on in these more private quarters which are somewhat hidden by sheer curtains. As we walk by, I notice couples naked in these private rooms – all of them - and some are kissing and touching each other or dancing erotically to the music. I look away, slightly embarrassed and think well I am in Greece after all.

Where would you like to sit, Roxanna? We can sit in a room here near the pool or in chairs overlooking the sea. It is up to you." I think about the private room being a little too cozy and opt for the sea view.

"I'd like to sit on the water if you don't mind." So we head toward the beach and find two chairs. Cristos orders a bottle of champagne, Veuve Clicquot, and proceeds to remove all of his clothing.

"I hope you don't mind, Roxanna; but this is how I enjoy the sun." He says it so matter of fact, as if it is an everyday occurrence.

"Not at all." I gulp and look away then sit down keeping all of my clothes on. As we drink our champagne, look out to sea and watch all of the naked people running around, I feel myself relax. The more I look around, I realize not all are young and beautiful. There are people of all ages with all different body types, but they aren't the least bit self-conscious about their bodies, but rather relaxed and happy. Most are lying on their backs with their arms behind their heads, naked for the world to see and enjoy. I start to giggle.

"What is so funny, Roxanna?"

"I was just thinking about how self-conscious I am and how hot I am in this heat. No one else seems to mind that they are naked as the day they were born. You have to remember I'm American. We don't sit around naked in front of just anyone!"

"Yes, I know. They don't do this on Cape Cod, but you do what you need to do." He pats my leg and says, "I'm going for a swim." I watch him walk to the water, and steal a glimpse at his manhood as he turns around and waves to me. It isn't every day I get to see so many men naked – such a wide range of flaccid sizes. I had no idea! The champagne and sun have gone to my head and I am giggling again – alone – in my chair – all this nakedness for my enjoyment -

Cristos is in very good shape for his age, toned and muscular as if he still works out regularly. He dives into the water and I imagine what it would feel like on my now sweating body as I wipe the beads of perspiration from my face and neck. Then I remember what Michael said to me before I allowed Valentino to sculpt me. *"Drop the puritan attitude that you have lived with…"* This is so silly…

"Well, it's now or never!" I remove my top and bra and then stand to remove my shorts and panties. O-o-h-h-h, how delicious I feel as the breeze ripples across my bare nipples and the rest of my damp body. I walk as quickly as I can to the water and then into it, hoping no one is looking. I dive in and feel the cool Aegean wash over me and shiver with ecstasy. Mmmmm… This is like making love. I swim out to Cristos who is floating above the sandbar, his manhood cresting the water-line.

"Ah, this is the life, eh Roxanna? Glad you joined the rest of us in Paradise." He closes his eyes and relaxes back into the water. I do the same and allow my naked breasts to be revealed to Helios and Apollo and all the other gods and goddesses of the Greek islands. We play in the water for quite awhile before retiring to the sand where we bake in the sun like lizards.

"Thank you for this, Cristos. I am still quite shy – even at my age. It's an American thing, I think. We are not as free with ourselves…quite inhibited I think."

"I know. I struggled with that raising my sons. Their mother was brought up very strictly in New England and the naked body was not to be taken lightly." A smile creeps across his sweet face, "I wonder what she would think if she knew I was sunbathing naked with a beautiful woman? I don't think that she would understand that it is innocent. I love her far too much to wander into the arms of another, even though you are very beautiful my dear."

"You flatter me, Cristos; and you're right. She probably wouldn't understand for I wouldn't either."

When evening comes, Cristos takes me to his house in the countryside, not far from Paradise Beach. After our afternoon sunbathing, I feel perfectly safe with him. It is a small cubical two-story building, white washed with red doors and stairways instead of the blues I have seen everywhere. The only way to the upper level of the house is via an outside staircase which is lined with colorful potted plants. Bougainvillea has grown all around the front door and is now growing up the side of the house. The chimney on top of the house looks like a church spire. Other than that, there is nothing fancy or opulent about it. It is very simple with clean lines, and painted with the sparkling white-washed paint that is used everywhere on the island. There are cacti and small trees on the property but no gardens…I am sure because it remains empty most of the year.

"How often has your wife been here, Cristos?"

"She has been maybe five times in the last ten years. She really is a homebody and when she is not teaching in the summer, she loves the Cape house in Falmouth. But this is my favorite. So we allow each other the freedom." We talk as Cristos makes dinner, and soon it is laid out on the table. There is fresh local white fish and salad, and bread, *keftedes, kopanisti* – a soft spicy cheese made from goats and cows milk and *sadziki* – a cake made from yogurt with garlic sauce, all of which he had stopped to purchase from the local market.

"It is nice to have companionship here, Roxanna. Thank you for allowing me to make dinner for you." I will be leaving the island tomorrow and going on to Kalamata. I love the quiet there and the smell of the olive groves which brings back wonderful memories of my childhood."

"What was it like to grow up in Greece?" I am curious about the culture which I know little of, aside from its mythology.

"Ah, it was wonderful." He has a dreamy look in his eyes as he looks upward, the cleft in his chin standing out in the low light. "We had little money but I never knew it. My father and mother always had food on the table and we always had clothes on our backs. Our olive groves were so large that as boys, we worked long days during harvest with my grandparents and parents. It was our way of life. The rest of the time, besides the menial chores around the house, we played in the groves on the hillside or went swimming. Life was sweet."

"I spent a lot of time with my grandfather whom I loved very much. At night, he would take me for walks down by the sea and there he would tell me stories of my homeland during the ancient times. I still remember his pipe as he stopped in the middle of a story, to take a puff and let the smoke out. I was always waiting for him to finish it seemed, and he would always take his time. It was like a game between us, one trying to move the other. He schooled me on how Greece came about: the Creation of the World with Gaia, Eros and Chaos, and the Battles of the Titans and the Giants. Then there were all the stories of the heros: Herakles, Odysseus and Achilles.

"The story of the fall of Troy has always been a favorite of mine." I am mesmerized as he speaks the words.

"Ah, yes, yes. Paris and the taking of Helen…Achilles, his sweet friend Andantilochos and Agamemnon…the ten year battle… I love all the stories. Roxanna, do you believe that they all existed?"

"The gods and goddesses?" He nodded. "Yes, I do. I have felt their presence before, and I can only go by my feelings and what I know to be true to me." I don't want to reveal my experience on Delos. "Yes, I believe they existed."

"Roxanna, you know that no one took Apollo seriously in the matters of medicine, so he passed these skills on to his son, Asklepios, who became a great teacher of medicine. He could cure illness and then schooled priests in the arts, to assist him."

"I had no idea. I never knew the name of his son although I assumed that he must have had children."

"Asklepios was extremely popular in his time, but Zeus was offended by his talents. He wanted to have the most power and didn't want men to believe that Asklepios might be more powerful than he, so he killed him with a thunderbolt. Of course that didn't put an end to it. There was a temple built in his honor in Epidauros in the 5th century B.C., and thousands pilgrimed there from all over the world to be healed. It is believed that when they made it to the temple and prayed to Apollo, that he would later come to them in their dreams and tell them what to do to be healed. I find this fascinating; don't you?"

I am lost in thought, thinking about that brief moment on Delos when Helios spoke to me about Apollo and the healing properties of the sunlight and now I realize my sole purpose for coming here to Mykonos was to be given this gift of healing – this information from the gods themselves, which is now being confirmed by Cristos. He is an angel that has come into my life and bestowed his vast knowledge upon me, and now this is a confirmation. Nothing is as it seems…

"I am sorry, Roxanna. I hope I am not boring you with my foolish preoccupations."

"No! Not at all! Please don't stop. I love the stories. I am fascinated by them. This is why I came to Greece – to hear all of this and to learn about the country I love so much."

"Please, do tell me when you have had enough, for I love them as well and could go on forever. Sometimes, I think I am my grandfather!" We both laugh as he rises to clear the table.

"Have you ever heard the story of the Sphinx?" My heart has just skidded to a halt and I can hardly get my answer out.

"No, I haven't."

"At one point in time, there was a monster with the head of a woman and the body of a winged lion who came to Thebes and started tormenting and killing everyone who crossed her path. She said she would stop only if she could be defeated and in order to do so, someone had to solve her riddle. The riddle was, *What being may have two feet, three feet or four feet - is the only one of all the beings who can move on the earth, in the air and in the sea - can change forms - and moves more slowly when it has three feet?*"

"If anyone came near her and had the wrong answer, she killed them. The King of Thebes at the time…I can't remember his name…proclaimed that if anyone could solve the riddle, he would make him king, and he would marry his beautiful daughter, Iokaste."

"Well, at that time, Oedipus was traveling to Thebes and had just killed the king - who unbeknownst to him was his father. When he arrived, he came upon the Sphinx and solved the riddle…by the way, the answer was *man*…and she – the Sphinx - was so outraged that she jumped from the rocks and was killed. Of course Oedipus became king and then married Iokaste who was actually his mother…but that's another story for another time."

"Cristos, I am confused about the Sphinx. So it was actually a bad thing?" I'm curious about the one in my dreams and at the Villa San Michele.

"No, no; not at all. This one in Greek mythology, the one in Thebes was a demon sent by Hera. It was either Hera or Ares…I can't seem to remember. Age must be catching up with me. In Egypt, the sphinx represents the Sun God with the head of a king or pharaoh wearing his headdress, and the body of a lion."

I am put to ease now knowing it is Egyptian and not Greek. But now this…the fact that it is the representation of the sun god…Helios…Apollo…I think of the Pharoah Ramses who some believe to be the reincarnation of the sun god… My head is swimming again. I refocus on what Cristos is now saying.

"…over 4500 years old…faces the rising sun in the east…so with its sacred association to the sun and the sun god, and also with the head of a pharaoh, it is actually a good thing. It brings luck and healing."

I must look exhausted, although I am not. I'm just overwhelmed with all of this information, but Cristos stops speaking. "It is time for me to return you to your hotel. I can see in your eyes that you are very tired, my dear." He smiles like a father does, and takes my hand as he guides me out the door and to his scooter for the ride back to town. We say our good-byes since we will probably never see each other again.

"It has been a pleasure, my dear. I have enjoyed your conversation and your companionship. I hope we meet again some day." He bends to kiss my hands and my cheeks, and I realize he will be gone in a moment as if I had never met him or known him…except for the imprint he has left upon my heart.

"It was my pleasure, Cristos. You taught me so much and thank you for your hospitality. I have enjoyed Greece more just by having known you. Thank you so much for everything. I will miss you and our conversations."

"Yes, I will miss you as well. Remember one thing…remember that feeling of love, will you? Good luck, princess!" He smiles and winks at me as I turn to enter my hotel.

I awaken on my last day in Mykonos and lounge in bed as the mist from my dream dissipates. In it, the Sphinx on Capri is speaking to me; but it is an imaginary dream, not like San Michele coming to me and speaking with me. This one is fabricated by my mind and the day's happenings I am sure. I can't even remember what it was saying except the sound of the voice like that of a woman's.

My next thought is of Cristos and I smile. What a wonderful man…such a passion for life. Come to think of it, I have only met wonderful, passionate men on my journey. I love their openness and their individual expressions of passions. I love the way Cristos talks about life, like it is a sweet dessert that needs to be described with each savory bite. I love the way he adores his wife, and the fact that he is not uncomfortable taking his clothes off, teaching me to do the same.

I think of the men on Capri holding their babies in their arms while they walk the streets as if the babies were trophies made of gold. They hold them up for the world to see - kissing and cuddling them as if they were the nurturing mothers themselves. I think of Marcello, Mario's son-in-law who told me how much his two year old son Luca meant to him, his chest filled with pride as he pounded lightly there with his fist. It was an expression of love for something so much larger than his self.

I think of the way they love women. The look in their eyes shows that they know the secrets and that they have figured out what it takes to keep a woman happy. How will I ever leave all of this – this place of expression and passion? Greece is like Italy for me, always teaching me something new, showing me yet another chamber to be unlocked inside my heart…showing me something new about myself that I never knew existed before.

I roll over on my stomach and tuck my arms underneath my pillow. "God, I love my life!" Then, with a smile on my face, I close my eyes again and bask in that feeling of no sound except the faint movement of life around me in the distance, and the birds moving quietly on the air as if they know not to awaken the late night party-goers as they sleep. My last morning here… I hate to leave this beautiful island.

CHAPTER 35

SANTORINI (THERA)

The story of the lost continent of Atlantis, is it fact or fiction…myth or a reality? I am reading yet another tour book I picked up at the Athens airport while waiting for my flight to Santorini and I am fascinated with it. It says that Plato wrote about Atlantis in his *"Dialogues of Plato."* He wrote that it – Atlantis - consisted of two islands, Meizon and Elasson. From his description of the islands, scientists now believe that they were actually Santorini and Crete. He even went so far as to say that Atlantis's city of Metropolis was actually the island of Strongyli, now known as Santorini and that the city of Vasiliki Politeia was Crete. What a feeling to be standing on Atlantean soil.

It is believed that this ancient civilization of Atlantis was destroyed in 1500 B.C. by a volcanic eruption which took place on Santorini. Even though Crete was sixty miles away, the 210 meter tidal wave at Santorini which was caused by the eruption, was 70 meters high when it hit Crete, and the waves reached the island within an hour and devastated the entire civilization within minutes. The towns and villages of Santorini were buried under thirty meters of pumice stone and when the volcano finally blew, it sank the central and western parts of the island, forming the caldera now known as Santorini.

Santorini has had many names. First it was known as Strongyli meaning *round*. Then it was called Kalliste, *most beautiful*. Then at one point in history, Theras, son of a Theban hero named Autesion, settled in Santorini and the name was changed to Thera to honor him.

In recent history, the name was changed to Santorini after the main church on the island, which honored St. Irene. It was called "Aghia Irini" by the Greeks, but "Santa Rini" by foreign sailors; thus, the name stuck. Today, some call it Santorini and others – mostly locals - still call it Thera.

After I check into my hotel which is called a traditional house, I follow the houseboy named Costos up the stairs that winds up and around many different levels, until we arrive at the very top floor. The vistas are awe inspiring and breathless, indescribable actually. From this height which I would guess to be about 1000 feet, I can see the caldera that has been left by the volcanic eruption thousands of years before. Santorini, the piece of island I am standing upon actually looks like the rim of the Grand Canyon as it wraps around in a half moon. At the end to my right, the little white houses look like snow along the edge of the rim. There are also a few tiny islands that dot the seascape before me.

"Oh, my God…" is all I can speak.

"You like?" Costos smiles proudly as if he owns it. He is young, probably late twenties with light-colored eyes and very short brown hair. He doesn't look Greek at all, but has a thick accent which I don't recognize. "There…" He points to the caldera. "Is called Nea Kameni - New Burnt Island. Behind is Palea Kameni - Old Burnt Island. You see?" I can barely see the tip of it with the slight haze of cloud cover from the altitude where we are standing…so high up in the atmosphere.

I am wondering about the names of the islands and Costos' interpretation of the translations. I would learn later that they were in fact exact translations, as strange as they seem.

"There, Aspronisi - White Island." He is pointing to a tiny island to the left of the caldera. He moves closer to me so we are at the same eye level, as he points out the land mass that is further back behind the caldera. "This, Therasia. Five. Five islands make up Santorini." He holds up five fingers to me before picking up my bags again.

I tip Costos and hurry out onto my deck with my camera and before I take any pictures, I bow down to the gods saying a prayer of thanks. Santorini takes my breath away. I am so high up that if there were any clouds, we would be in them! The cruise ships far below are teeny tiny little things that look like matchboxes and I can hardly see the other smaller ships that are next to them.

Yes, it looks like the Grand Canyon with its walls that spill down into the Adriatic Sea, which are the colors of the surface of the moon, all reddish blacks and browns. The contrast of the deep blue sea and the blue sky against the colors of the cliffs is a landscape I have never known before. I stand for quite some time thinking about Greece and the Greek gods that have been here before me. No wonder they chose Greece of all places on earth for Mount Olympus and their home.

My room is actually a small apartment with a sunken alcove where my bed is positioned. It is surrounded by windows covered with white cotton curtains trimmed with lace; and as I walk through the room, they dance back and forth in the breeze as if to greet me.

Off of the alcove is a small area with a couch, a sofa table and a large armoire for clothing. There are three steps that lead me into a dressing area with a large vanity and sink and then beyond that is the marble bathroom with a shower and window above it overlooking the sea. I can look out at the caldera while showering! Okay...this is heaven and I am up high enough for it to be so.

All is painted white - the walls, the floors and the countertops. The accents and the wood in the room including the large cabinet for clothes and the round lamp that hangs from the ceiling are the blue that Greece is so well-known for - a cross between cobalt and the azure of the sky on its clearest day.

I check with Cassandra, the woman at the front desk for the best tours of the island and choose a boat ride and tour of the caldera. I want to learn everything I can about how Santorini came to be this strange and beautiful place that looks so much like the face of the moon.

After the thirty minute walk to town, I choose the *funicolare* down to the port instead of the donkey rides that are traditional. Once aboard the boat, I take a seat up front next to the tour guide. We travel around the three inner islands - Aspronisi, Palea Kameni and Nea Kameni that Santorini seems to wrap her arms around as if protecting them. Then we ride along the coast of Thirasia, the largest of them all and the one that is the furthest from Santorini. But we do not go around it, probably because of its size and the time it would take.

Instead, we dock in Nea Kameni and a guide leads us up to the rim of the volcanic crater. Here, I learn that in the middle of the second millennium B.C., there was a strong earthquake and a volcanic eruption that took place on Santorini, Thera - as my tour guide calls it. It was so massive that it blew out a chunk of the middle of the large island which then filled with sea water. All that was left on top of the water was the crescent which is now Santorini, the further piece of land that is now called Thirasia, and the little island of Aspronisi. The two smaller islands which were the center of all of the volcanic activity were created by the volcano itself: New Burnt Island and Old Burnt Island. We are now docking at New Burnt Island or Nea Kameni.

Our guide is a cute young blonde woman in her early twenties, who has dimples and a vivacious, bubbly personality. She reminds me of the actress Kate Hudson. Although she speaks fluent English and was schooled in the States, she tells me that she has lived her whole life with her Greek father and American mother on Santorini, except for a brief four years in college in the States. It is she who has told me about the translations for the Nea Kameni and Palea Kameni.

Ali, short for Alexandria, jokes about how simple the Greeks are when naming their islands. She explains extensively about the history of Santorini which she prefers to call Thera, and says that there have been ten known eruptions, the last being in 1950 which formed the Palea and Nea Kameni islets.

Ali talks about how the Therans used to worship the twelve Olympic Gods of Ancient Greece and then the Egyptian deities who were brought to the island by the Ptolemies – Cleopatra's family. Today, most inhabitants are Greek Orthodox and Catholic. I learn that like Mykonos and Athens, Santorini had been occupied by numerous tribes, the Ptolemies of Egypt, the Romans, the Venetians, the Byzantines, Barbarossa - a Turkish Sultan who I know had also invaded and plundered southern Italy, including the towns along the Amalfi coast and Capri. I think that after this tour, I will have known more about Greece than most.

We hike to the highest point on the island, the Georgis dome, stopping along the way at the Mikri Kameni dome, the Fouque and Reck lava domes, the Niki dome and the great Daphne crater. The walk takes two hours and is pretty strenuous but the vista from the Georgios dome is inspiring and well worth it. I can clearly see Palea Kameni and to the east, a valley of gray and black lava fields known as the Liatsika lava left behind from the eruption of 1950. With Ali leading us, it's like going to camp, as she tells Greek jokes and sings Greek songs. She says that because she is Greek, she can get away with it and she is what makes the tour so exciting.

I arrive back in Thera in time for dinner and take the *funicolare* back up to the cliff tops of Fira where I walk the streets until sunset. I come to a place at the end of a street and stop to catch a glimpse of the sky and the sea. Then I see Frank's Bar…strange name for a place in Greece… It is a terraced bar that overlooks the sea to the west.

I make my way through the crowd and settle down to watch the magic of the sky as I relish the fact that I am in Greece. And Santorini is a place like no other on earth that I can think of…a crescent moon of an island with cliffs that rise up past the clouds and upward toward the heavens.

I wonder about Mount Olympus and whether all of the stories are true. Some of them have to be, for Helios had come to me. I think about the Sun God Helios and picture him with a crown of sun rays above his head standing in his golden chariot with his four winged horses pulling him across the sky. I think about the house of light that Axel Munthe has built and then I think about San Michele. Even in Greece, I can feel him calling to me. For a few more minutes, I revel in the scene before me and say, "Thank you, Helios." Then I blow a kiss to the sky, to the sun that has now gone to sleep, and to the sea before me.

Now, where to have dinner… As I walk the streets, I come upon a restaurant by the name of The SPHINX. Well with a name like that, how can I say no? I laugh out loud and a couple who are walking arm in arm stop to see what I am laughing about. This is cliff top dining at its finest and I am 1000 feet above the sea looking out over the edge…how dizzying if you have too much to drink, I think. There is a tapered candle before me, its fire dancing in the soft wind. The weather is warm. I think of Cristos and decide to have a glass of champagne to toast me and my adventure; this is what he would have done if he were here. The only regret I have is that the sun has already set and I will not see it from here.

The local shellfish is sweet and the champagne is delicious as its bubbles light up in the candlelight. I never for a moment forget that I am sitting on the edge of the cliffs, for I feel it every time I look out and see the lights of the tiny boats below, drifting upon the sea and of the buildings along Fira. This is a place where magic happens.

I think about magic and Natale enters my thoughts. I promised myself that I would call him when I arrived here and the thought of hearing his voice sends butterflies from my stomach to my heart, so I pay my bill and leave for the long walk back to the Altana to call him. By the time I reach my room, it's almost midnight which is perfect since he finishes work then.

My hands shake as I dial his number, afraid of what he might say to me - or worse, yet, not speak to me ever again. If he doesn't want to speak with me, I deserve it, for I haven't called since Venice. He is probably worried about me… I didn't even send a postcard…thought it too cruel since I'm off traveling without him. The phone is ringing now but it goes directly into his voicemail.

"*Ciao*, Natale; it's me, Roxanna. How are you? I know it's been awhile. I wanted to say hello and hear your voice. If you're angry with me, I understand. I'm still thinking about you and I miss you. I'll try back again another time. *Ciao*." I feel as if it's a lame message and wonder if he thinks the same. Why didn't I say anything else…tell him where I was…tell him that I love him? Because I am afraid... There is distance between us now - and time - and I don't know anything anymore. I lay in bed as the breeze blows kisses through the curtains that fall upon my eyelids.

Natale missed Roxanna's call as he was busy with the last few customers of the evening. When he finally picks up her message and hears her voice, his heart skids to a stop and he can feel his throat close. He has been thinking of her day and night since her last call from Venice, had wanted to go there and surprise her. But he didn't. Each night when he gets into bed, she is on his mind and the only thing that dulls the pain in his heart is a shot of grappa or pure exhaustion.

He doesn't know how he has survived this long without her. The last few nights have been a bit easier as her memory has started to fade away, slowly being erased by time. Is that a good thing?

In her message, she just says *ciao*. He listens to it five times, in hopes that he has missed something, anything that might mean she is on her way back to him...but there is nothing. He decides to walk the three miles home, in hopes that by the time he gets there, he will be physically exhausted. If not, he is prepared to sit up and watch the sun rise which is a ritual since she left Rome.

"Damned you, Roxanna!" He kicks the curb hard and feels the pain in his ankle. "This has to stop! I can't go on like this. No more...I am done...*Finito*!"

The curtains wake me as the cool breeze slips between them and they dance above my head. The only thoughts I have are of how the air feels and the sounds of living in the sky...then, I think about what I will do today. I want to sightsee as much as I can since I'm only here for a few days.

Breakfast awaits me on the lower patio where Cassandra has laid out tea, fresh breads, cheeses, yogurt with honey - a Greek tradition that I love - and assorted fresh fruits.

Costos has come by to chat and see how my stay is. I find out he is from Croatia and working in Santorini for the summer. We talk about which tour I should take today and he tells me that the Sunset Tour to Oia is the most beautiful so I decide to take it. He also mentions that if I am interested in going to the disco tonight, he will take me. I thank him and tell him that if I decide to stay up until midnight, I will let him know.

Before the tour, I decide to visit Oia for shopping and sightseeing. Oia pronounced "E-ah" is about ten kilometers from Fira, its white and okra houses carved into the rocks. It's a quaint village, quieter than Fira and with fewer tourists. The streets are small narrow lanes with flagstones and all are painted that sparking vibrant white color. Here, more so than Fira, the town is awash with color. The gates, doors, terrace floors and simple wooden patio chairs that are placed here or there, are all painted with bright colors of brick red, blue, fuscia, or yellow. Even the large decorative urns are painted brightly. There are bright umbrellas and colorful flowering plants everywhere. I spend the next three hours here before departing to see some of the beaches I have read so much about. They say in Santorini, you can choose whichever color beach you prefer, because there are black sands, red, brown, and gold from past volcanoes.

CHAPTER 36

After the beaches, I return to Fira and take the *funiculare* to the port in search of the tour that Costos has told me about. He said to look for an 18th century replica schooner. The sun is perched in the center of sky directly overhead and the heat has created a desert-like mirage, but the sea before me is not a mirage. It is real.

I cannot seem to find anyone who speaks English so I am having difficulty finding the correct tour. The only words I've been able to grasp since arriving in Greece are *ef hari sto* which I think means thank-you, and it took me about twenty-five times before I finally got it. I am at such a loss with this language. Now I understand what the expression "It's all Greek to me" means…

I finally manage to purchase a ticket. Don't ask me how since no one at the ticket counter speaks English today. On the front of the brochure is a picture of a schooner so I think it is this one docked before me. How many could there be at this one port, right?

This ship has massive sails and is called the Bella Aurora. I wait but do not see anyone around. There are no signs of anyone else waiting for a tour and if I were in Italy, I would assume everyone is on siesta. I stand here for ten minutes waiting, no other ship in sight. A young man in his twenties is on board sweeping the deck so I call out to him and he comes to the dock.

"Excuse me. Do you speak English?"

"Ah?" was all I get. Obviously he does not.

"Do you speak English?" He shakes his head as if to say no then holds up his finger telling me to wait while he goes through the cabin door. A few minutes later, another man who looks to be in his early forties comes out. They are both well-built and tanned, I imagine from a life of hard work on the ship. Again, I try.

"Do you speak English?" He shakes his head no as well. A third man approaches and he doesn't speak English either. *Mama mia*, I think! They keep trying to communicate with me in Greek and when I keep shaking my head no, they speak louder as if this will help. I hold my ticket up to them, point to it, and then to their ship.

Ah, now a reaction. The oldest of the three pulls them all aside to talk. They walk off with my ticket and a few minutes later, come back smiling and motion me on board.

Finally! I hope someone speaks English on this tour and then I remember that the brochure states there will be an English speaking guide. I assume they will be here later and everyone else is running late as is the case many times in this part of the world. It seems to be perfectly acceptable. Everyone is late and everyone else waits for them patiently – unlike us Americans.

Since I am the first to board, I have my choice of seating, so I move toward the very back where I will have the best view. As I am fully engrossed in my guide book, I suddenly feel the ship as it pulls away from the dock. I look up and realize that besides the three men I spoke to minutes before, I am the only other person on board. At first, I don't panic, just sit here stunned. After a few moments, I rise and walk over to one of the men.

"Excuse me, but where is everyone else?" He just stares at me with a questioning look on his face. I move to the next man and he starts talking to me rapidly in Greek and using his hands to express himself. He keeps moving them as if he were smoothing the wrinkles out of a blanket...and I think that if I was in Italy, this would mean *piano, piano*...easy, easy. He then motions with his hand for me to sit. I move back to my seat and try to collect myself. Now I am starting to panic.

What's happening? No one else is on board and I am here with three Greek men who can't speak a word of English. Where are they taking me? My imagination is working overtime and I am dreaming up different scenerios as to why they have taken me. Am I being kidnapped? Then a soft mist from the sea blows up with the breeze and pulls my hair from its clip, pushing the strands in front of my eyes. I pull them back and carelessly fastened them into place as one of the men comes over to me. He motions toward the two islands in front of us.

"Nea Kameni, Palea Kameni." He points to them as he says their names and then points to himself and to Roxanna and shakes his head as if to say "yes." I take this all to mean that we are headed there – just as the guide book says.

Okay, so this is a bit strange. Only me and the three of them are on this ship. At least they are going where they are supposed to. Finally, I relax and sit quietly, looking out over the water and feel the smoothness of the schooner as it cuts through the water. It's as if it were a knife cutting through an ice cream cake.

I say a quiet prayer and ask if I should be alarmed and the answer that comes back to me is "No."

"OK, so I guess I'll sit back and enjoy this tour." With closed eyes and my head tilted upward toward the sky, the sun feels good upon my face and makes me sleepy. But I am excited about seeing the rest of the islands in this crater known as Santorini. I'm still a little anxious about this predicament of being the only sightseer aboard, but I trust that all is well.

The trip to the volcano, Nea Kameni is smooth and the motion of the schooner as it cuts through the water is mesmerizing, calming my nerves. This ship is amazing with all of its beautiful wood and its great linen sails. Within forty minutes, we stop and one of the men drops anchor and we sit in the bay for about half an hour as the men jump overboard for a swim.

They motion for me to jump in as well, but I am not feeling comfortable enough. Instead, I sit looking over the edge watching them as they play like little boys, trying to out-dive and out-swim each other, laughing all the while. The youngest is about twenty-five and the others tease him constantly which seems to be a Greek tradition where the older men torment the youngest in the group.

They wrestle with each other, taking turns dunking and being dunked. Finally, they come on board and pull up anchor to move on to Palea Kameni, the smaller island. Here, they drop anchor closer to shore so I can swim in the natural hot springs that have been created by the volcano, which I do.

It is warm and refreshing and I cover my body in mud as they all do. I am actually having fun watching them play and swimming with them. There's a small church on this island and they motion for me to go and take a look. It's very sparse inside and no longer used, but I imagine that sailors used to stop in to say a payer of thanks for keeping them safe on their long voyages to far off places.

We have to swim from the thermal waters out into the cold sea to get back to the ship although the distance is not far, maybe 150 feet. The water however is a lot cooler than where we just came from. We are now heading toward Thirasia, the farthest of the islands and sail around its entire mass, not stopping. The men come to me and introduce themselves as best as they can.

The oldest, Apollo seems to be about sixty and he is the one in charge. He has silvery hair, long sideburns and a rugged complexion after being on the sea his whole life, I imagine. I cannot ask since we do not speak the same language.

The middle-aged one is Palo and as he tells me his name, he puffs out his chest and thumps it with bended thumb. He has indents in his face that almost appear to be dimples, but instead are deep crevices connected to the laugh lines in his cheeks. His hair is thick, long and black reminding me of Yanni, and he has it pulled back into a ponytail. I can tell he is the mischief-maker, always trying to pull one over on the others.

The youngest is Dino, which I am sure is short for Constantinos which it seems most Greek male names come from. He has the face and the body of a Greek god and dark almond shaped eyes with beautiful skin and thick hair that rests in big curls all about his head. He smiles all the time – as a matter of fact, I notice they have all been smiling.

Is it the work they do on the ship, living a life in the sun and on the sea? I try to imagine what it would be like, to sleep on a ship such as this and feel it in the night, rocking me.

I can tell they are close friends - the kind that would probably die for one another. I can see it in the way they are with each other. Even though Apollo and Palo tease Dino, Palo instigating it all, they are tight as I imagine they have to be, on a ship like this where all hands and eyes have to watch one another and become one as they master the sails.

As we circle Thirasia, Palo points to areas on the island and calls out Greek words, which I guess to be the names of the cities - Agrilia, Potamos, and Manolas. Occasionally, Palo calls to Apollo and takes over for him so he can come to visit me and communicate via sign language and Greek that I nod my head to occasionally, but barely understand. At times, I just want to end the conversation, so I nod my head yes so they will stop.

He is pointing toward the sky and the sea at the horizon and telling me something, but I don't understand. I think he is trying to explain where we are headed to next, and the only reason I understand is because I have read the itinerary in the brochure. We are to circle Santorini and then set sail to Oia to watch the sunset. Apollo also tells me that the name of the ship is the Bella Aurora as he points to the floorboards and spread his hands out saying the words in English. He is very proud of her.

Dino is playing music and I can hear it through the speakers on the deck. It is a mix of international artists and pieces that sound like a Buddha Bar compilation. This, along with the light of the day creating millions of dazzling diamonds upon the surface of the water, soothes my soul. This is paradise and I am sailing to the ends of the earth, somewhere in Greece where civilization began with the Gods of

Olympus. I can feel them now and think of Helios and Apollo. How strange that the pilot's name is Apollo? Is this another sign to remind me of him?

Dino and Palo now have their black tee shirts wrapped around their heads, and their bare suntanned chests and backs glisten brown and shiny in the sunlight. They look like modern day pirates, I think as I laugh to myself. As we get closer to the northwestern tip of the big island, the dance of the raising of the sails begins.

I watch in awe as both men work in unison – an extension of each other as they move quickly from one place to another working the sails and rigging. Dino follows Palo's lead as he seizes the lines to release them. They nod their heads and speak the unspoken language of sailors that have been at sea together for a lifetime. When the furled sail reaches its position high above them, Dino shimmies up the mast to release it, moving quickly from one area to another like a monkey. He unties the fasteners, and the heavy linen drops filling with the wind.

The schooner picks up speed and its sharp prow slices through the Aegean Sea as an Arabic singer croons his song to a rhythmic beat, so appropriate for the scene before me.

My heart is full as I take in a breath, amazed at what I have just witnessed. It's a dance – the dance of the high seas, between the wind and the sea and the men who know how to harness its energy. And in this moment, I think of Aeolus, the Greek god of the winds.

We move quickly toward Oia where we will watch the sunset since the book says that this is supposed to be the most beautiful place in Santorini to view it from. Dino brings Restina, Greek wine to me which I know is made with pine resin, hence the taste. He motions for me to come to the helm where Apollo is, and they have laid out a spread of appetizers of *keftedes*, stuffed grape leaves, olives, breads and cheeses. We enjoy the food and wine as we move along the coastline of Santorini toward its northern point where Oia lies.

I am blinded by the brilliance of the sunlight reflecting off the white painted houses and other buildings of a town high atop the cliffs. Dino has brought a mandolin and starts to play as Apollo and Palo sang. The wine, the wind, the music and the sounds of the ship as it moves upon the sea, relax me and I close my eyes. As we approached Oia, the sun is at the edge of the horizon and the colors of the sky and the sea begin to merge into orange and golden hues. Paradise…There is no place on earth that I would rather be than right here, right now…an end to a perfect day on the high seas.

Once again, the dance of the sails begins and both Palo and Dino take their places to lower them. Apollo must have put the music back on, for a Greek singer is crooning another perfect song. I move to my seat for the ride back to Fira. The colors begin to fade as the schooner picks up speed and when I look up, I realize we are not moving back toward the south and Fira, but continuing around Oia and to the north eastern side of the island. I jump to my feet in a panic and approach Palo.

"Palo, Fira is in that direction." I point toward the rear of the ship. "We need to go that way." I am now officially alarmed.

"Anafi. Anafi."

"No, Fira. I need to get back to Fira!" Dino, on hearing the commotion has gone to Apollo who asks for Palo to come.

"Fira is that way. Where are we going?" I ask Apollo as he approaches. He sees the look of uneasiness in my eyes.

"Anafi. Anafi." He pats my shoulder as if to tell me it will be all right and goes back to the helm. I sit down and try to chase the fear from my mind but it keeps rearing its ugly head and its crazy thoughts. Where are we going? Am I in danger and are they kidnapping me?

CHAPTER 37

THE CYCLADES ISLANDS

This isn't my tour, I now realize. How stupid of me to think so and to get on this ship in the first place! I reach into my bag for something warm but all I find is a damp towel. Palo sees me shivering and brings a heavy jacket, probably his own.

Okay. I am sleeping on the ship for the night, but what about the morning? What about tomorrow? And where will I sleep anyway? I know we are heading east away from Santorini because I can still see the lights from the now distant towns outlining the land mass. The three men come with a bottle of Ouzo and four cups. As I drink, I grimace because it's so strong and I don't really like the taste; but it warms my insides.

We're sitting together and they are talking amongst themselves, laughing and poking at each other while Apollo lights his pipe. They seem safe enough and kind enough…but can I trust that all will be well…should I fall asleep from this long day and the Ouzo.

In seeing this, Apollo brings me blankets and motions for me to lie down and go to sleep. I take his direction gladly; but at the same time, I try to keep one eye on them. Before I know it, I am out until I am awakened by singing and the sounds of the sea.

Dino is washing the deck and Palo is working with the nets that are on the starboard side. As I rise from the blankets, Palo runs only to return with a cup of Greek coffee which is thick and bitter. I assume it would be too much to ask for sugar and how could I communicate this anyway? Apollo comes to us with more coffee and breakfast which consisted of bread, cheese and some type of cold fish that doesn't look too appetizing, but I am so hungry that I devour it all.

Apollo tries to tell me where we are heading.

"Anafi." He points toward the helm. "Santorini." He points toward the stern. In the distance, I see an island that appears to be almost as big as Thera and guess that this is Anafi. What will they do here? There's no way of me knowing and my mind starts working overtime again. Maybe they really are modern-day pirates and have stolen this ship. What are they going to do with me once we get there? They're feeding me and taking care of me in some small way, trying to make me comfortable at least. No one has crossed the line with me or made any advances so this is good...a good sign, but I still have a knot as big as a fist in the pit of my stomach.

As we move into the port of Anafi, Apollo drops anchor and he and Dino prepare to take the dingy to shore, leaving me on deck with Palo. I guess I will have to wait and see what happens next. Time drags on as my mind runs wild and an hour later, they return and load crates onto the ship. What is in them, I wonder? Drugs? Guns? Maybe it's a smuggling operation. Do they have drugs in Greece? I wish I had read up on all of this before I left. As they pull out of the port, I look back toward the island and try to quiet my mind.

I notice that Anafi is all rock similar to Capri and about the size of Santorini. There is only one town visible to me on the entire island and it's at the very top sprinkled with sparkling white houses and buildings similar to Thera. I see the remnants of an old castle which I assume was left by the Venetians. I had read so much about Greek history before I came that I learned everywhere that Venetians conquered, they left beautiful castles behind. These I knew must be the ruins. I also noticed there were sandy beaches all around the island, unlike Capri.

After we set sail, I approached Palo.

"Where are we going now?" I point toward Anafi and say, "Anafi." Then I point to the horizon before us hoping he understands my question. He does.

"Ah, Amorgos." He mouths something that I think means east and points to Santorini. Then, he points toward the horizon and mouths Amorgos again, and another word I think means north. Another island...I sit down at my usual spot and watch the sea in hopes of catching a glimpse of a fish or a dolphin. Are there whales in the Adriatic? I'm not sure. Dino is busily polishing the wood while Palo polishes the brass. Well, if they had stolen the schooner, they wouldn't be taking such good care of it, would they?

It's almost noon for I can tell by the location of the sun overhead. My stomach is starting to make noises because it is empty and I realize with horror that I haven't brushed my teeth since yesterday morning.

"God, I wish I had a toothbrush." I've given up on makeup and brushing my hair since I don't have anything with me! I must look a wreck. And I laugh out loud at the thought of me on this ship in the middle of the ocean on the other side of the world with three pirates and me…in all my nakedness – sans makeup, toothpaste and lipstick! Silly woman, I think -

I lie on the deck, bathing in the sun even though I am covered in 30-sun block, which I remembered to bring on this tour. Who knows how long I will be out in it? Sitting alone with my thoughts and no one to talk to, reminds me of *Mio Paradiso* and my little villa.

There are no distractions here except for my own mind. After the fears die down and I am a bit more relaxed realizing they aren't going to harm me, I am able to just sit and enjoy the sun, the sea and the wind. It's as if I have my own sailing vessel and a fine one it is. It is a replica of an 18th century schooner with two large rectangular masts and two small triangular ones. The deck, rails and floor seem to be made of hand hewn wood that has been highly polished and there is bright, shiny brass everywhere. I know absolutely nothing about sailing ships, but I do know this one handles well…either that or Apollo has the gift.

Once again, they come with food, thank God. At least they are feeding me. This time, there is fresh white fish that I guess Palo caught with the nets he was working with this morning. There is Greek salad, bread, and olives and the wine is poured with the meal – just as the Italians do. Again, they converse with one another as I strain to hear any words I might recognize. But it's all Greek to me…

Apollo leaves and motions that they have reached Amorgos so I stand to look at the island and see that it is rocky and rugged with mountainous terrain. I notice a strange looking building built into the side of the mountain that reminds me of an old castle but now has crosses covering its roof. It is painted that glistening Greek white and looks as if it might now be used as a monastery. At the top of the island, there is another ruin of a Venetian castle and realize that they built them at the very top of the mountains and cliffs for safety, just like Capri.

This time, we dock on the island and both Dino and Palo leave and once again, I am motioned to stay with Apollo. They are met at the port and unload ten crates, giving them to a man in a black sea cap and a blue button down work shirt who pays them money. What could possibly be in them? I haven't seen any signs of guns on board, but who knows? Anything is possible.

Dino returns to the ship but Palo leaves hurrying toward the town, only to return ten minutes later with four packages wrapped in white paper. I imagine they are filled with either cocaine or marijuana. Maybe they're moving drugs from island to island? Palo returns to the ship and the other men slap him on the back as if to acknowledge his hard work.

He beams as he speaks to them in Greek, pounding his chest. I can't believe I didn't even buy a Greek-English dictionary for this trip! What was I thinking! *Stupido*…I say to myself!

I had been so in love with Italian, wanting to learn it and never forget it, that I didn't want anything else to interfere with it or cloud my mind. Now, because of my stupidity I am out here in the middle of Greece at the mercy of hand signals and charades.

Exhaustion has taken over my mind and it is finally resting…too tired to think. Now the rest of me can relax. There is nothing for me to do except watch the men as they work. The sun is high in the sky and it is mid-afternoon; and, I've been told - via sign language - that we are heading east for Ios. This is promising, since Santorini is also east.

Palo is teaching Dino how to tie a special knot with the rope and it has become a game. It's probably not your typical knot, but a puzzle or joke that he's playing on Dino, for he just can't seem to master it. Each time he fails, Palo laughs and talks with his hands as if to say, "It's so simple…watch again." After thirty minutes of this, Dino gets tired of the game and throws his hands up in the air as he walks away, leaving Palo laughing behind him.

The winds have picked up and the sky is starting to change, heavy black clouds moving in. Apollo yells for Palo and Dino to quickly lower the sails and they race to their posts. It's a matter of minutes before the job is finished, but the ship is rocking wildly with the power of the sea…the power of the sea…

I remember this term from Capri used by Enzo, a young man who works on a boat in the port of Marina Grande. I had asked for its translation in Italian and he told me it was *forza del mare*. I had been trying to arrange for a boat ride around the island but there was a storm moving in the next day and the "force of the sea" would be *quattro* – four, too high for sightseeing on a small boat. From this, I guessed the force of the sea now must be about a six or seven.

The winds whip the water up into churning waves that rock the ship violently and all I can do is hold on to the rail and hope I don't vomit, for my stomach is starting to turn. I keep holding my breath in hopes that this might help but I realize it's only making me feel worse. Now, a thin film of sweat has covered my clammy body as it does when seasickness overtakes you.

Suddenly, I am violently ill over the side of the boat, releasing all from my stomach into the foamy sea. My hair and face are now wet and I am shivering, not feeling so well, and probably green. I hear Dino yell behind me but I can't even move my head for fear I shall vomit again.

Palo comes running over to me, picks up my limp body and lays me down on the floor boards where it's dry. Then he instructs Dino to do something and he quickly comes back with blankets and a bottle of Ouzo. Palo talks to me all the while, soothing me, as I lay they in the moving boat, wishing it would stop. He takes something out of a small tin that smells like camphor and rubs it under my nose which seems to relax my stomach muscles as I breathe in.

He then wets a towel and places it on my forehead. After a few minutes, he motions to Dino who pours some Ouzo in a cup and while Palo holds my head up, Dino makes me drink. I think I might gag, but I don't. He won't take the cup away until I drink all of it. Then, he motions with his hands as if to say, "*piano, piano*…take it easy and rest." So I lay here on the floorboards, my eyes closed, drifting into a semiconscious state as the rain falls upon my face. I am lost in between the misery of the retching which has caused my stomach and chest pain, and the feelings of being comforted by the men, the camphor, the Ouzo and the blankets. Is this what it feels like to die at sea?

The rains have passed and the thunder and lightening has moved into the distance. I fall fast asleep. The winds have died down so the sea has relaxed and is eerily calm. When I awaken, I feel miraculously better. Who knows how much time has passed? I only remember how ill I felt and how Palo took care of me.

I sit upright, rest my back against the bench seat behind me, and watch Palo and Dino as they stand watch on deck. I notice the way they are standing with the ship's rocking, legs wide apart and feet firmly planted. The motion doesn't seem to bother them at all. I carefully rise to my feet and realize that if I too stand like them I am not bothered by the rocking, no longer fighting it.

On the darkened horizon, heavy rains fall and there is virga in the distance. How beautiful it is dancing up in the sky never touching the sea… Palo turns toward me smiling, and winks. I realize I am standing as they are, rocking with the motion of the ship, relaxing into it…surrendering…sort of like life, I think to myself. Instead of fighting it, go with it – become one with it. I smile for the first time that day and remember how good it feels to do so.

By late afternoon, we reach Ios and as we pull into port to dock, I look up toward the cliffs. This too is a mountainous island, but this one has many coves cut into the rocks, the crystal clear water moving in and out of them slowly. The white houses and the chapels remind me of Fira at the top of Santorini. This time, the three pirates motion for me to leave the ship with them and we walk into the port town and into a pub where an older man named Demitri comes to Apollo and kisses and hugs him.

Demitri motions us to a table where we sit, and wine is brought to us. Food is also brought and we feast for hours as the owner's wife brings dish after dish. I am feeling much better now that I am on land and my stomach is fed.

Palo and Dino sit quietly as the older men talk and tell stories, none of which I understand. I sit here with these people wondering if I should try to escape and go for help. Would anyone on this small island know how to speak English? Probably not. Or would I be better off staying with them in hopes that they might take me back to Santorini?

I look around and realize there are mostly men in the pub and only two women, all locals, I assume. They look like kind and gentle people, not like they're part of some smuggling operation. Then I realize these people don't do drugs or sell them for that matter. I can tell by the look in their eyes. It's a look of honesty – of good people you can trust with your life. They look like people that would take you in and take care of you if you needed it. As a matter of fact, it's the same look that I have seen in Apollo's eyes, and he is looking at me right now. I wink at him first then he winks at me and laughs.

After my meal is finished, *sadziki* with yogurt and garlic sauce is served. It is at this moment that I decide that this is another wild adventure I am on and that I have to trust that they will deliver me safely back to Santorini. Trust…Okay. I take a deep breath, allowing myself to finally let go of all the madness in my head and then I hear that familiar laugh…

"Is this some wild goose chase you have sent me on?" I ask him with my mind and not my mouth so no one else will hear, and I furrow my brow so he sees my seriousness.

"No, no wild goose chase, just a wild adventure! That's what you wanted, right?" And in an instant, he disappears and I am drawn back into the laughter surrounding me.

Apollo motions for Dino and Palo to go and in a few minutes they return with two crates. The owner smiles and claps his hand excitedly as if he is being given two crates filled with treasures. He calls for someone to bring him something to open them with and a tool is handed to him. When the tops are removed, he sees jars of olives, pickled fish, cheeses wrapped in paper, and bottles of wine that look like they are homemade for they have no labels no them.

Demitri takes both of his hands and grabs Apollo's face and kisses him hard. Then, they touch forehead-to-forehead. He is thanking him for the gifts, and this time there is no money that passes hands. After many kisses, hugs and back slapping, we leave for the ship.

CHAPTER 38

Once on board, Palo says to me, "Ios" and points to the island in front of us. Then he says, "Sikinos" and points out to sea.

"Santorini. I want to go back to Santorini. No Sikinos…please?"

"Sikinos" was all he says as he makes the motion with his hands of smoothing out the wrinkles in a blanket again.

"Yeah, yeah, I get it…*piano*…*piano*!" I say with deep frustration.

"Parla l'italiano?" Palo asks excitedly.

"Si! Si! Io parlo un poco Italiano! Tu?" I am almost dancing now. Finally!

"Un poco!" He points to his chest and nods his head up and down. Good! Let's see how this goes, I say to myself.

"Adesso, Sikinos. *Allora*, Thera." Palo tells me that now they will head to Sikinos but later they will go to Santorini. How much later I wondered?

"Quando Thera? *Oggi*?" I ask when exactly and if it will be today.

"No, *domani* Thera." Tomorrow. Okay…another night on the ship. This is pretty wild. Will anyone ever believe that this actually happened to me in this day and age?

"Okay, *domani*…*promessa*?" Palo laughs full and hardy, his head bobbing up and down and his teeth showing.

"Si, promessa!" He crosses his heart. I asked for his promise on keeping his word.

Tonight, my last night with my pirate friends, we watch the sunset as we enter the waters surrounding Sikinos. This island is like the others, topped with illusory snowcaps, the glistening white houses painted with the Greek paint. Palo tells me we will go into town in the morning to deliver *cosi* - things, and then we will leave for Santorini arriving by late afternoon. I am happy with this news and prepared to enjoy the rest of my captivity.

As we drink Restina and eat some of the food Demitri has given us, I relax and enjoy the stories and the conversations that Palo translates into Italian for me and most of them I *capisco*. Finally, I have to ask why they had taken me like they did. Palo talks with the others and finally says, "*per divertimento, e cosi vedere l'isoli...*" for fun and so that I could see the islands.

Another joke I am sure that was instigated by Palo...so I laugh and teasingly punch him in the chest. He laughs and puts his hand where I hit him as if he is bruised there and Dino and Apollo laugh at Palo as if to say the joke is now on him.

I look up into the heavens and the stars are winking at me as if to say, "Everything is good," and as I drift into slumber, in that conscious dream-state, San Michele appears before me and we are standing at the rail looking out to sea toward the horizon.

"So, sweet woman, you finally got it. It was all about trust and surrender." He is smiling at me lovingly.

"Why didn't you come to me sooner and tell me I would be safe?"

"Because it is your lesson...it is not about this voyage, but about your life. Surrender and trust. Haven't I always walked with you and kept you safe?"

"Yes."

"Haven't you always felt me near?"

"Yes."

"Then all is as it should be." He is smiling at me and I notice his eyes are as blue as blue can be. I have never seen such a color before. His eyes...so full of love for me.

"It is about surrendering to every moment in life and letting it take you like a lover. It is only good if you allow it to be. Now go and surrender to the rest of your life! Go and make love to it! And remember, if you need me, just call my name." With his index and middle fingers, he touches my heart; and at the same time, kisses the top of my head. Then he dissipates into the mist of the sea.

I awaken electrified, filled with energy. Every word he has spoken fills my mind and is held captive in my memory so I will never forget. I also realize for the first time, that I have actually had a conversation with him and have been able to ask a question and receive an answer before he has disappeared. Our encounters and relationship have moved to a new level. This whole adventure – this kidnapping by modern-day pirates is about trust and surrendering to life. Now, I cannot sleep, so I lie awake for hours, looking at the stars and contemplating all of it.

After our morning delivery to Sikinos, we have breakfast together before Dino and Palo are off to do their daily chores and I am left alone to contemplate this journey and my days spent on the ship. I am going to miss this life that I have fallen into the arms of. This part of my adventure is like having my own private schooner and crew to take me wherever my heart leads me to throughout the Cyclades. Greece - where the wind, the sea, the sky, the sun, the moon, and the terra meet to create magic. It has been a magical time with my pirates.

I doze in the sun and am awakened by a sensation that I am so familiar with. I have to express my passion on paper somehow and this time, it's not with paint but with pen. It is a poem and it's as if it has come from deep within me and will not let me rest until I put it on paper. So I write it.

THE PIRATE

He came upon her ship in fury
And took the men by storm.
They killed and maimed and stole her treasures.
All were dead by dawn.

He had dark ebony eyes and darkened skin
And muscles lean and tight.
He was a rogue in all his glory
Who sailed and stormed by night.

He saw the maiden dressed in white
Scurrying away in haste.
Her hair was long and golden red
Hanging to her waist.

Her skin was soft and creamy white,
So different from his own.
His heart leapt in pain at the sight of her beauty,
And her feeling of being alone.

And lost at sea with no one alive
But she who feared she'd die –
At the hands of this dark stranger,
With the deep, black, piercing eyes.

She feared for her life – her heart pounded.
She couldn't catch her breath.
She tried to run, but to no avail.
He grabbed her and brought her to his chest.

He gazed into her eyes of green
That burned into his soul –
Not because she feared him now,
But something else – they glowed.

She saw the love he felt for her,
The pain upon his face.
He grieved for all he'd done to her –
For falling from her grace.

He made a vow that he would keep –
To always be by her side,
And protect her from any harm,
And dangers in the night.

They sailed the seven seas together,
And their dreams were all fulfilled.
And as the years passed on and on,
Their love grew deeper still.

He was so in love with her beauty
As she slept in his arms at night.
She'd fall asleep to tales of his travels
And stories of his great flights.

It was a wondrous life they shared
Living high upon the seas –
After the fateful day when the pirate came,
And brought her to their destiny.

Surrender - it reminds me of another lifetime on the seas where I had to surrender then as well; for if I hadn't, I would have missed out on the greatest love of that lifetime. This time was no mistake...it reversed karma and changed history through eternity by taking me from my life, but keeping me safe and returning me back to it unharmed, nurturing me the entire time. It is my destiny, and theirs fulfilled...

When we finally reach the port of Fira in Santorini, none of us wants the journey to end. Palo is the first to break the mood by picking Dino up and throwing him overboard, Dino mouthing Greek words of protest all the way down until they are muffled by the water. Then, Palo proceeds to chase me around the deck until he catches me and throws me overboard, too! He then jumps in after us as Apollo looks over the rail belly-laughing at the horseplay.

I act annoyed but am just pretending to be as I mouth the words in Italian. The water is so refreshing and it feels good as it cleanses my body of the remnants of my life of no baths for these past few days. I try to swim to Palo and pound his chest in protest as I had done before, but he is too fast a swimmer for me. Eventually we all climb back on board to say our good-byes.

It isn't easy to part, but I hug them all and Palo takes my hand and carefully helps me off the ship, in that sweet and gentle way that he did when I was so seasick. I am going to miss my new friends – the Pirates of the Cyclades.

As I sit on the plane finally heading back to Napoli from Athens, I can't help but laugh out loud at Cassandra's concern with my absence from my room for the past few days. When I finally did return to my hotel, she was curious and thought I had met someone, fallen in love, and he had whisked me off to some far off place. She had wondered if I would ever return to fetch my things from the room and she was quite curious, asking questions; but all I would tell her was that I had found a wonderful adventure, and didn't divulge any more than that.

God, if she only knew, what would she think? I feel as if I have been gone forever and am now happy to return to my quiet little home in Capri for a rest.

CHAPTER 39

L'ISOLA DI CAPRI

Sleep comes so easily this night and stays with me for the next twelve hours at my villa in my soft bed of Italian linens…so much softer than the deck of the ship. There are so many dreams, one weaving into another. They are of the sea, the pirates, of Santorini, Mykonos and of everyone I met in Greece. When I awaken, I feel the peace and the magic of the island envelop me once again. I'm home and this time, I have no intention of leaving for quite awhile for I am feeling out of touch with everyone and everything and want to reconnect with my ancient roots here. God, I think. Have I connected with all of my ancient roots on this trip?

I never leave the villa this day or for the next few days, eating whatever is here; and then I sit gazing out over the sea, watching the boats cross the bay to Napoli, to Ischia, Sorrento and Amalfi. I watch the lizards and the cats as they lazily bask in the warm sunlight and when I am tired of sitting, I walk from one end of the *terrazzo* to the other, stopping at each flower, each bush and each grapevine to see them all and to note what new babies have bloomed or how much they have grown since I've been gone.

I am elated to be home. My last adventure was quite different than all the others in that I had no control over my surroundings, the events that took place or the people that I was with. I had to learn to surrender, finally giving up control and allow life to carry me; and if I could finally give up control to Apollo, Palo and Dino, I realize I can also do it here on Capri or wherever I am for that matter.

I make a vow to myself to always be open and to trust from this day forth. I smile as I think about this because I know that for me, it is something that's easier said than done. A chill runs through me as I suddenly think of not having the control lever in my hand, but then I remember San Michele and know he will always be with me, never too far away should I need him.

Should I continue to call him San Michele now that I know he is Helios and Apollo? This confuses me, but in my heart and my whole life, I have known him as Michael. So I will continue to call him the same.

The flames flicker a golden glow across the room and upon my plate as I sit in my little kitchen enjoying my dinner. Mykonos, Delos and Santorini are playing a slide show across my laptop and I have Italian music playing in the background. How beautiful is this moment? It takes me hours to prepare my meals - from picking food in the garden to washing each piece slowly - to removing all of the little creatures that hang on their leaves since this is an organic garden.

It takes me a lot of time to slice and sauté and then cook on the burners since I have no oven. I have become really good in the kitchen and all my food is delicious…I think I have found the formula to becoming a gourmet chef! Time! So I am eating a big salad with fresh lettuce, and sautéed greens in garlic and olive oil which reminds me of spinach. I have only sautéed it for three minutes so it is still firm and chewy and filled with iron.

Then, I have sliced tomatoes and have layered them with fresh basil from the garden and the mozzarella cheese that Mario brought to me today, a welcome home gift. I then sprinkle olive oil and balsamic vinegar with sea salt on the tops of them. Now I can't decide what is more exquisite…the food or the slide show before me!

Pictures of my travels are dancing across my screen - the Acropolis and the Plaka, dancing with Stavros. There are pictures of Paradise Beach and Cristos, Delos and Mykonos. There is a sunset from Oia and from Fira, and the brightly painted buildings of Santorini along with the view of the caldera from the rooftop of the Altana.

There are numerous pictures of my new friends – Apollo, Dino and Palo and my days on the ship. I have captured their mischievousness and their fun and games, but at the same time, their hard work as they raise and lower the sails and care for the ship. I see the deep lines in Palo's face as he grins at Dino the day they were playing with the knot; and I captured Dino's lean and muscular body as he walks the mast above my head to raise the sails. I had photographed Apollo as he sat in the tavern on Ios, that proud look on his face as his old friends, the owner and his wife praised him for his gifts. Now, I realize how much I miss them and will probably never see them again. Ah, the memories…This, I realize is the adventure of a lifetime, and one that most will never get to experience as I did.

"I love my life!" I am out of my seat now and dancing to the music of Sarah Brightman as if I am an angel twirling and whirling around my little Italian kitchen. I am free and light and happy and have roamed the world. And this day, this night, this meal is my crowning glory, for I have found freedom inside of it - freedom in roaming and surrendering to what comes next…a great love affair with the world – and it is so vast and so filled with passion and adventure that I can have all of it if I want to - if I open my mind to all of its possibilities…

I am so intoxicated with it, without even touching wine that I have to go to bed – and I gladly do so, for I wish my dreams to be of this, my memories of my journey. I sleep with the three of them this night, dreaming of the sea as I feel my bed rocking as though I am actually on the ship with them. I am laughing into the wind with Palo, Apollo and Dino and then I am on Ios eating in the pub as we had done. I'm walking through my dreams as if I am still there, just like I did with Capri when in California. Somehow, Greece has changed me. I am no longer the person I was before I visited there. It has brought a piece of myself back to me that had been gone for centuries.

The silence awakens me and I lie very still trying to pull every piece of my dream into my consciousness so I won't forget, and I play them over and over again before I release them. Finally, I move from my bed and the villa to venture out for food and supplies. How long has it been since I have been in the village, I wonder? I can't remember because time has twisted itself so that I feel as if I have been gone for a half year this time.

The first person I see when I arrive in town is Nunzio at the Ceramica Shop.

"*Ciao, bella; como va?* Where have you been? It has been a long time since I see you. A hug and kisses…

"*Ciao,* Nunzio. *Bene, bene*…and you? He has big smiles like everyone here.

"I am well. We are all well." He is talking about his wife and family.

"I have been to Greece – to Mykonos, Delos, Athens and Santorini. It was beautiful, Nunzio."

"I have been to Santorini, too and the view is beautiful, is it not?"

"*Si, si.* It reminded me of AnaCapri a bit because of how high up I was from the sea."

"Hmmmm…not me. I think it is very different, but it is okay. You know they say there are still many pirates that run the water around the islands there. I hope you were careful." I laugh out loud at this.

"Oh, you have no idea how careful I was, Nunzio! I have to go shop for food now. It's good to see you. *Ciao.*"

"Welcome back, Roxanna. *Ciao, ciao.*" He waves good bye to me as I turn toward the *piazza* and walk down *la strada piccola* toward Federico's studio.

"Ah, *bella…como va*? Where have you been? I have missed your smiling face." More hugs and kisses.

"*Bene, bene.* I have been to Greece traveling around a bit and now I am back."

"Please, come sit with me and tell me all about it." He takes my arm and walks me into his studio to the little couch. The tourists have not arrived on the first bus yet today, so we have some time to talk about my holiday before he has to tell them the story for each painting. "Can I get you something to drink, *bella*?"

"No, *grazie.* I'm okay. I missed Capri when I was gone but it was a beautiful trip."

"Yes, Capri does that to you. It is intoxicating like the scent of love. Once it grabs your heart and invades your senses, you are captivated and can never leave."

"Said like a true painter!" We both laugh at this. I tell my tales of Greece, leaving out the part about being captured and taken out to sea and the Cyclades for four days.

"Sounds like a wonderful trip. Where will you go next, Roxanna?"

"Federico, I am staying put for quite awhile. I miss my home here, believe it or not…all this traveling!" I am smiling as I say this because, I think how lucky am I? He turns to me and takes my hands in his and looks me in the eyes.

"*Mi amore,* have you started to paint yet?"

"No, not yet…soon, though." I find myself nervous as if I have done something wrong. He immediately releases my hands from his, rises from the couch and starts to pace, all the while saying, "*Mama mia…mama mia,*" rubbing his forehead with his hand.

"What in God's name are you waiting for, Roxanna? If you don't use this gift, it will be taken away from you! You are doing a disservice to yourself and to all of Italia if you do not paint!" I feel as though I am being scolded but know he is right.

"Okay *domani*, tomorrow. I will come and paint with you. I promise." He sits back down, takes my hands again and kisses each one of my fingers, one by one, talking in between.

"You…will come…at ten o'clock…and I will have…a canvas set up…and we will paint…until you are comfortable…and no longer fear…the paint brush…" He smiles at his silly joke and I start to laugh.

"I'm afraid, I guess."

"But what are you afraid of, *mio amore*?" His sweet eyes are filled with love for me.

"I am afraid I have forgotten how…and maybe won't be as good as I used to be." I feel the fear rise inside me and tears start to fill my eyes.

"Oh, *bella*…no…*interminabile*…it is never-ending. Once you have the gift, you will always have it. You just need to work the muscles of your creativity that you have abandoned for so long. It will all come back to you." I let one tear fall and he wipes it with his thumb. "You will be okay, *bella*. You wait and see *domani*. I will be with you holding your hand. We great painters have to stick together, you know." He is laughing out loud and now, I am too.

"*Grazie*, Federico. I will be back tomorrow at ten." I hug him and kiss his cheeks. "I have to go now. *Ciao*."

"*Ciao, ciao…domani.*" As I move down the street toward the San Michele Villa, I think of him and how sweet he is. Ever since I came to the island, he has counseled me, guided me and been a dear friend; and if I'm going to dive into the abyss of paint again, who better to have holding my hand, and what better place to be than on Capri with Federico?

I am on the grounds of the San Michele, looking out over the *Mediterraneo* with my hand upon the back of the great Sphinx. Since I come here so often, they let me in for free, and since the tourists have not yet arrived today, I am alone as if it is my own home, my own *portico,* and my own Sphinx.

The sea is calm as it always is and the sky has melted into it, the same color. It is so peaceful, so quiet. I only hear the beating of my heart and the sound of a distant scooter on the winding road far below. My attention is drawn to *Monte Vesuvio*. Out of the corner of my eye, I think I see smoke coming from one peak instead of two; but as I look more closely, I realize I must be dreaming, for it is the same as it was when I first arrived – with the top blown off giving it the appearance of having two separate peaks. I know that the last time it had one peak was in 79 A.D. when it blew off in the eruption that buried the cities of Pompeii, Stabiae and Herculaneum.

I've had this love affair with *Monte Vesuvio* ever since I arrived here and I sit and watch it for hours every day. It seems to give me strength when I am crazed with guilt for leaving my home and my children. It seems to quiet the voices inside my head. All I have to do is look at it rising up out of *Compania* as if it is ascending from the sea itself, a merging of the masculine and the feminine, my mother and father.

"Hello, I am Roxanna, daughter of *Mediterraneo* my mother, and *Vesuvio* my father. Welcome to our family." I am talking to the Sphinx as I belly laugh out loud. "And you are my brother Sphinx? Ha-ha-ha!" I can't stop laughing. Everything seems so real here, even the unreal - making it surreal. I hear the voice in between my laughter.

"It is all real, all of it." So I stand and watch my mother and father as they lull me into a state of softness as I stand there with my arm around my brother. *Mia famiglia...* When I do leave, it is only because the tourists have arrived and the grounds are now filled with their energy and their voices.

"I think it's time to buy paint supplies." I take the autobus to Capri below and walk the town in search of a shop that carries what I need, but before I do, I decide to go to the Quisisana to visit Raffaello, for it has been a very long time.

When I arrive at the Grand Hotel, I search the restaurant for him but he is not there. I ask the man at the front desk if he is in the hotel and he says he will check. When he comes back to me, he tells me Raffaello will be down to the lobby in a few minutes. What will I say when I see him?

I think of Natale and wonder if I will feel differently about Raffaello now. My mind wants to move to chaos and confusion about all of this and how I might possibly feel for two men, but it doesn't have time, now that Raffaello is walking toward me.

"Roxanna, *mio amore*. This is a surprise." His eyes are bright and happy to see me and my heart responds, reminding me of my great love for him. We embrace each other and kiss each others' cheeks, ever so slowly...as slow as we possibly can without giving ourselves away. Neither of us wants to part, but we know we have to.

"Raffaello, I have been traveling and just got back yesterday. I was in Capri and wanted to come to say hello."

"I am so happy and grateful that you have come." His hair has grown a little longer and the bits of silver stand out framing his face. He is one of those men who looks beautiful with this salt and pepper look. "Come, let's walk." He takes my arm in his and guides me out through the most beautiful gardens overlooking the sea; and as we walk, he tells me that he has worked the lunch shift and will start again at 18:00 for dinner.

"Since the first time I met you, Roxanna, I can't stop thinking about you."

"I think about you too, Raffaello." It's nice to know that we have met again after all this time." We both smile for only he and I know what that means to us. He places his hand over mine as we walk arm in arm.

"I thought you would be leaving the island to go back to America and I would never see you again."

"I would have come to say goodbye first; and I'm staying through the summer."

"I am very pleased to hear this," he says with a broad smile. I notice the lines in his face and how much I love them. I want to touch them but know he is a married man and this is too intimate a gesture in a public place. To take my finger and caress this line, this crease that runs along his mouth, would be like making love to someone's face…a secret touch that arouses the senses, both his and mine. I think he reads my mind or feels my thoughts, for he shudders…so subtly, but I can feel it.

"Roxanna, I miss you." He whispers now. "I have a room here where sometimes I rest in between my shifts. Please come with me." I know it is hard for him to ask.

"Raffaello, I can't." I stop and pull from him and walk a bit just to put space between us so I can speak the truth. "I met someone in Rome. I think I am in love with him and I can't complicate things and you are complicated, because you are married to someone else." I laugh at this. "And now I am also complicated because I am in love."

"It does not matter. I have two wives, her and you." We both smile again and try to make light of it, but we both know this reality.

"Yes, but life has taken us down a different path once again. Do you understand?" I can see the hurt in his eyes. Although he is married, I think he dreams that somehow I will be his alone. He walks toward me and takes my arm in his again and places his hand over mine, squeezing it to let me know he cares; and although it is just a touch between two hands, it is like a soft kiss.

"Capisco. But I am still yours and will be here for you. For now, we can stay like this." We are walking the garden facing the sea, looking out toward the Bay of Napoli. "It is a good life here, Roxanna, so beautiful – so peaceful. I hope you stay forever and never leave. Maybe someday we can be together?" I am not sure it will happen in this lifetime, but I agree just in case.

"Maybe…who knows where life will take us next? Every time I think I know, it turns out that I don't." After a pause, I tell him, "I have to go now." I pull away to face him and take both of his hands in mine and raise them to my lips to kiss them. We are at the edge of the garden and there is a tree blocking us from the hotel. He pulls me close and kisses my lips, so softly, so sweetly, so filled with emotion. It is a gentle, kind and loving kiss…the deepest of its kind, and I let him do so. It seems that it is a forever moment, although I am sure it is only a few seconds.

"Please come soon and I will feed you and take care of you, *mio amore*. I wait for you."

"*Ciao,* Raffaello." It is always so hard to part from him. My soul is now all turned up like whipped crème, soft and filled with air. Now what do I do with this? I walk away and look back to see him standing in front of the tree with his hands in his pockets and a solemn look on his face. I think that this might be the last time I see him; it is not an easy thing to walk away from this time - even harder than the last.

As I walk the town in search of art supplies, I think of both Raffaello and Natale – not comparing them to each other but of them separately and what I love about each of them. They are so different and of course I know Natale more intimately.

I wonder what he is doing this time of day as I walk by a gelato stand and see two lovers holding hands and sharing spoonfuls of gelato.

CHAPTER 40

I find a small store across from the butcher shop and the sign above the door reads *L'arte Forniscethe*, art supplies. Once inside, I choose all of the same things I left in Rome - two soft-haired sable brushes, one firmer one, a palette and knife, and eight different colored oil paints. They have no poppy seed oil so I have to buy the linseed instead. Then there is the stretched canvas, the thinner, primer and the alcohol.

Once back at the villa, I take out my sketchbook and look at the sketches I have made of Natale. It is time to paint him now that I am back home. When I see the detail I have captured, it's as if he has come alive and is right here with me. It is hard to digest and to deal with again because my heart is raw. I miss him all over again - now it seems like only yesterday…

This night, I fall asleep with thoughts of Natale and his face before me; then, these pictures are interrupted by Raffaello's face as if he is marking his territory ethereally somehow. My visions flip back and forth between the two of them until I fall asleep from exhaustion.

The dreams come and I am awakened by the screams of a woman. I bolt upright in my bed as I hear her cries in the dark. I try to listen more closely, but the sound disappears. Was it a dream at all?

I try to pull the memories to the front of my consciousness, but can't and all I remember is fire and people running…so unsettling… I get up for a glass of water and walk from my bedroom to the outdoors where the stars are shining brightly in a blackened sky. It is so quiet, I feel as if I am the only one alive as I stand here looking out to sea. Many lights across the bay are still burning brightly even though it is three a.m. Italians are such night people.

I stand out on the *terrazzo* listening to the sounds of silence until my mind grows more relaxed, the unsettling memories of the woman screaming fading. Then, I grow sleepy.

The next day, the heat and humidity seem to rise to a boiling point, so hot…hotter than I have ever experienced. It's almost too hot to walk into the village, but I know I promised Federico. I leave in time to get to

258

his studio at ten. The humidity is so intense that just the short walk to the end of the *terrazzo* leaves me dripping with perspiration. I decide to go anyway. It's not just for Federico, but for me as well. It is time to move on with my life and somehow, painting Natale today is the first step.

"Roxanna, you have come. Welcome." Federico is kissing me as he pulls me into his studio. I am nervous but feel that this is a time of initiation for me. Somehow, it feels so big – so sacred. What does it all mean? It's as though I can feel San Michele beside me in this sacred ceremony as I pick up the brush for the first time in two years.

"*Pronto?*" He asks me if I am ready.

"*Si.*" My hands are shaking as I lay out my supplies and place the paint on the palette. Yesterday, I prepared the sketch on the canvas so I could start painting it today. Now, Natale's face is looking back at me from it with his soulful eyes. I take a deep breath and say a prayer to all that I know.

I call forth Apollo the God of Healing, so that he will soothe my soul and it will be healed of whatever is ailing me as I paint. I call forth San Michele the God of Truth so that I am honest with myself in all of this. I call forth Santa Maria so that she will watch over me and guide me with her love and compassion. I call forth Athena, Goddess of the Art and then I call forth San Francesco because he loves me so. I don't stop there…I call forth my father *Vesuvio* and my mother *Medeterraneo*, and my brother the Sphinx to be with me, to give me power and strength through their love for me. Then I giggle nervously, because I feel insane…

I don't want to do this alone. This is not just about painting a canvas. It's so much more - it is my destiny. It is my release from this life and my entry into another world, through the doorway on this canvas. The new world I am speaking of is how I want to create my future from this day forward. As I pick up the sable brush and dab the dark sienna oil on the canvas, I hear music…a soft tune that seems to be coming from the ethers just for me. Then I am lost…

I never hear Federico as he guides me. I am lost in ecstasy and blinded at the same time, for I never see what I am painting, only feel it as if the brush is an extension of my fingertips. At times, I don't even see the colors I choose, but just know which ones to go to on the palette. I paint and paint and never stop for two hours. He is quiet now, watching me, not painting himself. He has put his glasses on and has his face so close to the canvas, not that I can see him, but I know he is there. He is in shock at what I am doing.

I feel like I am in another lifetime and this is like music to me, so natural. I am good and I know I am better for being here on this island for the rocks, the earth, and the sea feed me through my feet. Its energy - a gift - moves up through my legs and my body and then out through my fingertips. I don't even have to think about what I am painting or my technique…It just comes to me. It's as if my soul is the one painting and I am just the vehicle that carries the brush.

It is two hours before I come to my senses, needing water and needing to rest. Federico is wide-eyed now sitting on the sofa. He is speechless but jumps up quickly to take my arm and guide me to the sofa to sit. I can see in his eyes that he recognizes the state I have been in. It is a place he is very familiar with himself. He moves quickly to get me a glass of water. After he hands it to me and is sure that I can hold the glass without dropping it, he rushes to fill a plate with grapes and cheeses and pours two glasses of wine for us.

I have finally recovered although I am still in a daze. It is now 12:30 and upon my canvas is the face of Natale in oil. My heart stops for a moment. It takes me a few moments to realize the magnitude of what I have accomplished in such a short period of time.

"*Santa Maria*…look at what you have done. You did not tell me you could paint like this. This is *magnifico… il milione cronometra grande…molto bello…*" He is quiet now as if he were in a church wanting to take a moment for silence. I still cannot speak and do not, for if I do, I think I shall weep. I sit in the quiet. I drink only the wine and play with a few grapes. He understands, and we sit in silence for the next hour. Thankfully, no tourists have come inside the studio but only to look at his paintings that are on the outside.

After some time, he places his hand in mine and holds it there lovingly until I am ready to leave. I don't have to say a word, just kiss him and go. Before I do, he whispers to me with reverence.

"I will keep this for you. Return whenever you like and we will finish."

I have lost this day. I don't remember any of it, except that I have brought not only Natale back to life, but myself as well. And now, I have brought more pieces of my soul back to me and I am a richer, fuller person because of it. I sit on the *terrazzo* for the rest of day, not even knowing or caring what time of day it is. No matter… nothing matters in these moments.

I don't remember what time I go to bed. I also forget to eat dinner. Something has taken over me and I don't mind a bit. I'm somewhere in between breathlessness and bliss, and nothing matters. All is well. It feels like when you have made love and your lover has left you for the night and you are left with that space before you go to sleep. You are content with no worries and you know he will return to you, and there is nothing in this world that you want or need after him. That is the place I am in...

"Poppeus, where are you? Claudius..." The woman who is calling out is choking in between her anguished cries. She is running through old Roman streets as ash and large stones of pumice rain from the sky. The mountain in the background above the city is rumbling, the pointed summit is spewing liquid fire, and people are running for their lives trying to dodge the stones that are falling around them. The anguished cries fill the night sky which seems like daylight because of the fire.

A small boy falls to the ground as he is hit by a stone. His mother cries out to the fire god. "Please, not my child. Take me!"

The woman looks everywhere, trying to find someone to help, but to no avail. As the screams grow louder, I awaken with a start.

"My god!" I cry out as I wipe the perspiration from my face and jump out of bed and pace the floor. My heart beats wildly and I am nervously wringing my hands. Why is the woman so familiar to me? God, it's only a dream, I think; but it seems so real. I haven't had a dream like this in years. It's as if I'm there on the streets with the people...It starts to come back to me...a volcano had erupted and people are running for their lives. Is it Mount Vesuvio across the bay? Is the city Pompeii? I don't see the buildings because I am so focused on the woman and the children and the fire that is falling from the sky...and the large rocks of pumice.

I walk outside and look over the Bay of Naples in the direction of Vesuvius, but it's dark. Only the lights along its base are visible...possibly from the cities of the new Pompeii and Ercolano. I shiver as I feel a breeze come up behind me, brushing along the nape of my neck. I sit on the cement seat and look out over the quiet, dark sea as I contemplate what it would be like to die in a volcanic eruption.

Would it be by poisonous gas, or extreme heat that melts the body? Would I be buried alive by ash or pumice? I shudder at the thoughts and try to shake them off and forget the dream, but all I can think of is the woman with the long dark cloak and the look of distress on her face. She is young with dark hair and light colored eyes and I feel as if I know her.

It is almost five a.m. and I am so unsettled that I cannot go back to bed. Instead, I sit at the little table outside my window and watch the colors of the night fade and turn into daylight, hardly taking my eyes off of Vesuvio as if it will tell me its secrets. By the time I finish my tea at nine, the memories of the night before have faded and are carefully tucked away in the recesses of my mind.

The day goes as any other day here does. I walk into town and chat with my friends. I choose not to walk down to Federico's studio to paint for fear he will ask me what is wrong and I have to tell him. I cannot talk about this with anyone. It is too real….too unsettling…too close to me for some reason.

I continue trying to have a normal day, riding the *seggiovia* to the top of *Monte Solaro*, and sit overlooking Capri while I read the British newspapers and sip *espresso*. Then, as night falls, I visit the Caesar Augustus Hotel and my friend Bruno Pappini, the bar manager. We talk about the guests at the hotel, the Prince of Greece and Marisa Tomei who is staying here. The talk is light and I laugh at his stories. Then, I head back to the villa to go to bed with trepidations. I hope my sleep is without dream.

As I walk the path in the dark, I think about Natale and how lonely I am for him. I think about his smell and how his arms feel around me when he is being protective of me. I almost weep at the feelings that arise. I love Capri, but I love him, too. How can I leave here to be with him? How can I make a life with him when I miss my boys in America?

It's a puzzle too big for me to solve right now. I don't have the answers yet. I can feel San Michele's hand on my arm telling me to stay quiet and drop the thoughts; and I know when the time is right, I will have the answers I need. I continue to walk under the stars while I listen to the voices of families on the island all around me. I can hear them at dinner, some eating on their *terrazzos*. I can hear the sounds of giggling children playing and music coming from somewhere. It sounds like a woman singing Napolitano songs, possibly at a dance somewhere. *La dolce vita*, I think to myself – a sweet life.

CHAPTER 41

POMPEII

This time, the woman is running through the streets calling to me. "Help me, please help me." Her cloak is burned in some areas, singed with blackened edges, and her face and hair are covered in ash. She looks like a ghost. Her hands are clasped together as if in prayer and she is roaming around aimlessly shaking them. No one will help her for they are busy trying to save themselves. I can see her eyes. They are pleading with me; and in the background, I can hear the screams of others. People are running everywhere.

Suddenly, there is a loud rumbling of the earth followed by an explosion. The ground shakes and the woman falls. As she struggles to get up out of the warm ash, what seems like an avalanche of pumice stone starts to rain down upon the city. It's so heavy and the stones are so large that one hits the woman and she stumbles.

I am fully awake now and jump out of bed knowing I have to do something. I pace back and forth, same as the night before, and walk outside to look at the volcano across the bay.

"Damn you!" I scream at my father – Mount Vesuvius - with a clenched fist as if I am threatening him. "How could you do this?"

I know it's the cycle of life and it's as it should be, but I won't buy it this time; because I keep seeing the woman's beseeching eyes. I realize I need to go to Pompeii and at least be there, stand on the soil, see if I can feel anything. Maybe if she knew I had come, she'd be comforted somehow. How silly, I think but I don't know what else to do. How can I help the woman? She must be real or it wouldn't be a repeated dream.

I stay awake waiting for the daylight to arrive and ready myself for the trip and the 6:00 a.m. ferry which will have me in Sorrento within the hour. I'll go straight to the train station, the Circumvesuviana Sorrento and from there, the train ride will take an hour or so.

As I sit, I read the stops on the overhead neon sign: S. Agnello, Piano, Meta, Sieano, Vico Equense. If I can walk the grounds of the city, maybe I'll feel something. Maybe I can connect to the woman. Then what? How could I possibly help her? There's no way. She's in a distant time…79 A.D.

Scraio, Pozzano, C.mare Terme, C.mare Stabia. We are moving closer to Pompeii, crawling at a slow pace. Maybe if I'm in Pompeii, I can sit somewhere quiet and meditate. Maybe I can make a connection with this woman…maybe in one of the ruins? My mind is racing. Maybe in one of the temples I have read about…the Temple of Isis or Apollo…the Temple of Venus.

I will know when I get there. I'll surrender to it all just as I learned on the high seas, and allow life to move me wherever I am supposed to be to help this woman. I have to help her, or I will never be able to sleep again! V.Nocera, Pioppaino, Ponte Persica, Moregine…Pompei Scavi…

"Finally!" I race off the train hoping to get inside the city walls at once, but when I arrive at the gate, it's only 8:30 a.m. and the sign says the park doesn't open until 10:00 a.m. I look for a way in, maybe a fence I can scale, but I see nothing. So for now, I order *espresso* from a stand on the corner and wait until 10:00 which takes forever. Once inside, I walk aimlessly about looking for a sign from the heavens or something that will tell me where I should go. I move through the Porta Marina, the main entrance from the west.

If I could close my eyes and follow my heart blindly, I would do so, but the uneven Roman stones in the street are too dangerous. Each stone is bigger than my foot, and each set separately, with a gap that is probably six to eight inches deep in between it and the next one. I know this is from over two thousand years of erosion. If I should lose my footing, I could sprain or break an ankle so I have to walk consciously and very carefully.

I stop to read the map as I come to each intersection in this large city. The Porta Marina is also called the Sea Gate because it faces the sea and was the gate to the Forum Plaza which was the nucleus of Pompeii at one time; from here, I move onto Via della Marina and come to the Temple of Apollo.

"Here," I think. "This is where I need to be." I move into the center of the temple, across the grass which used to be a marble floor, and then up the stairs to the altar. The columns, the roof and the statue of Apollo are gone now and only the floor remains. I sit down and close my eyes in hopes that I will receive a message… nothing…nothing comes to me. I linger for almost an hour, trying desperately to connect. My legs are cramped and my spirit dampened. "I thought this would be easier," I say out loud. No one is around. I am alone, my words falling upon deaf ears both in this world and the next.

I move about the grounds of the temple area and then back out to the street. Next is the Temple of Jove, the city's main sacred site, where I sit and try again…nothing. I go from one sacred site to the next trying to connect with the woman or to be guided to where she might be. I don't know what I am doing or what I can do, even if I do connect with her. I spend the day roaming through the streets in hopes of feeling something – anything at all. After the temples, I move to the smaller Forum Baths, and then on to the larger Stabian Baths. I roam throughout the insides of the buildings and the grounds, to no avail.

All day, I walk the streets, moving through the temples and public buildings, the gardens and the Grand Theater. I never stop to study the frescoes. My head is spinning and I feel lost. It is late afternoon by the time I stumble upon the Temple of Isis. It's a small temple that sits upon a high podium with four marble columns and two niches where the statues of Anibus and Arpocrates stood two thousand years before. Now, only two of the four columns remain and the statues are gone. All that is left is the stone platform that was once the altar and the stairs that led up to it.

As I sit here with my head in my hands, tired and hungry, I hear a faint whisper, "…Go to Herculaneum."

"Why? What will I find there?" But nothing comes back to me. I pull my *Circumvesuviana Autolinee* map from my pocket and look to see if I can find its location. There...Herculaneum. It lies beneath the new city of Ercolano …and it is eleven stops from Pompeii to its north…God, it's already three o'clock...will I make it before they close for the day?

I head back out the gate and to the train and board for Ercolano, which is the newer city that was built around the old ruins. As the train moves north toward Napoli, I think about the dream, the woman in it and her surroundings. Maybe it's Herculaneum instead of Pompeii. After all, there were three cities that were destroyed by the volcano in those three days that August in 79 AD - Pompeii, Herculaneum and Stabia. Waiting to arrive at my destination, I read the guide on the three cities.

Stabia had been a vacation spot for many, with large villas scattered throughout; and Herculaneum, a seaside resort for many of the wealthy. Pompeii on the other hand was a flourishing coastal city, and residential center inhabited by noble families who brought their wine and other agricultural products there. I read on about those infamous days.

When the mountain blew its top, spewing tons of molten ash, pumice and sulfuric gas miles into the atmosphere, all three cities were buried. A ground-hugging avalanche of hot ash, pumice, rock fragments and volcanic gas, called a pyroclastic flow rushed down the side of the volcano estimated at 100 kilometers per hour and the temperature was said to be greater than 500 degrees. Whoever survived the poisonous vapors were engulfed by molten debris or suffocated by the blasting heat wave. I shudder at thoughts of what the people went through.

Within forty-five minutes, we arrive. I jump from the train in search of the now lost city of Herculaneum which lies at the foot of Mount Vesuvio on a cliff overlooking the sea, and I walk up a long, narrow road the distance of a mile before I arrive inside the city. Once I reach the main entrance which is in the northeast corner, I have to cross a bridge which takes me to the eastern and southern sides before entering by a bridge in the southwest corner of the site. I'm exhausted from my long day and all of the walking I've done, but I keep going, haunted by the woman.

I am amazed at the size of the villas and houses as I roam the streets. Some take up entire blocks! I try to tune in to wherever I am supposed to be – to whatever is calling to me, but I feel and hear nothing. I pass the House of the Inn and the House of the Wooden Partition. I walk by the House of Neptune and Amphitrite and then the House of the Beautiful Courtyard. After this, I stop to rest at the Forum Baths.

I enter the women's section where the floors are mosaic tile with octopus, morays and Triton with dolphins. It has survived well I notice, as I sit on one of the stone ledges that must have been a bench.

"Where are you? How can I help?" I ask out loud. I am clearly frustrated and with exhaustion setting in, I am losing my patience. "I must be insane! What the hell am I doing, chasing some stupid dream! What am I thinking? This is too crazy!" I am too tired and dejected to move, so I sit for half an hour or so before I rise to leave.

Eventually, I make my way to the north end of the inner city and a broad porticoed plaza with a wide brick arch at one end which looks to be the city's public area. Again I sit, but nothing comes to me; so I move on to the Sacred Area, a compound that encloses two places of worship - The Temple of Venus and the Temple of Four Divinities…nothing.

I give up and try to find my way out of the city. By this time, it is almost 7:00 p.m. I know the ruins are closed, because I see no one in the streets. I realize I need to leave, but am having trouble finding my way back. I come upon the Villa of the Papyrus to the west, overlooking the sea, where the sun is now hanging low in the sky. It is a large complex with many large rooms and a breathtaking view. I walk through them in awe of what remains of the tiled floors and frescoed walls and ceilings. It is grand. There is a large garden with replicas of statues and I imagine the originals have been moved to the museums. There is an area where a swimming pool used to be and a rotunda-shaped belvedere. I roam throughout, mindlessly walking. I am drawn here and cannot pull myself away from this place. I just don't want to leave.

So I sit on the belvedere, looking out over the bay. I watch the sun and rest my aching back against a cement wall with my eyes closed. This is when I have the vision - a woman in a long white dress with a green sleeveless over coat draped over one shoulder and clasped at her waist. Her sandals are brown leather with straps up her calves and she has a golden band woven through her hair. She looks to be in her twenties and is standing inside her home at the edge of a pond where a swan lazily moves through the water in between the lily pads. There are two boys playing a game of stones on the tiled floor at the feet of someone who I assume to be her husband, their father. He too is dressed the same in a white pleated caftan with an overcoat that is green in color.

I can hear their voices and the foreign language that is so unfamiliar to me. The children are giggling as they toss the stones into the circle, some type of game I am not familiar with. The father is giving them instruction or advice on how to play as the woman looks on smiling. The scene changes and I see the husband and wife walking across the belvedere, the man giving her a red hibiscus flower, fastening it to her hair.

They walk to the edge of the rotunda holding hands and then stop to kiss. And at this moment, I realize this is their house, their villa. They must have been wealthy people for the villa is huge and magnificent. I see the woman's face close up and hear her husband call her name, Corelia Pthengis as he speaks of his love to her. This I know to be true because of the way he is holding her face before he kisses her…and it is then that I realize she is the same woman in my dream! It is her! Finally I have found her! And they lived in this house, the Villa of the Papyrus. Just as I am trying to comprehend all of it, the scene changes and I now see the husband and his two young sons standing on the belvedere looking east toward the volcano as it shoots fire and smoke into the sky. Suddenly, the vision fades.

I'm desperate to know more, but nothing comes and I realize I have to leave to go in search of a bed and something to eat. I am starving and start to feel weak from exhaustion. I finally find my way out of the site and into the outer-lying city of Ercolano where I check into a small hotel. There is no way I can make the trip back to the island tonight. I have missed the last boat and I am in desperate need of sleep.

CHAPTER 42

By the time I eat, it is 20:30 (8:30 p.m.). The restaurant is quaint and conveniently one block from my hotel which is why I chose it. I sit on the outdoor patio and watch as people walk by, all the while wondering if any of them ever feel what I do or see what I see in my dreams. After all, most of them I assume are living on top of a buried civilization here. Is there any connection at all…do they feel it? Are any of them haunted by past memories of these people that died thousands of years ago? I go back over the facts as I try to make a timeline in my mind. There was a seventeen hour span between the first and second eruptions so why didn't more people escape?

"Something else, *Signora*?" The waiter is standing before me and is removing my plate. Lost in thought, I say, "No, *grazie*, just the check." A few moments later, he returns with a small fluted glass of Lemoncello.

"When I was a child, I used to have bad dreams. I dreamed of fire falling from the sky and people running for their lives. I could hear children screaming and crying and I would awaken in the night crying for my mama."

I snap to attention as the young man speaks. Why is he telling me this?

"Do you still dream these dreams?" I am curious.

"No, but I have never forgotten the sounds of their voices. It is sometimes not easy always living on top of a buried city. I know there are so many more down there that have never been found."

"Yes, I can only imagine what it would be like. Do you know anything about that time?" There are only two other tables with patrons so the young waiter has time to talk.

"I have been to the site many times. I played there when I was a boy and pretended it was where I lived. I remember how they dressed and the game I played with the stones. The houses were so big and everything was beautiful. I remember a painting on the wall of an old building, with Hercules at Mount Olympus. I always stopped and looked at that painting. It was my favorite."

"It sounds like you might have lived there during that time."

"Yes. I think so." He smiles and walks away. I reach for my guide book and leaf through the section on Herculaneum but there is no new information that I haven't already read. I'm curious to know more about this family and the house I have just seen in my vision.

"*Scuzi*, what is your name?" The young man has come back to the table and I would like to talk with him again.

"Crescenzo, after my father." He smiles.

"Nice to meet you, Crescenzo; I am Roxanna. Do you know anything about the House of the Paparyus and the people who lived there?" I look at his face which is a darkened bronze color. His eyes are green and his hair is lighter than most. He speaks English well.

"*Si*. When I was in school, I studied our history, and that is Herculaneum's most famous house." He has taken a seat across from me and continues. "The villa was built by Nero's family. Nero's first wife Poppeae had a brother named Claudius Drusus. He built the house for his wife, Corelia Pthengis." I know I have gone pale. It's true. My vision...the name I heard...

"Their main home was in Pompeii and this was where they came to spend the summers. Have you been to the villa, Roxanna?"

"Yes, today."

"Then you have seen the library." I suddenly remember a large room but didn't realize it had been the library. He continues. "When the ruins were excavated three hundred years ago, they found thousands of scrolls that were charred and some covered with hard ash. They are still trying to find a better way to open them without damaging them and losing a lot of the text. Most are philosophical texts written in Greek. They believe that since Claudius Drusus was related to Nero through his sister, that there are more valuable scrolls buried deeper under the library in a hidden room. Our people have been looking for Caesar's "Civil War" and believe that the only copy is in that house. But they have not found it yet."

"Why haven't they excavated further?"

"I don't know. There is still so much to uncover. Maybe soon, they will start."

"Did you ever learn in school if they had any warning that *Vesuvio* was going to erupt?"

"There was a half a day in between the first and second eruption – the big one. Maybe most thought it would be as small as the first and that they would survive. Many left but many stayed behind. I read that the eruption came down in layers...first light pumice, then heavier pumice. I am sorry. I have to go back to work now. More Lemoncello, *Signora*?"

"No, *grazie*. Thank you for all of your help." He smiles and bows politely as I rise from the table. My mind is exhausted and I am lightheaded. It's the feeling you get when you are either intoxicated with life or Lemoncello…or maybe too much information that does not compute inside your brain…

Back at my hotel, I immediately fall into a restless sleep and dream of the volcano. I can feel the stress and anxiety as if I am truly there experiencing it all. I am in Pompeii running through the narrow streets, along with others and I feel panic as the ground shakes beneath me. At one point, I lose my footing on the stone road and fall to the ground. Quickly, I pick myself up in fear of being trampled. I'm running beside a woman who is crying loudly and even though the language is not English or Italian, I understand her. She is crying out for her husband and sons, calling them by name.

Claudius…Drusus…Corvinus…where are you? Please, save them. Help me find them!" She reaches for my hand as we run side by side. In the dream, I am consciously aware that I am back in time but have the sense and the presence of mind that I am also not from there. My memory is from here as I recall all that I have learned today and from the waiter in the restaurant tonight. In her foreign tongue, I speak.

"How can I help you? Where are they?"

"They traveled to Herculaneum on an errand for Nero. He is very angry. I am afraid they will not make it back. Where shall I go? What shall I do? My babies…" She is distraught and confused as I try to think as the fire falls from the sky hitting our coats, raining down all around us.

Suddenly, the dream changes and the woman is gone. Instead, I am in a cold room – a very large room and there are three people with me. There is a loud explosion and the earth moves. One of the boys cries out.

"Papa!" When I turn, I see Claudius and his sons.

"Sshhh…it is all right." He tries to calm them as they climb into his arms. There is a lighted torch hanging on the wall next to them and a lantern on a table. He looks up in surprise as he sees me for the first time.

"Blessed Isis! You have come to save us!"

"I am not Isis. I am like you." I do not know what to say to calm the man for I am as filled with fear as he is. "Where is this room?" I hope I don't frighten him with this question.

"It is underneath the library, a hidden room. This is where we store the sacred scrolls. No one knows where this room is, for it is far beneath the house. Where did you come from?"

"I came through the door," I lie. "Where is your wife?" I ask, removing his attention from me.

"She is in Pompeii. I pray to the gods that she is safe." I can see the pain on his face and the tears in his eyes. "My love...my sweet wife, Corelia..." He is weeping and it causes the boys to cry. I feel helpless but know somehow, I have to ease their pain.

"It will be all right. She is safe - Pompeii is safe." I lie again. "I can't explain to you how I know this or where I came from, but it is the truth, for I just saw her."

"Ah, I knew you were sent by the gods!" He starts to prostrate himself before me. "Please, protect us and save my Corelia. I will be lost without her. She is my life, my love." He lowers his face to the ground and places it in his hands. He weeps quietly trying not to upset the boys again. I get down on my knees before him and take his hands.

"As you wish... I smile into his eyes. At once, he relaxes and the children stop crying. They come and sit in my lap as if I am their guardian and protector and they ask me where I have come from, and if I have been sent by the gods to protect them. I say yes and tell them of Mount Olympus.

Their father has come close and the oldest goes to him; and it isn't long before all of them close their eyes and they listen to my fabricated stories, the stories I have made up to calm them. Then, in an instant, they take their last breath. It is a quick and painless death as the suffocating blast of the heat wave hits us.

I am the only one who survives and I know why I have been saved, for in one single moment, I am transported back to Pompeii running through the streets next to the woman again. We are running hand in hand through the square, past the marble statue of Augustus and the public fountain.

"We need to go back to your home now. Take me there!" I know that soon, it will be the end, and the safest and most comfortable place to die will be inside. I pray that Corelia's death will be as peaceful and as painless as her husband's and children's.

"This way." We are coughing now from breathing in the sulphur and the thick gray ash. Our faces are covered and we look like ghosts. There is no longer any color in this world – only gray – the gray of the dying. We try to run now, but the pumice rocks that have fallen are covering the streets and are up to our mid-calves making it difficult to wade through them. Our progress is slow as we make our way up *Via della Fullonica* and then onto *Vicolo del Fauno.* The sky is getting darker as if a huge cloud has covered the city.

We walk past the Dancing Faun with its arms raised and a smile on his face. The ash and pumice have covered the pool of water he is standing in. Turning now onto *Vicolo di Mercurio,* we arrive at the House of the Vetti where the woman lives. Just as we approach the outer atrium and are trying to wade through the rock, a large explosion hits and the sky lights up within minutes. Dirt and fire are raining down from the heavens and our cloaks have caught fire so we quickly remove them as we enter the archway into the inner portico that has the pond in it – the place from my vision when I was sitting in Herculaneum.

"Is there a lower room in the house?" I stop Corelia, thinking it will be safer for the time being.

"Yes, follow me. It is the store room for the food." We run now to the back of the house and down a passageway to a darkened room. Corelia lights two lanterns and places them in the corner and we both sit on the floor. She throws her arms around me and starts to weep, and I realize she is but a young girl still.

"Claudius… Drusus…Corvinus…I love you. I pray to Isis and to the gods that they keep you safe."

"Where are they?" I am trying to calm her by getting her to talk.

"Nero was here and requested my husband go to the other villa in Herculaneum and bring back some sacred scrolls that he said belonged to him. There was an argument between them; but my husband lost. Nero is brutal and killed my husband's sister fourteen years ago. He beat her to death when she was with child. Since then, there has never been peace between Claudius and him. I am surprised Nero didn't kill him, too."

Now, her mind has moved from her loved ones and is focused on Nero.

"Where are your sons?" She started to weep again.

"My babies…Drusus…Corvinus. They need me. They are probably so afraid right now. They begged to accompany their father. It was a trip that would only take a few days so although I said they were too young, he insisted. He told me they would be well and he would take care of them. He wanted to show them they were big boys." She continues to weep.

"I am sure they are all right. The winds are blowing the debris from the volcano southwest toward Pompeii. That means that Herculaneum will be saved." It is another lie, but I want to put her mind at ease. I know the outcome of this and it will be the same as my experience in Herculaneum.

"Do you really think so?"

"Yes, I do." I pat Corelia's arm and she laughs.

"How ironic that yesterday was a holiday…*Vulcanalia*." I had read that August 23, 79 AD was the day before the eruption and it was also a holy day – a day where the people threw live fish into bonfires as a sacrifice to appease the God of Fire, Vulcan.

"Why is he so angry with us?" She starts to cry again.

"It will be all right, Corelia. You will be with your family soon enough. All will be well." I hug her. And at this moment, a blast of heat sucks the breath out of our lungs…

I bolt upright in my hotel room bed and cough, gasping for air. My body is covered with sweat and my sheets are wet. I jump from the bed and run to the window, hanging my head out trying to catch a breath of the night air. I have felt death twice tonight – heard it – breathed it – and, it is too much for one human!

I have been with all of them when they died and now I know that it wasn't a painful death after all. As long as they are together now in the next world, maybe this is all I was meant to do.

The sun is rising and I am sitting at the window watching the night change into day. How glorious a sunrise… I have gained deep respect for *Vesuvio* this night – who has the power to change all things – to bring life and to take it away. I think about my life and my age and that we have such a short span of time on this earth for each lifetime that it is wise to know what one wants so that one might go after it…

On the train back to Napoli, I hear the voices of two people, a man and a woman. As the sound of the rickety car scrapes along the steel tracks, I think I hear a faint whisper. "Thank you…" and children's laughter in the background… Maybe it is my imagination, but it soothes me nonetheless.

This is all I need to hear. I know they are together and all is well. The memories of Corelia's and Claudius' love for one another make me realize how lonely I am for Natale. His face comes before me and I start to weep quietly. Although it has been almost two months since I left Rome, it seems like it was only yesterday. I think about his soft touch upon my cheek and the way he holds me at the base of my back as he looks into my eyes. I feel his lips upon mine as he kisses me. I sigh and close my eyes so that the tears no longer escape from me.

What do I want from this life of mine I ask myself? What am I searching for? I think of my sons and how I love them so, and then I hear him.

"Once you no longer have to ask yourself these questions, you will know…" His voice fades as we arrive in Sorrento at the train station.

CHAPTER 43

On the hydrofoil back to the island, I feel at peace as *Vesuvio* grows more distant on the horizon. The waves are noticeably high today and the boat rocks causing me to lose my footing. I slip backward and fall into someone.

"*Scusi.* I am so sorry."

"No problem." He is American.

"It got rough all of a sudden." I turn to look at him.

"There is a storm coming in. It will be here this evening. My name is Joseph – or as they say in Italian, Guisseppe." He smiles, extends his hand to me and I take it.

"I'm Roxanna…nice to meet you, Joseph. How long are you on the island for?"

"A month; I have a villa in AnaCapri."

"That's where I'm staying." We both laugh, and I forget about Pompeii, Herculanuem and *Vesuvio* for a moment.

"I come every summer for a few months but this year, I've been so busy that unfortunately, I can't stay as long. How long have you been here, Roxanna?" He is about forty, has dark hair and eyes and a very well-defined, very muscular body. He is wearing jeans and a sleeveless shirt with *ITALIA* written across his chest.

"I came in April and never left, although I have traveled around Italy and Greece a bit; but I always come back to Capri. It's my favorite place in the world." I know I have that dreamy look in my eyes. I can feel it as I look up to see the shape of the woman's body called Capri taking form on the horizon.

"I know how you feel. I fell in love with it fifteen years ago and dreamed of living here until seven years ago when I was finally able to purchase a small villa. Now my dream has come true. You'll have to come for dinner, Roxanna. I have friends joining me tomorrow and you're invited – we're calling it a Welcome Home Party for Joseph. " He laughs. "Will you come?"

"Yes, I'd love to."

"Good…I'll give you my cell number so you can call for directions and everyone is arriving around eight o'clock. Oh, are you traveling alone?"

"Yes, yes. I am." I think of Natale again and my heart aches with heaviness causing me to take a big breath. It's not smooth, but slow, long and deep and this is what catches his attention. Joseph notes the change in my face and I become embarrassed.

"I'm sorry."

"I understand. Love is not for the faint of heart. I too miss someone, but in my situation, it's a little different. Gay relationships are a bit more complicated than heterosexual ones." Now it's his turn to look out toward the horizon, sigh and take a heavy breath.

"We have something in common, I suppose. I would love to come to your dinner party tomorrow."

"Good. You can be my date then. We'll set tongues wagging all night. They'll wonder if I've gone daft and turned straight. We both laugh. The boat ride becomes increasingly rocky so we walk precariously holding on to the seats as we try and find somewhere to sit.

I learn that Joseph lives in Malibu and is a screenplay writer, and I realize that I have seen some of his movies. His ex-lover is a married man, a well-known heterosexual actor in Hollywood, who has decided to stay in his marriage because of his career. The relationship lasted two years and the break-up is only a few months old, so the wound in Joseph's heart is still fresh. Although he is very masculine and a definite head turner, I see how fragile his heart is and instantly want to befriend him, for I know his pain.

He's very handsome with his dark hair and eyes of Italian descent – one of the reasons he loves Italy so much. His relatives are from Milano but he, like me has fallen in love with Capri. He has this beautiful bright smile that is accentuated by his great tan. I see the way women are staring at him as if he were a GQ model which is what he looks like. If he hadn't told me, I would have never guessed he was gay.

As we sit and chat for the remainder of the ride, I find myself laughing hysterically at the way he speaks about things. His sense of humor is as infectious as his smile, and he is telling me about Richard, his ex-lover.

"…and Roxanna, he is gorgeous! The first time I laid eyes on him…oh baby…I thought I'd died and gone to heaven. I almost dropped my drink in my lap! He has the face of a god and the body to match. I tell you, I was twisted in knots for weeks before I got up the guts to ask him out for a drink."

He's still talking as we dock and disembark. We exchange phone numbers and I promise to call him for directions.

"How silly of me; do you want to share a taxi, Roxanna?" The cost is twenty-five euro, a bit expensive, to the top of the island, so I was planning to take the bus.

"I'd love to." It would give me a chance to spend more time with my new friend who I am immediately smitten with. As we round the corner of the winding road that leads from the port, through Capri and then up to AnaCapri, Joseph gasps.

"I am always amazed by this view. For fifteen years I have come here, and I never get tired of it. It's as if I am seeing it for the first time all over again!"

"I know. I feel the same way." Joseph has this spark that I love. He sees and feels the same way I do. We are kindred spirits, he and I; and because of him, the memories of the last few days have faded from my mind, thank goodness. We have reached the *Piazza Vittoria* and our taxi driver unloads Joseph's luggage.

"Tomorrow evening, Roxanna. I'll see you then." We hug and kiss.

"I'm looking forward to it. I'll call you tomorrow afternoon."

"If you have trouble getting through, leave a message. You know how it is on the island with cell phones." We both laugh knowing the service is not the best here. The feeling is as though the volcanic rock beneath us is saying, "No, you are not supposed to be on your cell phones but engaging in life instead…"

I decide to walk home, bathe, change and go directly to Federico's. I've decided I want to finish Natale's painting – need to finish it. I feel as if I'm somehow running out of time, although I don't know why. By the time I reach his studio, it is 13:00 hours and he is sitting on a stool outside his shop chatting with another shop owner. Immediately, he jumps to his feet.

"*Mio amore…como va*? I am so happy to see you. Are you ready to paint again?" He turns, waves to the woman he is sitting with and takes me inside. Although I saw my painting two days ago, it still surprises me. Its likeness is so close that I am stirred up again.

"I'm ready." We don't speak but get right to work. I work with the finer brush for the detail work today and am a little more conscious then I was the first time. Only because of the detail do I force myself to be. But after an hour or so, I am lost once again and never really become conscious until it is finished at four o'clock. When I step back, I am amazed that I am the one who painted it.

"*Molto bello…Perfecto…magifico*…I-yi-yi…M*ama mia*…you are a master, Roxanna. He is kissing my cheek as he stands behind me with his arms around my waist. He is so excited, he can hardly contain himself. "You are *incredibile*, unbelievable. Have you always painted like this?" He moves toward the canvas now. Look here, the eyes - you can see into his soul. The nose is *perfecto*…the dimples in his cheeks…are they truly like this?"

"Yes, yes they are." I realize how precise it is and love what I have painted.

"This is the man you are in love with. I can tell. No one paints like this if they do not truly love who or what they are painting, for the art is their expressed *passionne.*"

"Yes." That is all I have to say, for I am thinking about how to send this to Natale. How long will I have to wait for it to dry? Two months? Three? Maybe I will write to him and tell him I have finished but the paint is still too wet to mail. He should have it, not me. I can paint another. Yes, I think it more important that he have it so he knows how much I love him.

"Here…I have something to celebrate!" Federico leaves and returns with two glasses and a bottle of Moet and Chandon champagne. "I've been saving this for something special and this is the time." He pops the cork and pours each of us a glass which we raise to the painting and to each other.

"To you, Roxanna. Welcome back! You are a great Italian master now – as good as the rest of us. To You!" I take a sip and as I swallow and let my breath out, I feel as if I have fallen backwards onto a feather bed, the down rising up around my body embracing me. I feel that I have found myself…another piece of me…a very large piece. Then I realize Vittorio is singing "*Tu Sei* - For You," on the CD player. I find myself weeping with joy and at that moment, Federico takes me in his arms and we dance to the music.

A celebration for me…I can't explain how my heart feels…as if it has been birthed here, as if it is now new and it in turn has birthed me, this new woman. I am dancing in the arms of Federico, as if we are making love to the music. He is humming the song and I am singing "la-da-da-da-da"…along with him. It is the perfect moment in time – one that I will always cherish…and in this moment, I understand Elana…

"*Mio amore…*" He takes me by the hand and we sit on the sofa as the music serenades us in the background. Pouring more champagne into my glass, he says, "In order to find a great love, you first have to fall in love with yourself and in order to do this you have to learn about yourself. I think you have learned much about yourself here. I have seen you become more beautiful every day since you have arrived on the island. Do you know what this means, Roxanna?" He takes a sip.

"This means that this is your home, for it feeds your soul…and you cannot live somewhere that does not feed your soul." He kisses my forehead.

"Thank you, Federico. You have been such a beautiful friend to me." I am embracing him.

"*Ti amo.*"

"*Ti amo troppo*…" He starts to laugh.

"You love me too much? What does this mean? Is this a bad thing?" He cannot stop laughing.

"I meant to say I love you, too. It's not *troppo?*" He hugs me again and the mood lightens.

"Roxanna, I am going for a swim at the *Grotta Azzurra*. After the tour boats leave for the day, we can go inside and swim. Would you like to come with me? It would be the perfect ending to our celebration." I think for a moment that it will be like a baptism for me in my birth waters, the sacred waters of Capri – my mother and father both there for the ceremony.

"Yes. I will go home and get my suit and meet you in the *piazza*."

"I will be there at 18:00 (6:00 p.m.). *Ciao, bella.*"

"*Ciao.*"

We meet at 18:00 and ride his scooter through Linaro and La Selva, the little pockets of AnaCapri until we reach the cliffs above the Blue Grotto where we walk down the long flight of stone steps.

"Be very careful, Roxanna." He is holding my hand taking care of me as if I am his little girl. We reach the bottom and he whistles to a man who is sitting in a row boat resting in the sunlight surrounded by the diamonds of the day that have spilled onto the water. The man takes my hand and I step into the boat, Federico following.

We enter the cavern through the small opening where there is a rope hanging across the entrance. We have to hold on to it and lie on our backs in order to enter the cave. Once inside, the color is that of an opalescent electric blue if you can imagine this. Because the cave opening is so low and narrow, it doesn't allow light to enter so the sunlight penetrates the sea water and reflects upward into the cave, against its walls, creating this electric blue. As the light reflects off the white sandy bottom, it creates an opalescence so that along with the blue, everything in the grotto appears to be dripping with a silvery light. The entire cavern is covered in it as I see the silvery raindrops before me dripping all around us.

The boatman starts to sing and the rock walls echo it back to him as if in answer to his questions. Federico slips over the side of the boat and is already in the water swimming slowly to the cave wall. I, on the other hand am still in the boat looking out to sea through the mouth of the cave where we entered. It's like being at the North Pole, the water a shade of blue that is uncommon to the rest of the world and the air as different as the water is.

I feel like a sea nymph who has just found her home and I want to stay here and sleep in this opalescence that is edged in silver. I imagine that if you make a wish here, it will come true. I feel it to be so. I wish to know intimately what I have been searching for. I wish to know all the secrets so I can be finished with all of this and settle into my life as it is, never going backwards but only enjoying where I am right now.

"Come in, come in, *bella*." I am roused out of my fairy dream by Federico who is asking me to come into the water and swim so I too slip over the side of the boat, the oarsman holding it steady for me. The water is cool and my body tingles, loving it.

This is sublime…luxurious…spiritual…sacred…this is like a dream…I say this to myself so he cannot hear me, and I start to giggle like a little girl.

"Ah, *bambina*, little girl…you are happy, no?" He is happy that I am happy and I am happy that I am here in this place inside the *Grotta Azzurra* and inside my life finally! I swim from one side to the other, from one end to the other, all the while listening to the music that is being sung to us by the oarsman. After thirty minutes or so, Federico says it is time to go, so we leave and are dropped off at the stone steps for the climb back to AnaCapri.

"I am so happy you joined me, Roxanna. A perfect day in *paradiso*…"

"Thank you, Federico. You have no idea how much I enjoyed this."

This night back at *Mio Paradiso*, I choose vegetables from the garden for my dinner and listen to my Vittorio CD on my laptop as I prepare my meal in my little Italian kitchen. When I am finished and the sun is setting over Ischia, I twirl and twirl on the *terrazzo* as I celebrate my awakening to my life. As I tuck my self in between my sheets for the night, I tell my self, "So this is what it feels like to have peace in your heart…"

CHAPTER 44

The sun is shining brightly as it always does on Capri. I know that Cristos said Delos was known to always be bathed in sunlight, a place that Helios blessed daily, but I know that Capri is the same. Why else would Axel Munthe write it to be so. "*… like a temple to the Sun, where I would seek knowledge and light from the radiant God whom I had worshipped all my life….light, light everywhere...*" Yes, this has to be a mirror reflection of Delos with its light and its energy. Why else would I be here, or Munthe, or San Michele who is actually Apollo, who is actually Helios? Enough, I think! No need to spend time trying to figure anything out but just to enjoy all of this. Some things need no explanation.

I have much to do before the party tonight. I have to call my boys, write a letter to Natale, mail it, pick up flowers for Joseph and also a great bottle of *vino* as a welcome gift. Oh, and I have to call him for directions!

The letter to Natale is short telling him I am back in Capri for the rest of the summer and that I have finished his painting and that hopefully, it will dry soon so I can get it to him. I don't say that I will mail it or that I will bring it to him myself because I can't say what I will do then. I am not ready to make any decisions yet and after hearing my sons' voices, I miss them and am thinking that it is time to see them. But, for now, there is a party to think about.

When I arrive, I first notice the music that is coming from Joseph's villa, an Italian opera singer belting out an aria. As I walk through the gate, I realize how large the villa is…quite impressive with its balconies and a long portico that runs the length of the house on the bottom level. It is surrounded by gardens and people are milling about everywhere.

"Roxanna! You found me." He kisses me, happy that I have come. He is dressed in white linen slacks and a white linen shirt that hugs his body, and his shoes look as if they have been hand woven by the Caprese shoemaker in the village.

"Joseph, your home is beautiful!" I hand him the big bouquet of flowers from the island's only florist and a bottle of Brunello from Toscano.

"*Grazie,* they're so beautiful." He smells the bouquet. "Come…I want you to meet my friends." He takes me into the house for a glass of Prosecco and then introduces me to about thirty people, most whose names I cannot remember the moment I leave them. There are both Americans, some from the movie industry, and Italians.

There is one man in particular who I do remember because I have seen him at the port. He has a gorgeous long white linen shirt on that has his insignia emblazoned across the pocket and white linen slacks with almost the same woven loafers that Joseph is wearing. They must have the same shoemaker, I think.

"A pleasure, Roxanna; I am Alberto and this is my wife Francesca."

"He is the most sought after designer in the world right now, Roxanna. You have to get a pair of his jeans…they're all the rage. Remember his name – Alberto Bruno." I have seen his jeans and his scarves on many of the women throughout Italy, and he is very famous in America.

"I know your work, Alberto, nice to meet you." I shake his hand and then his wife's. "Nice to meet you, Francesca." She is very beautiful. I love her thick black hair and her hairline as she has it all pulled tight and piled up on her head. She is dressed exquisitely and her clothes have fine lines, her shoes are high-heeled sandals with jewels on them, her toes painted a shimmering white. She has a beautiful necklace around her neck like the one Sophia Loren had on the day I saw her in Capri; but hanging on Francesca's is a large blue stone which I think is an aquamarine.

"*Incantato* - enchanted. You are every beautiful, Rossana."

"*Molto grazie,* Francesca." I realize that this is a very "in party" with very "in people" and I check myself for just a moment to see if I am okay with all of this. I am …so I smile wide because I'm excited. I love my new friends! I spend most of the night mingling and talking with everyone. There is an American playwright here and an actress that comes here every summer. A gay couple who are friends of Joseph's have arrived and he says they will be staying with him for a few weeks. I am also introduced to Michael who is Richard's best friend. Joe's ex – Richard, that is.

The night goes on into the wee hours of the morning as we mingle, laugh, dance, and talk…I am having a wonderful time and Joseph has taken me by the arm into every circle he mingles with. I feel as if I am his date and I know some are questioning our relationship. He, in the meantime is loving it, setting everyone's tongues wagging. He was right when he said they would wonder if he had gone straight. I am having fun.

By 2:00 a.m., I am getting sleepy and we are with Alberto and Francesco. They are talking to Joseph about taking their boat down the Amalfi Coast for a few days. Alberto is begging Joseph to join him as he did the year before.

"You must come…it will only be a few days. Please, Joseph." Alberto is begging him, telling him he is the life of the party which I can see he truly is. He is contagious and you want to be near him because you know you will have a good time if you are. It's not so much that he is a partier, but that he has this effervescence about him. He has a freshness about him due to his direct honesty, and he is sincere, too. He isn't pretentious by any means and everyone loves him. I feel sorry for Richard for breaking up with him. I'm sure he must be missing him right now.

"Okay…if you do come, then I promise to take you to Africana…" At this, Joseph's face lights up.

"I'm there! What time tomorrow?" We're laughing. Joseph has always wanted to go to Africana, a very cool nightclub hidden in an obscure place somewhere on the Amalfi Coast which I am told all about the next day on the drive down to the port. I would find out about this place later, like the fact that once you are inside, it's like being in an underwater cave that is the color of the Blue Grotto. The only way to enter is from the cave-like entrance from the sea which I assume means you need a boat to go there. It's also only open from June through August, so timing and the sea is everything.

"Be at the dock at noon...you know my boat, yes?" Alberto and Francesca are leaving. "Come *mio amore;* we are sleeping in tomorrow!" We all laugh as we say *arrivederci,* and as he kisses my cheeks, he says, "Oh, and please bring Roxanna." He turns to me, "I won't take no for an answer, Roxanna. *Arrivederci a domani!"* I stay to help Joseph clean up and we talk about tomorrow and the boat ride.

"Roxanna, don't be fooled by him. This is not a small yacht and this is not a little boat ride down the coast. Pack for four days! You will need dress attire as well as casual attire. These two know how to live it up and this will be a four-day long party!"

"I don't think this is my thing, Joseph. I'm just a simple girl." I think of the peace and quiet I have not had for months now, running here and there all over Italy and Greece…

"I won't take no for an answer! If I have to go, then you must come as my date! I need you, *bella*! Please...for me?" I'm laughing because he is on his knees begging me.

All right...but I don't have a thing to wear!"

Then we'll have to go shopping in Positano and Amalfi, doll!" I'm giggling – another adventure.

"Okay, but I have to go to bed now or I won't be awake in time! *Ciao, bello.*"

"*Ciao*, gorgeous." I leave and find my way home just in time to fall into bed and into the arms of sleep...my lover for the next six hours...

CHAPTER 45

AMALFI COAST

I am wide awake thinking about what I will wear since I've been buying clothes as I go. As I walk to town with my carry-on bag, I stop by a small boutique I've had my eye on and purchase a linen skirt, blouse and a pair of strappy sandals. These will have to do until I go shopping with Joseph and I am sure that will be an adventure! Joseph meets me in the *piazza* where we take a taxi down to the port.

"Wait until you see this so-called boat, Roxanna…" I wonder what it will be like, for I haven't a clue. I have never been on a yacht before. We are walking through the port town after being dropped off by the taxi driver. The private boats and yachts are docked at the far end on the other side from where the hydrofoils dock.

"Here we are." We stop before a huge ship named *Mio Francesa* which is anchored in the bay. This has to be a mistake…but Joseph proceeds to get into the motor boat that is docked waiting to take us to the ship.

"Wait…is this really it?" It looks as if it belongs to a king or something." Joseph takes a few steps back and comes to get me.

"Are you surprised, doll? It's a luxury superyacht, 300 feet long, holds up to 38 passengers, has 20 staterooms and 36 crew members. There is internal LAN for internet access, a digital PBX telephone system, a health fitness center including a world-class spa with saunas, steam rooms, cold plunge pools, jacuzzis, a massage parlor, beauty salon, a gymnasium…do you want me to go on?" I am dizzy with all of it… I don't answer in time so he continues as we walk on board.

"Oh, did I mention two speed boats for water skiing, diving equipment, wind surfers, about eight jetskis…I'm exhausted just talking about it! But you wait, doll…you're going to feel like a princess, you'll be waited on as if you are royalty." As soon as we step on board, Alberto is there to greet us.

"Ciao, ciao. Benvenuto."

"This is amazing, Alberto."

"*Grazie*, Roxanna. I named it after my beautiful wife…only the best for her. She is my life, you know." Francesca has come up behind him, hears his compliment and slips her arms around his waist.

"Ah, darling…there you go again… always flattering me…that's why I love you so…Good to see you both. Come, and I will show you to your rooms." We walk the length of the ship, walking through a bar and lounge area with plush chairs, a grand piano, and a fountain surrounded by glass and mirrors. Then we walk through a theatre room with a wall-to-wall flat screen and a bar off to one side. Next is a formal dining room that seats forty-eight which is done in gold and salmon tones with custom drapery and fabric and a mirrored ceiling.

There are more rooms decorated just as lovely before we arrive at the outer dining area on the deck at the far end which is also formal. There are white linen table cloths and large candles adorning the tables. The floors are a golden toned movingui wood from the Ivory Coast in Nigeria; and there is a sitting area surrounding the dining area with long white couches with pillowed teak seating. I am in awe.

"Would you like to see the spa before I show you to your state rooms?" Francesca is proud of her ship that carries her name. "We want you to enjoy yourself while you are here. I say yes, and Joseph smiles as he is enjoying my excitement.

We take the elevator down to the lower floor where we enter what could be a world-class spa. A golden door opens and we enter a round marble room with surround-windows to the sea. I am blown away! Everything is white marble with blue accents and an iridescent blue cast from the ocean outside. We enter room after room and each one has marbled walls, floors and ceilings. There is even a waterfall in the lounge area where you can sit and relax while waiting for your massage or whatever treatment you are having.

My senses are on overload as I move from one sauna, steam room, cold plunge pool room, massage room, shower area, aromatherapy baths, jacuzzi room, dressing room or powder room to the next. It's like a city – you could live here forever and never want for anything! Joseph is still quietly enjoying this, a slight smirk on his face.

"Come. Now I take you to your rooms. We take the elevator up to the next level and find our rooms. Mine is as big as my villa on Capri with a king-sized bed in the middle of the room, and an overhang held up by four columns that cover it like a fan made of ostrich feathers. It is white and gold with golden bedding, golden drapery over the windows that semi-circle the room and mahogany wood everywhere. I feel like Cleopatra for it is that regal.

"Roxanna, this is your room. I hope you like it."

"It's fabulous, Francesca. *Molto grazie*." I am pleased. I stay behind and fall backward on my bed as Joseph follows Francesca down the hall in search of his room. I'm so happy I was talked into coming. If I had known that it would be like this, I wouldn't have hesitated for a moment.

I spend part of the afternoon in my room lavishing in its exquisite beauty just lounging or sitting in my upholstered chaise looking out to sea. Then I roam the ship with Joseph for awhile exploring, when we come across a library filled with many first edition books in Greek, Italian, and English. I'm in heaven as I pull them off the shelves and place them in a pile just because I love them. I can't read the ones written in Greek, but I can hold them in my hands and flip through the pages.

I find many books on Michelangelo: The Sculptures of Michelangelo, The Drawings of Michelangelo and Michelangelo E La Sua Scuola. There are two on the works of Raphael and a copy of Dante's Inferno. Then there is the Roman Empire: The Rise of the Roman Empire, The Fall of the Roman Empire and A Greek-Roman Empire Power and Belief under Theodosius II.

I find Greek literature: The Plato Dialogues, Plato - the Man and His Works. There is a copy of Dionysios Solomos, Greece's national poet. There is the History of the Byzantine Empire, Mystical Hymns of Orpheus, The New Posidippus - A Helenistic Poetry Book and the Complete Works of Aristotles.

"Joseph, I could die here or stay forever with all of these books piled around me! I love these books!" I am now lying on the floor with piles of books eight or ten high all around me.

"What are you going to do with all of these, doll? You can't possibly read them all, and we have dinner in just a few hours!" I giggle at him as if I've had Prosecco but we have not had a drop.

"I know. I'll take a few to my room to read. You go. I'm going to stay here for awhile. Is that all right?"

"Anything for you, doll. Oh, but first, we need to hit the boutique on the upper deck. I saw this gorgeous midnight blue gown that would look stunning on you! What do you say?" I think of that fact that I am no longer working…

"Okay. I'll look, but it depends on the price tag. I'm out of work, you know."

"Don't worry about a thing! I'll buy it for you – after all, you are my beautiful date. Whatever the cost, it's yours! Consider it a gift!" I leave my books in piles so I can claim them later and we move to the upper floor where the shops are located.

"Roxanna, it's made for you! You have to have it! It fits your body like a glove and your breasts…" It does fit me like a glove – this new figure I have acquired as of late.

"Stop! I'm shy!" I giggle. I don't usually accept gifts this expensive from strangers – it is 2,100 euro – but I guess Joseph is no longer a stranger but a dear sweet friend. I'll pay him back.

"Okay, okay. I'll take it, but I'm paying you back, once I get back to work."

"Who are you kidding, sweetheart? You are going to find a gorgeous Italian man, fall in love with him and live happily ever after here and never work again! Since I know your future, consider it a gift. After all, who else do I have to spend my money on?"

"Don't say that. You'll fall in love again. Trust me, Guiseppe…" We laugh, but I know he's hurting inside.

We've dropped anchor off the coast of Solerno, the southern most part of the Amalfi Coast and Alberto has given word that we will dine on board the ship tonight and visit the mainland tomorrow. Dinner is formal. It's on the outer deck so I dress in my midnight blue sequin dress that fits me like a glove – or better yet, the skin of a mermaid. The only thing missing are my fins, but my black strappy heeled sandals replace them perfectly - for land and not sea. Joseph knocks on my door promptly at 19:55 (7:55 p.m.) perfect timing and when I open the door, he is awestruck.

"If I were a straight man…you wouldn't be leaving this room tonight…"

"Oh, stop…" I am flattered by his remarks. By the time we reach the deck, there are about thirty people there. Some faces I remember from the party the night before but most are Italians I have never met before, probably close friends of Alberto and Francesco. The couple is greeting everyone as they arrive.

"*Molto bella.* I knew that dress would be perfect for someone. You look fabulous. I chose it myself in Milano for the boutique, Roxanna…because it was so beautiful."

"*Grazie*, Francesca. I adore it." She has on a clingy black gown that hugs her body down to her hemline and then it fans outward. Her neckline is low cut with thin spaghetti straps and she has a very large radiant cut diamond hanging from her neck; and her beautiful Italian hair is piled high upon her head.

We join the others and are seated for what seems to be a ten course meal which I lose track of after the first six courses. I am picking at my plate and not eating much, as I feel myself bulging out of my dress. Everything is so good and the wine is the best – Brunello di Montalcino, Fornacina 2000…smooth with elegant tannins… sangiovese… I've died and gone to heaven…ah-h-h-h-h.

The dinner lasts for four hours and I cannot take another sip of even this incredible wine as there is no more room left in my body. I sit listening to Alberto tell stories about the pirates that raided the towns up and down the Amalfi Coast in the 16th century.

"…and of course there was a time when Amalfi's population dropped considerably due to the pirate attacks, probably between 1510 and 1555. Everyone along the coast here and even Capri, Roxanna…" He turns to me as he says this…"knows who Barbarossa was - a Muslim born in Greece and a lieutenant general in the Ottoman Navy who led fleets up to 135 galleys through these waters with his three brothers. Their mission throughout their entire life was to fight against the Knights of St. John, the Maltese Knights, the Papacy in Spain, the Holy Roman Empire, the Republic of Venus and every other Christian led fleet who had inflicted serious damage against the Ottoman Empire or the Turks back then." He took a drink of his wine.

"He and his brothers were ruthless, calling themselves the Barbary Corsairs…you know pirates from the Barbary Coast of Africa which extends from Egypt to the Atlantic? Although he and his Corsairs raided Sicily, Spain, France, and Greece, he particularly loved ravaging, plundering and ransacking every port town along the coast here including the islands of Procida, Ischia and Capri." He turns to me and Joseph again.

"Have you been to the Barbarossa Castle in Capri?" We shake our heads no.

"He built a great castle there above AnaCapri; and you have probably seen all the forts that are still standing on the island that were built then. He probably loved Capri because of its cliffs – not an easy place to surprise someone in the middle of the night."

"Of course the Christians everywhere hated him for stealing all of their sacred artifacts from the churches. The Corsairs despised them so much that most times, they pillaged just to throw everything into a pile and set them on fire. They were ruthless." Alberto stops to take a breath.

I can see that this is a subject dear to his heart because he is a seaman himself.

"You know they carried razor-sharp rapiers...the two-edged swords with sharp points? And they wore metal helmets and breastplates...which was common battle dress back then..."

Everyone is silent, looking out toward the lights of Solerno probably wondering if pirates still exist today. I am wondering the same thing. Will we be safe sleeping on board tonight? I had heard stories of the pirates who stole on to the cruise ships around Greece recently. The cruise lines had tried to keep this quiet from the rest of the world. Alberto is still talking.

"Did you know that Barbarossa was never his name to begin with? His name was actually Yakupoglu Hizir - meaning Hizir, Son of Yakup. Barbarossa was his brother Oruc's name, who was killed in battle. To honor him, Hizir dyed his beard red, took his brother's name, Barbarossa, and then took command of his fleet." Alberto was shaking his head.

"This beautiful coastline...pillaged and plundered for almost an entire century...you know he wrote his memoirs – five volumes called "Memoirs of Hayreddin Pasha," but then they were fictionalized and retitled, "The Mediterranean was Ours." They truly believed it was theirs for the taking..." He is still going on about them when he is interrupted.

"Darling, enough about Barbarossa...maybe our guests would like to dance." Francesca reaches over and kisses her husband on his cheek.

"You're right *mio amore*. Those Greeks...you have to watch them every minute..." Everyone starts to laugh but I am thinking about my time in the Cyclades... I think that if this is the life they were born into and this is all they really know, are they bad men, or could they possibly have had good hearts? I am thinking about my pirates...

We dance the rest of the night away which helps me to digest my food. When I fall into bed, it is 3:00 a.m. and I fall immediately to sleep with the feel of the ocean cradling me in her arms as if I was her baby...and I remember I am, for she is my mother...

Late morning has come and we are in *Vietri sul Mare* the closest city to Solerno. We have come to see the local artisans who paint the *ceramica* that the town is so well known for. Everyone buys the hand-painted ceramic dishes from the locals as they sell them from their garages inside the thousand year old buildings. The architecture is ancient. Each place of business or residence has a hand-painted tile outside its door telling what family or what business resides inside. The wine shop has a large sign made of hand-painted tiles of a vineyard scene - a man stomping on grapes - and there are bottles of *vino* painted along the edges.

The flower shop has beautiful hand-painted tiles depicting a woman in the fields picking flowers. Along the shores of the town, we see 15th century watch towers everywhere, necessary to warn of corsair invasions. As we move into the town, we visit the Church of Saint John the Baptist, the Chiesa di San Giovanni Battisa. I love how ancient this old town by the sea is.

By 13:00, we are back on the ship traveling to Ravello, a small 19th century town in the hills high above Amalfi. Alberto takes us on his own personal and favorite tour through the Palazzo Sasso, to the Villa Rufolo built for and by an aristocratic mediaeval family in the 1200s. From there, we move on to the Cathedral with its doors by Barisano da Tani that was founded by the Benedictine monks, and finally to the Villa Cimbrone, a cloisture with expansive grounds and gardens.

This is one of the most beautiful villas I think I have seen with its belvedere looking out over the southern coastline. Alberto tells us that this estate and its vineyards and gardens have been sold continually over the centuries, until in 1940 Lord Ernest William Berckert purchased it and converted it to this astounding villa.

There is a *palazzo*, a castle, a tower, the cloister, a crypt, and a tiny villa for a small child which is called the *Rondinaia*. A belvedere with busts of men lining it offers a spectacular view of the sea, the sky and the horizon. As you leave it and move into the gardens, there are terraces with marble statues throughout. The Belvedere of Mercury, the Grotto of Eve and the Temple of Bacchus are hidden as if they are beautiful secrets somewhere lost in the secret gardens. I love this place and wish I could stay longer, but Francesca wants to take me to the jeweler in town.

As we walk into a little shop, she is telling me how her husband always surprises her with a gift when they come here, which they do quite frequently. She says that this is their favorite spot along the coast and they stay at the Villa Cimbrone which has now been turned into a boutique hotel for the rich and famous. She also tells me that Greta Garbo once lived there while she had a secret lover which the Italians still talk about. As we enter, a tall man swoops down upon Francesca, gathers her up in his embrace and starts kissing her face all over as he speaks to her in Italian.

"Oh, Giovanni, so good to see you, *bello*." She turns to me and introduces me to him, Giovanni, who is a fourth generation coral carver and jeweler. He kisses my hand and takes me inside to show me his designs as Francesca leaves to find her husband who is walking behind us with some of the others. In half Italian and half English, he shows me the cases he has lining the walls and explains that his family has made carved crucifixes and other sacred objects for the *Vaticano* all of their lives. He shows me an 18K gold crucifix that has just been returned to them after the Pope's death which is encased in glass with a papal seal on it.

Before I take my eyes off of it, he has me by the hand and is quickly taking me into a back room through a small door. I am only alarmed for a millisecond, for as we enter, I realize this is a huge room as big as a half my villa, and there are religious artifacts everywhere - boxes filled with trinkets and bureau type cabinets with pull-out drawers filled with jewelry. I see statues of saints including Antonio and Francesco.

He tells me the history of each work of art, who it was made for and by whom in his family. When he sees my eyes linger on the one of San Francesco, he opens a drawer and very carefully picks out a small case with a papal seal on it. Inside is a piece of the cloak San Francesco wore along with one of his teeth. I touch the outside of the bag and my eyes well up with tears as if he is right here holding me in his arms. I am speechless as he moves me from one drawer to another showing me similar packages. I don't know if my heart is overwhelmed because this one belongs to Francesco or because I feel as if I am in the Vatican, but this has been a sacred gift to be able to view these pieces.

By the time he takes me back through the door, Alberto is paying for a set of 18K gold and lapis earrings for Francesca which she now has on. They are rows of little round lapis balls laced onto long golden strings. I have taken control of my emotions by now and tell her how beautiful they are.

"*Buonasera, bella*." The jeweler is kissing my cheeks and squeezing my hands as he says good bye. It's as if we have become intimate, our hearts coming together in a sacred way. I know he felt my joy and I respected that he allowed me to feel it quietly.

"*Molto grazie.* I am honored by you." I bow slightly, although I don't know why...only that I want to. I walk quietly with the group as I contemplate this place. Is all of Italy blessed with the saints and every religious being who ever walked? Were they all born here? Joseph interrupts my thoughts.

"Are you sad, doll?" He sees that I am quiet.

"No, just a religious experience I guess you could say..." He takes my arm in his and kisses my face, and we walk in silence as if he knows it is something I am yearning for in this moment. Time passes and he finally speaks.

"That's what I love about you, Roxanna. You're real. You're not afraid to feel – and you're not afraid to express your feelings. If I were straight..." We both laugh out loud and I pinch him, lightening the mood. What another great gift to come all the way to Italy to find Joseph. I feel as if we have been friends forever and that I can tell him everything. I make a note to myself that I want to talk with him about Natale. I know he will be honest with me.

We stop and mail postcards before going back to the ship for the night. I mail one to Elana and my boys, but not to Natale. My letter to him should have arrived by now. I wonder how it was received...

It's mid-week in Rome and Natale has picked up his mail. He is on his way to work so he tosses it carelessly into the bag hanging on his scooter without even looking at the envelopes and with only a quick thought that he will open them tonight when he returns from work.

When he finishes his shift, he stays at the restaurant until 2:00 a.m. sharing drinks and conversation with his friends since there is no one waiting for him at home. He is getting used to his life once again now that his heart has finished with Rossana – or so he thinks...

When he arrives home and parks the scooter, he takes his bag into the house and sits on the *terrazzo* to read his mail. He is in shock that she has written. Nervously, he fumbles to open it, wild thoughts in his mind. Has she gone back to America? Met someone else? He tries to swallow as he opens the fine paper with a few short paragraphs on it.

That night, he never sleeps...his heart confused once again...

CHAPTER 46

Our great ship is sitting between the towns of Amalfi and Positano and before us lies the little town of Praiano which is sprawled out over the base of Mount Sant'Angelo. Alberto and Francesca are standing next to us on deck. Alberto points toward land.

"Left is Vettica Maggiore and to the right is Praiano." He is dreamy-eyed as if he has fond memories and Francesca squeezes his hand and kisses him.

"*Chi vuol vivere sano, la mane a Vettica, la sera a Praiano.* Do you know what this means, Roxanna? It means that for a healthy life, morning hours must be spent in Vettica and evenings in Praiano." He laughs. "I used to come here in the early 70s. This was the hot place to be in Italia. Every beautiful film star was here waiting to be seen. This is where I took my darling Francesca when we were very young." He kisses her hand.

"We try to come back here whenever the club is open - which is only three months out of the year." He is talking about Africana.

"Yes, except last year, we were away for most of the summer. It's good to be back." Francesca smiles while Alberto puts his arm around her waist.

We take the small boats to the cave at Africana and Joseph is beside me squeezing my hand, as excited as a boy of fifteen anticipating his first kiss. Once inside, I feel as if I am in an aquarium surrounded by walls of water. There are two caves, one for the DJ and the other for the main bar and dance floor, and stalactites and stalagmites hanging everywhere. Even the floor itself is a window to the sea with big fish swimming beneath our feet as we dance! I wonder if they are as mesmerized by the beat of the music as I am by them.

The color of the lighting is that opalescent electric blue like that of the Blue Grotto on Capri. This along with the walls to the sea and the manner in which we have arrived, has left me breathless! How much more can a body take with all this adventure, romance and passion that takes my breath away all the time? Is it healthy? What if it isn't? Would it be so bad to die like this – in these places? I think not!

The music is a cross between Buddha Bar and a Euro Disco Beat, pulsating and undulating, inviting you to move your body, although no one is dancing yet since clubs don't come alive until midnight here. It's only 22:00 hours…two more hours to go…

"Doll, they have a martini called the Africana made with Amarula. It's sort of a chocolate martini made with this liquor from Africa that you can't buy in the States. Want one?" Why not? So I say yes. Joseph is the perfect date and we dance for hours, never tiring. I think our energy is coming from the sea. When he hands the drink to me and I taste it, I love its sweet chocolaty taste.

The music is gyrating for hours on end. I dance with Joseph and a few of the Italian men who ask me as I sip my martini in between the songs. Somewhere in the middle of the night – or morning, I should say, there is a commotion and the dance floor is cleared. Three local fishermen come in and dredge a sinkhole in the edge of the dance floor, and with nets start to pull fresh fish up through the floor. I am dancing around in glee as I watch this bizarre occurrence. Alberto explains to me that this is a tradition at the Africana and the fresh fish will go to the local restaurants for the day's menu. I am amazed and have been giggling for hours, dancing, giddy with pleasure…another reason to continue this lifestyle I am now living.

Somewhere around four in the morning, Joseph has met someone, a gorgeous young Italian man with thick, dark hair and that beautiful hairline that I love. He looks Sicilian or from somewhere down south. He has that strong nose, dark eyes and dark colored skin. They are dancing now and I have lost my partner but no mind. My feet are aching a bit in my stilettos, but I am very happy to have bought them.

At 6:00 a.m. after a long night, we take the boat back to the ship with an extra person – Luciano, who is with Joseph. I'm happy for him. He deserves to be loved by someone who appreciates him. As I look out toward the yacht, I hear Joseph telling him about the spa on board.

I fall into bed and into sleep, only to be awakened by a knock on my door…of course it seems like only minutes have passed, but it is actually late-morning.

"Roxanna, come! We're leaving for Positano in thirty minutes. Come up for breakfast." It's Joseph and I can hear Luciano with him.

"Go away! I need more sleep!" I'm exhausted from this lifestyle.

"It's almost noon! Get up! We'll see you upstairs." I can hear them laughing as they walk away. I lay there with my eyes closed and think that I can't miss anything because who knows when I will be back; so I pull myself from the bed and quickly shower and dress for *espresso*.

"*Buonojourno*, Roxanna. Did you sleep well?" Francesca is glowing in her yellow caftan with sandals to match and she doesn't look a bit tired. She must have a secret.

"It was not enough! *Espresso*, please..." I tell the waiter who is standing before me. I realize I sound like a princess, but tell myself it's acceptable behavior for a woman on a superyacht who is being waited on as if she is royalty.

"We will come back in time for a nap today. Don't worry. It was fun, no?"

"Yes, it was amazing. Thank you so much for inviting me on this cruise." I am gushing, and can't thank her or Alberto enough.

"Roxanna, it is our pleasure. You can come along anytime. I enjoy your company and I know Alberto does too. You are very real and real people are hard to find in our circle...we have lots of money as most of our friends do, and for some, the money overshadows everything. These are the ones who don't like themselves too much so they try and find an image they want to project to others." She is very smart I think.

"Francesca, you are the one who is very real, but thank you for the compliment. I am still honored to be here." Just then, Joseph and Luciano come to the table for breakfast.

"We had to buy Luciano something to wear today since he's coming with us." Luciano is smiling at his good fortune.

"Where do you live, Luciano?" I ask. I live in Napoli in the winter and in the summer I live in Amalfi." He is on the thin side but nicely built and the bones in his face are strong. I guess him to be in his early thirties. We finish our food and our much needed *espresso* before leaving for Positano.

As we come in by boat, there lies before me a brightly painted town that seems to be all about color, and the houses seem to sit like steps all the way up the mountain. They climb up its front like grapevines and all are painted either rose, yellow, white or red. When we arrive at the shore, the beach is covered by rows of green umbrellas over bright orange chairs. On the far side of the beach are two rows of twenty little boats that are painted white on the outside and have bright yellow insides.

We walk to town and visit the *Chiesa di Santa Maria Assunta* with its majolica-tiled rounded dome of yellow and green, then browse the shops walking up stepped paths everywhere in between the buildings. There are secret passageways and lanes all made of stone that make me feel as though I am in a medieval village from a thousand years ago. Soon, we take the motor boats up the coast to Amalfi; but before we do, we head toward three little islets and motor in between them where the sea water is that Mediterranean aquamarine color.

"You know of the sirens, Roxanna?" Alberto asks.

"Yes, I do. On Capri there is the Rock of the Sirens in Marina Piccola."

"Yes, the legend is particularly strong throughout *Campania*. But here, it is much more. Look there." He is pointing toward the peninsula. "That shrine was dedicated to these winged sea deities. And here..." He is pointing to three little islands. "These are called the *Sirenuse*, and are believed to hold the three bodies of the sirens: Ligea, Leucosia and Parthenope."

"You know the story the Odyssey?" We say yes, but he tells it anyway and I don't mind one bit because he has great stories. "Men who have died here through the centuries were believed to have been hypnotized by these creatures with their mystical powers, but I think they were probably either tired or drunk on Italian *vino* or mesmerized by the beautiful Italian women who are everywhere!" He laughs at his own joke and he is having so much fun with it that we laugh too.

"*La Grotta dello Smeraldo* – the Emerald Grotto." We have moved further south and Alberto our tour guide points to a cave. "The water is an emerald green color due to the sunlight which comes into the cave through an opening underwater."

As we come upon it, Amalfi's coastline is almost as colorful as Positano's with row upon row of brown cabanas with bright green awnings, and further down on the beach are rows of white boats with bright blue covers.

As we walk into town, we pass the Amalfi pier and enter the square where there is a monument of Flavio Gioia who invented the compass. Then we move through the main street and come to *Piazza Duomo* where I am faced with a fountain, Saint Andrew, the patron saint of the Amalfi Coast, the fisherman saint, and the protector of seaman. It is a beautiful fountain with Andrew standing high atop a stone platform with little angels beneath it. Beneath them is a naked woman sitting in the water holding each of her breasts in her hands as they squirt water.

"Joseph, look!" I'm surprised and can't help but laugh.

"Yes, I nicknamed it the "Boobie Fountain!" He winks at me and grins.

"Alberto, who is she?" I ask.

"She is a mermaid." No story, I think to myself? But he is on a mission and walking toward the great church before us. We all make the trek up the fifty-seven steps after him and meet at the top. *Chiesa di Assunta*, Our Lady of Assumption – just like Positano… but this one is enormous. Its structure is Romanesque but with much Baroque accent and decorative work. It also has a lot of Moorish arches and frescoes.

Even the bell tower is mixed – its lower half Romanesque while the upper portion is Moorish. Inside is the Cathedral of Saint Andrews and its front atrium is designed in a unique pattern of Moorish arches that run into a series of marble columns. The inside walls are made of huge two-tone tuff stone blocks creating a design. The main door is grand and made of bronze cast in Constantinople in 1060, and then set into a marble portal.

Once inside, my breath leaves me again as I view the sacred artistic works before me. The ceilings and walls are incredibly beautiful with their gold and white tones and golden gilded and frescoed walls and ceilings. There are beautiful sculptures and oil paintings everywhere. The architecture of the interior goes from gorgeous Romanesque to Moorish inlaid stone of different colors in the crypt room.

There is a 17th century bust of Saint Andrew in gold-plated copper that is so detailed it looks as if he has been cast in the gold himself. It's like a museum, there is so much to see, and of course, I sit for a bit to enjoy the feel of the place. As we exit the great church, we come to the Paradise Cloister which is surrounded by four porticoes and as you look into it, you see a series of delicately designed ogival arches that rests on top of small marble columns. The gardens are… so beautiful… I don't think I will ever tire of visiting churches in Italy.

It's time to go back to the ship for a nap before dinner so we pile into the boats and motor our way back up the coast toward Positano and the yacht.

Dinner is a quiet event, and afterwards, I choose to go to my beautiful room to be alone and to pretend I am Cleopatra as I gaze out over the Amalfi Coast. Tomorrow morning we are heading back to Capri. There will be so much to do when I return. I have been away far too long with all the traveling I have done lately. As I sit and look out over Positano, I contemplate my latest adventure and my newest, dearest friends.

Before falling asleep, I wonder if Natale has received my letter yet.

CHAPTER 47

HOME

As I walk the distance to my villa, I drag my suitcase behind me with one hand and my stunning midnight blue dress in the other. Such an incredible dress…and an incredible time… I walk past the man who has been building a new rock wall around his garden and notice that it is now finished. I see him coming out of his gate with a wheel barrel filled with tree branches and weeds and he smiles at me.

"Journo."

"Journo, signora." I love it here so much that I can't imagine living anywhere else. I have finally found my happiness. I no longer even have the need to know how Helios, San Michele and Apollo are connected, for my soul knows and this is all that matters. I love them all. San Francesco is here, too. Who knows…maybe Axel Munthe is the reincarnation of Francesco? All I know is that I love this place and the San Michele Villa and grounds as if it were my own home.

I walk slowly. My heart is trying to breathe and it is difficult because it is swelled with love and gratitude for all of this. If I had not been open to Capri coming up on my computer or open to San Michelle coming into my dreams, I never would have come here at all. And now, there is nothing else that I need to search for. I have found everything right here; and in the process, I have learned so much about myself.

I have learned how to surrender to life, and how to follow my spirit to have what I desire instead of pushing so fast and furious to get it…ahhh…Power vs. Force! This is true power! Once I learn to trust, I know I will always be taken care of, for I already am.

I have learned that the sunlight and the sea, the earth, the rock and the wind heals the body if I walk upon it, sit in it, become one with it. I am now healed of everything that ever ailed me. I feel like a twenty-year old and look like one, too. Hadn't Antonio, Bruno and Natale told me so? I laugh out loud as I walk down the little lane past all the villas with their altars holding their Madonna with flowers at her feet.

I have learned that love doesn't always hurt – this is a myth. It is warm and even hot like sitting near a bonfire at night…so hot that you know it has the power over you if you get too close to it…it will singe your soul…but you have to be singed at least once in your lifetime or you have not tasted love!

I have learned the depth and breadth and height of my own soul intimately. There are no recesses left that I have not seen, nor felt, nor bled from.

I have learned that there are many kinds of love and that you can love two people at the same time, but the one that you take to bed at night – the one that you wake up to every morning, the one that is in your dreams and the one that takes your breath away - is the one true love for you. He has captured my heart and that's why I can't stop thinking of him. I sigh with this thought…

I have also learned that it's okay to talk to spirit – or not talk to them for a while – like I have in my life - and then start up again – because they love me whether I am talking to them or not, guiding me along, whether I am listening to them or not; and they too are all connected to each other, working together for me.

Now that I have figured this life of mine out, what do I do next? I open the gate to *Mio Paradiso,* walk inside and close it before dropping my suitcase on the ground to twirl in the sunlight and blow kisses to the sea and the sky before me. I am so happy…laughing out loud – big and hard…

"Rossana…"

"It's you." I start to weep and then I run into his arms and remember them. I can't control myself as I am all over him, knocking him to the ground trying to crawl inside him. My soul is ignited and the cells in my body are fizzing like little champagne bubbles rising up inside a glass. They are dancing feverishly as I kiss him truly, madly, deeply. Then, here, under the Mediterranen sun, under the blue of the sky and against the aqua backdrop of the sea, we make love in the grass on the *terrazzo* as if we have been waiting for each other forever.

He makes love to me so passionately, so carefully and I make love to him in the same way. I want to make sure I remember all of his parts and the feel of his skin beneath my fingers. I want to remember his chest, how it feels, and the shape of his body. I want to taste him all over and feel him in my mouth, and then have his kisses whisper love to me.

Our love making is feverish, hot in the 102o heat of the day, but we pay no mind - we are too enmeshed in each other. After we both reach that place our souls take us to together where we are touched by the Divine and where we are the only ones who really exist in these moments, we stop to look into each others' eyes.

"I love you," we say in unison as if it was rehearsed - but of course it is not. We both laugh a little.

"*Mio amore*. I receive your letter and had to come and see the painting for myself. I had to see you, too. I cannot sleep. I cannot eat. I am too in love with you, Rossana. I feel like I get hit by a big truck and I can't recover."

"Oh, Natale, I'm so sorry. I wanted to call and come to you, but I knew it wasn't time. I had to find myself. I had to find my own happiness first. But now, I have found it."

We are on the ground still and he pulls me up so that I am sitting facing him. He cups my face with his hands, pulling it to his. Then, he kisses me softly on the lips, all the while speaking to me in his native tongue before he begins in English.

"Rossana, I love you so much that I will do anything to be with you. If you want to move to America, I will go with you. If you want to live here, I will come here to be with you. I love you this much. Now, will you please say yes? Will you marry me?"

"Yes, I will marry you now." Now it's my turn to take my hands and cup his face as I bring it to mine to kiss him ever so gently. When I open my eyes, I see tears have filled his. "Oh, Natale..." I start to cry, for I am so happy.

For the remainder of the day and night, we stay at the villa and make love over and over. We cannot get enough of each other. He tells me he has been here for two days waiting for me, sleeping in the sun chair in the grass with only the mosquitoes to keep him company. He tells me he is hungry so I feed him from the garden, and then we talk all night long. I have much to share with him and when I get to the part about being kidnapped by the modern-day pirates, he jumps up and starts to curse, half in Italian and half in English. He paces the floor as he runs his hands through his hair.

"Shit!" ...which sounds like *sheet*... "Santa Maria! *Tutto cattivo* – very bad! *Mama Mia*! Jesus Christo...damned *Greco pirati*- Greek pirates!" I laugh and try to calm him down. We talk into the morning and watch the sun rise over the villa behind us. We have tea on the *terrazzo* as we watch the sea and the sky change and the first hydrofoils of the day as they move to and from the island. I take him into town for breakfast and then to Federico to see his painting.

"*Bella,* this is me! It is I, Natale! My face...*magnifico*! I am so happy." He kisses me and Federico smiles wide.

"Ah, you are the one she loves." He grabs Natale's face and kisses him. "You are a very lucky man, Natale. She is *un tesoro* – a treasure." He looks at me to make sure I understand the word.

"*Si, si. Ho uomo di fortunato.*" I take good care of her. We are to be married soon. She has accepted me!" For the first time, I see this look of pride on Natale's face and it suits him well. And, since it's for me, it suits me too. We leave the painting with Federico so it can continue to dry and say our good-byes.

"Come again, Roxanna. We can paint." He blows a kiss in the air. As we walk out of the shop, we bump into Joseph and Luciano who has come from Amalfi for a few days to be with Joseph. They have lots of bags and have been shopping for Luciano who is grinning wide. He has a brilliant smile and is more handsome today than the others. It must be the love I think.

"*Ciao, bella.* Who is this?" He knows but wants to be sure before blurting out his name.

"Joseph and Luciano, this is Natale." They greet each other and we talk about our latest adventure with the Brunos aboard their superyacht. I can tell Natale likes Joseph immediately, feeling comfortable with him - so comfortable that he suddenly blurts it out.

"We are getting married!" There is that look again. Joseph is jumping up and down as excited as if it were his own engagement.

"Congratulations, you two! We'll have to have a party! Let me plan one for you, doll! It will be my gift to you, an engagement party."

"Joseph, wait - I'm not sure when Natale will be going back to Rome. I..." But Natale has cut me off.

"I am not going back. I am here with you now. So we have the party soon." We say good-bye for now and promise to talk later. Natale places his arm around my shoulder and pulls me close as we walk, just as I have seen the married men in Capri do to their wives.

"Natale, what about your apartment? We should talk about what the future holds and where we will live. And I have to see my sons…think about how I will do this." He stops me short and turns me to face him.

"You change your mind?" He is very serious.

"No, I am not going to change my mind…just details. We do this together." He kisses my forehead and then we walk on to the San Michele Villa so he can meet my brother the Sphinx and make a wish upon his back.

This night, we fall asleep in each others' arms very early, and I dream I am married to this beautiful Italian man who adores me and treats me as if I am the Madonna herself.

Morning is filled with surprises as I awaken to someone calling my name.

"Debbie…are you here?" I hear a voice from the past outside my door. "Debbie, it's us. I have the kids with me."

"Mom, are you here?" My heart races as I find my clothes and run to the door. There before me is Ed, his wife Cynthia, Josh and Devon. I run to both of them at the same time and wrap my arms around them.

"Oh, my God! You are both so big! You got taller! I have missed you so much!" I smother them with kisses.

"Okay, okay, Mom! Stop!" We all laugh.

"You have grown up, haven't you? I can't believe you came all the way over here! What made you do it? I thought you were in Hawaii?" Cynthia speaks up.

"Are you kidding? Thanks for coming here, Debbie. I've always wanted to see Italy but could never get Ed to take me…so when the boys were missing you, I thought it was the perfect opportunity! I can't thank you enough!" She gives me a big hug and Ed laughs.

"Mom, this is a really cool place!" Devon is walking toward the cliffs to look out to sea and Josh follows.

"Ciao, I am Natale." He has come up behind me and extended his hand to Ed.

"Nice to meet you, Natale." After pleasantries are exchanged, and I show them around, we have *espresso* while the boys explore.

"We booked a room at the San Michele Hotel at the end of town. We have a room for the boys, too; but if you'd like them to stay here with you, it's okay with us. We'd love to have a little time to explore the island alone." Cynthia grabs Ed's hand and I can see she is clearly excited to be here in this romantic setting.

"We would love to have them here with us."

"Yes, I would like them here to know them." I smile as he tries to express himself.

THE END

EPILOGUE

So you are probably wondering what happened to Roxanna and Natale after *espresso* with her ex-husband and his wife? Well let me tell you...

Josh and Devon thought Natale was pretty cool and loved the fact that their mother had someone else who stole her interest besides them. They also loved the fact that twice a year they got to travel to Italy for a few months to be with her, and also to explore and enjoy the young, beautiful, Italian girls.

Joseph was so excited about their engagement that he called Alberto and Francesca to tell them and the three of them planned a surprise engagement party that week at Joseph's villa. Everyone Roxanna knew and loved in Capri came and even Elana showed up as if she had a sixth sense. She had decided she needed a bit of a holiday from her beloved Venezia and wanted to surprise her new friend on Capri. It was just her luck that she arrived on the island the day of the party! Oh, and that is where she met Massimo....

Enrico got Natale a job at the Caesar Augustus Hotel and Alberto hired Roxanna to design a line of women's evening wear for his company. She and Natale stayed on at the villa, a gift from Enrico. She worked at home and spent time at Federico's studio where he set up space for her so that they could paint together.

The wedding was a huge affair off the Amalfi Coast on the Bruno's superyacht. Roxanna's sons, Ed, and Cynthia came back for it in September along with a crowd of her girlfriends from the States who had been living vicariously through her emails. While there, the single ones were looking for Italian men to fall in love with hoping to find a dream such as Roxanna's.

Alberto designed her gown and Natale's suit; and her sons walked her down the aisle as Joseph, her loving friend, looked on weeping with joy.

And what of Luciano? Joseph fell head over heels in love with him, and he with Joseph. So they exchanged vows themselves and split their time between Malibu and Capri.

And for the honeymoon…Well Valentino sent a letter to her that he had finished the sculpture and asked her to call him. When he found out she was getting married, he invited them to his castle and family vineyard for their honeymoon.

But it didn't stop there…Alberto and Francesca offered their ship for a cruise to the Cyclades in search of her *Greco pirati*!

Truly the Beginning!

ARTIST'S PAGE

Gergana Injev was born in Sofia, Bulgaria in October of 1969. Even as a child, she was a gifted artist and studied with private masters at a young age. In 1993, she moved to Irvine California to marry her husband and continued studying with private artists and teachers in southern California.

In 1995, she studied art and fashion design at Irvine Valley College, Santa Ana College and Rancho Santiago College. Over the next few years, she won "1st Place in Fashion Design for the State of California," and 1st Place in Fashion Illustration for the State of California."

Gergana's talents are varied as she has painted in water color, pencil, acrylic and oils in the Abstract, Baroque, Figurative, Graphic Art, Impressionistic, Neoclassic, Realist and Renaissance styles.

Currently, she is working on a collection in preparation for her first exhibition.

AUTHOR'S BIO

Over the past eight years, Gail Michael has written eight books, four of which have been published. She penned her first in 2000, "I Am a Thousand Winds That Blow," a few months after her mother died from lung cancer. Since then, she has written both fiction and nonfiction. "The Passions of Roxanna" is her first fiction to be published.

In both classes, Gail gives her readers an inspiring look into her own life, in hopes of assisting them with changing their lives in some small way.

Gail has also lectured throughout California and New England on subjects she has written about: *Mother-daughter relationship;* S*urviving Grief and Loss; Shifting from Inner Conflict to Inner Peace; Change Your Life by Changing You; Age is a State of Mind so Live Like the Immortal That You Are;* and *the Dance...How to Romance Your Life*.

When not writing, Gail works as an executive for a fitness equipment manufacturer in Irvine, California. Whenever she can, she travels back to her new homeland in Capri, Italy.

ALSO BY GAIL MICHAEL

I Am a Thousand Winds That Blow

Depression
Floating Through it Without Drugs
- An Alternative to Antidepressants

Looking Into the Eyes of the Snake

CPSIA information can be obtained at www.ICGtesting.com
Printed in the USA
BVOW062017211112

306221BV00003B/7/P